Sisters of the Stone

∞

Judith Manchester

This is a work of fiction. Names, characters, places, and incidents either are the product of the author's imagination or are used fictitiously. Any resemblance to actual persons living or dead, business establishments, events, or locales is entirely coincidental.

Jansen Cape Publishing

ISBN-13: 978-0692533604

To those who journey inside to self-discovery.

One

She lifts her stiff shoulders, too many hours in the car, and yet, when the road narrows and twists at last alongside the familiar river, Sydney Foster feels the tug of a smile. The river is swollen at this hour by the tide, and the salty breath of marsh grass fills the car. With it, a first flicker – a sense that maybe she was right to come back – pokes up through the doubt that's been building all day, with each mile closer to this place, and Sydney drives on. Past the harbor. Past gray shingled Cape Cod cottages and peeks at an azure bay, quiet scenes that burst through breaks in the low scrub pine. But when the shore road meets with the low wooden bridge set on pilings, Sydney stops the car.

Across the bridge, Ponokanet waits. A mile in length, the island's breadth is half of that, and Sydney remembers every foot, every path, each turn of its shore. This is it. This place is why she left California so far at her back. In the past week, she has driven three thousand miles across the continent on a simple hope that here on Ponokanet she might discover a new way to be in this world. Maybe here …

Beside her, the gray cat complains through its wire crate.

"We're almost there," says Sydney, and the Subaru clatters over the planked bridge. The island's one road is more a narrow lane, made of packed gravel and stone dust meant to keep wheels from sinking in too much sand. The road turns, then climbs, leaving the blue of the bay at her back. When the island levels, she is suddenly in a forest of long-needled pine. Sunlight breaks through the limbs and casts thin arm-like shadows onto the road. Shadows that bring Sydney back to days when she pedaled a bike along this same road, pedaled under the same limbs. Those days, years ago, were hard and yet, here she is at age thirty-nine wanting to return.

When the road opens onto the circular drive, her breath catches. Her grandmother's house sits on one side of the clearing. They buried her grandmother seven years ago, in an ancient graveyard just outside the village. All the town, it seemed, turned out to say goodbye to Eva Foster. Now the house – in fact, the entire island – belongs to Sydney and to Sydney's mother in equal share. Even so, Sydney still does not think of the place that way. Ponokanet and this house belong to her Grandmother Eva and always will.

Sydney looks to the steep pitch of the roof, to the front porch with its tall windows like dark warm eyes, inviting. She imagines her grandmother, half-expecting Eva to come running from the porch with lanky arms outstretched. But, of course, Eva does not.

No one does.

Sydney is alone.

For ten months and a day she's been alone.

With two hands she pulls through the obstinate curls that frame her face. What if even here she cannot invent a new Sydney? What if it is too late, impossible at age thirty-nine to change spots, to become something other, something better? All this effort, all the miles, East Coast to West Coast, how could it possibly make a difference? Here or there, Rick is still dead. And here or there, she is still to blame.

No. She was right to come back. She has to believe it. She has to believe in the island's tonic. Sydney squares her shoulders and steps out onto the gravel drive.

"Here we are," she says, lifting the cat from the crate. How sad really that Cat is all she wanted to bring from California. A cat named

Cat, a cat who found Sydney, not the other way around. A few days after Rick … after the crash, this gray ball of fur came to the screened door meowing. At first Sydney fed her out in the yard. A few scraps of chicken. Milk left in Sydney's cereal bowl. That's when she started calling the cat Cat – a nameless name to keep the relationship impersonal. Unattached. But Cat persisted, until the door was opened one rainy night and Cat ran in, slept the remainder of that storm curled into a ball against Sydney's feet. And that was it. They became a pair.

In the golden low light of disappearing day, Sydney sets Cat loose. The cat darts for the moment behind what looks to be new evergreens at the side of the house. In front, along the porch rail in wooden planters lined up end to end, flowers grow – lush orange petals with delicate stems. But how on earth do flowers grow ripe and full in front of a house so seldom visited?

It certainly couldn't be because of her mother, Alison. Alison never stays put long enough to nurture anything, least of all flowers. Even so, Sydney glances over her shoulder to see if she missed a parked car, maybe across the yard by the barn, missed some sign that Alison might be here.

There is nothing. Just the barn with its broad door closed and the empty drive.

During the past week, she tried a dozen times to call her mother. But with each try Alison's away message clicked on and Sydney left only a simple request, 'Call me.' She wants to tell Alison her plan to stay here on Ponokanet, but she needs to talk to the real Alison, not a machine. She needs to hear the response. Whatever that response, it will have two meanings. The spoken one will be something like, 'oh, my, what a pleasant surprise. If only I could get away from my busy life here in Connecticut to visit with you.' And there will be the underlying message, the one Sydney needs to hear, the one that says as long as Sydney is on the island, Alison will stay away.

Alison has not called back. So, in a little while, after a much-needed soak in the old claw-foot tub, Sydney will have to try calling her again.

She returns to the car for the small bag of groceries she picked up when coming through the downtown of Orleans. She digs in the bottom of her purse for the key to the house. And hanging on to the slightest of hope, she climbs the porch step. She places the key in the door to her grandmother's house, the door to Sydney's new life – whatever that might be.

The door swings open.

"Make yourself at home," says Sydney as Cat leaps in, tail flicking. Sydney, too, steps inside the island house.

The hallway smells of wood polish, a lemon scent that is not her grandmother's. But the moldings and wide pine floor still show dark against pale buttery painted walls, and something like comfort washes through her. This house – it remains the one place that ever felt like home. She can't even say now that the small stucco house in Santa Rosa felt truly comfortable in a belonging kind of way. It was Rick's house and although they lived in it together for most of five years, she held no claim to the house, no loyalties to it now. When Rick's mother announced that the house was to be sold, Sydney surprised herself as much as anyone and merely packed a suitcase, wanting nothing more than to drive as far away as possible.

And Ponokanet is as far away as she could get. Here, the entire continent is at her back. Only the vast Atlantic and an unknown future lie beyond.

A sigh leaves Sydney empty.

She looks to the stairs that will take her up soon to the small back bedroom. That room is to be hers again for a while. She doesn't know yet exactly how long she will stay, only that she wants to see the four seasons again. When Sydney was a child, Alison shipped her off between school years to spend summers here with Eva. But by the age of fourteen that young Sydney grew surly and street smart, skipping school, smoking pot, which proved to require too much of Alison. She left Sydney here to finish high school, left her here for Eva to fix.

That girl of fourteen hated being here as much as she hated Alison for giving up on her. Gradually though, as months turned into a long year, that angry girl woke to discover she was looking forward to the turn into a next new season. She watched summer slip into the warm russet and gold of autumn. She bundled under a woolen coat and hat to walk in the muted world of a winter snow. Walked in a yellow slicker through the damp tenuous start of a Cape Cod spring. Through the seasons a troubled teen grew and became somehow strong. The seasons – this much Sydney could have again.

The possibility pushes her with the bag of groceries through the living room and on into the kitchen. Cat sits looking out through the French doors to the backyard, and Sydney opens the doors wide.

Salt air brushes past, soft, moist and warm.

Cat strolls onto the deck and claims a spot at the far edge. Beyond spreads a field of bearberry, leathery leaves like lawn for a hundred yards to the island's high rim. A distant crash of waves sounds on the beach below. That break of waves, the repetitive rhythm, will be her companion here. Her new lover. Her constant. In this solitude she will have space and time.

She considers going for a walk, barefoot along the path behind the barn and down onto the beach, but there's an ache behind her eyes. She craves a tub. So, no. There will be no walk. She pours Cat a dish of food, and with the rattle of pellets from the bag Cat comes running.

A click – the front door latch. Leather soles – high heeled – sharp on the entry hall floor.

A woman's voice, "Sydney, where are you? I saw the California license plate and knew it had to be you."

In the kitchen, Sydney clutches her middle as if punched. "No. It can't be."

But there is no mistaking. Alison has arrived on Ponokanet.

Two

Sydney looks to the same jeans and rumpled T-shirt she has worn since five in the morning, and she groans. Cat gazes up wide-eyed, and Sydney exhales, strokes the soft gray back. "It's okay," she says, trying to believe it, looking to the door, then back to Cat. "We'll survive this, too … somehow."

Sydney stands straighter, digs to find the adult she is, and she walks out of the kitchen to greet her mother.

In the front hall, at the foot of the stairs, Alison holds to the banister post, appearing polished as ever in a sundress, lime with narrow straps at the shoulder, and sleek chin-length hair the rich color of redwood. The two, mother and daughter, they make a comic difference.

Or it might be comic if the difference ended there.

Alison's green eyes scan Sydney. "Aside from being too thin, you look lovely."

Sydney roughs through her hair. Seven years since Alison last saw her – not once since burying Eva have Alison and Sydney been in the same room – and this is all the woman can say, 'aside from being too thin …'

"It's nice to see you, too," says Sydney.

"How long have you been here?" asks Alison.

"Less than an hour."

"You should have told me you were coming. I would have arrived earlier and had the place ready for you."

"You don't have to do anything for me. But I did try to call. Your Connecticut house. Your cell phone. I even tried calling here. You never answered."

Alison touches the drop of beach glass that hangs from the silver chain at her neck. "Good heavens, that's right. My cell phone ... it's been off all this time." She reaches deep inside a straw purse, pulling from its depths a silver phone. "Edward and I went north to Quebec City, the old part. And I turned off my phone." And quickly she adds, "So tell me. How long are you planning to stay?"

"I'm not sure," says Sydney, which more than ever is absolute truth.

"However long you stay, it'll be nice." Alison, smiling for the first time, looks to her own bulging suitcase that rests by the door. "I'm here for a week or so, but there's plenty of room. Can you stay that long? We can catch up."

Surely there is plenty of room, but no amount of space would be enough. They'll end up in an argument. They always do. But Sydney bites back any words. She needs to think about this. She wants more than the week. Much more. And if that requires spending seven days with Alison in trade for months alone on the island – there has to be a way. There has to be.

"Are you all right?" asks Alison. "You look tired."

"I am. It's been a long day. A long week of driving."

"You drove all that way? Why, for heaven's sake?"

"I had the time." But Sydney looks away, hating the fact that she opened this path into what would certainly be her mother's next question.

"But what about your stunt flying? The aerobatics?"

"I've told you. I don't fly anymore."

"Still?

Sydney says nothing. No answer would make a difference. Alison does not get it – has not understood from day one why Sydney stopped flying. 'It's time to pick yourself up by the bootstraps' – if Sydney has to hear that again …

"I'm going to get my suitcase," says Sydney. "And I want to take a bath. As I said, it's been a long day."

"That's a good idea," says Alison. "Freshen up a bit, and I'll get us dinner."

But the gesture of peace falls at Sydney's back. Already she has walked out onto the porch, and her hands grip the railing. If only Rick were still here. If only …

Her hands go sweaty, and again she is slipping back –

High above the patchwork of California grape fields, Sydney flies alone, harnessed in the single-seat cockpit. Her hands hold steady on the control stick, feet gentle on the rudder, and she waits.

"Thirty seconds to show time," Rick's voice clear through her headphones. "You ready?"

"Ready," says Sydney, and her plane rolls to the right.

Rick, she knows, will come at the airfield from the west in his own Pitts, a squat double-winged plane, blue stripes on white, same as hers. They will meet over the runway. Climb together above the tide of onlookers that have flocked to Chico's Municipal Airport to watch. She smiles at the thought of him careening toward her now.

"Three seconds," says Sydney into the small dot mike at her chin.

"Let's give 'em their show." In his voice she hears the crooked grin and his excitement.

On the horizon, the blue and white of Rick's plane. Their mark appears, a white X on the paved strip below. Sydney checks air speed. Lowers the nose.

Altitude three hundred feet.

The claw propeller churns, loud like the late Pavarotti at a reverberating hum, and Sydney enters her air space, to the right of the X, the crowd reduced to a blur of liquid color. Ahead, so close, Rick's plane a flash of blue, and Sydney snaps the control stick to her lap. Climbs, nose up. Vertical, the same as Rick. Two Pitts in unison, wingtip to wingtip. Straight to the sun, adrenalin sweet in her mouth.

She checks altitude. Holds back on the stick, holds the nose to the sun, her airspeed dropping. The nose falls back. The plane's belly is suddenly up, and Sydney hangs in the straps, the earth her ceiling, blood heavy in her face as she counts …

Two …

One …

A quick twist to the stick. Too soon. An error, but she is upright, and she waits, the split second made up. The stick is jammed forward, and her plane dives into perfect spiral, down through the practiced spin – she and Rick in graceful duet.

Altitude five hundred feet. The ground rising up.

Four hundred.

She locks sight on the X, like a skater in a spin selecting a point, keeping balance, riding through the spin …

Three hundred.

Two.

She yanks the stick. The Pitts levels.

A glance left, but where is he?

"Syd …" Rick's shout through the headset.

On the ground a burst of orange. Tongues of flame. And the black billow of smoke. Still, a span of a second before the reality strikes. Her gut twists. Bile rises in her throat. Bile that Sydney tries to swallow, tries but cannot hold back the vomit.

Despite her grip on the porch rail, Sydney's hands shake, and tears are wet on her face. She can't keep doing this. Somehow she has to move on. Move forward. And that can only happen here. She has to stay. Seven days with Alison – an eternity but a price she's willing to pay for a long line of solo months here on Ponokanet.

An approaching crunch of wheels over gravel turns her head.

A green pick-up drives into the clearing. The driver, a man in sunglasses and dark midnight hair tied back in a sort of ponytail, nods to Sydney as he passes. He parks in front of the barn, climbs from the truck, long legs in faded-out jeans stepping down onto the gravel. When he walks toward Sydney, she steps out from under the shade of the porch to meet him.

Three

"You must be Sydney," says this complete stranger. "I recognize you from all the pictures."

All what pictures? ... She wants to ask, but the man extends his hand. He appears not as young as Sydney first thought. A few gray hairs show in the black.

"It's nice to finally meet you," he says while slipping off the sunglasses, exposing dark eyes. Eyes that aren't quite Asian, although the cheekbones are. "I'm Tien Dinh Nhu. But it's easier to call me Ty."

Sydney presses at the ache behind her eyes, feeling two steps behind in this conversation. "Are you here to see Alison?"

"No," he says. "I'll check in with her later."

"Mr. ... Ty, I seem to be missing something. If you don't want to see Alison, then why are you here?"

She feels the hesitation while his eyes search her face. "I'm sorry," he says. "I assumed you knew. I live here. In the barn."

"You live here?"

"Yes. I take care of the house and the gardens. In exchange, I live in the apartment your mother put together in a wing of the barn."

"I see." Sydney kicks at a shard of gravel. She knows nothing of any apartment in the barn. Alison never mentioned it. But why would she when Sydney is so seldom here? Even so ...

"It's good that you're back, Sydney." The man nods, then walks away towards the barn, his gait limber, like a lean runner who's been devoted to stretching the hamstrings and hips.

Sydney kneads at the headache. This man, a stranger, living here. She'll have to talk to Alison about that. It'll lead to a fight, but what choice does she have?

Her heels dig into the gravel as she walks toward the Subaru.

Alison's black Lexus sits too close to the rear of the Subaru, and Sydney has to stand at the side to drag her suitcase from the Subaru hatchback. She carries the suitcase across the gravel, up the few porch steps and into the front hall.

Alison calls from the kitchen. "Dinner's almost ready."

Sydney, with the one free hand, holds to the stair rail. She could skip dinner. Keep it safe and sleep for a week. But her empty stomach grumbles at the idea. Besides, there is the subject of the caretaker.

"Give me ten minutes," says Sydney, while with suitcase in hand she climbs the stairs.

The door to the first bedroom is open. Instead of Eva's hint of lilac, the scent of oversweet gardenia drifts from the room. The chenille bedcover is stacked with silk pillows. Alison's unopened luggage rests on a bench at the foot of Eva's bed, claiming its space. The room ... the changes ... they stab her heart, and Sydney closes the bedroom door. She pushes forward, starts along the length of pine floor that will take her to the back bedroom. This, more than any room, she hopes will be the same.

In the doorway Sydney stops, an open palm to her chest. Time has stopped in this back room. Against the wall is the single bed with its same eyelet cover, as if waiting for her all this time. The same maple rocker. The tall five-drawer bureau. In one corner, suspended from the ceiling by clear nylon thread, hangs the model red and white Cessna, an exact replica of the plane in which Sydney learned to fly. All those years ago, over the course of one long winter, she built the model from balsa and paper, and she hung it there from the ceiling herself.

Amazing. From that Cessna a whole world opened. Learning to fly. Taking on the aerobatics. Airshows and competition. The medals.

And finding Rick.

Sydney sets the suitcase on the bed and opens it. The photo lies on top of her things. Rick's face staring up. Rick's buzz-cut hair. His eyes the same sky blue as his flight suit. Sydney picks up the photo. Touches on that grin that seemed to mock life and the risks he took in flight every day. Rick, so alive.

Her palms go wet.

With heart pounding, Sydney slides down onto the rug, her legs unwilling to hold her. Lungs have no air.

The claw propeller churns, pulling her away from the fire ... from Rick. Lungs find no air to breathe. But she has to think. She has to get back on the ground.

Or not.

She banks the wing. Turns back toward the chimney of black smoke. A hand swipes at tears but there is only one thought now. To get to the fire.

As if through a wall, she breaks into the smoke, surrounded by oily black soot, blinded to either up or down. The cockpit fills with fumes of burning fuel. She can meet him there at the bottom. Tell him it was her mistake ... her break in timing. Tell him she is sorry, and now they can be there together. All it would take is a jam of the stick and the plane will drop, vertical down inside this black tunnel.

Both hands grip the stick.

Searing heat fills her lungs.

Jesus. No. Neither curse nor prayer. Simply panic. A coward.

Sydney rips at the throttle. The plane scrambles out and up, away from the smoke. The act of landing, of rolling the Pitts to its intended spot on the tarmac takes place in some automatic subliminal space. She sits stilled in the cockpit, stares out but sees nothing, aware only of the acrid stench of vomit that covers her lap.

It is Jean, the plane's mechanic, who first comes to her. Jean who flips open the canopy. Who unhitches the harness, tugs and steadies Sydney as she climbs from the plane, as Sydney shuts her eyes to sirens. It is Jean who wraps arms around her,

Jean who won't let her run to the fire, saying it's all over, there is nothing anyone can do for Rick now.

"Let me go. Let me go." Screams as if spewed from someone else, someone else gone mad, someone else clawing at one of the few who cares about her.

"It's all over," says Jean again.

And it's Jean who keeps her from collapsing when her knees buckle under.

Even now, all these months later, the visions are too real. Jean once suggested Sydney see someone – a therapist who could help her work through the grief. But it isn't so much the grief. It's knowing it was her fault. No amount of talking could wash that away.

Nothing can take away that one blip in timing. It put Rick off balance. Her error sent him down.

Sydney tastes blood where she's bitten through her lip. With one finger, she wipes at the lip. The blood is proof she's still alive. In that one moment in the air, when it really counted, she'd chosen to live.

She unfolds her body, and with the framed photo she crosses the room to the bureau, opens the top drawer and places the photo inside. Slowly, she closes the drawer and walks away to the window.

The sun has slipped behind the bay. Sea and sky show in deep tones of rose, color like paint brushed out from the horizon. Through the doorway, Cat patters in to weave at her ankles, and Sydney picks up the gray cat.

"How do you do that? How do you know?" she asks because Cat always finds her when the ache hits so hard.

She puts Cat on the bed, and Cat picks a spot, lies down, purring as if never before so comfortable. Sydney scratches behind a velvety ear, taking that bit of pleasure before heading to the old claw-foot tub.

Four

Weetamo
When the long days meet the short, 1588

Night would soon lift its blanket of darkness and still Weetamo did not sleep. Outside, beyond the simple dome-shaped hut, the sea rolled and ebbed, and Weetamo rose from her sleeping mat. She slipped past her father and mother, both deep in sleep, and Weetamo considered how the years had made those two people tired, for it was not so long ago that she could not have left their wetu even in the darkest hours of night without being heard by her father, Tackanaw. But this night she must.

By nightfall of the coming day, her people – the Ponokanet and those of many villages – would gather in celebration. There would be fire and dance to thank the great spirit of the sun. This her people did always when the long and short days met. And, too, by next nightfall, she would be wife to Nohtok.

Nohtok. Nohtok.

Her heart beat to the rhythm of his name. So loudly her heart beat that she feared it might leap from her chest if she did not escape the walls of the dome-shaped hut, if she did not feel the fresh, damp air of the shore.

In a line of many, she found her dugout canoe. If the gods beneath the sea remained serene, the dugout would reach the island shore in time to see the sun begin her wedding day. For Weetamo, the island was a special place, where the gods welcomed her with the touch of a gentle breeze. She would go there in times like this, when her heart was either heavy or too full, and she would sit at the highest bluff until the heart settled in a place of calm.

Today her arm was strong. The paddle sliced the low swells with easy rhythm until the bottom scraped upon the white sand, and Weetamo pulled the dugout high onto the island's beach. She found the path and climbed upward to the top, wove in among the many pines to her sitting place by the great stone, at the forest edge where the island ended and the sea began.

The large stone stood out of place and alone in this land built of sand, and with the tip of her fingers Weetamo touched where the hard gray surface rounded, to trace over the resemblance of a sloping forehead. As a young girl, Weetamo had heard from her father the story of the stone maiden. He had sat here by this great stone with Weetamo at his side, and he spoke of the goddess, daughter of Kietan. Being the most powerful of all the gods, Kietan, at great sacrifice to himself, sent the young goddess to earth in the form of a maiden to watch over the Ponokanet. But bitter cold and the winds of winter blew in off the sea, and Kietan found it necessary to turn the maiden into stone, so that her spirit could survive within and continue to watch over the native people.

How sad it seemed – a woman trapped in stone for eternity. Tackanaw had explained it as a great honor bestowed upon the goddess. Yet, Weetamo felt the sorrow even today, and she whispered to the woman in stone. "I am here to sit with you once more, my sister."

The two, Weetamo and the stone, sat in silence, waiting. At last the arced tip of gold lifted itself above the earth's rim, and Weetamo felt the first tender rays touch on her face. And her thought was of Nohtok. By nightfall she will be his wife. Tonight she and Nohtok – their bodies and their spirits will be one.

Suddenly, the breeze went still.

From behind, in among the pines, a man's voice spoke in a strange unfamiliar tongue. Twice before, Weetamo had heard such a strange tongue spoken by men from a white-winged ship. Pale-skinned men that traded with her people, exchanging such things called ax and pot for the pelts, furs and bone beads carved by the men in her village. Neither time had the winged ship brought danger, but Weetamo did not want an encounter. Not alone.

She would hurry to tell Tackanaw of the men.

Weetamo stepped quickly along the path, wove through the thick forest, eager to reach the dugout that waited on the shore. She could see her way easily now in the morning light, and she broke into a run.

A twig snapped.

Heavy steps plodded through the brush.

Weetamo opened her stride. But her foot caught. Her hands thrust forward to break the fall. There was laughter. The deep laughter of men. A hand grabbed hold, its grip surrounding her arm, and she was pulled hard to her feet.

She set her shoulders and faced with narrowed eyes the pale-skinned man with hair that grew on his face. And a second, smaller foreign man, squat and laughing. Both wore layers of clothing not made of animal skins, and with the breeze at each man's back, the horrid unclean scent carried to Weetamo. The man who gripped her arm stood tall, with eyes that held the gray of foreboding clouds. In the other hand he carried a weapon, what her father once called a musket. When this man spoke in sharp words, the shorter squat one moved aside and spit through blackened teeth onto the sand. Yet, Weetamo did not feel the real danger until the squat one walked down the steep path to the shore and pushed the hollowed dugout many paces distant into the bay.

The one who held her glanced to the dugout that bobbed on a wave, and Weetamo grasped at his inattention, pulled her arm from the pale man's grip. But before she could match her first step, the man grabbed her, tighter, more vicious this time, bringing a sharp pain to her arm. He pushed her forward, forcing her to move ahead of him, and together they descended the path.

On the flat shore, her captor spoke again in the unfamiliar tongue. Whatever meaning the words held, they made the squat man laugh. Weetamo stiffened at the grin that spread across the tall one's face. Yet, she fixed her eyes hard on his and did not allow a hint of her weakened courage.

The tall one dropped his musket. The grin was gone. His eyes gleamed stern as they lowered over her body. With an opened hand, he pushed against her chest, causing Weetamo to stumble backward. He stepped in and pushed again, this time with such great force that Weetamo fell to the ground.

She turned onto her belly, pulled against the sand, tried to get to her feet. To run. But strong fingers clutched at her long black hair. The stranger coiled thick strands of it around his fist, tightened his grip, and Weetamo could not move any farther.

The raspy voice of the squat man spoke at her back. He raised phlegm and spit again, and the two men laughed together. Fear pounded in Weetamo's chest.

Nohtok raced the dawn. Each pull on the paddle went deep. Sweat warmed his bared chest as his dugout sped across the rolling swells. He had woken early, his heart remembering that by next nightfall Weetamo would be given as his wife. For the rest of his days as man upon this earth, he would have the privilege of both her softness and her strength.

But he would not see Weetamo until again the darkness came unless he found her now before the day began. And at this early hour if, like him, Weetamo had risen restless from sleep, she would be at the great hill surrounded by the sea.

The white cliffs grew larger, closer, and Nohtok worked his paddle against the water, caught in that space between rhythm and the effort. He saw the empty dugout first. Aimlessly it rode on top of low swells far out from the island shore. The dip of his paddle became quick, its stroke deep, and Nohtok kept his eyes trained on the beach ahead. Each stroke brought him nearer until his eyes fell upon the figure of a man on the beach. Not a man of his people. This one wore the strange, loose clothing of the trading men. The man was stout and stood bent forward, hands rested on his knees. Then Nohtok saw the second man low on the sand. But it was the cry of a woman that caught in the air.

Weetamo.

As if in one motion, he placed the paddle down and pulled the whalebone blade from its sheath, raising it high over his shoulder. His eyes beaded on his target. With the power of a practiced hunter, his hand released the blade.

The blade cut, silent through the distance.

The stout man fell in a slump to the ground.

The weight of the tall man was suddenly on her, her body pinned beneath him, her arms held above her head. He lowered himself closer still, until the coarse hair of the foreign face scratched her neck, and Weetamo bit with clamped teeth onto the cheek of the man. Her body writhed under the weight, but bile rose in her throat, forcing her clenched jaw open.

His open palm hit. The force turned her head into the sand, and the rough grit ground against her face.

As if beckoned by her will, the warring screech of Nohtok came loud across the beach, and Weetamo felt the heaviness of the tall one roll aside. She pushed against the sand. Forced her legs to scramble away. Forced control. Not until then did she see the body of the squat man lying face down with a blade of her people in his back.

For a moment only, she hesitated as Nohtok ran with his knees high through the shallow water of the shore. But the tall, pale-skinned man had found his musket, and he aimed it ready for Nohtok.

Weetamo pushed to her feet, thrust her body against the arm of the tall man. The man lurched, and a loud fire shot from the musket.

Nohtok – he did not fall. He leapt across the distance, and the two men, Nohtok and the pale one, crumbled together to the ground. While their bodies twisted and rolled toward the water, Weetamo hurried to the body of the squat man. She pulled the blade from his back, warm blood rushing over her hands. She turned, ready with the blade. But Nohtok's dark muscled body straddled the paled stranger, and he held the hair-covered face beneath the water until the struggle stopped.

Her hand shook as she bent to rinse the blade. When Nohtok came to her, she let the blade fall into the water. He took both her hands gently into his, and he drew her to her feet. His eyes scanned over her trembling body.

"I am fine," she told him.

"He did not hurt you?"

"No," she said. "Because you arrived, I am not harmed."

"Come," said Nohtok with one hand still holding her own, and the two ran together toward Nohtok's dugout canoe.

She waded with him into deep water and scrambled into the canoe, knelt in front as Nohtok worked the paddle, pressing the canoe forward. A musket fired. Then another. The dugout held to its quick smooth pace, telling Weetamo that Nohtok was not struck. But a third shot fired. The rhythm broke, and Weetamo turned to see Nohtok fall forward, nearly loosing hold of the paddle before he regained position. On the island shore, more men in traders' clothes gathered. A fourth shot fired, but Nohtok, this time, drove the paddle hard. The mainland came steadily closer. The shouts of the strange-tongued men faded.

Weetamo stepped out into the spill of shallow waves and pulled the dugout onto the beach. She looked back to the bay and across to the island and saw no sign that the foreign men had followed.

But Nohtok …

Blood, thick and red, gushed from beneath his shoulder. She had him sit so she could rinse his wound with the healing water of the sea. The wound was open and too much of the flesh was torn. It would need the bruised flower of the elderberry.

Her own village was closest. There she would tend the wound of Nohtok.

Five

Night filled the hut, and with Nohtok standing so close at her back, Weetamo fingered the mat woven with bulrush. This one mat and the many others that lined the dome hut did not need rearranging. Each had been tightly woven and placed on the walls of the wetu carefully by herself to provide warmth come time of the snow. But on this her wedding night, the hand of Weetamo needed to be busy.

Never before had she felt so tentative, so unsure.

As a child, when the people of many villages had reason to meet, she had watched Nohtok play with the other boys and had felt respect even then. Yet, because she was not allowed to take part in the games of boys, she had not known his friendship until many more passings of summer. When at last she came into womanhood, her body giving of itself in cycles with the moon, Nohtok had spoken of his fondness for her, and Weetamo had easily expressed the extent of her feelings. Tonight, however, a great silence grew around them.

Beyond the walls of the wetu, drums and whoops of laughter bore on into the darkness. In ceremony, beneath a spark-filled night sky that smelled of fire and wood smoke, Nohtok had taken her as wife. Members of every village had followed them as far as the doorway. Now they were suddenly alone.

The hands of Nohtok took gentle hold. He turned her body to face his own, and she leaned to the caress of his hand upon her cheek.

Still Weetamo could not meet his eyes. Thunder beat in her chest as she walked behind him, inspecting the poultice that covered the recent wound. "Perhaps Nohtok should rest. You have not had time to recover."

"How can I rest?" He held her to him, and she felt his solid breadth, the strength of his arms surrounding her.

"Nohtok." The simple whisper of his name let tension go, and with his arms around her, she felt the warmth of Nohtok become her own warmth. Slowly, she stepped back and let the dress of soft hide slip to the floor. His finger traced her collarbone from shoulder to her throat, followed the line down between her small, rounded breasts, and her breath escaped.

He led her to their bed of mats, and Weetamo lay down on the softness. No longer timid, she waited as Nohtok removed his loin cover and let himself down next to her. Their bodies touched, melded. And in the flickering dimness of the small fire's light, the two were joined.

Night held no sound but the lolling break of the sea. She did not know when the celebration outside had ended. The chest of Notok rose and fell slowly beneath her own. They now lived as one. Yet, with that thought came the overwhelming feel of loss, and a tear spilled down onto her cheek.

The gentle thumb of Nohtok brushed the wet trail away. "Why?"

One word but it was a question so large she feared the answer. "I am happy, Nohtok. Never before have I felt so much joy. Yet, a part of me walks to that other side where I have met grief. On that other side, I feel the loss of an earlier Weetamo, for I have always been that other, the daughter of Tackanaw, a maiden of Ponokanet people. Now my spirit joins yours. My love for Nohtok is deep ... so deep that I fear the loss of myself within it. What is to happen to that earlier self?"

"That Weetamo is here beside me still. She is strong and yet she bends to life like a birch. Because the birch bends, because it grows, this does not mean the birch no longer is a birch."

She placed her head onto the chest of Nohtok, listened to the heartbeat. She felt the tenderness in him. And the two, Weetamo and Nohtok, did not see the rising dawn, for at last they slept, both body and spirit intertwined.

Six

Sydney
Evening of Friday, August 31

She steps into the pants, cotton scrubs she wears as pajamas. The only clean shirt in her suitcase is a yellow t-shirt. She hesitates, remembering Alison in the lime-green dress, then pulls the t-shirt over her head. She hates it though – hates that she even considers what Alison might think. It makes her feel like that sad little girl again, the girl who learned late that she couldn't win approval no matter how she tried.

Barefoot, Sydney walks down the stairs.

In the kitchen, the table is set for two. Two plates, each with Caesar salad topped with chicken. "I'll shop for us tomorrow," says Alison, "but tonight I made do by stretching the few things you had in the fridge."

"You don't need to shop for me." Sydney stands at the side of the table, not quite able to push herself into sitting down.

Alison takes a bottle of white wine from the refrigerator, wine that did not come from Sydney's grocery bag. "What happened to your lip?" asks Alison while pouring into two stemmed glasses.

"I bit it." And Sydney sits, if for no other reason than to get at the meal and to change the subject.

Alison looks to Sydney's lip, to where the lip has swollen into a cushion of raw flesh, but surprisingly Alison lets the topic drop. "I see you've brought a cat," she says. "All the way from California?"

"I couldn't leave her behind."

Alison, still in lime green, sits at the table, across from Sydney, and the clock on the wall ticks through the silence. Sydney cuts into the sliced chicken on her plate. She pokes at it with her fork.

"Ty called," says Alison. "He said he met you out in the yard."

"Briefly."

"You'll like him. He does so much around here. He wanted to know if we needed anything before he settled in for the night. That's so like Ty. So thoughtful."

Sydney sets her fork on the table, meaning to feel her way. But the Ty situation irritates, like nettle under her skin. "Why is he here?" she asks. "Why do you have some man living in Eva's barn?"

Alison matches Sydney's glare. "First of all, it's no longer Eva's barn. And Ty is here because most of the time I am not. This place, it doesn't take care of itself, you know."

"I know but …"

"Sydney, really, he's a very nice guy." Although the fire has cooled in her eyes, still Alison leans in. "Ty stays to himself. I never really see him unless he's outside working. And besides, the insurance costs less if someone is living on the property."

"I understand all that. But I'm here now. And I'd like to stay for a while." Sydney folds the linen napkin, plunks it onto the table as if in some finality. "Look. I know I haven't been here in years. I haven't been any help. But since Rick … since he died, things have felt all wrong. I'm all wrong. I can't explain it exactly, but I thought … I thought it would be good to have some time alone. Some time to get my life back together. I just thought there'd be more solitude here, that's all."

Alison wets her lips, glances to the crumpled linen napkin that lies on the table. "Seems to me, you don't get back into life by isolating yourself. But that's neither here nor there. As I said … Ty is no bother. And if it makes you feel any better, Everett is the person who recommended him."

As if knowing she's hit a chord, Alison sits back and sips her glass of wine, looking smug because it was Everett – the man who, those years ago, taught Sydney to fly. He'd been Sydney's instructor. More importantly, he'd been her friend. Everett gave her reason for being. She has planned to see him tomorrow, to drive out to his small airport and visit. He's a big part of why she came back to Ponokanet.

"You said it yourself, Sydney. You don't know how long you'll stay. And Ty ... he's good at everything he does." Alison sets her glass of wine on the table, leaving a smudge of red lipstick on the glass rim. "You've seen what he's done with painting the house and with all the flowers. I'll never find anyone better."

Sydney pulls through her still-wet hair. She hates losing, even to a logical argument. There is still the irritation deep below the surface. It makes her want to scream. "You used to hate this place even more than I did," she says, hearing the tightness in her own voice. "You hated everything about Ponokanet. Isn't it odd that now, all of a sudden, you find this place so ... so important?"

Alison takes a second sip of wine. "I didn't hate everything. Just being stuck here in the middle of nowhere. But people change, Sydney."

"Do they?"

Alison glances away, infuriating in the way she avoids looking at Sydney, merely smoothing the linen napkin on her lime-green lap. "Let's not fight, Sydney. Let's eat dinner. And tell me, what are your plans while you're here."

A sigh blows warm and heavy over Sydney's swollen lip. For now, the argument, round one at least, has been lost.

"Would you like more wine for the living room?" asks Alison.

"No. None for me," says Sydney while putting the last of their plates into the dishwasher.

Exhaustion is in every muscle, and Sydney says goodnight, glad to be going upstairs. But Cat meets Sydney in the front hall, and both look to the screen door. Sydney opens the door and follows Cat out onto the porch.

The moon shows no more than a silver sliver over the barn roof, but countless stars pierce the blackness. The Big Dipper and the summer triangle of Aquila shine like pinholes pricked in patterns, the same patterns that Sydney once poked through the old lampshade in her grandmother's small library. Sometimes at night, the young Sydney would sit alone with only that one lamp and read about the constellations. As she read about each one, she used a needle to poke its pattern, yellow stars in a darkened room. Memorizing them – the names and patterns – it fed a need to learn all there was to know about the sky in which she flew.

Tonight, on the porch, the thick darkness smells of the sea. All around her, waves wash onto the shore. And Sydney thinks about seeing Everett in the morning. He is a rare person. One of those few whose strength flows like extra milk to those who need it.

She hasn't told Everett she's come back. She hasn't wanted him asking why. He believes she's stronger than this. Braver. Yet, she is eager to see him.

Behind her, the tall windows give a soft hint of light from far back in the kitchen. Alison is in there, but only for a week. Seven days. Sydney looks to the darkness, to the depth of sky. The seven days will pass, she supposes, while she holds on. Then she will have her seasons.

In a few minutes, when Cat returns from a stroll somewhere out beyond the porch, Sydney will go up to her room and lie on the narrow bed. She'll call Jean back in California and let Jean know she's arrived safe on the island. Then sleep, Sydney hopes, will follow.

Seven

Sydney
Early Saturday morning, September 1

The first full day begins in shades of gray. Across the yard, the barn
shows in charcoal against a dusty sky, and the pines stretch from sleep
in ashen silhouette. On the front porch Sydney slips into running
shoes, glances to the Subaru because this morning she wants, more
than anything, to drive to Everett. But the sun isn't up. She must fill at
least a couple hours before going to see him. So, she'll go for a run and
catch the sunrise along the way.

With the back of a hand, she touches the tender bottom lip.
The lip is not so sore today, and she takes it as a sign of all things
getting better. She steps down from the porch – a first step but not a
small one into a new life.

The path, as she remembers, begins behind the barn. She jogs
lightly across the yard, not wanting to be heard by the man who sleeps
inside. But when she turns the corner, at the back of the barn, she
stops and has to stare. A new glass room, a kind of solarium, has been
added on. Even in the early gray light, Sydney can see inside to the
shadowy forms of plants. All kinds. Potted ones on shelves. Tall leaf-
topped stalks that reach from floor to near the top. No curtains, no
darkened glass prevent her from looking in at the profusion, the
abundance of it all.

The plants, in here and in front of the house, they are obviously
the work of the caretaker. He lives in there somewhere behind all that

incredible growth, and Sydney wonders what kind of man uses his time creating space for flowers. Her only experience with growing things was with a row of marigolds beside the bungalow in Santa Rosa. She'd bought a few cardboard flats of yellow, and while on her hands and knees, she poked each plant into a hole, filled in around it with rich dark dirt from a bag, trying in earnest to do it right. The next day, she and Rick left for three days of hiking in the Sierra Nevada. When they returned, they stood together over the barren row, Sydney shaking her head at the hard brown dots that once were sweet yellow blossoms. Rick, in his usual pragmatic way, said only, "We don't need flowers anyway. Better to spend your energy on a plant we can eat."

Sydney closes her eyes to push away the memory, and she concentrates on the distant soft wash of sea over sand. When her breath settles, she jogs on, away from the barn.

The path at the edge of the woods lies nearly hidden under wandering bearberry, but enough shows and Sydney's pace quickens, each footfall light as she enters in among the pines. The run feels good. Where the path forks, instead of turning down onto the beach, Sydney follows along the island rim. Through pine boughs she sees that the tide is out. The beach spreads far, bare and flat. The distant water, indigo in the low light, murmurs and snakes in moody curves across the pale sand. How different the sea is in this protected bay, so different from the raw open Pacific that pounds the California coast.

Before, in the years she spent here, Sydney never really liked the sea. She preferred the sky. Speed in flight thrilled far more than any ship held by viscous water. To escape the ever-present sea, she rode her bike down over the bridge to Everett and to his small airport two miles away. With Everett, she learned to fly above it all. The sky, being up there in it, soaring thousands of feet above the earth, that had been everything – her world – a world in the heavens.

But no more. No more soaring. No more love affair with the sky. Beginning today, she must make close friends with this bit of sea.

On the horizon comes the first thin show of pink, and Sydney opens her stride. If she hurries, she'll get to the stone before the sun actually appears. The sunrise was something the young Sydney seldom climbed out of bed to see. But Eva touted the sunrise as a great event – the heaven's 'magnum opus' to hear Eva tell it. After any session with a sunrise, Eva returned to the house all smiles, and Sydney, sitting half-awake with cereal in the kitchen, merely listened as Eva talked of color spilling like paint across the sky.

The path ends, and Sydney stands at the rim of the island, beside an enormous boulder. About a dozen of these giant chunks of stone lay scattered across the outer Cape, giants left behind eons ago by melting glaciers. But on Ponokanet there is just this one, and as pink deepens on the horizon, Sydney sits with her back against the hard gray stone and she gazes out.

The sky turns to magenta.

A breeze picks up off the water, cooling the warm sweat on her skin, and the same breeze slips through the tree limbs, causing the pines to whine. Less a whine really than a call - *Be you. Be you.*

It's her imagination. She knows that. But the words – *be you* – she's heard them before. Years ago. They were Eva's words.

At fourteen, that first autumn after Alison discarded Sydney here on the island, Sydney picked a fight at school, a knock down and roll on the floor fight with a girl who had called her a freak and a loser. Eva was called to the school to bail Sydney out of the principal's office. Afterwards, in the car, Eva reached across the front seat to examine the bruise on Sydney's face. "Looks sore," said Eva, and Sydney burst into tears, tears that had been building for weeks behind a wall of spiked hair, ear piercings and self-isolation.

"Sydney, at your age life can seem too hard," said Eva. "But that's because you're learning how to be you. That's your biggest job right now ... too find out who you want to be in this world. And it has to be your choice, Sydney. The hell with what anyone else says. What's important is that you be you, be who you want to be and go for it with all your heart."

Today with the stone at her back, Sydney draws a breath heavy with the scent of wet tidal muck. *Be you.* Good advice then. Good advice now. But the question is hanging there. Who is this thirty-nine-year-old Sydney going to be?

Sydney pulls knees to her chest, wraps her arms around them. On the horizon the first molten arc appears.

On the beach below a man appears.

The caretaker.

In easy fluid motion, he sits cross-legged on the beach, his face to the rising sun. The hair has been freed this morning, freed to fall below the man's shoulders and black wisps catch on the light breeze. In that silhouette, his back to the high cliff, he looks to be a statue, a Buddha-like form, and Sydney wonders why this man Ty is here. What need brought him to live in the quiet solitude of Ponokanet?

The sun's arc slowly lifts – lifts until the sky rids itself of the reds, takes up instead the golden hues of daylight and the sun comes to full round. The caretaker stands, causing Sydney to stand as well. She moves farther back, not wanting to be seen. But Ty never looks up. He merely walks his easy gait barefoot back along the beach.

This Ty then – he is an early morning person.

In a burst of old memory Sydney recalls an argument she would toss back to Rick whenever he asked her not to jog alone early in the morning. She was safe at dawn, she'd say, because all the creeps of the world had just gone to bed, asleep after their long night of stalking.

Sydney checks her watch. There's time to jog the remaining rim around the island. Back at the house, she'll shower and sit on the deck for a while with some juice. By then, it will be late enough to go to Everett.

Alison stands at the kitchen counter pouring a cup of coffee. She wears a pile robe and no make-up at all. Her skin looks thin and paler than Sydney remembers. "Hi," says Sydney before carrying the carton of orange juice to the counter and filling a glass.

"I'm going shopping later," says Alison. "At the mall and then to an outdoor furniture place on Route 28. We need a few new chairs for the deck. Would you like to come along?"

"I can't. I'm visiting Everett."

"How about some breakfast then?"

"No, thanks," says Sydney. "I have to shower first, but then I'm going to the airport."

"So early?"

Sydney takes a swallow of juice, and in her head she counts, making it to five before she notices. Alison's eyes are wet, as if she's been stung.

"I just hoped that you and I ... well, another time maybe," says Alison, and with coffee mug in hand, Alison walks from the kitchen onto the deck.

Sydney finishes the remaining juice but watches as her mother sits alone, staring out to the bay. So, what did Alison expect? Friends? Oh, yes, let's share secrets and go to the mall.

Cat scampers into the kitchen from somewhere in the house. Sydney fills the round food dish on the floor and scratches behind one gray ear before climbing the stairs to shower.

Eight

The last stretch of road on approach to the airport runs beside an open field. On the grass, a few planes sit lined up in a row, their wings tied down with rope. Here, there are no flashy stunt planes designed to sustain the pressure of forced G's. These are a half dozen ordinary pleasure planes that include an old Aeronca and the red and white Cessna that's been tied in that field since Sydney first started coming up the road. This morning she smiles at seeing the Cessna at the end of the row. She can almost smell the old vinyl seat, the light scent of oil. She drives on past and parks in front of the tin hangar.

The wide hangar door is shut, so Sydney walks to the far side. But even the side door is closed. She rattles the knob, but the door won't open. All those years ago, inside this hangar was where she found him. If not in flight, Everett would be inside, standing on the old stepladder, bent over the engine of one plane or another. He'd work and at the same time listen to her endless questions. Questions because Sydney wanted to understand how a plane could fly.

Everett answered every one.

As incredible as it seems, he never minded her hanging around. Or at least he never showed it. Instead, whenever she pedaled in and set the bike against the hangar wall, those slate gray eyes of his lit up. She'd find a stool or just sit on the cool of the concrete floor and start with the questions. And Everett would give that girl all the answers, all the whys and hows of flight. Sometimes, the best times, he dropped whatever he was doing, leaving wrenches laid out on an old rag, and he'd take her up in the Cessna, to show her the feel of the aileron or the knack of keeping the nose to the horizon.

Sydney rattles the doorknob again but with the same result.

The second option is to try the wooden structure that serves as an office. She leaves the car by the hangar and walks the fifty yards.

But things are not at all how she remembers them. Above the office door, bolted on, is the same familiar sign, Dean Aviation carved into the wood, but the gold lettering is weathered out. The once blue background and the hand-painted red and white Cessna are equally faded and cracked. Even the building – its siding of cedar shingles has gone beyond weathered gray to black and twisted, beaten down by the Cape Cod sun and wind and rain. In the distance, on the old macadam runway, tuffs of grass grow in the cracks.

It's like entering the wrong kitchen, feeling not right with things out of place. Everett was always meticulous with the airport. This place had been his father's before it was Everett's. And Everett would never let it decay like this. This airport is everything to him.

Inside the office, two men and a middle-aged blonde woman stand together. The woman is in the midst of telling a fly story. She tells how she once flew the old Aeronca low over the outer beach, a buzz dive that uncovered two youngsters, a boy and a girl who ran naked up into the dunes. The story ends with something about a good roll in the sand, and the men laugh.

When the laughter ends, Sydney asks when Everett will be in.

"Don't expect him much before noon."

"Not until then?" asks Sydney, because Everett never missed a morning or a fly story.

The woman crosses the small office to where Sydney stands. "Is there somethin' I can help you with?"

"No," says Sydney. "I was just hoping to see Everett."

"You're a friend of his?"

"Yes, I am."

"Then you know he's tired these days. He takes his time coming in. But he's home, across the field in the house if you want to go say hello."

But Sydney hears little after the first few words. "What do you mean he's tired?"

"You know, from the cancer."

Sydney's mouth opens but nothing …

"You didn't know about the cancer?"

"No," says Sydney. "I haven't seen Everett … not for a long time."

The woman eyes Sydney, a scientific eye to a new specimen, before a warm smile pulls across her face. "You're Sydney, aren't you?"

Sydney only nods because words are stuck, a mass in her throat.

"Well, Sydney, I'm sure glad you're here. My name's Nora." Nora puts out a hand and shakes Sydney's with a solid grip. "You go see him," says Nora. "I know he's up because I just came from there myself."

Except for the university and the eight years spent flying rotor birds for the Air Force, Everett has lived all his life in the house on the far side of the field. Yet, Sydney has never once been inside. Back then there was no reason to cross the field to the house. The planes and Everett could be found at the airport. But today she walks the distance, her mind taken up by what she's heard.

Cancer.

Everett is sick and she had no idea.

Sydney presses to her chest, to the crush of panic.

Last year Everett had told her about the first cancer. He wrote about it in a letter, saying he'd been fighting non-Hodgkin's lymphoma. He also said he was in remission. She thought he was cured.

But now, again?

Tears burn but Sydney fights them. She won't meet him that way – not crying. She knocks on the front door. In his letters, they haven't been many but still, he never mentioned this new cancer. Why? Maybe he doesn't want her to know. Maybe he wants to keep the fact that he's sick from everyone but those closest few, those who absolutely have to know. And she isn't one of them.

She'll wait to see his face, to see if he smiles, glad that she's come, or if he hesitates, shifting his weight, a signal that she should simply say hello and leave.

But before the door even opens, Sydney knows no matter what look she sees, she will not leave without sitting with him, without hearing what he has to say. Everett once understood her like no one else. She needs him again. Everett is going to have to let her in.

Nine

After sixteen years as wife to Nohtok, in the season of warm sun, 1606

The tidewater creeped in toward shore, and the shallow footprints of Weetamo filled with the wash of gentle incoming water. She lifted the reed basket, and the basket strained under the weight of white-shelled mollusks. Her gathering was done.

A dugout glided toward land, and joy swelled Weetamo's heart, for leaning hard against the paddle was her son, Cononchet. Though having known only the span of fifteen summers, he moved with both body and courage of a man. Yet, there were times when Weetamo could not quell a mother's fear, times when her only son left the narrow land of her people to defend their sister tribes against the Narragansett. It was because of his courage and skill that he had been chosen, so Weetamo silenced her fear and showed only the face of pride when her son left alongside his father on such a journey.

On this day the task of Cononchet had been but to carry back the bones of the giant blackfish. Recently, during strong wind and rain, the gods had offered up the great fish. The length of three men, the sleek black and white body of the blackfish had washed onto the shore of the island and left there as the bay water drained. Already the clan women had paddled out and cut away the meat. They'd brought the great oily slabs back to be smoked and dried. Before the sea could reclaim all remains, Cononchet and three others had gone to gather the ribs and the spine bone, to be carved during the cold of winter, shaped into tools and beads of decoration. But something now seemed not right. No giant frame of bone dragged on the bottom behind the dugouts that pulled up onto the beach.

"Mother," called Cononchet when he stepped out from his dugout. "I have seen the great vessel with wings, white like the night moth. Perhaps they are traders. I have returned to tell my grandfather that the foreigners are near."

A boy's excitement spilled into the voice of the man, but Weetamo's heart turned heavy, a stone in a river. As if many summers had not passed between, she felt the slap of the foreigner she once encountered – a man dressed in clothes not of animal skin and who stank of filth. No foreign vessels had come again to the village since that day. No enemies. No traders. No men from across the sea.

But now …

Weetamo pulled against her need to run. She must think clearly, not react with the frightened heart of a young girl. So she did not keep pace with her son and the other young men that ran toward the village, toward Tackanaw, who was now the village elder. Instead, with laden basket in her arms, Weetamo walked slowly along the path. She spoke to the spirit of the wind, asking it to turn direction, to turn and to carry the winged vessel on back across the water.

Tackanaw soon blocked the path, his aged and sinewy body backed by that of Nohtok. Cononchet stepped to the side of his father. The rubbed wood of their bows caught the rays of sun and glistened, and Weetamo saw the same glisten in the eye of her son.

She stopped there in front of Tackanaw.

"My grandson has told me that foreigners approach," he said.

"And you believe they will come here?"

"There is no way to know, Weetamo. We go to the beach. If the foreign men bring their vessel to shore, we will meet them there, not in the village."

"And what will you do if they come?"

"We will meet them as guests, but we are ready if they mean harm."

Weetamo glanced to her son. "Their number may be many," she said. "You are but three."

"My daughter worries needlessly. The men of our village are hidden nearby. Each quiver carries many arrows." Tackanaw looked to the bush and pine that lined the meadow before he turned again to Weetamo. "To meet the ship with all our men," he said, "might be considered a threat by the foreigners. But to face possible danger without our greatest force ready would not be wise."

Nohtok came to her and touched briefly upon her arm. "The other women have taken the children and gone to the dense cover of the cedars. I ask that you go with them."

Without reply, Weetamo stepped aside, and she waited as the men passed. But she did not seek out the safety of the cedar forest. She crossed the low meadow, not taking any path, to where the bayberry and juniper grew thick, providing a line of cover between her and the beach. She caught a glint of rubbed wood no more than ten paces distant. Setting down her basket, she lay on her belly beneath the low branches and watched as the great vessel folded its wings far out from shore.

A smaller boat lowered over the side to the water and filled with a handful of men, men who rowed until they reached the shore of the Ponokanet. All wore hair blunt-cut and short, and most grew hair on their faces. But not their leader. Not the man who stepped first out of the boat and walked to Tackanaw.

Tackanaw stood particularly straight, and he announced to the foreigners that they had arrived at the village of Ponokanet people. The leader nodded in a way that lowered his eyes from the face of his host. Yet, Weetamo did not trust the eyes. She did not trust that subtle sign of submission.

When the foreigner spoke, although his words fell as broken

pieces, the words were recognizable as words of the Ponokanet tongue. "We wish trade. Friends," he said so that everyone heard, and he slowly pulled a strip of brightly colored cloth from inside his heavy cloak. The cloth was followed by a gold bracelet. Both he placed in the hand of Tackanaw. "For you. Many more in the boat."

"What is it you want in exchange for these things?"

The challenge in Tackanaw's question was heard even by Weetamo at her hiding place. But the stranger, planting feet slightly apart on the sand, met Tackanaw's steady gaze. "I have seen before pieces of bone and wood carved by your people. And beads that were very beautiful. I wish to make a trade. Treasures from France for treasures from Ponokanet."

"I am an old man," said Tackanaw. "In my lifetime I have met men from your France and from other places far across the sea. Some have come with weapons. And my people have been harmed."

"I am not those men. I ask you to consider that."

Tackanaw looked deep to the faces of the other trader men, then again to the face of the man who spoke for them. But from her place beneath the juniper, Weetamo watched only the face of her father. Across its leathery lines she read his concern. She knew he considered within him the lives of his children, and their children, and theirs. As sachem, it was his duty to consider not only this moment but also the moments for those generations that follow. In her heart, Weetamo wished for her father to send these men away, back to the far shores.

"Cononchet," said her father. "Find Weetamo. Have her select items of value and bring them here. We will trade with this man."

Weetamo withdrew from her hiding place. She lifted again the basket of white shells and met her son on the path.

"We are to bring items for trade," he said. "It is Tackanaw's wish."

She walked briskly in front of her son, taking him to their wetu.

Leaving the filled basket by the low entryway, she stepped inside. Only then did Weetamo speak the words she felt. "Tackanaw is wrong to do this."

"But he is sachem," said Cononchet. "He knows best what we should do."

Weetamo worked at selecting items, inspecting the knots on a string of black-shell beads, eyeing the perfection of pattern on a bulrush mat. With those items held now in her hands, she faced the son that stood tall before her.

"Age, Cononchet, has great benefit. But no long line of decisions can be completely without error."

"These men have brought cloth of colors I have never seen. And bracelets that shine of sunlight. I ask my mother how trading for these things can be wrong."

"Our ancestors have lived since the beginning of time without this cloth or these bracelets."

"What you say is true," he said, "but have you not enjoyed the foreigner's metal pot in which you and your own mother have cooked?"

"And have you forgotten that your father was once wounded by one of those men from across the sea?"

Her son shifted his weight, and his eyes glanced briefly away to the floor. "No, Mother, I do not forget the story of my father's wound. But this foreign man said it himself … he is not the one that used the weapon. Does not every man deserve to be judged on his own merit?"

"Cononchet grows wise. He makes me very proud. But I tell you, my son, that I am worried for our people."

"Then you still disagree with my grandfather?"

The shoulders of Weetamo sank low but only for a moment. She drew a breath and set her shoulders once again, her spine ready. "I am but one voice," she said to her son. "The possibility of traders has many times been discussed with the elders, and today Tackanaw made his decision. We are to trade. Come, take those baskets. And the fur robe. The traders may find it useful.

That night in sleep the vision came –

Air hung heavy with the stench of rotting flesh, the flesh of her people. Weetamo sat by the pile of dead – young and old heaped onto the pile, the arms and legs sprawled and limp. She tried to hold the babies, but they were too many. The pile grew too large. All the while, the malicious spirit Hobbamoqui laughed from a blackened sky, and the dead babies cried.

The golden sign of a thunderbolt crackled across the blackness, giving Weetamo escape from the dream. She had been sitting upright when her eyes opened. The wetness of heat covered her body. With Nohtok in sleep at her side, she lay back on her mat, tried to match the rhythm of his breath. But even with her eyes opened to the quiet of night, the vision remained and fear gripped around her heart.

Ten

Weetamo
After passing twelve seasons of the sun, 1618

While gray came to her hair, the Ponokanet people respected Weetamo for her wisdom and her way with the gods. But today, no matter the promises she made to Hobbamoqui, the mightiest of all vengeful gods, nothing stopped the dying. No matter the numbers or how desperately Weetamo pleaded, the sick did not heal. And in the dim light of dawn, beneath Hobbamoqui's powerful hand, Weetamo feared for her son. His body lay so still. Earlier, in the darkness of the night, he had moaned and his eyes had opened when Weetamo washed his body, wiping the oozing blisters that had invaded every space. But no sound came from him now, no flicker of recognition. Fever had taken him into a distant sleep.

She lifted him to her and cradled his head on her lap. Cononchet lived in the body of a man but he was her son – her boy. Never before had pain cut so deeply into her heart. Silent tears fell. And Weetamo rocked her son.

Two days earlier she had walked to this village of her son's wife. Weetamo had been sent for, requested by the mother of Awashonk. Awashonk was a quiet girl, young, and already she and Cononchet shared a son. But like so many others, both Awashonk and Cononchet fell ill with the strange new sickness. Weetamo had spent these two days in the wetu of the sick, placing a poultice of shinleaf on the blisters and forcing Cononchet to sip the broth steeped with wych elm bark. This tending should have been the work of the pawaw, but the sick were too many. The pawaw stopped by only to bleed those in need and to beg the spirit world for the return of health, before he moved on to the next body lying hot and swollen by the crusty sores.

All this Weetamo did while Awashonk was tended by the girl's own mother, though the mother, too, was weak with fever. Awashonk, however, had gone quickly. At the last high sun, the village people, those who were well enough, walked to the burial hill, high on the far side of the narrow land, and there they had placed the girl's body toward the southern sky.

Soon Cononchet would be carried there also, to be set to the southwest so that his spirit might find the home of Kietan, the great ancient one that lives in the sky. With certainty, Weetamo knew the spirit of Cononchet was worthy and would find its way to the ancient one. But she was not ready to let him go.

The weakened voice of Cononchet came then through blistered lips, and Weetamo met the eyes of her son looking upon her face.

"Mittark," he whispered.

"He is with your father. Your son is well."

As the eyes of Cononchet closed, Weetamo held him close, clinging to his fleeting spirit, but the eyes opened again.

"Mittark. Care for him," the voice scarcely a whisper.

"Mittark is a part of me, just as you are a part of me. I will care for him."

"Goodbye, Mother."

"No ..."

But her son's eyes stared blankly past her. She heard the wails of anguish as if from someone else, but while she held close the body of Cononchet, she knew full well the anguish was her own.

The paddle cut slowly through the calm water. Weetamo did not hurry. Patiently, rhythmically, she paddled toward the white cliffs. Mittark sat low in the bow of the dugout, with only the back of his raven hair and the small but arrow-straight shoulders visible to her. She watched him more than she did the water ahead.

He had spoken little since the death of his mother and father. Half his village had been taken by the sickness. It was too much a loss for a child. Yet, he would survive. She would see to that. She would show him that love does not die with change and loss.

The dugout scraped bottom, and Weetamo stepped out into the shallow water. Already the bay held the first bite of the cold to come, and she let the cold ache seep into her ankles while she dragged the dugout through the shallows to the sand of the shore.

"Come," she said. "I have a special place to show you."

Though the boy had seen five summers, she bent to lift him and held him against her. More than ever, he craved this affection, this tenderness, and Weetamo gave it, knowing that it filled her own need as well. She carried him this way across the beach until they came to the path that would lead them up the high cliff and into the dense forest. She set her grandson down and took his hand, and the boy returned her hold with his own tight grip.

"This path will climb that steep hill," she said. "At the top there is a place that always brings happiness to your grandmother. Would you like to go up there with me?"

The boy nodded his answer.

"Come then. I will show you."

Together they walked, staying close along the path. When the earth flattened, they walked a short distance more, to where a clearing opened and the great stone rested at the edge of land.

"Here," she said. "This is my special place."

Weetamo sat at the base of the high stone. She asked the boy to do the same. He pulled his knees to his chest, wrapped his arms around them as he looked out to the bay.

"A long time ago, when I was just your age, my father sat here with me by this same stone." Weetamo spoke softly while she, too, kept her eyes forward over the calm indigo water. "My father told me how this stone came to be." And leaving out no details, Weetamo retold the story of Kietan, how the most powerful of all the gods had sacrificed his own daughter, how Kietan had turned her into this stone so that the Ponokanet might be watched over and protected.

"I believe," said Weetamo, "the spirit of the goddess sits here with us even today, a sister to the Ponokanet."

With story ended, Weetamo sat quiet while the sea moved on. The honk of geese sounded in flight across the sky, but Weetamo herself said no more. She waited, longing for the child to speak.

At last he turned his young face. His gaze lifted to Weetamo, and he asked her, "Why did the goddess not protect my mother?"

"I think the sickness was too new, even to the gods."

"But I heard what the pawaw said. He said my mother and all the others were being punished by the gods." The boy looked to his knees, and the back of one small hand brushed at his cheek. "The pawaw said my mother must have done something evil."

Weetamo wished to hold the boy, to take him into her arms. But she did not. She sat, instead, at his side with barely his shoulder touching her arm. "Mittark, I will tell you what I know in my heart. No evil ever came from your mother or your father. They were gentle and kind and did always good toward others. The pawaw speaks from ancient rulings held in his head, not from the sense of his heart."

Mittark sat silent. But Weetamo waited, and she watched the workings of thought move across the boy's face. In time, she spoke again. "Do you hear that? Do you hear the sea falling on the sand?"

The boy looked to her. "Yes," he said.

Such a tiny voice but Weetamo filled with the sound of it. "And do you hear the wind?"

Mittark looked to the tops of the green pines. "Yes, I hear the wind."

"During times when I sit here," said Weetamo, "I listen to the wind because on that wind are the voices of those I love, all those who have gone on. They sing across the pines. And if I sit still enough, very still, I can feel them. They caress my face and arms, like this." And with the gentlest of touch, she drew her fingers across the cheek of Mittark, drew her fingers down along his slender arm. As she took her hand away, she whispered, "Close your eyes now and feel. Feel the tender wind."

Weetamo opened her own eyes early to see that Mittark's were closed. The gentle wind whispered on the pine, and a narrow stream of tears fell unchecked down the boy's angled cheek.

"I feel it, Grandmother." The eyes of Mittark blinked, then opened wide. "I feel it." And when his arms reached out to Weetamo, she clutched him to her chest.

"You will never be without your mother's touch. You will never be without her love. You need only to be still and feel." Her voice broke, but Weetamo caught her breath, and she held to her grandson.

Eleven

Sydney
Saturday morning, September 1

Shoulders sharp beneath a summer shirt. No hair. No eyebrows. Eyes set back in a sunken place. And when he wraps his thin arms around Sydney, the thread that is holding her together gives out. In the doorway, she clings to Everett, her face pressed to his chest, and she cries.

"Damn you," she says, not yet willing to let go or to have him let go of her. "Why didn't you tell me?"

"It's good to see you, kid," said Everett, giving a gentle squeeze before stepping back. "Have you got time to sit?"

"Of course."

Everett looks at her, a long gaze. "Gad, it's good to see you," he says again and when he turns, Sydney walks with him into a small living room. The room is neat, without clutter or even dust. The end tables and the floors shine with polish, not what she expected at all, not in a house lived in by a sick man.

To aid in the simple act of sitting, Everett places a hand on the arm of the chair. The crusty cold sore on his upper lip cracks and thin blood seeps from it. He pulls a tissue from a box by his chair and dabs at the sore. Red spots the tissue. The bald skull reminds her of those posters, children wracked by cancer, their hollowed eyes pleading for donations that might help find a cure.

But Everett is a long way from young. Last April, he turned

sixty-one, and Sydney wonders if age is a factor in beating cancer – or losing.

She shoves both hands deep into the pockets of her shorts. With Everett, not knowing what to say is new. A first. He's frail. It turns the cards and makes her feel suddenly the stronger. An irony that backs Sydney against a wall of shelves.

"Would you like me to make us some coffee?" she asks.

"You go ahead. Make some for yourself. I like the smell of it, but it doesn't like me these days."

"Then, no thanks." She looks away, to anything but the gaunt face. She turns to the bookshelves at her back. Each shelf holds photos in frames. Most are of her. Snapshots of the younger Sydney. One as a teen standing with the red and white Cessna, taken the day she first flew solo. One with her riding the bike toward the camera. One when she was very young, before she'd even started school. In it, she holds her grandmother's hand, the two of them on the beach, with Everett beside them. Sydney recognizes the cliff in the background, the path coming down off the island. She picks up the photo and looks closely, warmed by the image of Eva almost youthful and strong. "Where did you get this?" she asks because this is the only photo on the shelves that was taken before she'd started coming here on her own to the airport.

"Your grandfather took it. He was still alive … still living here then, and your grandmother threw quite a party that day. Your fifth birthday. She invited half the town." Everett, as pale as he is, smiles. "You were quite the kid."

"Quite the difficult kid, you mean." She sets the photo back in its place on the shelf. "There must be something I can do. Have you had breakfast?"

"Syd, it's okay," says Everett while leaning back in his chair. "You don't have to do anything except sit here with me for a while. Tell me how you are. What are you doing here in Wells Creek?"

"I wanted to see Ponokanet. And you." Sydney sits and rests her hands on the arm of the chair, trying to be comfortable. With another tissue, Everett pats his lip. "I'm so sorry," she says. "I didn't know. Are you in pain?"

"Nah. Just a little wrung out now and then."

"Are you in treatment? What are they doing to help you?"

"Chemo mostly. Some pretty wild doses. Too much time spent on my hands and knees in front of the great white bowl."

All too clear the image – Everett on his knees, at the mercy of poison. "I wish you had told me. I would have come back sooner."

"Exactly. I couldn't do that to you. You've been fighting your own fight. I didn't want to throw this on top of everything else. Besides I've got plenty of help around here. Too much sometimes."

"I'm glad at least for that."

"Look," he says, moistening his cracked lips, "they keep telling me I've got to eat. So on second thought, how about putting together a couple of banana shakes?"

"Banana shakes?" She shrugs and forces a smile. "Does that come with a learner's manual?"

His laugh eases her. It always did.

"On the kitchen table," he says, "there's a blue booklet. Page twelve."

In the kitchen, Sydney finds the booklet – *Eating Hints for Cancer Patients*. She has to read the recipe twice before any of the words sink in, a slow osmosis through the obvious elephant in the room – cancer.

She finds the blender on top of the counter. Everything looks scrubbed clean. Open shelves on the wall are stacked neatly with plates and bowls. Who keeps this place so immaculate? Even if Everett was once a tidy housekeeper, he is incapable of keeping this much order now. He couldn't muster the energy. At the sink, Sydney smells the dish soap. The scent of strawberry. And it hits her. All this cleanliness is the result of a woman, someone important in Everett's life.

Her heart grips with something like jealousy. But that's crazy. Everett is like the father she never had. He deserves to love someone. And to be with a woman who loves him. Even so, even though it's ridiculous, Sydney feels replaced.

"How you doing?" calls Everett from the other room. The strength in his voice surprises her. Without the visual proof of him in front of her, he might not be sick at all.

"I'm doing fine." She has to be, and she starts the search for what more she needs. Bananas. Milk. Vanilla. She mixes them in the blender, its small motor roaring in the otherwise silent house. At last, she pours the mix into two glasses and carries them to the living room.

In his chair, Everett's head has leaned back, eyes closed, eye sockets so sunken and gray that Sydney stops in the doorway, struck in her gut.

"Come on in," he says, even before he opens his eyes.

Sydney places the glass of banana shake into the thin veined hand.

"So how are you, kid? Really."

Blood pulses in her neck, and she walks back to the chair. Takes a sip of the shake. "I'm better," she says.

"So you don't beat yourself up anymore?"

"Not every minute of every day."

"Just every other minute, right?"

"No, I ..." But she meets Everett's gaze. "Right," she says. "Now, drink up."

Everett takes a slow swallow, as if testing to see if it hurts, and Sydney looks to his hands, the raised purple veins, long fingers that splay around the glass. "Syd, I'm glad you're here. I've been worried about you. How long you staying?"

"I'm not sure. But I was thinking maybe a year."

"That long?"

Outside the window, grass is growing through cracks on the

runway. And the sign by the office door, it was all faded. "I'm going to stay until you beat the cancer. I can help around here."

But Everett leans forward, elbows resting on his knees. "Look, don't get me wrong, Syd. It's great having you here. But staying alive is my work. You've got your own work to do. When are you going to start flying again?"

"I'm not," she says, and her eyes fill against her will. "Can we talk about something else?"

"If you have to."

"I do. And I need to help you."

Everett takes a second swallow from his glass and sits back in his chair. "Come to think of it, I could use a break from Nora and Ty. One talks too much and other comes in but just sits and listens to me and my old war stories."

"I met Nora on the way in," says Sydney, talking through the tightness still in her throat. "I like her."

"Yeah, Nora's quite a gal. Thanks to her, I hardly lift a finger around here. She does the morning stint. The breakfast and whatever she thinks needs to be done. Makes me feel like a goddamn invalid. And Ty, he does the dinner check-in. By now I guess you've met Ty."

She thinks back to the morning sunrise, to the unusual stillness of the man as he sat on the beach. And Sydney nods that yes, she's met him.

"That Ty," says Everett, "he's an interesting guy. I met him in Saigon. Carried him out in a helicopter when he was twelve. He's had his own fight. Have him tell you his story sometime."

Because she has no intention of listening to stories told by the caretaker, Sydney doesn't answer. But she does notice that in the short time she's been here at Everett's, the hollow space around his eyes has grown darker and his posture more drained. She wants to stay with him, to hear about the airport and what is or isn't happening with it. Instead, she brings her glass into the kitchen to wash it.

"You should rest," she says. "I'll come back another time."

When she returns to the living room, Everett sets his nearly full glass on the table by the chair. "How about I call Ty," he says. "I'll tell him he doesn't need to stop in tonight, that I'm having dinner with you."

"I'd love that."

Everett walks with her to the front door, holds to the knob as if to rest his weight, what there is of it, and he asks her, "What do you hear from your mother?"

Sydney intends to laugh, but the sound comes from low in her chest, more like a groan. "Would you believe … Alison's on the island."

"Well. Well. How's that going?"

"Pretty much the same as always."

"It's been a long time since you two spent any time together. This could be a good thing, couldn't it?"

Sydney raises an eyebrow. "Let's just say I'd rather come here for dinner." She puts her arms around Everett and hugs him, gently this time for fear of breaking something. "Rest. I'll see you at five. And I'll bring dinner."

"You don't need to bring anything. The freezer's full of chicken soup."

"Then what else would you like?"

"How about some rum-raisin?"

Ice cream. Always, rum-raisin had been his favorite.

She leaves Everett in the doorway and starts across the field. Because he can't see her face, she doesn't care that tears drip from her chin. Death is so final. One last breath and then gone, forever. She can still feel the coarse powder of ash in her hand, see the cloud of it falling through the air. Rick tossed away. Rick, what was left of him, had been cremated – a horror knowing his body was put to fire that second time. But that wasn't her decision to make. She had no rights. No marriage certificate to claim ownership. But in the end, Rick's sister hiked with Sydney to a high ledge in the Sierra Nevada, and from there they tossed Rick's ashes.

Eva was simply put into a hole. Dirt shoveled on top.

And now ... good God, not Everett ... not Everett, too.

She walks deliberately tall because Everett may still be standing in the doorway. Turning, she sees him there, and she waves. Everett waves back, and she is glad to have walked so far, so that he can't see she is crying.

The road is a blur in front of her, and she swipes at the tears. When in front of the bridge, she pulls the car onto the side of the road. She finds some tissues and blows her nose.

Planks rattle on the bridge, and the green pick-up bounds onto the road. When the truck stops beside the Subaru, Ty leans to the open window. "Everett called. He told me you're having dinner with him tonight."

"Yes. I am."

"It'll be good for him, having you there."

She believes that. Even more, she believes being with Everett will be good for her. "He's so sick," she says.

"Yes, he is. But if anyone can beat this, Everett can."

Sydney nods, but her eyes fill again.

"I'm heading into town," says Ty. "Need anything?"

"No. Thanks. I'm all set."

A moment passes. A gull squawks from its perch on the bridge, and Ty puts the truck into gear. "Take care," he says, and the truck moves on.

Sydney looks across to the island. Chances are Alison is still on the shopping spree. The house will be empty and offer all the solitude a person could want. So, why not just go home to Ponokanet?

Because she can't. She doesn't want to. Not right now. What

she wants – what she needs is something to take her mind off Everett. Somewhere where no one talks. No questions. Just pure diversion.

She breathes in. Breathes out. Ty said he was going into town. Because it's Saturday of Labor Day weekend, the village center will be busy. She could get lost there in the crowd. And on Main Street there's a small ice cream shop. She could pick up the rum raisin.

Twelve

Tourists swarm the village center, the vacationers identifiable by their sunburns and bathing suits worn under their shirts. Sydney moves among them, in and out of shops and galleries. She browses and she observes, while the knowing grows – knowing she will be here to help Everett, and the stiffness in her neck slowly drains.

In the village, one thing becomes obvious. Art plays an even greater role in Wells Creek than she remembers. Sculptures, made from every medium imaginable, stand everywhere, both in and out of doors. Pottery, in the natural colors of earth and sea, lines the shelves in one shop after another. What Sydney is most drawn to are the paintings. Most are done in the softer strokes of watercolor paint. But on a slight hill just off Main Street, in the ornate gallery rooms of what once was a sea captain's home, she finds hanging on the walls Cape scenes rich with the texture of oils.

She moves from one painting to the next, noting each artist's variation, the style of stroke and use of color, until she comes to one scene in particular. This painting she knows. She has seen it before. The harbor with its heavy-hulled fishing boats tied to the pier. And distant behind the harbor, rising from the sea, are the cliffs of Ponokanet. In the lower right corner, written in broad sweeping script, is her grandmother's signature – *Eva Foster*.

This painting used to hang above the mantle in Eva's house.

Sydney studies the incredible detail of Eva's work, the ratted clothes of the fishermen, the rope sacks loaded with white-shelled clams. Such an incredible piece. Always Eva possessed this special talent. Her slender hand moved with brush as if by magic along the canvas, seeming to pull scene and light and shadow from the brush itself.

Scene and light.

For Sydney, a former afternoon begins –

Eva stands before an easel. A girl of twelve stands also with an easel of her own. Her chestnut hair, not yet hacked or dyed, hangs at her back in a single long braid. In her hand is a paint brush, and she dabs with it at the canvas. But the girl's jaw tenses from the trying. No matter how soft the touch of her brush, sunlight refuses to dance on her painting, not like it dances on the blues and violets of her grandmother's canvas.

The girl takes up black paint in the broadest of the brushes. "It's simple and stupid," she says, and she smears black across her poor depiction of the sea.

"You must give yourself time," says Eva. "Craft comes with practice."

"No," shouts Sydney. "It's ugly." And she runs, taking two stairs at a time, down from Eva's studio under the eaves.

Today, Sydney feels the price her grandmother paid for taking in that angry girl. Eva was so patient, simply urging Sydney to do her best. To be her best. Eva did not deserve that girl's sharp adolescent chip.

"We're very fortunate to have that painting."

Sydney turns to see the saleswoman there at her back.

"The paintings you see on this wall," says the woman, "have been donated to help raise money for our new hospice house. This one in particular would be an excellent choice if you were to buy it. The artist was a local woman. She passed away several years ago, so they'll be no new work of hers available for sale."

"Someone donated this painting?"

"Yes. The artist's daughter. A very generous gift."

Hospice House. It's a good cause. But this particular painting – how could Alison part with it? It was Eva's favorite. It belongs on Ponokanet.

The saleswoman presses. "If you decide you like it, I could wrap it for you?"

"Oh, no thank you. I was just admiring it." Sydney places her back to the saleswoman, but only to look again at the detail, the mist, at the play of light. And she looks at the price tag. When flying, she made decent money. But she and Rick lived loosely. They thought nothing of traveling to places like Switzerland and Italy, even Malaysia once to hike in the mountains there. Money seemed merely a means to an end – excitement. The two of them fed on it.

She wouldn't change the way they lived. But Eva's picture. If Sydney doesn't buy it, where will it end up?

Before she can change her mind, she seeks out the saleswoman.

In her grandmother's living room, Sydney takes down the woven tapestry that more recently claimed the space above the fireplace. In its spot, she hangs Eva's painting. This is where it belongs. Buying back Eva's favorite, bringing it home again, in a small way repays a debt owed. It feels very just. Very right.

How long will it be before Alison notices the painting has been returned? Sydney makes a bet with herself that it will be days.

She steps away to admire the painting, and with that step she is back again to the twelve year old Sydney being taught how to paint. That had been her last art lesson. In fact, it had been the last time Sydney climbed the stairs to the attic studio. Twenty-seven years have passed since that angry afternoon, but today the need to see Eva's work space pulls Sydney to the front hall and up the stairs, and higher still, taking the narrow steep stairs that lead to the studio under the eaves.

Thirteen

Ruth

On the land of the Ponokanet, August of 1635

Mittark, grown to manhood, stood today on a rise of land at the edge of dense forest, looking out to the clearing beyond. Three men of the paled skin cut and felled trees. One Mittark had come to know, even trust, for he who called himself Wells had lived there along the river for four passings of the snow. Wells had lived there alone, in peace with the forest and with the Ponokanet people.

But this day Wells was not alone. Along with him were two more men of the paled skin. The one yellow-haired and new to manhood worked at hitting an ax to the low dark flesh of a cedar. The second was heavy set with chest large for the man, and it was he who worked beside Wells stripping a fallen cedar of its limbs.

Because Mittark just now returned from the trading lodge at the Manomet, he carried two wool blankets in a wrap of softened hide. The blankets would keep his grandmother warm in the cold time ahead. In the pouch at his waist there were beads of glass that she would sew on deer skin as decoration. Also, he carried the iron blade brought as a gift for Wells. But as he looked out over the unfamiliar faces, he thought to pass wide around the clear water and return to his village unseen.

Wells saw him then, and Wells motioned to Mittark to come, to enter into the clearing. Because of this, the native set his shoulders and walked the gentle slope to the clearing of Zebadiah Wells.

Greeted by a handshake, Mittark returned the handshake in English custom before giving the blade in its sheath to Wells. "In return for the tool called plow you gave to my people," said Mittark in the English tongue learned from this foreign neighbor and from those at the trade post.

"Thou need not have done this, my boy," replied Wells as he pulled the carved handle for the sheath. "But, aye, 'tis a beauty."

Mittark nodded but then announced he would go on now to his village. "The day ends, and I have been gone long."

"But thou must stay and share a meal. Come," said Wells, "meet a friend." Wells turned to the elder man that had stood quiet at the side of the fallen tree. "This be Jacob Sears. He has come from Plimoth, just as I did, tired to death, he says, of the narrow preaching of the Saints. And beyond stands his son, Elias."

The son, with ax now rested on end, holds his gaze on Mittark.

"These good men," said Wells, "help me clear trees for a barn. They share my house until they discuss with your people a purchase of land."

Mittark's eyes narrowed. He did not like this exchange of land for trinkets. These men of a foreign place had a strange way of possessing land, as if it were but a necklace or pot to be given or owned. Wells was only one, but here now were more.

"Let us walk to the house," said Wells as he picked up the ax that lay at his feet. "A stew is readied, prepared by a woman this time, not a meal scorched by myself." Wells laughed from his belly and led the procession toward the small house at the edge of the water.

In his heart lay the wish to refuse this offered meal, but the honor of friendship pushed Mittark forward to walk with Wells.

But when Mittark stepped in through the doorway, he saw the one who cooked, the one with hair the color of corn silk, her hair mostly hidden beneath a headpiece of fitted white cloth. When she turned, he saw the eyes as violet-blue as flowers of the field.

"Ah, Ruth, 'tis good to have thee here," said the booming Zebadiah Wells as way of greeting the seventeen-year-old Ruth.

Ruth's small, oval mouth opened to speak, to return the greeting. But words caught in her throat. Her eyes widened. Behind Mr. Wells stood a near-naked savage. Flesh the color of dark iron-filled earth was covered only by a breechcloth of hide. To his shoulders long coarse hair fell black as ever she had seen. And hanging from his neck on a thin cord was the sharp talon of some large bird of prey.

"This young man goes by the name of Mittark," said her host before he and the native sat at the table.

Ruth feigned strength by the turn of her back, and she pulled the wooden ladle through stew that steamed in the kettle by the hearth. When her brother, Elias, entered the square room, his hands still dripped wet from the outdoor washing bucket. He came to Ruth with a wink of his eye, and he leaned to her ear.

"It seems we be in need of another plate," he whispered. "We have company."

"But a savage, Elias. He is to sit at our table. If Mother were here ..."

"Ah, but Ruth, she is not." Elias reached to hold lightly both her shoulders. "We live now in the native's land. An adventure, remember?" He winked once again, and Ruth answered with a weak smile.

Their father came last through the doorway, and Elias went to the table, taking a seat beside his father. From a shelf on the wall, Ruth gathered the last of the wooden bowls, and as she filled the bowl with hot stew, she considered her brother's words, words that were indeed true. Just two weeks after burying her mother on the hillside of Plimoth, her father had announced he would make a new life far out on the peninsula with the peculiar name of Cape Cod. Ruth had pleaded, not wanting to be left behind. She preferred to go with him to this wilderness, believing it would be an adventure. In the beginning, Jacob had been firm. Ruth was to stay behind at the settlement, to be brought up proper in the ways of the Lord, and this hypocrisy she did not neglect to point out when challenging her father, saying he could not possibly consider leaving her in the strict narrow-minded hands of those he himself wished to escape. At the very last, Jacob consented. The three had left together on foot with what little they could carry.

However, coming here had not been the adventure she had hoped for. She so missed her mother. And she missed her friend, Beatrice. She longed for them both. And she longed for something more, something without shape or words, and the longing hurt.

The trencher was full and Ruth turned, only to see the dark eyes of the savage looking across at her. So quickly his gaze turned away that she considered being mistaken. Perhaps the savage had not been watching her. With heart beating wildly, she gathered courage and made her way to the table, making the decision to serve the guest first, savage or not. When the others had been served, she sat on the bench beside Elias and pretended great interest for the meal in front of her.

The native sat across from Ruth, and as she lifted her spoon, she dare not raise her eyes. She had seen native men, of course. On many occasions, one would pass by the settlement outside the stockade. Two had even shared a home with families of the Saints, helping to plant and aiding the elders in dealings with the local tribes, but those two, most gratefully, had covered themselves with the shirt of a civilized man, unlike this raw savage that sat at the table now and expected to be served supper.

Lifting her spoon a second time, Ruth dared glance to the dark-skinned face and the bared chest, but her glance caught on the talon, the black pearly hardness of it. She returned to eating her stew but not without imagining the savage with arrow aimed at such a magnificent bird of prey. Around her, conversation centered on cutting trees and the building of a new barn that was soon to be erected. Mr. Wells also planned to add a shed roof at the side of this house to make room for the brewing of beer, as he had found that hops grew in the meadow not far. With barley unavailable, he had also discovered a taste for beer fermented with pumpkin grown by the natives. This had become the customary talk during the past week of living here in this remote land.

But of a sudden, Mr. Wells asked Mittark, "What news doest thou bring from the Manomet?"

"The Manomet hold anger." Such clear enunciation of English came from the mouth of the savage that Ruth's spine straightened, her eyes open circles. "Men of the Bay Colony force Williams to leave. But the Manomet want Williams to stay. Williams deals fairly."

"That be no surprise," said Mr. Wells. "Williams was always a free thinker. That's not looked on kindly by the Colony."

The conversation went on but with very little added by the native Mittark. Mittark spoke only when asked a question. He never again looked to Ruth. For that, Ruth gave thanks to the Lord, and she continued with the chore of swallowing her supper.

Fourteen

Ruth

Two months after serving supper to the native, October of 1635

When Ruth lifted her wool cloak from the peg by the door, she saw the manner in which her brother eyed the cloak. But this morning Ruth was done being left behind. Of late, each day Elias left the house with the native Mittark. Together the two fished or hunted, seeming to enjoy each other. Ruth, however, remained alone throughout most of the day. That must change. So, this morning, despite her brother's dubious look, Ruth placed the cloak across her shoulders.

"Thou may not go with me," said Elias.

"I see no reason why not."

"Because I go with Mittark. My sister shall not go running about the forest or kneeling in a dugout like some wild native. It would not be proper."

"Not a day passes that does not find thee doing those things."

"But I am a man."

"I am only female, Elias, not a child." Her words snapped at her brother as she buttoned the cloak at her neck, but even as she lifted a defiant chin, her eyes grew wet. "I thought thee, of all people, would understand. Each day Mittark comes for thee. The hunting and trading take thee out and away. And father has Zebadiah. They work as if they were brothers. I have no one. 'Tis is not as though I can invite the local women over for tea."

Elias pulled through his hair where it lay straight over his ears.

"If thou were not the dearest thing to my heart, 'twould be far easier to teach thee a proper manner. Come along."

The door opened, and though graveness remained in her brother's tone, the light had returned to his eyes. Ruth kissed him quickly on one cheek before stepping in front of him and out into the air.

Leaves had colored with reds and gold, the marsh grasses gone to russet, and the bright sun warmed the morning. The plot of land had been traded for, and the Jacob Sears house had been completed, at least the one main room and loft. It would be enough to keep them sheltered through the coming winter, huddled together as a family between the home of Zebadiah Wells and the Ponokanet.

Briefly, while bent down to brush away a clinging pine twig that scratched through her stocking, Ruth considered that Mittark might disapprove of her coming along. But that possibility did not prevent her from stepping quickly to catch up again with Elias. They would meet Mittark and look for whales. This would be a morning surely to stand out against the former long string of mundane.

By the edge of the salt creek, Elias steadied the dugout. The dugout was now his, in trade for an ax, and Ruth knelt in the front. The tide had turned, and the current in the creek ran strong toward the bay. Elias scarcely needed to paddle as the dugout rode the current, rounded a wide bend, and there ahead, on the shore where river spilled into the bay, Mittark stood waiting.

The native's only concession to the change of season was the wearing of leggings made of hide. Over the course of summer, because Mittark so frequently visited with Elias on the stone slab step just outside the door, Ruth had become somewhat accustomed to the bared flesh of shoulders and chest. But today in the sharp morning light, she looked long at the native where he stood, his back to the blue of the sea. In his stance was a grace and strength not commonly seen among young Englishmen. The sight of lean muscle, the beauty of the angles, so different from the roundness that had come during the past year to fill out her own clothing, this brought to Ruth an unfamiliar stirring, brought such warmth that she needed to shift position and look away to the cool air of the sea.

The dugout neared, and Mittark greeted Elias. The two spoke of the small whales that Mittark called the blackfish, and they spoke of good tide. Only then did the native say hello to Ruth. He did not ask why Ruth was there, but the question showed in his eyes before he turned and slid his own dugout into a low wave.

The two dugouts headed to the small island that lay not far from the mainland. Only yesterday Ruth had overheard Mittark telling that many blackfish were seen that morning in the bay. She had listened with the door open to the sunlight while she kneaded dough, and the native on the doorstep told Elias how on occasion, during a storm of wind and rain, the spirits beneath the sea would send a blackfish up onto the sand. The great body would thrash and die there, robbed of breath by the whale's own weight. When this occurred, the Ponokanet thanked the gods for their gift before cutting up the freshly dead. They portioned the meat and carried away the largest of bones, leaving the innards for the next tide to wash away.

But when told that Elias planned to build a shallop during the cold of winter and would use it to hunt whale, Mittark did not agree to hunt with Elias in this boat called shallop. He argued that the whale should not be hunted for intentional kill. The whale, said Mittark, has lived beneath the waves since the great shifting of Mother Earth, a time when his people, the ancient ones, were forced from a land beyond the large water, forced to sail in search of high ground. The whale, he said, traveled with those ancient people. The whale guided his ancestors to this place of sand and rivers. The whale carries in its memory that history.

The white cliffs with a top of green appeared closer now. Elias paddled swiftly behind the dugout of Mittark, and as they slid into the shallows, Ruth removed her shoes but ignored the cloth stockings and the hem of her skirt, and she stepped into the water. She pulled at the bow end, dragging the dugout high onto the beach.

Behind them rose steep ragged cliffs. Mittark walked before her setting the pace until they came thankfully to a more gradual slope, where they climbed to the top. A narrow footpath led in among the outstretched limbs of pine. That shaded world became a quiet calm, a chorus of sea and gentle wind. So lovely was the chorus that Ruth stopped on the path.

"Listen," said Ruth. "The breeze is like a song sung by angels."

The native and her brother stood at either side of her, but it was Mittark who spoke. "What is that word, angels? I have not heard it."

The dark eyes were on Ruth, and she met them. "Angels are but souls without a body to dwell in. They speak in all kinds of ways to us mortal beings, guiding us."

"My sister speaks too bluntly of her own beliefs," said Elias, breaking in quickly. "Her words have often upset our mother and angered the Congregation."

"The Congregation doest need being angered." Ruth pulled her cloak close around her. "They are blind to their own double tongue. Just as blind as the King and his own church."

"That be true enough, Ruth, but let us not discuss it now." Elias set his hand upon her arm, nudging her forward. He began to talk of whales, and he questioned Mittark further about this smaller whale called the blackfish.

On any other day, in another place, Ruth would have been hurt by her brother's rebuff. But not this day. She was happy enough to be along. As they walked, the native in front of Ruth and Elias behind, Mittark spoke of the journey that blackfish take each spring and again before the cold and snow, roaming the sea through the seasons, always the same, north to south and back again.

Ruth listened as they walked. Yet, she soon determined not to look up from the path, for when she did, she faced the broad shoulders of Mittark, saw the sunlight glisten off taut skin. Just for today it would be best, she thought, if Mittark were better covered. Or at least he might rid himself of the high cheekbones and precisely cut chin and replace them with ugliness. Perhaps a portly middle. Ruth smiled at the imagined figure. But no, admittedly, she would not change one thing about him.

In this line of three, they followed the footpath for some time, crossing the breadth of the island to where the western cliffs looked out onto open bay. The water below rippled and slithered along the shore, looking much like a long silver snake moving over sand. No sooner had they arrived there at the rim when Mittark pointed out to the bay.

"There," he said. "See the black fin. There are many. They are the blackfish of which I speak."

The water beyond tossed and roiled as if in a kettle on the hot fire. Scores of sleek black backs arched and writhed on the water's surface, feeding, she supposed, on what they could find in the warm protected waters of this cape bay.

Elias began to pace. "If only I held a harpoon."

Mittark, like Ruth, watched silently until the bay waters quieted and the black backs could no longer be seen. And Mittark pointed again, directing their gaze west, to the thin line on the horizon. "There is the Plimoth from where Elias and Ruth have come."

"Plimoth? That close?" asked Ruth, for it had taken four days of walking to reach the house of Zebadiah Wells.

"Close for the bird to fly," said Mittark. "Not close for man who follows the footpath as Ruth did come."

With her hand, Ruth shaded her eyes, hoping to see better the land of the settlement. But Plimoth remained only a distant gray line. She thought of the thatched-roof cottage and her mother who lay there on the hill beneath the dark earth, and homesickness welled inside, causing Ruth to turn sharply away.

"What upsets Ruth?" asked Mittark.

"Nothing. 'Tis nothing," she said.

But Elias came to her side. "Ruth is missing our mother, I would guess. We buried our mother only weeks before leaving the settlement. My sister feels greatly the loss, as I do."

"I know that loss," said the native, and Ruth looked up to the glisten of raven hair and eyes warm on her face.

"Has thy mother passed on also?" asked Ruth.

"Passed on ... I do not know this word."

"Passed on is to die. To go on to a place other than this world," said Ruth. "Has your mother gone on to another world?"

"Yes. Awashonk lives now in the spirit world."

In that small circle of three, Ruth moved in a step closer, curious and wanting to know. "When did she die ... or go on to this spirit world?"

"I had seen but five summers when both my mother and father died."

"I am so sorry, Mittark. I cannot imagine that double sadness."

Mittark held his gaze on her face, as if taking that moment to prepare his words. "I am no longer held by sadness," he said. "I have known my grandmother better than might have been. Weetamo has been my gift from the gods."

"What a lovely thing to say of another person. I would like to meet her, your grandmother."

"That cannot happen."

"Why?"

"Weetamo is angry," said Mittark, slowly, hesitantly in the way he glanced for just that moment to the trees. "Weetamo is angry that your people have come to live so near."

"But we do no harm."

Giving no answer, Mittark started back along the path.

For Ruth the pain was immediate. How could one's heart be so deeply hurt by a simple turn of another's back? Elias took her by the arm then, pulling her forward.

Fifteen

Ruth
Four days later, 1635

With autumn sunlight splashing in through the open doorway, Ruth peeled down one stocking, then the other. She set them atop the stool by the door. Plucking up the reed basket from the floor, she glanced back to the stockings with a quick grin, for she was being very much the wayward child. The misgiving, however, was forgotten as soon as the morning air struck warm on her face.

With basket in hand, she walked the path along the salt creek, letting the grainy white sand mold to the shape of her bared feet, savoring the feel. In the past, it would have been the chore of Elias to dig at low tide for the white-shelled clams. But Elias had left with the rise of the sun to make his way to the trade post with dried pelts of deer and fox. He would not return until the Sabbath. And Jacob was off for the afternoon to assist Mr. Wells with the raising of the new barn. Alone in her chores, Ruth had thought of supper and wanted for the sweet briny meat of the clam. It would take only a few holes dug to have the basket overflowing, leaving ample time to wash the shells, then steam them over the fire.

She took her time along the path, coming to where the creek opened into the bay, the creek giving only a thin trickle over the sand this afternoon, for the tide was far out, leaving but a few shallow pools trapped between rippled sand and patchy green mounds of eelgrass.

Eager for this new chore, Ruth started out over the flats. Soon her feet were in the ooze of bottom mud, and the mud squeezed up between her toes to blacken her feet and to stain black the hem of her skirt. Because she had but two skirts, she set the basket down and went about fashioning a solution. The rear hem she pulled forward between her ankles, pulled it upward and tucked that rear hem into the front waistband, forming a new piece of apparel not unlike a man's loose breeches. It seemed a practical invention with but one error – the makeshift breeches revealed the pale white flesh of leg all the way to the knee.

She glanced behind but saw no one. Her makeshift solution would stay. She tied the ribbon of her white pinner cap, tugged the bow tight beneath her chin before setting out again to dig for clams. Gulls argued above her head as she bent to the mud. Her fingers dug in, feeling for the shells, for the round hardness. One after another, she scooped them out. In short time the basket could not hold another one. She straightened up, stretched the tightened muscles in her back and breathed in. She had come to love the smell of salt and even the strong odor of bottom mud. Most of all, she loved the murmur of the calm sea as it inched its way back in toward the shore.

In a shallow tidal pool, she rinsed mud and grit from her hands and from under her nails. Lifting the overfilled basket required both hands, and when she hoisted the basket to her, black mud bled through to soak her blouse. The wetness brought a shiver as the weight of the clams settled in her arms. Thus, with basket brimming, Ruth started back toward the dry sand of shore. She kept eyes down, looking out for sharp broken shells or even worse, the feisty little claws of a crab. She stepped carefully but even so, of a sudden, her foot slipped on the slick mud. She stumbled, nearly dropping the basket, she herself close to ending in a heap.

A deep laugh carried from the shore.

"Hello, Ruth," said Mittark from on the beach where he stood, not trying at all to conceal the grin or eyes that laughed.

"What is it that amuses thee so?" she asked, feeling his jest at her expense.

"Ruth wears the dress of a sauncksquuaog."

She stood in front of him now, and she adjusted the weight, pressing the basket to another hip. "Whatever is a saunk squog?"

At her attempt with his language, Mittark laughed. Ruth wanted to be put off, but instead she, too, was smiling.

"Sauncksquuaog," said Mittark. "A strong woman who leads. A sachem. But even the sauncksquuaog wears clothes that allow work. Ruth wears such clothes today."

She glanced to the muddied hem tucked in at her waist. "I thought it a fine way to make breeches."

But Mittark looked out to the distant water, all signs of laughter leaving his face. A different, darker thought moved behind his eyes. "I was on my way to the house of Ruth," he said.

"My brother is not there. He has gone to trade."

"This I know. I have need to speak to Ruth."

"To me? What about?" And she shifted again the weight of the basket, for it grew heavy in her arms.

"I have spoken to Weetamo about the sister of Elias. Weetamo asks now that I bring the English sister to our village."

"But I thought ... "

"I told my grandmother that Ruth hears the voice of spirits, your angels on the wind."

"And because of that, she has changed her mind? She wants to meet me?"

When a hawk screeched from its slow, high circle above their heads, Mittark raised his face to watch. A small muscle twitched across a cheekbone. "Yes. Weetamo asks that Ruth meet with her."

The thought of sitting with Weetamo made Ruth's heart race. And her father would argue. He'd pound his fist on the table at the mere mention of her going off alone into the Ponokanet village.

Even so, to meet Weetamo …

"I accept your grandmother's invitation," said Ruth. "I would like to meet her, very much. When would she like me to come?"

"On your next day. When the sun begins descent in the sky, I will go to the house of Ruth and walk with Ruth to my village."

"I will watch for thee," she said. "And please tell Weetamo I look forward to my visit." Mittark started away, but when Ruth called out his name, "Mittark," he faced her again. "Thy grandmother," asked Ruth, "will she know my English words?"

"No, not well."

"Then how shall I speak with her?"

"I will stay and give meaning to the words."

Ruth watched the native walk away over the sand, watched when at the edge of woods he turned and looked at her. She did not wave as her hands still held the basket. She waited there on the shore until Mittark, his face without expression, turned again and disappeared into the forest.

"I shan't change my mind, father. Not even if thou shake thy fist twice more. I am the only English woman within four days walk. Thou cannot bring me here and then not allow me to make acquaintances."

Jacob sat at the table that rested tight against the wall. "Ruth, you cannot go traipsing about with a savage native woman?"

"She is a sachem. A wise elder. And she wishes to meet me."

"Look at thee, dressed in filth, wet through. And with bared feet. Already thou be looking more like one of them than my own Christian daughter."

Jacob had surprised Ruth by returning early, while Ruth was rinsing the white clams in water she had carried from the pond. Her feet and clothes remained stained from the mud, and she tugged now at the hem of her skirt, pulling it from her waist, and the skirt fell to cover her bared ankles.

Jacob scratched at the back of his head. "Ah, Ruth, I see that I should not have brought thee here."

"I do not regret the decision, father. I wanted to be with thee, and I still wish for that."

"Yes. Yes, I know. And I must allow for where we are."

Her eyebrows lifted with the softening of her father's tone, giving hope to a thin possibility. "Does that mean I may go with Mittark to meet his grandmother?"

Again Jacob scratched at his head, and his hand stopped there to knead the back of his neck.

"I shan't go back to living at the settlement," said Ruth, hoping still to impact her father's decision.

"No. I can see that sending thee back is not an answer."

"Then I may go?"

"If it's what thou needs, then yes, you may go." But Jacob lowered his head and rubbed at his chin. "Ruth," he said, "your visit with the old woman be not all of what I need speak of."

"Then what? Tell it, for I know that look."

"What I have to say, 'tis a good thing. Thou need not worry," said Jacob. Yet, he looked to her with a deep seriousness, one Ruth hadn't seen in her father's eyes since the horrid morning he had told that her mother was dead. "Thou must listen, Ruth, to what I have to say. 'Tis not always in thy nature to hear me out."

Ruth crossed her arms over muddied chest, for the sun had gone low, leaving her to stand in the long cool shadow of the house. "All right. I shall listen."

"As you said, Ruth, thou be no longer a child. I begrudge that loss, but the fact remains that thee have become a woman. And now, just today, Zebadiah has asked to take thee as his wife."

"What?" She had heard her father's words, but her mouth remained open with disbelief.

"Hear me out, Ruth, for Zebadiah and I have discussed this. It appears he finds my daughter to be lovely, a woman ready to take a husband. Contrary to me," said Jacob with a brief smile, "Zebadiah feels the wilderness agrees with thee."

"No."

"He be a decent man, Ruth. And he cares for thee."

"And he be twice my age. What of love, father? Zebadiah is lonely. 'Tis all."

"And what about thee? I have heard thee speak of loneliness."

"Not in that way. Believe me when I say I prefer the company of thee and Elias."

Jacob walked the few steps that took him to Ruth. He reached with his hand so that she thought he might touch on her face. Instead, he drew his hand back and let it fall, awkwardly at his side. "I loved thy dear mother," he said in a voice gone soft. "And the greatest stroke of good fortune was that she loved me in return. That is what I would want for thee."

A burn came to her eyes, and she feared tears would come as she slipped her hand into Jacob's, just as she had done so often as a young girl. "I want that as well, father. I want love. But it would never be so with Mr. Wells."

"All I ask of thee is to consider Zebadiah."

Her feelings would not change. But Jacob has asked her to at least consider, and for Jacob's sake alone, she will not speak today with the strict truth. "I will not give my decision yet," she said, while taking her hand from his, and she walked barefoot across the cooling earth toward the house.

Sixteen

The attic door swings open, and Sydney steps into stale air. Air that holds the lingering hint of turpentine. The space is lit by the mid-day sun that streams in through a row of skylight windows.

Installing skylights, as Sydney remembers, was not an easy decision for Eva. Although Eva longed for more light in the studio, she balked at altering the old house. She believed with windows in the roof, the house would lose its authentic self. Then, one day in the shortening days of autumn, Eva announced to Sydney that the house had spoken to her. The house, she said, would enjoy being opened up to more light.

Today the attic space does not feel as large as it once did. On a table at the rear gable, an old paint-stained apron lies ready. Beside it, a tin box, the same tin box used by Eva. Sydney lifts the cover. Inside are all widths of brushes and countless tightly capped tubes of color. A wooden rack along the sloping eave holds a dozen or more canvas boards stacked on their sides, a few blank, not yet touched by the artist's brush. But the others – eight, nine – Sydney leafs through them. Several are completed seascapes, scenes of rosehip bushes and dunes, each left behind in the rack unframed.

But the last one is different. This last is a portrait of a woman, her hair long and straight and black as night, with eyes as dark centered as eyes can be. Hanging at the woman's neck is a string of odd beads that look to be made of bone. The touch of light and color is again incredible and the painting hauntingly beautiful. But the signature at the bottom corner – *M. O'Brien* – this is not Eva's work. Odd. But all the rest, everything about this room is Eva's.

Sydney turns from the rack of paintings, and she spins slowly to take it all in. Eva's world left intact. But she notice another canvas, one that is sitting on Eva's easel, and Sydney walks slowly to it. On a small eight-by-twelve canvas board, Eva has captured the red and white Cessna, with Sydney and Everett in front of a wing. Sydney the lanky kid. Everett tall and lean even then, his dark hair tight with curls. How perfect it is, like discovering an old photograph, except this, too, is Eva's work.

It's clear in this one painting how much her grandmother understood. Eva knew that flying and Everett were that girl's salvation. She never questioned the hours Sydney spent at the airport. Never questioned why Everett instead of Eva. And with paint Eva captured the two of them, Sydney and Everett together, to be held in time forever. Sydney picks up the painting, eyes wet and overwhelmed by the sense of Eva there in the attic room even now.

To others, this painting of the Cessna might have little value. It lacks scenic beauty. There's no depiction of a traditional Cape Cod scene which tourists and local collectors would snatch up. But to Sydney this one is a favorite. She will have it framed and hang it on the wall in her room.

Cat calls in a throaty meow and appears at Sydney's feet. Sydney strokes the smooth gray back, and Cat follows when Sydney carries the new-found painting down the narrow stairs to her bedroom.

Late afternoon, when Sydney walks the main stairs down to the front hall, Cat zips ahead, tail flicking. Sydney turns the corner into the living room, but is caught by surprise. On the edge of the sofa sits Alison. A new fire burns in the hearth.

"Oh, there you are," says Alison, her green eyes latching onto Sydney. "Come in and have some wine."

Sydney glances to two glasses waiting on the pine chest in front of the sofa. Between the two glasses sits a plate of Eva's English china, the familiar pheasant pattern neatly ringed with peeled shrimp.

The whole scene feels like bait on a hook.

"No, thanks," says Sydney.

She walks past the sofa, into the kitchen. Cat food rattles from the bag as she pours it into a bowl for Cat, who glares as if not fed in days. With Cat eagerly crunching, Sydney goes to the French doors and looks out, and she recalls the image of her mother sitting out there alone this morning, Alison so close to tears.

Sydney feels the slump of her own shoulders. This is ridiculous. She can't avoid Alison completely. To even try will create a scene. So Sydney resets her shoulders and walks back into the living room.

"I changed my mind," says Sydney, when she sits on the far end of the sofa. "I'd like that glass of wine."

"Perfect," and Alison raises her glass, as in a toast to Sydney.

Sydney manages a smile. She reaches for the glass. The wine is chilled and delicious, and she lets a sip slide down her throat. "Thank you," she says. "It's very good."

Alison gazes into the fire. From the far side of the room, the grandfather clock ticks.

"So," says Alison, "Eva's picture. It's back."

"You noticed."

"You thought I wouldn't?"

"I didn't know for sure." Sydney sets the wine glass down on the wooden chest, feeling her good intentions slipping. "Tell me," she says. "Why did you give it away? Why didn't you just donate money?"

"They didn't ask for money. They asked for one of Eva's paintings. What's this about, Sydney? Why are you angry?"

"I'm not angry. I'm just trying to understand."

"Are you?"

"What's that supposed to mean?"

Alison sits back against the sofa. "I don't want to fight. Please. Let's just look at it this way … the painting is returned and Hospice House has the money. It couldn't be better."

With the small shake of Alison's head, the sleek mahogany hair sways, catching a glimmer from the firelight. Early on, there were times when the young Sydney sat close to her mother on an old worn sofa. In those times, Sydney would twist her mother's hair around a finger and wish her own hair to be that sleek and shiny. She wanted the polish and glamour. But later, all of that ended, and Sydney longed only for the mother.

Alison takes a single shrimp between two fingers and nips a portion.

"Everett has cancer," says Sydney, shocked at her own voice, shocked that she would bring this raw fact up with her mother.

"Yes. I know."

"What? You knew but you didn't tell me?"

"I saw him recently with Ty. They'd come by in Ty's truck to pick up something. It was obvious that Everett was ill. He asked me not to write you about it. He said you had enough to deal with, and frankly, I agreed with him."

"But I would have come back sooner. I would have …"

"Just exactly what would you have done, Sydney? I mean, it's good you're here, I suppose. But there's really nothing any one of us can do."

Sydney pulls through her hair. "That's not true. Everett needs help doing about everything. And the airport. It …" She stops, feeling the uselessness of this argument. "I think I'll take a walk."

Sydney sits with her back to the stone, knees to her chest. Clouds have come in, and with them comes a cool breeze that hums through the pines. Off the tip of the island a buoy clangs. How did her life get so turned, a life so upside down? When Rick was twelve, his father died of a heart attack, but his mother, sister, and Rick remained close. More than once, he told her how the three had counted on each other, in small ways and big. Sydney envied that closeness. That sense of family and belonging is something she's never known. Alison never married, at least not until three years ago when she married Edward. Sydney never knew a father. She knows his name. Alison gave her that much. A name and a picture cut from a newspaper. He was a theater director. He gave Alison her first job as an actress in New York.

A gull squawks from down on the beach, angry that another has stolen a bit of food, a razor clam ripped away from its yellow beak. A few sandpipers skitter through a shallow wash of waves. The stillness of the moment fills Sydney with an ache, the ache of missing Rick.

Over time, Rick would have grown restless in this spot by the sea. He was a man of doing. He loved to fly, 'to test the limits of plane and man,' he said. He loved to hike. And laugh and dance – not to the slow stuff so much as the old rock and roll. Especially the ethnic dance of his Greek heritage, his favorite the fast beat of the Syrto.

Oh, God, with Rick life was so good. With Rick, life finally made sense. She wants him here, to look out with her at the steel gray of the sea. She wants the feel of him as they move together on the dance floor. The feel as they move together in bed.

The sadness is too deep for tears.

An onshore breeze pushes new through her hair. The low sun strikes her face. The afternoon is disappearing. So, with the past heavy in her, she lifts herself and stands. She has to shake off this mood. Push forward. The good side of forward is that soon she'll be having dinner with Everett.

Seventeen

Sydney
That same Saturday, at six

"And the first time I tried to land … remember it?" asks Sydney while leaning an elbow on Everett's table. During the course of chicken soup she moved past his thinness and the cracked lips, and she's now simply glad to be with him. Everett laughs, and so does she. "When I touched down that first time, I about bounced us both out of the cockpit."

"Yeah, but on the next try you could have poured coffee on touchdown and not spilled a drop."

"Mmmm. Those days with you were good," she says, looking to the wan face of this man she adores so much. But when Everett shifts position on his chair, she gets up and clears their soup bowls from the table. "Why don't you go in the living room and rest for a minute? I'll bring us in some rum raisin."

"Good idea," he says, and he unfolds his tall frame, leaving Sydney alone in the kitchen.

It is only six o'clock, but already Everett looks tired. She supposes it is the chemo. At this very moment, poison is at work in his body, trying to kill the cancer. Chemo would make anyone tired. And because it will tire Everett more if she stays much longer, Sydney quickly sets the few dishes into the dishwasher before scooping out the rum raisin into two bowls. She carries the bowls to the living room.

Everett, in his chair, is asleep. The gaunt look and the stillness in him bring tears to her eyes. He sleeps even as Sydney sets a bowl on the side-table by his chair. But when she sits opposite, in the same chair she sat in that morning, Everett opens his eyes.

"I was just thinking," he says, "how good a pilot you are. A great one, but then you know that. So I want you to tell me, kid, why you aren't flying again?"

Sydney looks to the bowl on her lap, to a lamp, to anything but to Everett. If she answers, the words will choke her. "I can't," she says, needing to leave it at that.

But Everett sits straighter. "You can't? What the hell is that supposed to mean?"

The coarseness of his words brings her hand to her throat. "It means I won't."

"I'm sorry, Syd, if you don't like what you're hearing. But you can't give up things that give you joy. Come on, flying gave you your wings."

She shakes her head. "I can't. I don't deserve it."

"Deserve what? A chance to move on, to find happiness and grow old?"

"I can't talk about this. Not even with you. You don't know what it's like." Tears won't stop, even as she swipes at them. "Every day I relive it. I see Rick's plane on fire. Every day I watch him burn. And I know he's dead because of my mistake."

"Kid, no one, including the FAA, believes that. They did their investigation. You were not the cause of Rick's crash."

She can only stare at Everett. He, of all people, knows that in the air every second demands attention. And for that split second, she took Rick's attention. Why won't Everett believe her? "You weren't up there," she says, and she gathers enough breath to go on. "We were straight up at the top of vertical, our two planes wing tip to wing tip when I snapped to the roll. I've told you. I snapped to the roll too early. It distracted Rick. Because of me, he ... he's dead."

"I don't buy it." Everett rubs on sharp pointed knees. "He was too good a pilot, Syd. Focused as hell when up there. Something else went wrong. It was a hot day. That can effect speed and lift. You know that."

"Yes, but ..."

Everett holds up a hand. "Let me finish. Let me ask you this. Would Rick be blaming himself if it had been you that crashed? No. And why? Because you stunt pilots fly at the edge of limits all the time. Where you go, there is no margin. Every time you go up, you know the possibility of a crash is just this far away." He squeezes his thumb to finger, leaving no space between.

"But it was my error. That's what makes this different."

"No, Syd. Rick's death was ruled pilot error. His error," says Everett, his voice too strong, so opposing the frail body from which it came. "Something else happened that day. Something else."

With both hands, Sydney covers her face. "I have to go," and with a few steps she is at the door.

"Sydney, stop. No one leaves here without finishing their rum-raisin."

She does stop, with her hand on the door, and she breathes. "Then don't be mad at me. I can't do this right now."

"Ah, Jesus. I'm not mad. I'm worried, that's all. I want to see the light shine in your eyes again."

"I want to stay. But lay off, okay?"

Everett leans back in his chair, spoons a small mouthful of ice cream. "Okay. Now come eat your rum-raisin."

Hers, most of it, has melted. She stirs it with the spoon. "All of this," she says, "the crash and Rick, it's why I came back here. I had to get away from California, away from the reminders and expectations. I know I have to figure out a lot of things. And I will. I just don't want to fly, okay?"

"All I'm gonna say, kid, is that life is too short not to live it."

"You sound like Rick."

"Do I?"

Everett is ashen – the flush of argument drained from his face.

"I've worn you out," says Sydney while she collects their bowls. "I'm going to leave. But I want to come back in the morning. There's something I want to do."

"What's that?"

"I want to fix the sign over the office door. Paint it. It looks awful. Like nobody cares. "

Everett rubs at his throat as if it were sore. "I don't know, Syd. I appreciate the notion, but if you've looked around at all, you know the place needs a lot more than a new sign."

"But you have to start somewhere."

The sore on his lip splits open, and he reaches into a pocket for a tissue. Pity knots in Sydney's throat.

"Okay," he says, dabbing at the bloody lip. "I guess it's time you give us a new sign."

Eighteen

Sydney
The next morning, Sunday, September 2

Sunday it rains. Long wet strings of it run down from the visor of Sydney's Forty-Niners cap as she walks to the hanger. Inside she finds all she needs – a toolbox with various wrenches and a ladder. Needing two trips, she carries each of them outside to the front face of the office. Even in this wet, she is feeling better. In her own way, she can help Everett. Besides, this is the twenty-first century. Medical science cures people. Statistical odds favor living. So, while science works at saving Everett's life, she will work at saving his spirit.

"Ya need some help?" asks Nora, who seems to appear from nowhere wearing a gray plastic poncho.

"You could hold the ladder when I'm up there," says Sydney while setting the ladder against the office front. She climbs near to the top wrung, feels the steadiness as Nora leans body weight at the bottom, and Sydney stretches to reach the sign. With the wrench she gives a yank to a nut that holds hard to a large bolt. The nut loosens.

"I hear tell you're a damn good pilot," says Nora. "I hear, too, that you won't go up any more. Why's that?"

The wrench jerks, slips off the metal nut. "I decided not to," says Sydney, placing the wrench teeth back around the nut. She pulls hard. Then tucks the nut into the pocket of her yellow slicker.

"I heard, too, that you were flyin' stunts with your guy when he crashed. A damn shame," and Nora clucks with her tongue. Looking up into the rain, head emerging from the gray poncho, Nora resembles more a wet dog, hair slicked to her face, and Sydney feels the urge to boot her away.

"Well, Nora, it seems you've heard the whole story."

"You never know the whole story 'til you hear it from the horse's mouth."

The second bolt is not as easy. Sydney tugs, but the bolt has rusted and the nut resists.

"And it's a shame about Everett," says Nora. "But he'll beat this thing. He's a good man, even better on a cold lonely night, if you know what I mean," and Nora gives a throaty chuckle.

Sydney has to force herself not to stare, force her hand to work with the wrench. But Everett and Nora?

"Don't get me wrong," says Nora. "I don't take his attention as anything serious. Wouldn't do me any good if I did."

"Everett said you've been a lot of help since he's been sick," a kinder response than any Sydney feels.

"I like helping him," says Nora, not missing a beat. "And that Ty, he's been a help, too. Ty … now there's a real gentleman. Every young woman in town's been trying to jump him. Don't seem to be having much success though. Sarah Santos, now she's come the closest. I thought for sure they were an item. We all did. Didn't last long though. Don't know what happened there. Neither one is talkin' about it."

A hard yank on the wrench and the ladder rattles under Sydney's weight. The final nut gives out, and Sydney slides the sign off from the bolts, lowers the sign to Nora's reaching hands. Sydney is glad to be done and glad to be off the subject … any of them.

But Nora persists. "This place sure does need some spiffin' up. I was afraid Everett was gonna close the door on Dean Aviation."

Sydney waits until her feet stand on solid ground. "Everett would never do that. He'd never shut down the airport."

"Well, I sure hope you're right about that. But he's already closed the flight school. And ya can count a week's worth of plane rentals on one hand. Don't know why he keeps me in the office, though I'm damn-sure glad he does."

"The airport's not going to close." She sounds more convinced than she feels. The airport is in bad shape. But all they need is an overall plan.

Using both hands, she takes back the sign from Nora.

"Are ya gonna stop in and say hi to Everett?"

"No. I stopped in before coming to get the sign. Besides," says Sydney, "I'll be back at five to have dinner with him."

The ladder and tools are put away, and Sydney carries the sign to the car. She'll take the sign up to Eva's studio. It can dry there before she starts work on it.

On Ponokanet, rain falls heavy again. Smoke swirls from the chimney. The air smells like burning wood as Sydney scurries from the car, half bent from the weight of the sign. Before she can set the sign down onto the porch and free a hand to open the door, the door swings open.

Standing in the doorway is the caretaker. Behind him is Alison.

"Let me give you a hand with that," says Ty as Sydney steps inside, and he lifts the sign from her arms.

"What on earth is that thing?" asks Alison.

"The airport sign. I'm going to paint it."

"Here?"

"It'll be easier here than to work from a ladder at the airport."

"Then give me your jacket," says Alison. "It's dripping water all over the place."

Sydney looks to where drips of rain have pooled on the floor. "I'll take care of it," she says, but when she slips off the rain slicker, Alison snatches it up and walks away with it toward the kitchen.

Sydney pulls fingers through wet tangled hair and looks to the caretaker, whose only sympathy shows in a grin.

"Thank you," she says, and she hefts the sign from him.

Alison's heeled shoes click across the living room floor. "I was showing Ty the painting you bought," says Alison when stepping in with a towel. "Did you know that Ty is the one who started Hospice House here in Wells Creek?" This as Alison bends to wipe up the floor. "It was his hard work that got it going."

"No, I didn't know that. And you don't have to clean up after me. I would have done it."

"So I'll be off the island for a few hours," says Ty. "If you need anything, just call my cell phone." And he walks out onto the porch, holding to the screen door until it clicks shut.

"Now there's a decent man," says Alison.

Sydney shifts the sign to the other hip and starts for the attic.

It is mid-day when Sydney stands in front of the warm flame that burns in the downstairs fireplace. She has left the rain-soaked sign to dry on Eva's easel, and she has changed out of the wet clothes. Still, she is chilled, and the fire feels good.

Cat lies curled on a sofa cushion, opening only one eye to look at Sydney before tucking her chin deep between two front paws.

"You're getting lazy," says Sydney.

Dishes clink in the kitchen. Alison calls, "Sydney, is that you?"

"Yes," she says, "but I'm going to get a book to read," and she escapes to the hallway, crosses into the small room that remains as Eva's personal library.

Rain beats at the windows while Sydney looks to the wall of shelves, each shelf lined with books. She searches among the titles until she notices a row of photo albums, eight of them lined up along the bottom shelf. Sydney picks up the largest of the albums. On the cover, written in calligraphy script, is the name Alison.

Sydney flips through the pages, each one filled with photos, beginning with a tiny baby wrapped in a blanket rimmed with silk, the little girl growing as the photos move forward. Several are of the young Alison with a man that Sydney recognizes as Charles, Alison's father. In his face, Sydney can see much of her own mother, the round peach-like cheeks, the mahogany hair. She turns the pages hastily, curious to see the years pass by, until one page near the end of the album. On that page, one photograph makes her go to a window in hope of better light. The figure in the photo with Alison is definitely Everett. The two stand together in front of the island house, Everett with his arm across Alison's shoulder, the porch rail at their backs. Alison looks to be in her late teens, Everett not much older.

"What's that you're looking at?" says Alison when stepping into the library with two mugs of coffee.

Sydney slaps the album shut. Returns it to the bottom shelf. "Just some old photos."

"Don't stop because of me."

"No. I'd rather read," says Sydney because reading is a solitary act. Looking at photos could invite commentary.

"I brought you some coffee. Milk, no sugar. Is that okay?"

"Thank you. It's ... it's perfect," says Sydney, and she accepts one of the mugs.

"Why don't you read in the living room? It's warmer in there."

Sydney doesn't trust the attention. But wind gusts, tossing rain against the window. She knows this is foolish, and it's disappointing to think she and Alison still behave like two clashing dogs when caged together. Today just might be the day for one of them to take the better road. Determined to be that person, Sydney first slips a book of short stories by Isak Dinesen from a shelf. With the book of short stories in one hand and the mug of coffee in the other, she follows her mother into the living room.

Nineteen

Ruth

An afternoon with Weetamo, October, 1635

Ruth pretended sweeping the broad stone step at the door, but in truth she watched the sun, watched as it started its downward slide toward the treetops. The skirt she wore, the finer of the two she possessed, was made of deep green cotton and sewn by herself only a year before, and the hem swished about her ankles in sync with the rhythm of the broom. In her stomach, while trying to imagine sitting with Weetamo, excitement and even a bit of fear tumbled as stones tossed by an anxious sea. And Mittark still had not arrived.

Upon hearing a splinter of wood, she ceased the sweeping and looked across to where her father chopped hard oak that he had taken from the forest. Seeing Jacob intent on his task, he fit and strong despite his forty-seven years, brought warmth to Ruth's heart. Her father's strength ran deeper than muscle. He was, as her mother once said, steady at the keel. Ruth had not understood the meaning so completely until that moment of looking out from the step to her father, the ax striking again and again. Yes, Jacob was so truly steady – constant to his own virtuous path, and that steady keel had caused her mother to love him.

Did Zebadiah Wells possess any of that deep steady strength? He did, of course. She had observed it herself. The man's strength was more hidden but present behind his robust manner. But if Ruth were to measure, her father would be full and Mr. Wells but half way to the top. She knew no other men really, unless she was to include Elias. And Mittark. It was difficult to think in such ways of Elias. To her, Elias was still a boy, her brother, but she determined he would measure well. And Mittark? Inner constancy was his way – the only way he knew. For Mittark, the measure would spill over from the top.

Mittark then entered the clearing. He walked not toward Ruth but toward Jacob. The ax came to a halt and rested on the ground as the two men clasped hands in greeting. Ruth saw the contrast, her father grayed and fair, and the other dark with hair and eyes black as pine tar. But, too, Ruth saw the likeness, two men surviving in the wood, and she smiled.

Briefly Mittark glanced her way, and Ruth nodded in greeting. But the two, Jacob and Mittark, spoke further. As they did, Ruth lifted her cloak from the hook by the door. Over her arm, she carried the quilt she had decided upon as a gift, and her feet scarcely touched on the sandy earth as she crossed the yard.

From a woods thick with juniper, Ruth emerged with Mittark into the great clearing that was the village of the Ponokanet. The clearing spread wide, bordering along the shore for a distance of perhaps one hundred strides. Scattered about the cleared land were a dozen or more dome-shaped dwellings, a few more with their ribs of bent sapling poles exposed and without the cover of woven mat and hides, as if not quite finished. Smoke that smelled of roasting meat carried on a light breeze.

Hoots of laughter came like musket shots from behind. Turning, Ruth's eyes opened round. A pack of entirely naked boys – no more than four to six years old – ran into the clearing. They jabbered in foreign sounds as they darted past Ruth, so that she stepped closer to the tall, straight-spined Mittark at her side.

"Come," he said. "Weetamo waits by our wetu."

Ruth followed past squared patches of earth tilled as gardens, mostly cut in this month of October and bare except for the broad leaves and orange of pumpkins. As they walked, at the very center of the clearing, a fire pit held a line of yellow flame. Wild turkeys, plucked and golden brown, were stuck belly-up onto a sapling rail that spanned the pit. The two women at the fire watched with dark eyes intent on the one who walked with the grandson of Weetamo.

Against the walls of her chest, Ruth's heart pounded. Beads of perspiration pushed out at her temples, wetting the silken hair at the edge of the clean white pinner cap. Never before had she felt so lacking of composure. Wanting the cool air on her, she unfastened her cloak, slipped it off and placed it with the quilt she carried on her arm. When again she looked ahead, her eyes caught on the leathery face of a sitting woman.

Weetamo. Ruth needed no introduction. The face was old and lined deeply by many years, the body thin and wiry in stature, wearing long white braids and a loose dress made from the soft skin of a deer. Yet, sinewy muscle coursed the length of the old woman's arms, and Ruth imagined the lithe girl that was once Weetamo.

Mittark stopped at the side of his grandmother. He spoke first in his own language, the words directed to Weetamo. Weetamo, in return, spoke back. Ruth willed her heart to settle, and when at last Mittark addressed her with his English, she was taking the second long slow breath.

"My grandmother wishes Ruth to sit," he said more clearly than she'd ever heard him speak, he laboring more carefully on the English words, so that Ruth wondered if Mittark, too, might be without his customary ease. That possibility helped to calm her. She looked to the woven mat of bulrush reed that lay on the ground beside the elder woman and realized it was there that she was supposed to sit.

"I thank Weetamo for this invitation," she said while purposely turning her eyes to meet with those of the grandmother, and Ruth sat down upon the mat, folding her legs beneath her skirt.

Weetamo began in the language of quick hard sounds, Mittark giving meaning behind each phrase. "My grandson tells me Ruth enjoys this land between two waters."

"Yes," said Ruth, glancing only quickly to Mittark, careful to keep her eyes on Weetamo, for she wished to observe each telling expression on the grandmother's face. "The waters here are lovely. Of all the beauty, I particularly like the smells. The sweet scent of the marsh grass and the salt that hangs on a fog-filled morning."

Ruth waited for Weetamo to receive the meaning, listened as Mittark seemed to struggle with what must have meant 'fog-filled'.

"So, Ruth is happy to leave behind her own people and to live here in this place of the Ponokanet?"

The question came through Mittark, and Ruth considered carefully, for it was not a simple question and she suspected it was intentionally so.

"I was torn in two," she began, "when my father announced that he and my brother, Elias, were leaving Plimoth. I had friends, and I was safe there. But I had a great emptiness inside me, for we had, only a few days before, buried my mother. I was so very sad and could not bear losing my father as well. So, I made a choice. I chose my family, and I came here with my father and Elias."

Ruth waited until the sounds of Mittark's retelling ceased, then she continued with more. "I have learned to be happy in this place. But not a day goes by that I do not think of Plimoth, of my friends, and of my dear mother."

Weetamo nodded as if perhaps she understood, but no smile, no ease came yet to that old face. Still, Ruth sat braver for having told the truth of her feelings, and she began again.

"I would like to tell Weetamo that I admire her grandson. He has been a great example to follow."

"Example? What is that?" her interpreter questioned.

"An example ... something to follow, to copy because it is

admirable and good. Mittark hast been someone to copy because he is admirable." When Mittark waited, staring to a place behind Ruth's eyes, she nodded toward the grandmother. "Go on, please. Tell her."

"In what way does Ruth copy my grandson?" asked the elder woman.

"I have learned that your grandson, too, has an empty place in his heart where his mother once was. The loss for Mittark was even greater than my own, for he lost his father as well. Yet, I have watched Mittark, and he does not remain angry or always sad. He is able to laugh and to love. In that way, I try every day to be as Mittark."

Again, Mittark waited with his eyes on Ruth, but he went on then to give the meaning to Weetamo. Weetamo spoke quickly.

"My grandmother asks how Ruth knows of her grandson's loves and sadness."

"I was on the island, there in the bay," and Ruth pointed to where the cliffs rose above the water. "One day we were there together with Elias, and Mittark spoke of thee. He spoke of his mother and father and of Weetamo. He said he no longer was held by great sadness because of thee, because Weetamo showed him love and that Weetamo was the greatest gift the gods had given to him."

As the meaning flowed through the strange sounding words of Mittark to the native woman, wetness filled the old eyes. When Mittark was done, Weetamo spoke but briefly, her attention given now to her grandson who stood at her side. Mittark in turn answered in the language only they shared.

"What is it," asked Ruth. "What did she say?"

"Weetamo asked if it was true that I shared those words with an English girl. I told her it was true."

"I see." Ruth turned back to Weetamo, choosing her words as she spoke. "My father, too, seems surprised that I find friendship here among another people. But I have learned that beneath our differences, we are quite the same."

With eyes held on Ruth, Weetamo fingered with large-knuckled hands the string of beads worn at her neck. Strung on a thin cord of hide, the piece was made mostly of beads of bone. Each bone piece had been cut round and smooth, and between each set of three there lie a thin purple shard that Ruth recognized as the colored inside edge of the quahog shell. As an adornment, it was oddly beautiful.

A whooping shout, and the young boys ran again across the clearing. A woman at the fire called out to them, and the boys slowed, each to receive a slab of meat sliced from the hindquarters of a roasting turkey. Ruth considered the boys' nakedness, their complete lack of modesty or shame. Though the sight of their maleness brought color to her cheeks, she was not repelled. In that group of small boys was the simplicity and freedom of these people, their natural blending, as if they were but one of many creatures of the forest.

The feel of the grandmother's gaze caused Ruth to look away from the children, to look down to her own hands, and in that moment she spied the colors of the quilt peeking from under the layers of wool cloak that rested across her lap. "Please, Mittark," she uttered quickly. "Tell Weetamo I have brought her a gift. I had wished to give it when I first arrived, but in my excitement it was forgotten."

Ruth slid the folded quilt from under the cloak and extended it toward Weetamo. "I would like thee to have this quilt. My mother and I worked together through one winter cutting squares and stitching. 'Tis made of mere scraps of cloth, but I thought Weetamo would like the colors and pattern of flowers."

The leathery face lifted to Mittark, though Weetamo said not a word. A moment passed, then another, so that Ruth felt the hollow churn of her stomach, fear that Weetamo would not want the quilt, that Weetamo would not accept a gift from an English girl.

"Please. Take it," said Ruth in a voice soft but clear. "I know Weetamo could never feel for me as she would for a granddaughter. But I would very much like for Weetamo to be a friend."

Slowly, Weetamo lifted the quilt from Ruth's hands. She set it across her own lap, and while dark gnarled fingers smoothed out the cloth and traced a pattern of yellow and russet flower, the native woman spoke low in guttural sounds.

"My grandmother says that the blanket is stitched well. The flowers are like those in a field."

"Tell her that I am pleased that she likes it."

The stiff old fingers of Weetamo went to the necklace that rested on the high front of the deerskin dress. With hands that shook with the effort, Weetamo raised the necklace up over white plaited hair. In silence, she placed the bone beads over Ruth's head, over the pinner cap, and the beads fell softly into place.

"These beads," said the old woman through the English of her grandson, "were carved and smoothed by Mittark's grandfather during a time of long snows. The bone is of the whale. This is right because the whale knows always his journey, and from his bones he lends his wisdom to those who wear them. The beads are a gift to Ruth so that Ruth may know her path."

Ruth touched on the hardness of the beads and pressed them to her breast. "Thy gift is too great. I am honored. I shall wear the beads with pride, knowing that they were once worn by Weetamo."

Sparks crackled in the pit, shot into the air as three men dressed in deer hide walked into the clearing. The sky had gone well past dusk, and Ruth knew she must set out for home.

"I must return home now," she said. "My father expects my return before supper." She stood, and not knowing what better to do, she took the hand of Weetamo and gave it a firm handshake. "I thank Weetamo for having me here and for my beautiful gift."

Weetamo squeezed lightly Ruth's hand in return, and she spoke again with the strange-sounding Ponokanet words.

"Weetamo asks that the girl with eyes as light as the sky come again to the village," said Mittark.

"And I would like to speak more to the woman who extends great kindness to this stranger."

Ruth then said goodbye, and she followed at the side of Mittark across the clearing to where the path entered the forest. Among the juniper the light had turned to gray. The moon had risen round and full above the trees, and Ruth stopped along the soft needled path to place her cloak about her shoulders.

"Thou need not take me the entire distance," she said. "I know the way well enough."

The native faced her and beneath the light of the moon their eyes met. "I wish to know that Ruth is safe."

A silence fell between them.

In her ear was the pulsing beat of her heart. "If you wish it," and she stepped past Mittark, her cloak brushing carelessly against the muscled flesh of his arm.

She walked not knowing how swiftly her feet moved along the narrow path. Her mind was elsewhere – on Mittark, on the warmth that swelled in her with him so near. And, too, she carried the weight of knowing her feelings could be told to no one, not even to Elias. Not even Elias would understand the strange workings of her heart.

Too soon the two stood at the step.

"I thank thee, Mittark, for taking me to Weetamo." Although speaking to the native, Ruth looked off toward the moon and the shadows cast by juniper, for she dared not meet those eyes. She dared not risk that Mittark see in her face all that she felt.

A bolt of laughter shot from within the small house. Voices in conversation. Her father was not inside alone.

"I best go inside," she said, hearing the regret in her voice.

Mittark nodded his only goodbye before he turned and walked away. She watched his strong gait, watched the way the moonlight etched his silhouette against the fallen darkness.

Ruth waited until Mittark disappeared in among the juniper

before she climbed the one step to her father's house and opened the door. In front of her, with hand clasped to a tankard of beer, stood Zebadiah Wells.

Twenty

Not at all wanting to, Ruth entered the single room that was her father's house. Mr. Wells set his tankard to the table and wiped the wet frothy brew from his lip. His beard appeared trimmed and combed, and he had about him the feint scent of lye soap, his shirt made clean by washing, unlike the shirt of Jacob which was still marked by the day's stain of earth and sweat. Inside, the cool air that had smelled of sea was gone, replaced by the heat and smoke of the wood fire that burned in the hearth.

Jacob stood at the bench by the fire. His expression fell serious, his brow creased. "Zebadiah will be joining us for supper. The meal be started in the kettle," he said, "rendered as stew by myself."

"You need not have done that," said Ruth, perhaps hard. "I told thee I would return in time to prepare the supper."

"Aye, thou hast returned and safely. I be thankful for that." Jacob walked the small distance and touched his lips to her forehead. "Now sit with our visitor whilst I fetch more wood for the fire." That said, her father walked out the door, leaving Ruth to the company of Zebadiah Wells.

She removed her cloak and placed it on the peg by the door, feeling all the while as if watched by Mr. Wells. With purposeful steps she went to the hearth and stirred the stew.

"Jacob told me of thy visit with Weetamo," said Mr. Wells, who stood stiffly by the table. "Had I known, I could have warned thee of the old woman."

"Warned me?"

"I have been to the Ponokanet village many times. Even when accompanied by Mittark, the woman spurns me, the Englishman. She never speaks."

"She distrusts foreigners, 'tis all. 'Tis no different than the English at Plimoth who build a stockade to keep out the savage. My feeling is that both fears are misplaced."

"Aye, Ruth, thee may very well be right," said Mr. Wells. But when his gaze lowered to the string of bone beads about her neck, an eyebrow lifted, and Ruth was reminded of the necklace.

"The beads, Mr. Wells, were given to me by Weetamo," said Ruth, allowing pride.

Mr. Wells rubbed a hand over the smooth planked surface of the table until Ruth feared he might rub a hole.

"Ruth," he said at last, "I would prefer that thee address me as Zebadiah."

"I think that unfitting, Mr. Wells, thou being older than myself and not of family."

"I be not that much older. 'Tis but a difference of eighteen years."

"Mr. Wells, I …"

The door opened and Jacob stepped in, split firewood cradled in his arms.

Ruth, wanting distance, went to the kettle. She put the ladle to her lips to test the stew's warmth, and while seeking out rye for making biscuits she wished only to get through this meal. She stirred the batter, then spooned the thick mix on top of the stew, keeping her back always to the table and to Mr. Wells. Her father, all the while, spoke with Mr. Well and drained his own tankard of beer. When the biscuits had risen up light, Ruth served the men and sat then at the table.

But Jacob looked to the bone beads. "Ruth," he said. "There be little I forbid, but I ask thee to remove that adornment. I shan't be staring at such a thing."

Her mouth opened to argue, but her glance caught on Zebadiah Wells. She would not give argument in front of him. So, without words, Ruth walked back across the room to a shelf by the hearth. She slid the string of beads up and off, and carefully, she set the beads beside the remaining last trencher.

Throughout supper, she listened little to the conversation, although she did hear her father speak with excitement about the pair of oxen he and Zebadiah now shared. The beasts of burden had been traded for at Manomet and were sheltered in the barn of Mr. Wells. All else that was spoken passed by Ruth as she ate bits of corn and beans from the stew, leaving the remainder in her trencher to grow cold. She felt no hunger, only a great need to return out of doors, to be alone with the isolation that pressed within her.

At last her father lit his cob pipe, and Ruth was free to clear the table and to scrub the trenchers while conversation went on without her. She held her pace slow, though she wanted to run when from the shelf she lifted the bone beads. With the beads held hidden within the folds of her skirt, she slipped past the men, out the door and into the night.

The sharp air of night showed in shades of black and gray under an orange moon. Sitting on a split log that served as a bench, Ruth could not imagine a moon more beautiful, and she fingered the beads. This form of adornment, she knew, would never be allowed at the settlement. Adornment was considered a sin. But this gift from Weetamo was not so much an adornment as it was a treasure, one Ruth wished to keep close. Knowing it was defiance, she slid the beads on again over her head, and she tucked them beneath her blouse.

Her heart torn by loneliness, Ruth looked to the wide forest of juniper that separated her father's plot of land from that of the native

Ponokanet. She wondered where Mittark might be – what he might be doing at this same moment. More than anything, she wished Mittark would walk now into the clearing, the moonlight upon him.

"May I sit with thee?"

At her side stood Zebadiah Wells.

"I was enjoying the quiet of the night," she said, hoping Mr. Wells would heed the subtlety and leave her alone there.

He sat on the low seat next to Ruth, his hands coming to rest upon his knees. He cleared his throat and stroked his beard, so that Ruth came to feel a small portion of pity for the man's unease. She determined to help the discussion along, the sooner to have it done.

"What is it, Mr. Wells, thou would like to say?"

He rubbed a hand along his trouser leg. "I believe Jacob hast spoken to thee of my fondest wish."

"I be not certain of what wish thou speaks to, but my father did mention thy wish to take a wife."

"Not any wife, Ruth, but thee."

Ruth shook her head, perhaps too vehemently.

"Please," he said. "Before you speak, I ask thee to hear my words, not thy father's."

She folded her hands and looked to Zebadiah, but not to the eyes, for she could not. She looked to the graying of his hair and to the trimmed lines of his beard, and she readied to listen.

"Life for me, living in this wilderness, can be lonely. 'Tis true," began Zebadiah. "And the company of a wife would be a blessing. But 'tis thee I have come to want at my side, Ruth. 'Tis thee I desire. Thou art lovely and strong both at once, and I would be greatly honored if thou would agree to be my wife. It need not be so immediate. Thou be young still and might need time to begin thinking of me in that way …
to think of me as a suitor. I ask only that I may call on thee and on occasion walk with thee at my side along the path with the hope that thou could one day accept me as husband."

His words came as sincere. That sincerity freed her to speak. "The very truth is I do not wish to marry. Not thee or any other."

"You be so young. In time thou will certainly have a change of mind. The day will come, and soon I suspect, that thou will feel the want of love ... the want of a husband and a family."

The urge to turn away caused Ruth to squirm on the log bench. Yet, she would have this done. "The question, however, was asked today, Mr. Wells, and I answer thee as only I can now."

For the first time Zebadiah Wells took his gaze from her face, he seeming to notice only then the full round moon. "I thank, thee, Ruth, for honesty. And I tell thee here tonight I will not stop the hoping for a change of heart. Should that day come, I will know it and ask thee again."

Ruth, in silence, held her gaze on the silhouetted trees until Zebadiah stood. Softly, he said goodnight and headed off toward his own small cabin not far into the woods.

In the loft that was her room, Ruth lay awake waiting for sleep. At last sleep did come but it was restless.

Zebadiah reached for her, taking tight hold of her arm. But as she struggled to be free, the figure was no longer Zebadiah Wells. Mittark, tall and lean with muscled limbs, released her arm.

"Come to me," he whispered, low and pleading, and his hand brushed her cheek. She pressed her body to him, suddenly aware of her own nakedness, her skin hot against the dark flesh of the native, and his arms encircled her.

A moan rolled from her throat, and Ruth woke to the sound. She lay unmoving, her breath heavy, her sleeping gown wet with perspiration. The black quiet of night filled the loft, and she curled to a ball, knees to chest, regretting the dream had ended.

But how could it not end? She knew not where it could go. She knew so little of what happened after the nakedness. There had been times when she had heard her mother and father on the far side of the curtain that separated her own sleeping space from theirs, heard their sounds of pleasure, and Ruth had lain there in the dark, curious even then. Of course, she had seen animals mate. A rooster jump fast on the back of an unsuspecting hen. A goat ride the back of the nanny. But a man and a woman ...

Her hand traced a hip, up and over her belly to the tip of her breast. She whimpered at the pleasure of it.

She turned to her stomach. Then back again onto her side. It was no use. Sleep was lost.

In the dark, Ruth crept from her mattress. Below the loft, in his bed, her father's breathing had turned throaty and loud, but still he slept. And remembering that Elias was not there to hear her, Ruth moved quickly to find her clothes and slip them on. She wanted the salty air and the moonlight.

A brief touch proved the necklace to be there at her throat.

One rung at a time, she lowered herself down the ladder. Jacob's breathing caught – ceased, filling the house with a suspended silence, and Ruth waited. The fire had burned too low and filled the room with the smell of stale ash, but she dared not stoke it. Instead, she remained at the bottom rung for what seemed endless minutes until her father's breathing again rose and fell in sleep's slow rhythm.

At last, with cloak over her arm, she stepped out into the dampness of night. Like shadowed giants under the moon's light, the junipers rose beyond the clearing. An owl hooted. The feathered creature sat at the very top of a juniper, the owl the color of newly fallen snow. As if frozen, the owl boldly stared back. The great wings then spread, and the owl lifted away, lost in among the boughs. For some time, Ruth looked to where the owl had been. She had never seen an owl so purely white. Never seen an owl so close. This one – it was magnificent, a perfectly designed creature, the eyes so human.

In the dampness, Ruth shivered. She ought to go back inside. But that could wake Jacob, and surely he would take up again the topic of her refusal to Mr. Wells. When she told her father the outcome with Zebadiah Wells, the look on her father's face had been that of disappointment. "I worry about thee," he had said, and Ruth had felt the weight of his worry. But in this darkness, she felt only the isolation from even Jacob.

Huddled inside the wool cloak, Ruth set out on the path. She walked quickly, winding her way alongside the murmuring salt creek. When the tallest of trees ceased to be and her path was sided only by low oak, the break of waves could be heard washing onto the near shore. She knew now where she was headed, and in her hurry she lifted her skirt hem out of the way of scrambling feet.

She broke out suddenly onto the open stretch of shore.

The tide was full, the shore narrow. At water's edge, drenched in silvery light, stood Mittark – he and Ruth face to face, so close, and Ruth stepped back, so full of surprise.

"Hello," she said, hearing breathlessness in her voice.

"I did not think to see Ruth so early at the water."

"And Mittark? Doest he roam often in the night?"

Mittark looked away to the black of the sea and to the blazed silver path sent down across it by the moon. "In night a man sees what cannot be seen in the day."

"What Mittark says is true. Just now I came upon a snow-white owl. Never before have I seen one so entirely white."

"The white owl possesses great spirit and the courage to hunt alone," said Mittark. "The gods have honored Ruth by placing this white owl in her path."

"Doest thou truly believe that?"

"Yes, it is what I believe."

A sigh escaped from somewhere deep. "I wish I could be as strong as thee in all that I believe."

"Ruth is strong."

"Mmmm, perhaps at times. But tonight I feel without any strength at all."

"I ask if Ruth walks in this moonlight because she battles in her sleep."

She nodded, but was reminded, too, of the dream that had woken her. Heat rose on her face, and Ruth could only hope that the night was enough to hide her color.

"The night soon ends," said Mittark. "Come. I will show Ruth a beauty as great as that of the white owl."

"Where are we going?" this as she scurried to match the stride of Mittark.

Twenty-One

Mittark dragged the dugout into the water, and Ruth knelt in the low bow, not having yet an answer to where they were going. The dugout lunged forward. The weight of Mittark settled behind her, and they moved swiftly, the black water lapping at the sides. She heard his breath, strong with cadence to match the slice of the paddle. Her father would disapprove. He would be angry knowing she was with Mittark in this way, alone. Yet, nothing could have stopped her. Knowing this, her heart beat louder.

The dark form of the distant island moved closer with every stroke of the paddle, and Ruth believed now that they were headed there. The night sky was turning to gray, and when the dugout scuffed up against the island shore, Mittark leapt out onto the sand.

"This way. We must hurry," he said, leading her across the beach and on up the path, climbing the cliff to the top, same as that day with Elias. But they did not turn to the back of the island as before. Instead, Mittark took a more winding path along the east-facing side. The sky lightened to the palest pink as they moved through the pines. The forest opened then, and a level place spread before them, a clearing nearly filled by an enormous stone that stood so tall and wide they needed to walk around it.

Beyond the stone, the high cliff fell away to the sea and to a red horizon, set on fire by a sun not yet seen.

"The wait is not long," said Mittark, and he sat on the earth, his back to the massive stone.

Ruth sat also, and she pulled the cloak around her. That and the batting of bearberry vine beneath her gave a nestled sort of warmth, and she waited with the silent Mittark at her side. The sun appeared first as a mere arc of red, then lifting, sliding higher and higher, at last to a perfect molten circle, brilliant above the dark thin line of mainland, so brilliant that Ruth's eyes burned and she needed to look away. But the glance caught on the line of cheekbone, the straight raven hair held by a thin string of animal hide worn tight around his forehead. The Mittark before her now was real, not a dream. So easily, if she dare, she could reach out to touch and to know the feel of this native man who sat so entangled with her emotions.

Her hands pressed hard against one another in her lap, and the breath she swallowed tasted of the dampness. "Mr. Wells has asked me to marry him," she said, her voice nearly lost in the soft breaking of the sea onto the shore below.

A muscle twitched along a cheekbone. "Wells is a good man."

"Yes, but I do not love him."

"Will Ruth marry him?"

She shook her head but did not speak because tears welled and she would not show Mittark tears.

"What does the father of Ruth say about this."

"He does not approve of my decision."

"Perhaps Ruth will change her decision. Perhaps Ruth will honor the wish of her father."

"No. Never. I cannot." She looked to Mittark, met the dark of his eyes. He was beautiful, the day's first light on the angles of his face, and when his glance lowered to her mouth, the nearness brought courage. With the back of her hand, Ruth touched on his cheek, and her fingers felt along the coarse thick strands of hair.

"I have dreamed of this," she said. "I want thee, Mittark. 'Tis thee I want to touch … to feel." Her hand slid down the animal hide that was his shirt, brushed over its softness. When her fingers pulled down along the course of his arm, Mittark spoke rapid words of his own language, words she did not understand, and she let her hand come to rest upon his. "I wish I knew thy thinking. I wish I knew thy very thought."

"At this time, that would not be good," he said, at last in the words of English. He took her hand, drew it away from himself and set it back upon the earth before letting go.

With the sting of tears, Ruth looked to her hand that had been so bold. "Is it that Mittark finds me lacking? Am I not pretty enough?"

"Ruth lacks nothing. She has only beauty, of face and of spirit."

"Then why won't you touch me?" she asked while wiping at the thin line of wet that ran down her face. "Why don't you care for me?"

Again Mittark spun words of his language, and he leaned back against the stone. "I care," he said. "So strong is my want of Ruth that it frightens me."

Her heart beat as if hooves of wild horses galloped inside. And in the yellow light of morning, Ruth undid the button that held the cloak about her, and she let it fall to the ground. She removed the cotton cap and the pins, shook her head so that her hair fell loose.

Mittark's eyes gave not so much as a flicker, until with gentle touch, he reached to her, only to trace the line of the bone beads at her neck. "This is not the path Ruth should choose."

"I choose thee." Slowly, Ruth stood. Her fingers moved about the buttons. One by one, pieces of clothing fell atop the wool cloak. And with air biting at the pale young skin, she knelt down and took hold of the deerskin shirt, slid it up and over, exposing the native's muscled chest. When her nails caught on the taut flesh, the skin quivered.

"Ruth does not know what she does."

"But I do," she said, knowing only that she wanted his touch in return, the feel of him against her, and so easily Ruth wrapped her arms around him, her body pressing to his. A groan came from deep within him, and she felt him yield, felt his breath warm.

His arms surrounded her, and Mittark lay back onto the ground taking Ruth with him, receiving her weight upon him. His hold, his every touch was tender, and she understood then the gentleness within a man's strength. But even as she told him this, his touch became bold, as if a hunger had come upon him, roving, pressing, waking every surface, every part of her, and she held to him. There was only the need, the heat between them as he moved above her, finding her, and she felt the hardness of him enter. Felt his hesitation, the resistance given by her maiden body, and she heard her own insistent plea. "I want this, Mittark. With thee. No one else." And she lifted her hips to meet him.

From his lips came words not of English. Then a seer of fire, quick and gone. Gently he moved, and she moved with him, wanting the pleasure. Want became eager. Her flesh burned. There was his breath and the smell of heat and sand and pine. Until so suddenly, her body exploded, rippled with unfamiliar sensation, stopping her very breath as she wrapped herself tightly to him. Mittark pressed further, deeper with an urgency that did not fade until he called out her name, and he lay spent upon her.

When she opened her eyes, he was there still.

"I love thee, Mittark."

He held her as he rolled off to the ground, and he pulled her to him. "I know of love," he said. "I have loved Ruth since that first day in the house of Wells." But Mittark drew away from her then. He stood and stepped into the leggings as he walked to the cliff's edge, his back to Ruth. "I have spoken to the gods about Ruth."

The meaning was not in his words but in the way in which they were spoken. She understood, and the knowing cut as a knife through to her heart. With the silence between them, Ruth dressed, needing the steadiness of the stone as she smoothed wrinkles from her chemise and then the skirt. Somehow her hands managed each of the buttons. Not until the cloak was secure on her shoulders did she ask and dare to hear the answer. "And the gods," she said, "have they answered thee?"

Mittark came to stand before her. He set his hands upon her shoulders, hands that held her at a distance. "I cannot have Ruth. Not as wife. Ruth is not of my people."

"Are these the words of thy god or are they from the heart of Mittark?"

"What is one is the other," he said. "It can be no other way."

"Then thy gods are cruel. And thou be foolish and blind to everything but our differences. Where it is important, we are the same, Mittark. Love belongs between us."

"Answers are not found in love only. In each question, a man must consider his children's children."

"But we would have children."

"They would not be of my people."

"They would be of thee."

"And they would be of Ruth."

He let his arms drop to his side. Although his eyes moved over her face, his vision seemed to have gone inside himself, and Ruth waited, a corner of her soul still believing in the power of wanting.

"When the short days again meet the long," he said, "I will take a wife from the Pamet village."

"No," she said, backing away but held there by the massive stone. Mittark stepped closer, set a hand again on her arm, but Ruth pushed the hand away.

"I feel Ruth's anger, but I ask her to understand the battle that wages in my heart. Ahead there are two paths. Only one can be chosen. I must choose the path of my people."

"Mittark lacks courage. He dares not look beyond his narrow world." She wished to be angry, to hurt him with words as he had hurt her, to tell him he could not have it his way. He could not have her love and the love of another. But if she were to speak these words, they would forever be a lie. No matter how great her hurt, she would love always this wild and beautiful man. So she turned away, walking quickly around the stone and down along the path.

She did not speak, even from the bow of the dugout. Behind her, Mittark paddled in slow melancholy rhythm. But Ruth could not slow the rise of emptiness.

On shore, as Ruth stepped from the dugout, Mittark took her hand and held it in his. "I do not wish to bring sadness to Ruth. Ruth's sadness is my sadness."

She looked to their hands before lifting her eyes to Mittark. "If that were true ... if thou hurt as deeply as I hurt at this moment, thou could not let me walk away." She slipped her hand free of his. With it, she swiped at silent tears, and she stepped forward alone toward the salt creek path and home.

Twenty-Two

Ruth
The long winter passes into summer, August, 1636

Ruth sat on the bench Zebadiah had fashioned for her beneath the limbs of a high oak, shaded from the heavy August sun. Winter had given way to spring and now miraculously to lush summer. The infant, Constance, suckled at her breast, and with the scent of milk faint on the child's warm breath, Ruth felt the first tendrils of contentment, lost for so long, beginning again, uncurling low like the early tenuous shoots of the fiddle fern.

Ruth hummed a lullaby while in the distance, in the open field Zebadiah walked behind the plow, and the steady plodding of the oxen played into her song. But of a sudden the oxen were commanded to whoa. The plodding ceased, and Ruth looked outward to see the cause.

The straight proud figure of Mittark stepped out from the forest into the field. Wearing only the breechcloth of summer, he walked to Zebadiah. Because of the distance, Ruth could not make out the words exchanged between them, but Zebadiah looked repeatedly to her as the two men spoke. When Zebadiah again gave command to the ox, the plow pulled forward, and Mittark started toward the high oak.

Ruth thought to take leave inside. She had not spoken even once with Mittark since that dawn spent together by the great stone. Nor had Mittark seen the child she had born. However, avoidance was imprudent and fears better faced. Ruth sat straighter. As she pulled the sleeping baby gently from her breast, she covered herself and waited.

"Hello, Ruth," said Mittark when he stood before her, but his glance fell to Constance. He touched on the thick thatch of raven hair that already covered the infant's head. Ruth saw in Mittark's eyes the unasked question, but never would she grant the answer.

"I've named her Constance. 'Twas my mother's name." That was all she would give him.

"The cheekbone and the hair black as the night, they are not of Ruth's mother."

Their eyes held.

A gull complained from high overhead.

Then the robust voice of Zebadiah cut in. "Did you like the gift, Ruth?"

Only with great effort was she able to look away from the challenge and turn to her husband. "What gift, Zebadiah?"

The answer came not from Zebadiah.

"I come to the house of Wells to bring a gift from Elias. I have seen Elias and his new wife on my return from the Manomet. The two wish soon to see the new daughter of Ruth." Mittark unrolled a wrap of hide and took from it a small quilted blanket of pale soft colors.

At the mention of Elias, her shoulders wanted more than anything to slump, for she missed Elias so very much. But to Mittark she would not show even this. Ruth accepted the quilted blanket in her free hand and laid it across her lap. "A lovely gift," she said, the words falling empty.

Zebadiah faced the tall native. "Will thou stay awhile and talk with an old friend?" he asked, his voice amiable, though Ruth knew it to be too much so.

"I have been away long," said Mittark. "I must return now to my village."

"So be it. Another time then." Zebadiah shifted his weight, moving one step closer to Ruth.

Mittark nodded his goodbye to Zebadiah.

Then, too, a nod to Ruth, and Mittark turned to leave.

"How is Weetamo?" The question came unbidden as Ruth watched the sun strike on the native's back. "I heard she was ill during the cold of winter."

Mittark looked out to some place beyond the clearing before he turned to look at Ruth. "Weetamo has passed. Her body is on the hill beside the body of Nohtok and beside her son, my father. Her spirit is with theirs. For Weetamo it is good."

"But for Mittark it is sad."

"Yes. For me, there is sadness."

Her eyes clouded with wet, and there was a moment that held, one moment of connection, of shared grief and loss. Then Mittark walked toward the north, and there was only his back and the silence.

Constance squirmed.

Zebadiah requested his noon meal.

Ruth crossed the short distance and entered the house. She placed Constance into the cradle. At the foot of the wide bed she shared with Zebadiah, she knelt down at a wooden chest and placed the new small blanket inside. She reached then deep into the bottom of the chest, searching until her hand touched on the coarse bone beads. She thought of Weetamo – the old leathered face. And she saw, too, the angled face of Mittark. Her hand lifted as if to touch on the image, as she had done that early dawn by the stone.

"Come join me, Ruth," Zebadiah called from the table.

Ruth smoothed the garments back over the beads, waiting out the ache in her heart, then closed the lid.

Twenty-Three

Sydney
Sunday morning, September 2

The fire in the hearth throws yellow light across the room. A spark crackles, and Sydney begins to read, for the fourth time, the first paragraph in Dinesen's book. She's distracted. By Everett. And the airport. And she can't get rid of the chill. The hot coffee helps. But even with Cat beside her on the sofa, Sydney can't get warm and she shivers.

Barefoot, Alison leaves the chair where she has set up to paint her nails. She goes to the worn wooden chest that just today has replaced the maple coffee table, and she takes from inside the chest a soft pile blanket.

"Would you like this blanket over you?" asks Alison.

"Okay." Even that one word comes slowly because Sydney is confused … the coffee, the blanket … never has Alison shown this much consideration in one afternoon.

Her mother spreads the blanket over Sydney's lap. "You should've dried your hair," says Alison. "I have a dryer if you didn't bring one."

Sydney doesn't use a hair dryer. The hot air makes her curly hair frizz. But Alison has no way of knowing that. Knowing such a personal thing requires shared space over time. "No, thanks," says Sydney. "It'll dry here by the fire." She places the book open across her lap but looks to the wooden chest. "Where is Eva's coffee table?"

"Oh, that old thing," says Alison. "It was falling apart. And the chest was up in the front bedroom just taking up space, so I had Ty help bring it down here. It works all right, don't you think?"

"It doesn't matter what I think. But sure. It works fine," says Sydney, and she turns to the opened book, pretends to read the first paragraph one more time as Alison puts another log on the fire, stokes the flame with the metal poker. But it is all too unusual, and Sydney watches, wonders just what Alison will do next. Even as Alison sits back down on the large upholstered chair, Sydney is watching.

"Why are you staring?" asks Alison.

"I'm not staring. I'm just ..."

"Just what?" A splash of coffee spills onto Alison's lap. But rather than jump up and run to the kitchen to wash out the spill, which is what Sydney expects, Alison ignores the spill. Her eyebrows pinch together to show a crease above her nose. "Can't we talk? Can't we even sit in the same room?"

Sydney ruffles through damp curls. No, they cannot talk. Not about anything important. Neither one of them can speak an ounce of truth, not without arching backs and growling.

Sydney glances to the fire and remembers the new pledge to keep the higher path. "Mom, let's just sit. I don't want to fight."

"Why does it have to be a fight?"

"I don't know. You tell me."

"Please." Alison places her mug onto the side table by the chair. She dabs at last at the small spill on her lap. "I want to hear what you've been doing ... what your plans are. See? There's lots to talk about if we can just forget the past."

Alison may as well have slapped her, and Sydney turns from it. "What's that mean, to forget? Does it mean to forgive? To excuse the fact that years ago you left me behind? That you've never given me credit for anything without a backhanded criticism thrown in? No. I wish it was different, but I can't forget any of those things."

Alison leans back in the chair, a sigh deflating her. "I know, I've hurt you. And I'm sorry. I also know it's taken far too many years for me to say that. But really, Sydney, by the time I left you here on the island, I had no clue what else to do with you."

"You could have given up the theater. You could have stayed here, too. You were my mother."

Alison bites down on her lip, reminding Sydney of herself in that one gesture, and she wonders if such a habit is learned, copied.

"Yes, I suppose I could have left my career ... given up my dreams," says Alison. "But it wouldn't have worked. Not then."

"Why not?"

"Because I ... I couldn't come back."

"So, instead, you threw me away."

"I did not throw you away. I left you with the only person I could count on. But I couldn't stay with you. At the time, ironically, I was angry at your grandmother."

"At Eva?" As if someone just said the world was flat, Sydney sets her mug down on the chest, tries to take in the absurd. "How could you be angry with Eva? She was gentle and ..."

"And not at all like me, right? Well, that's for certain. I'm just like my father. Bold. Directive. The only difference between my father and me is that I don't drink to the point of taking my disappointments out on other people."

"What are you saying? That your father was a drunk?"

"Oh, yes."

"But Eva ..."

"I don't know how she stood it." Alison sits straighter in the chair, looks down to her lap. "When I was very young, I liked it when he drank. He'd get loud and funny. He'd sing and hug me and give me anything I asked for. Then, after a few more drinks, he'd disappear into his room, and I'd see no more of him for the night. It took me a long time to realize that even though I was done dealing with him early in the evening, my mother was not. When she finally kicked him out of the house and out of our lives, I blamed her. I fought with her for years. The day after I graduated from high school, I took a bus to New York with forty dollars in my pocket. I stayed away."

Eva never shared much with Sydney about Charles Foster. He left, according to Eva's telling, because they were no longer compatible. They had nothing in common. They'd fallen out-of-love, Eva said.

As for Alison, Eva defended her always, arguing tooth and nail that Alison, like any young woman, needed to follow her heart's dream.

"But you didn't have to stay in New York," argues Sydney now. "You could have come home when you found out you were pregnant. Eva would have taken you back."

"Oh, Sydney. Looking back always makes it look clearer. I'm sure Eva would have let me come home. But I couldn't. It was different back then. I couldn't come back to this simple place pregnant and unmarried. Besides ..." Alison meets Sydney's gaze, her eyes as dark green as Sydney has ever seen them.

Alison stands, walks to the fireplace, her back to Sydney.

"Besides what?" asks Sydney, waiting for the answer, any answer, wanting more of this truth they are suddenly swimming in ... or drowning in.

Alison shakes her head, without turning from the fire. "It doesn't matter now. What does matter is that I wasn't enough parent for you, and if I'd kept you with me any longer, I would have lost you to the streets and to drugs."

"And when you asked Eva to take me, what did she say?"

"Eva is the one who asked me. She said she couldn't just sit by and watch anymore. That you needed more attention than I was able to give."

Sydney pulls the pile blanket up close, covering her chest. Eva was the one who thought she needed saving. It was Eva's idea to have Sydney stay on Ponokanet. But still ...

"A real mother wouldn't have agreed to give up on her only child."

Alison turns to meet Sydney's glare. "I told you. I didn't know how to be a mother. I didn't know how to save you. I had to hope that Eva did."

"Why didn't you tell me all this before?"

"At first you were too young. Then it wouldn't have made any difference. You were already angry, and I knew what that meant. You wouldn't hear a thing I had to say."

Alison's phone chimes, but she does not move to answer.

Sydney ignores the chime. "You could have visited more."

"Yes. I could have. I should have."

"You could have been more of a mother."

"I wish I had."

Still there is the chime of the phone. Alison, with tears in her eyes, clears her throat and picks up the phone. While walking back into the kitchen, she talks to Edward about his arriving the next day. Sydney looks to Cat and scratches behind one gray ear while trying to imagine her mother angry at Eva. At eighteen, Alison left Ponokanet for her own dream, and in doing so left Eva here alone.

The same as Sydney did.

Sydney, too, fled off. To college, to California, as far away as she could get.

Her eyes burn. If she could take that one thing back, in this moment Sydney would. She would not have left Eva. She should not have left Eva here to grow old alone.

"Edward will be here mid-day tomorrow," announces Alison, her bare feet silent as she walks across the wood floor. "And I've invited some friends, the Cavanaughs from Shore Road, to come over about five for some drinks and a Labor Day barbeque."

Sydney feels surprise open on her face.

"I hope you don't mind," says Alison. "And really, Sydney, I hope you'll join us. It would be nice for you to get to know Edward."

"I'm not sure. But I'll let you know," says Sydney. She leaves the sofa, picking up the Dinesen book as she stands. Company wasn't in the plan. She can't imagine ever sitting an entire evening with Alison and Edward and guests she doesn't even know. "I think the road trip is catching up with me," she says. "I need a nap."

As she walks out from the living room, Cat follows at her heels.

Twenty-Four

At five o'clock Sydney sits parked in Everett's driveway. The Subaru engine still runs, the windshield wipers beating out a banter. Beside the Subaru sits the green pick-up. Dinner was supposed to be with just the two of them, her and Everett. It's selfish but she doesn't want to share Everett with this Ty person.

The alternative, however, is to not go inside.

Sydney turns off the engine. With the grocery bag in one arm, she walks through the rain toward the back door. Her hope is that Everett and Ty will be in the living room. She can call out hello from the kitchen and go about the business of preparing dinner.

As it turns out, Ty is also backdoor company.

When Sydney opens the door, Ty stands inside holding a mesh bag that bulges with white-shelled clams. Even with the one arm filled, he helps Sydney slip out from her slicker, and the back of his hand brushes across her shoulder. An inadvertent touch, light, but it sends a current through her, making her step away. Since Rick, not once has her body responded to touch, inadvertent or otherwise. She feels betrayed … her body forgetting grief.

She hangs the slicker on one of three pegs by the door.

"Ty brought us some little necks. You remember those, don't you, kid?"

Looking to Everett, Sydney smiles. "How could I forget?"

"I'll see you folks later," says Ty when he sets the bag of clams in the sink.

"Oh, no, you don't," says Everett. "We eat those things only if you stay and help us do it. We'd like that, wouldn't we, Syd?"

Two pair of eyes settle on her. Everett wants him to stay. She can hear it in his voice. "Of course," she says. "Someone has to teach me how to cook them."

Reluctance shows in the shift of his eyes, but Ty agrees to stay for an hour, saying only that he has to meet someone at six. He rinses the clams and lets them soak in a pot of cold water and corn meal.

"Why corn meal?" she asks.

"They take it in with the water. It helps wash the sand out of their bellies," he says while he fills a second kettle with water and puts it on the stove to heat.

Sydney unloads the bag she's brought and begins to peel potatoes. When mashed, the potatoes will be soft, something she's quite sure Everett will eat. She feels Everett watching her from where he stands by the refrigerator.

"How's your friend, Jean, doing these days?" asks Everett. "Is she still working on engines?" He takes two beers from the refrigerator, hands one to Ty and the other to Sydney before he sits at the table. Everett has met Jean. It was at the first competition in which Sydney flew as part of the Chico flight team. Everett traveled all the way to California to watch Sydney compete. He and Jean joked together and even danced a few times that evening at a local pub. Sydney watches him now as he stretches his legs under the table. He takes a swallow of what appears to be a half-full glass of ginger ale. On his face, Sydney sees a lightness. Everett is enjoying himself.

"Jean's still the best mechanic there is," says Sydney. "She's the only one I'd ever let work on the Pitts." Because she regrets already mentioning the Pitts, Sydney takes a swallow from the beer.

"What's a Pitts?" asks Ty.

"It's a biplane ... two pair of wings," says Everett, picking up where Sydney did not. "Syd flew a Pitts when she was stunt flying."

On the stove, the kettle cover rattles, and Ty removes the cover. He spills the whole bunch of clams into the boiling water, and there is no more talk of planes.

At the table, Sydney scoops a mound of opened shells onto Everett's plate. "This is good," he says. "It's good to have friends around." Everett is eating. His throat seems less sore than the day before. When he asks about the sign, Sydney tells him the wood is drying in Eva's attic, that tomorrow she'll start painting it.

She dips another clam into melted butter, and feels her shoulders relax. "I didn't know how much I've missed the taste of these things."

"Did I tell you that I met Ty in Vietnam?" asks Everett.

"Yes, you did." And because Ty as subject means that Sydney will not be, she accepts Everett's bait. "Were you in the military, Ty?"

"No. I was still a kid back then. I'd been given a job to care for the gardens around the American embassy."

"Don't be so damn modest," says Everett, jumping in. "You did a hell of a lot more than that." He takes a moment, noticeably a little too long, to swallow a tender clam before going on to explain. "Ty was twelve when I met him. But he'd been working at the embassy for two years before that. He knew the city and its people, and he knew how to speak Vietnamese and English. So, lots of times if the guys at the embassy needed someone to talk to the locals, they'd call for Ty."

"And so you helped the Americans?"

"Some."

"Where did you learn to speak English so well?"

Ty lets the question wait until he pulls meat from a shell. "I spent several years in a Buddhist monastery. I studied there. English was an important part of my lessons."

"A monastery? Was that common for young boys to do?"

"No. Not common." His eyes move over her face, but Sydney, looking in, can see his thoughts are elsewhere. Then the eyes are still.

"My father was French," says Ty. "When the French were defeated at Dien Bien Phu, my father returned to his own country. I stayed with my mother, but I was half French. In Vietnam that was considered lower than the dogs that ran in the street. My mother couldn't guarantee my safety. In the monastery, I was safe."

Sydney takes a delicious cold sip of beer and sets the bottle down again. "And your mother," she asks, "did she live with you in the monastery?"

"No. The world of a monk is very much a male world. My mother was not allowed to stay."

"So your mother just left you there?" Disbelief is in her voice, and she looks to Everett for confirmation.

Everett simply nods his head.

"I was four," says Ty. He puts his elbows on the table, seemingly resigned to the telling. "My mother saved my life by begging the monks to take me in. At the time, I was able to speak two languages, French and Vietnamese. The monks thought I showed promise as a student, so they agreed to keep me."

"But you were only four."

"Yes, I was young." He glances to his watch and then to Everett. "I really do need to be going. As I said, I'm meeting some people in town." Clearing his plate from the table, he rinses it in the sink and sets it in the dishwasher. "I'll see you tomorrow," he says, a nod of his head directing the words to Everett. Then he is gone, the door closed against the rain.

"Well, I guess I chased him out of here fast," says Sydney on a long exhaled breath.

"Don't worry about it," says Everett. "I told you Ty wasn't much of a talker."

"Did he ever see her again?"

"His mother? No, he didn't. He went looking for her once after he'd been in the states a while. He went back to her village, some place just north of QuiNhon. There was an old woman there who remembered her, remembered Ty even. She told him how the village had been attacked and burned by the North Vietnamese. The men had tried to fight. The women and children tried to hide. But Ty's mother had been found. The story wasn't pretty."

"My God."

"Yep. I guess Ty spent some time after that in Saigon, at that monastery again, trying to sort things out."

"So he lived as a real monk?"

"I'm not sure about that. To be honest, we haven't talked about it all that much."

"I can see why. He'd be out the door in a huff every visit."

Everett laughs a little.

Sydney gets up from the table to serve the rest of their dinner. Everett wants only a small serving of the mashed potatoes. The baked haddock she wraps in foil and puts it into the refrigerator for another meal, but she can't shake the image of that small boy left on the steps of a monastery, his mother walking away.

She puts away the last of the dishes, sits again across the table from Everett. The warm room, Everett just across from her, the setting has grown comfortable.

"How's it going with Alison?" he asks.

"Things are better. We actually talked this afternoon. Without claws." The mention of Alison reminds her of the photo in the album. "Were you and Alison good friends growing up?"

"Depends on what you mean by good friends."

"You know, did you hang out together in high school? Did you ever date her?"

Everett sits back against the chair, pulls in one stretched-out leg from under the table. "What's this all about?"

"Nothing really. I found a picture in an old album today, that's all. It was of you and Alison taken in front of my grandmother's house. I guess I just never thought of you two together."

The hand that has wrapped his glass of ginger ale slips away, only to come back and draw a wriggly line in the condensation on the glass. "We dated a few times one summer."

"You actually dated my mother?" Sydney pulls in her chair, eager like some schoolgirl wanting the scoop.

"This is a small town, kid. Smaller back then. I probably dated just about every girl there was."

"Then how come you never married?"

"Whoa. This is getting kind of heavy, don't you think?" He shifts some in his chair, as if the wooden seat is suddenly too hard."

"You don't have to tell me," says Sydney. "I was just curious."

"I don't mind telling you. I never found the right girl."

Sydney could sit there all evening, intrigued by this side of Everett that she's never met. But he rubs at the back of his neck. The shadow under his eyes has gone darker. Sydney lifts the slicker from the peg by the door, kisses Everett on the cheek. "Good night," she says. "I'll keep you posted on progress with the sign."

By the time she climbs into bed with the Dinesen book, her mind has gone back to Everett – his comment that he'd never found the right girl. It makes Sydney wonder. Why hadn't some woman snatched him up? He's an interesting man. And even now, racked by cancer, he's good-looking. As a young man in the photo, he was GQ gorgeous.

It's sad, sort of, but she supposes there are people who never find the person they are meant to be with. Just as there are some who lose that one person and never want another.

Twenty-Five

Sydney
The next morning, Monday, September 3

In the attic Sydney dabs with gold paint, but the gold merges with the wet blue of the background, turning an iridescent green. She should have known that would happen. Now she'll have to wait for the first paint to dry before trying again to work on the sign. Patience has never been her strong suit. Under the scratch of frustration, she cleans the brushes and puts them away. She intended to bring the finished sign to Everett later in the day. But that isn't going to happen.

She goes to Eva's chair, turns it so that it faces the opened gable window to look out at the front yard. The old weathervane on the barn roof – a whale, heavy and tarnished green – is swimming northwest. On the ground Ty walks from the corner of the barn. He wears jeans and a dark t-shirt, and seeing him, a warmth coils low inside Sydney. There is something beautiful about him, not just in his face but in the way he moves with such a calm, centered being.

It's not fair that her body is attracted. It's primal, and she doesn't like it. Doesn't want it. It magnifies missing Rick, and her body is a traitor.

Cat runs from the corner of the barn and catches up with Ty, who bends down and strokes Cat's back. Cat winds herself around his leg, and Sydney shakes her head. It seems her body is not the only traitor around here.

Through the window, she watches the caretaker climb into the truck. She thinks about the four-year-old boy who coped with being left behind. She would ask him someday just how he did that – how he survived and remained whole.

Or more than likely she won't ask. That kind of conversation could emerge only through a sense of trust and safety, something found between people close, between friends.

In the yard, as the truck pulls away, Cat scampers toward the house, and a black Ford Explorer drives in over the gravel. Edward is at the wheel. He hits the Explorer's horn, and Alison comes into the yard. Rotund Edward, as round in the face as he is in the girth, climbs from the Explorer and holds Alison, a truly affectionate embrace as the two meet in front of the house. Edward speaks something and Alison points to the attic window. Sydney sits back, away from view, and looks to her watch.

It is after ten. In a few minutes, after she gathers more will, she'll go down and say hello.

"That dress looks lovely on you," says Alison while arranging crackers on a plate. "You should wear blue more often."

A compliment but still backhanded. Sydney barely shakes her head before turning to the open French doors at the back of the kitchen. She's agreed, against better judgement, to be at Alison's dinner party but only for appetizers and a glass of wine. Just long enough to be polite.

With a martini in the hand that rests on his paunch, Edward sits on the back deck with the Cavanaughs. "Are you in love with him?" asks Sydney while looking out to Edward, remembering the way he'd taken Alison into his arms when he arrived.

Alison has been scooping hummus into a bowl, but with the question, Alison's hand goes still. "In love with who? Edward?"

"Yes. I watched him with you this morning. It's obvious he loves you."

The refrigerator door opens, and Alison refills a glass of white wine. "Of course, I'm in love with him. Edward's fun. He's kind and good company."

"I have friends that are good company and fun. That doesn't mean I'm in love with them."

Alison turns to Sydney, a smile softening her face. "But friends can fall in love, don't you think?"

"I don't know."

"So you and Rick, you weren't friends first?"

The mention of Rick cuts deep, and Sydney reaches to the pain. "I loved Rick first. I loved him even before I really knew him. I loved what he did, who he was."

"I see." Alison sips her wine before placing the stemmed glass on the tray with the crackers. "I think I'm too old to fall in love with the image of a man. I need to try him on awhile to find out if he's comfortable. And Edward. He's comfortable."

"Rick was comfortable."

Alison crosses the kitchen, close to where Sydney stands by the open door, and Alison reaches tentatively and takes hold of Sydney's hand. "I'm sure Rick was comfortable. All I meant was that for me, now, at my age, it's different."

"What about my father? Were you friends, or did you love him first?"

Alison drops Sydney's hand and returns to the counter where she picks up the tray of hummus and crackers. With tray in hand, she comes back to the doorway and stops beside Sydney. "I loved him first," says Alison before she slides past Sydney, out onto the deck, her long silk islander dress forming to shapely thighs.

Sydney starts to follow, but Ty has come into the yard and he steps up onto the deck. With hair tied back wet, as if freshly showered, he shakes hands with both guests. Sydney had no idea he'd been invited. When Ty agrees to a beer, Edward leaves the group and walks past Sydney into the kitchen. "Come join us," says Edward. "I'm just getting Ty a beer."

She looks out again, and Ty is watching her. Their eyes meet before he turns back to the conversation that continues around him. Sydney is shaking her head, even as she lifts her chin and joins the party.

"So, Sydney," begins Elizabeth Cavanaugh, "I understand you live in California. Are you enjoying your stay on the island so far?"

"Yes, I am," she says, knowing that it is not a complete lie.

"What is it you do in California?"

Sydney moistens her lips, resisting the urge to rake through her hair. "I worked at a small airport not far from Santa Rosa."

That at least is the truth, even though after Rick she hardly showed up at all at the airport. Brady was kind, sympathetic, letting her do some phone answering and general clean-up around the place. He was waiting, she supposed, for Sydney to change her mind and fly.

"Sydney is a pilot," says Alison, apparently not able or willing to leave the point alone. "A stunt pilot. I'm very proud of her, but it frightens me to think of her in the sky performing all those loops and twirls, whatever it is they call those fancy maneuvers."

"That's funny. I didn't know you were frightened." It's a slip of sarcasm, and color rises on Alison's neck. Even so, Sydney turns to Elizabeth Cavanaugh. "My mother has no more reason to be afraid. I'm no longer a pilot."

"Oh, why not?" says Elizabeth after sipping from the martini.

The eyes of everyone look to Sydney. All faces are shaded by the great striped umbrella, except for Ty's because he sits with legs outstretched, his distance from the group hardly measureable but apart.

Sydney looks to her mother. "Because I killed a man."

Elizabeth's mouth drops open.

Alison is shaking her head.

"I'm sorry, but I just noticed the time," says Ty, and he pulls his long legs up close to his chair as if preparing to leave. "I promised Sydney her first sailing lesson at six, while the tide is still up."

"That's right. We wouldn't want to miss the tide," says Sydney, jumping in, grateful for any getaway.

Ty thanks Edward for the beer and Alison for the invitation to join them. Then he touches the small of Sydney's back and whisks her away, around the house to the edge of the gravel drive.

"Thank you," says Sydney.

"Then you didn't mind?"

"Mind? No. I was about to leave anyway, and it would have meant an argument with Alison later."

"So, would you like to sail?"

"No, I …" she says, while pulling through her hair.

"They're going to know it was a ruse if we don't go."

"I don't know a thing about sailing."

"I said it was a lesson, didn't I?"

She studies his face, the man who works as caretaker, who tends flowers, who helps Everett, the man who somehow knew she needed to be out from under inquiring strangers.

"All right," she says. "What do I need to bring."

"It's not much of a boat. Just a little Sunfish. You pretty much sit on the water. You're going to get wet."

Twenty-Six

Lydia
Boston, Massachusetts, late summer, 1754

Rain descended on the ship and onto twelve-year-old Lydia Fenton. Pasted by the torrent, the white shirt clung to her slim strong body. The canvas breeches, permitted during those summer weeks at sea, were little protection from the deluge as she wrapped her legs to the yardarm. She tied the lashings around the lowered sail, rendering it useless to the brig and to the wind. Only then did she sit stilled, perched on the great spar with windswept hair, wet and black, slapping about her face.

"Get below." The ship's Captain shouted to her from the deck, hands cupped to his shaven face, but Lydia selected deafness to all except the hiss of the rain on the sea. She lifted her cheekbones to it so as to savor the sting and the brief time remaining before she would return to the bleak wooden house on the hill. The Captain let her be, as Lydia knew he would, because Captain James Fenton was also her father. On board his ship, she had been climbing mast and rigging since her legs could walk the deck, and though he often attempted to treat her differently than the rest of his crew, Lydia had determined to ignore all such attempts. So, like the rest who worked the rigging, she watched from her sitting place high above the deck as the dark blur of Boston's mainland moved closer.

The raspy bark of seals greeted them as the ship brushed past Castle Island, its old brass cannon pointed outward, and Britain's flag snapped in the wind there above the fort. The seals followed for a time but soon fell back, turned away, leaving only the rolling wake to widen at the back of the ship.

On deck, Caleb stepped out from the forecastle, lifting his collar to the soaking sky, and he looked up to where Lydia sat. "You keeping watch up there," he called, "or just daydreaming again?"

"Up here I do the work of two men."

"Aye, you do that." Caleb stood briefly gazing upward, then without further word he walked on toward the Captain.

Now a man of twenty, Caleb Willoughby served as first mate. He had sailed with her Papa for as long as Lydia could remember. Resembling more the paler population of Boston, Caleb was fair skinned with hair bleached white by the summer sun. But what Lydia admired most about Caleb's look was his eyes. His eyes possessed the color of a dark winter sea. She thought him handsome in a rough, seaworthy way. And for all the summers she had sailed aboard the Heaven's Mist, Caleb, even more so than the Captain himself, had kept an eye to Lydia and seen to it that she was safe and fed.

She watched where he stood with her Papa at the wheel, and she regretted in that moment Caleb's turn into manhood because there was not much play left in him. That was one part of growing up that Lydia planned to avoid. One day though, when she was a woman, she would find a man like Caleb, straight and strong, a man of his word and a lover of the sea. They would sail away to live all their days on a grand merchant ship, like the ship her father would next command, a ship built to sustain the high seas in the business of trade for the King. But for now, she was content with the work at hand, for Lydia loved the sea, the smell of its salt and the taste of its wind. And as Boston's harbor appeared off the bow, she climbed the ratlines down to the deck, ready to tie off the staunch brig to its cleats on Long Wharf.

Like ants impervious to any rain, porters in leather aprons scuttled over the wharf, busy at the work of unloading an English schooner that sat next to the Heaven's Mist. Already the Heaven's Mist had been emptied of its cargo, the tallying metered out at the counting house with the lace-collared merchant, Mr. Hurd. Business done, Lydia walked the length of wharf toward King Street, all the while keeping but a few steps behind her father.

She passed oxen that trudged ahead of a cart weighted with large wooden crates, each crate filled with what Lydia guessed to be London's finest fabric and furniture, hauled from the hold of the British ship. And she thought again of the day at the end of summer when she would sail on board her father's newest ship. Together they would sail across the Atlantic to Liverpool's docks, and those of Spain and India and perhaps even Madagascar. Already she knew the shores of Massachusetts Bay as well as she knew the road home, for she had sailed the bay's limits for as many summers as she could remember, glorious summer months when she was released from the stern teachings of the tutor. With cargo of candles and onion and flax, she had sailed on the Heaven's Mist as far north as the St. Lawrence and as far south as the Hudson. But the great ocean and the world beyond ...

"Stop your dreaming girl and keep pace." James Fenton ceased his wide stride, looked back and called to Lydia. "We've seen enough of this rain," he said while wiping the wet from his eyes. "It's time to be at home with the taste of a hot meal."

Lydia reluctantly stepped wider, leaving the sea a little farther behind. "You will tell Grandmother Brimmer that this year I'm going with you at summer's end?"

"I promised that I would discuss it, and that much I will do."

"But I have to go, Papa. I can't stay in Boston alone."

James Fenton waited the moment it took for Lydia to trot to his side, and he placed an arm across her shoulder. "You'd not be alone. You would still be living with Grandmother Brimmer."

"It's the same thing."

"Lydia, the woman is mother to your own mother. You can't think that badly of her."

Lydia crossed her arms, wet spooling from her long dark hair. "I won't stay with her."

Her father stared down to Lydia, and she thought he would speak again. Instead, he took a sudden step forward into the rain, and Lydia did the same, keeping at his side, her face turned to the mud that oozed out from beneath her shod feet.

At the corner of Sun Court and Moon Street, on the level crest of a long sloping hill, rested the squared house of Martha Brimmer. Grandmother Brimmer. Lydia's father opened the door, and Lydia stepped inside.

The smells of dinner pervaded the front hall. Beef gravy, she was certain. For six weeks at sea she had eaten only old Jake's cooking, and now, as a rivulet of rain dripped from the tip of her nose, and despite the knot in her belly that came with returning home, Lydia's stomach growled.

"You best get out of those wet things," said her father, and he bent to remove his own muddied boots.

"Yes, Papa." And she turned, but not before hearing on the polished wood floor the heavy footsteps of Martha Brimmer.

The woman stood not as tall as James Fenton's shoulders, she wearing a dress of rose cambric linen, and as Lydia walked past, Martha Brimmer stepped quickly aside, brushing at the skirt as if somehow Lydia could have soiled it. "Land sakes, James," the woman sputtered. "Get that child into some decent clothes."

Lydia's wide-set brown eyes met those of her father. She saw sympathy there, though he did not defend her or the clothes she wore. So, in silence Lydia walked to the stairway and began the ascent to her room. She had not reached her door before the next words followed sharp from behind her.

"The girl's getting too old for your times at sea. For heaven's sake, James, you must consider her age. It isn't right, a girl, and one of her station, dressing as a boy and behaving like one as well."

Lydia closed the bedroom door hard, and a small grin tugged at her lips because door slamming never failed to roil Grandmother Brimmer. But the door opened just as quickly as it had closed, and in walked the slender, yellow-haired indentured maid, Anna.

"Look at you, Miss Lydia, matted down like a wet cat," said Anna while reaching for the towel that waited by the washbowl. Anna dried Lydia's hair, rubbing it back and forth, forth and back.

"I can do this myself," and Lydia took hold of the towel, letting it fall at her side.

"Of course, you can. But your grandmother wouldn't approve, would she? Now, let's get you put together."

She squirmed while the servant girl peeled away layers of wet clothes, and with the discarded towel Lydia covered the tiny breasts that had budded over the summer. "I'm glad you're here, Anna," she said. "But I'm sorry you have to answer to my grandmother."

"Serving Mrs. Brimmer is no hardship from where I've been. And in the length of three years more, I'll be free to do as I choose."

"And what will that be?"

Anna took a cotton shift and petticoat from a drawer of the clothes press. "I'm not sure," she said while sliding the shift and then the petticoat over Lydia's head. Then the skirt and the blouse with its short tabs and puffy sleeves. "Perhaps I'll stay a lady's servant and be paid a wage for it. Or perhaps I'll marry and have me a wee little girl like you."

"I am not little any more. I've grown. And at summer's end I am going across the sea with Papa. In his new ship."

On Anna's face an eyebrow lifted. "Are you now? Well, that ought be a fine adventure. But I don't believe your grandmother's mentioned it."

"That's because she doesn't know yet."

"I see," said Anna while reaching for the hairbrush. "Shall I fix your hair, or would you rather do that yourself."

"By myself, please."

"Then it's time I return to the kitchen." The neat, trim Anna handed Lydia the hairbrush and marched out from the room, closing the door with what Lydia thought to be intentional quiet.

Lydia crossed to the window to peer out through the long needles of rain to the row of pear trees, and the rain clattered against the house. Slowly, Lydia started to brush at the tangles in her hair. Hers was raven colored hair that glistened even in the dim, gray light of a summer's storm. Her mother's hair had not been black, but more the color of hay. Her father's simply the color of an old chestnut. But Lydia had seen the same midnight color, coarse and thick and straight like her own. For one day each summer, her Papa sailed the Heaven's Mist to Ponokanet. Each time, Papa lowered the skiff and with Lydia in the bow, they rowed the mooring's distance to the high snip of land that was home to Papa's brother, Ralph, and his mother, Constance. Constance would greet them, waving from the top of the high cliff, her black hair blown by the wind, and Lydia had made note. Made note, too, of the smile and the warm eyes as dark as her own.

Turning from the gray of the out of doors, Lydia set the hairbrush upon the bed. She went to the clothes press and reached deep under a stack of folded cotton shifts. At the bottom she found the small, red velvet pouch, and she took the pouch with her to the bed. She cherished the feel of the velvet on her cheek, but the pouch had the power to make her sad. That sadness could sometimes last beyond the time spent with it, so Lydia wavered now at the choice.

She braided her hair, then coiled and pinned the braid high on her head before setting the detested frilly mobcap in place. This she did only because it was easier to wear the silly thing than to receive her grandmother's opinion of a girl with hair left uncovered.

With hair done, Lydia returned to the bed and took up the soft velvet pouch. She drew a breath, loosened the drawstring and took from the pouch the wide bracelet made of gold. Her finger traced the delicate leaf pattern engraved on the front of the bracelet, then turned it to better read the initials on the underside. *C.B.B.* – Corinne Belle Brimmer, her mother's name before marrying Papa. Lydia rubbed on the glistening gold, trying to conjure her mother, the mother who nine years ago had fallen ill and died of the consumption. But try as she might, all Lydia could see in her mind was the face in the large portrait that hung downstairs in the parlor room. Nine years had erased everything else – the images, the smells, the feel.

"It's absolutely absurd … the mere notion of a girl at sea. And for as many as three years. Perhaps more. You can't be serious, James."

Lydia had rounded the corner at the bottom of the stairs but stopped herself there upon hearing from the parlor the voice of Grandmother Brimmer. It was not Lydia's habit to eavesdrop, but neither was it her habit to interrupt when serious conversation was underway. At the moment she considered the latter of greater importance.

She heard the pouring of liquid into a glass and guessed it to be her father filling his favored snifter of brandy. She waited, abating all but the smallest bit of breath, until her father spoke.

"I'm the only parent the girl has, Martha. Is it better that I leave her home with none?"

"Of course, it is. And if you insist on this insanity, I'll fight you on it, James. That girl is a Brimmer. And no matter how hard you try, you can't turn her into the son you never had."

"You're wrong. That's not what this is about at all."

"Isn't it? Of all the Captains of all the ships in Boston, how many let their daughters go traipsing about their rigging for weeks at a time? And wearing breeches?"

Lydia heard the pouring of more liquid, and her eyes widened with the waiting. It was Grandmother Brimmer who spoke again. Her voice had faded, the slap of leather soles taking her further from the door, and this required Lydia to inch closer, leaning her face to the carved wood doorframe, risking discovery.

"Even with that aside, James, it's your calling to the sea that you're always putting first. Years ago, when you married my daughter, you could have stepped into the business of my husband's counting house. But the sea came first in your heart. Oh, yes, you stayed near to Boston for my daughter's sake. For that I was somewhat grateful. And up until now you've stayed close for your own daughter's welfare. But again the sea is winning."

"Then you think I shouldn't go at all."

"What you do with your own life is not of my concern. But the girl stays here, raised properly among the genteel and Christian."

Again the slap of leather soles, taking her grandmother back across the room. She came to stand not an arm's length from where Lydia listened behind the doorway, and Lydia bit down on her lip.

"Consider her future, James. She's near to becoming a young woman. On board your ship, what young men will be in her circle?"

Her father's snifter settled hard on the side table.

"And are you truly willing to risk her safety on board that ship and in filthy ports around the world?"

"You're right," he said. "I suppose I knew that all along, but I needed to talk it out before I could tell Lydia. She'll not be happy about the decision."

"She's a child. She'll take what's given her."

As Lydia turned, she slipped on the slick floor, caught her balance and fled, not noticing that her buckled shoes sounded sharply on the floor or that she'd left the front door open to the rain.

Twenty-Seven

Down the hill, onto Ann Street she ran, feeling her chest would burst, but still Lydia pressed on, darting among the market carts that cluttered Dock Square. The rain that streamed down her cheeks tasted of the salt of tears. It didn't matter. Nothing mattered. Not the tears. Not hateful old Grandmother Brimmer. Not even her Papa.

At the sight of the sea, the smells of tar and fish heavy in the air, Lydia slowed, for she knew then exactly where she would go – what she would do. In her satchel on board the Heaven's Mist, she'd find the second pair of breeches and a cap that would hide her hair. Then she'd go to Dowe's Wharf, or perhaps as far as Adam's wharf where the clerks and porters didn't know her. She'd check the board to find when the next packet was to sail for the outer harbors of Cape Cod. She had no money, but looking like a lad eager for work, she might earn her passage. And her Grandmother Constance might take her in.

The Heaven's Mist rested against the wharf, high in the water now without its cargo. The boarding plank remained out, lowered to the wharf. So climbing aboard would be easy. But she needed to get aboard in secret, without Caleb or anyone seeing her make way to her tiny cabin and to the breeches.

Navigating the narrow boarding plank like the sailor she was, Lydia scurried to the top, and there at the ship's gunnel she listened for the slightest sound of any crew. Hearing no one, she slipped off her buckled shoes, soaked now with mud. With one shoe in each hand, she stepped lightly toward the forecastle, toward the door to her cabin. The door scarcely squeaked on its hinges, first as she opened it, then only slightly more as she pressed it ever so gently closed.

Beyond the thin walls, rain drummed on the deck. She heard nothing more. But inside the cabin, standing so still in the dull light, Lydia clutched the muddied shoes to her chest. Like a stone tossed into the sea, the truth sank deep. She had lost everything. This ship. Her Papa. She had no one.

Her eyes squeezed shut, squeezed the fear. In its place an image started, the coarse black hair, the woman with a smile and a gentle hand raised, waving to Lydia from the cliffs of Ponokanet. She would not be alone, not if Grandmother Constance would have her, not if she kept her senses about her.

When the ship rocked and creaked on the turning tide, Lydia crossed to the leather satchel and reached inside for the breeches.

"What are you doing here?" It is Caleb standing there, who appeared somehow inside the door.

"I've come for my breeches," said Lydia.

"To wear to dinner, I suppose."

"And I should need to borrow your boots," she added as she straightened, the knee-length breeches hanging from her hand.

"What be the problem with your own boots? Have you out-grown them since last I've seen you?"

"Of course not," she said, bristling at humor made at her own expense.

New footsteps hit upon the deck, and so soon her Papa stood at Caleb's back, his face reddened beneath the soaking. Caleb stepped away, and Lydia was left with only her father's gaze upon her.

"Lydia," he said on the sigh of great relief, and he crossed the short space. He knelt on one knee and reached to the breeches still in Lydia's grip. "What plans did you have for these?"

With a daring that came from an unknown space, Lydia told her Papa, "I plan to go out on my own."

"Tonight?"

"Yes."

"Lydia ..."

"I won't go back. Not to that house."

Her father pulled through graying hair that curled in wet whimsy at his temples. "Lydia, I'm sorry you learned of my decision that way. I had hoped for a chance to speak with you, to explain my reasons."

"There's no need, Papa. I understand. You do not wish the burden of caring for a girl." A knot tightened in her throat, causing her voice to quiver and her eyes to fill. The briny tears spilled over her lashes, and there was nothing Lydia could do but wipe the flow away with the back of her hand. "It's all right, Papa," she said, forcing her voice a little louder. "I'm old enough now."

Her father placed his arms around her, tried to embrace her, pulling her to him, but Lydia stood rigid, her arms stiff at her side. "You cannot go off on your own," he said as his arms fell away from her, and he stood. "You're but twelve years old. And Martha ... your Grandmother Brimmer can give you everything that I cannot."

"I'm not going back," and her chin jutted with determination. "I'm going to Cape Cod to live with Grandmother Constance."

"With my mother? And you would like that?"

"I should like to know her better. And as long as you no longer want me, perhaps she will."

"Good heavens, Lydia. It isn't that I don't want you. You're my little girl, and I love you, very much."

"But you love the sea more."

"One has nothing to do with the other."

One had everything to do with the other, but Lydia chose not to argue. She stood quietly instead, face lowered, the breeches dangling.

"Come, Lydia. It's getting late. Come with me now, and we will settle this all out in the morning."

"No." Never had she so defied her Papa, and she felt the heat rise on her cheeks. He stared a moment, looking somewhat like a startled rabbit, until he scooped Lydia into his arms. "No," she said, and her fists pummeled his chest. But her Papa only held her all the firmer.

"Stop this, Lydia. I'm taking you home."

"Put me down. Put me down," her fists struck again and again, and she twisted, her legs kicking at the air. But her father ducked sideways through the doorframe, taking Lydia with him, her unshod feet hitting against the door.

Only when he reached Dock Square, did her Papa set her down. He held, however, tightly to her hand. Lydia plodded, mud spattering onto the hem of her already soiled dress. She would not ever speak to him again, and she would find a second chance to run.

"You can't prefer that land of barbaric fishermen to the opportunities of Boston. James, you're the girl's father. You must be reasonable … and firm." Old Grandmother Brimmer dabbed at flushed cheeks with the lace-trimmed handkerchief. Fine beads of perspiration had broken out in that humid hour of the evening. Although the rain had ceased, heat lightning flashed beyond the windows.

With posture rigid, Lydia stood at her father's side. "I'm going to Cape Cod," her words aimed at her grandmother's angry face.

"Be quiet, child, until you are spoken to," said the grandmother.

"If I leave her here in Boston, she will run again. I'm sure of it. She wouldn't be safe."

"She wouldn't run if she feared your punishment."

Her Papa took hold of her hand. "Come, Lydia," he said, and he turned toward the door. But Grandmother Brimmer was at his heels.

"Look at her, James. Is it not enough that the child so resembles that dark skinned half-breed? It's unthinkable that you would send that child out there to be raised by the likes of such a woman. I won't hear of it. Not with a half-breed."

Half-breed. The word was new – unfamiliar. Yet, Lydia felt the sting. The very sound of it was evil. "Grandmother Constance is not a half-breed," she shouted, her fist raised as if ready to strike. "You're simply mean, and I hate you. I hate you."

Her Papa grabbed a quick hold on her arm. Lines creased his brow and his neck colored, but he let go of Lydia's arm and simply held her hand. "You seem to forget two things, Martha," he said, more calmly than Lydia thought right. "That woman of whom you speak is my mother. She raised me, and I feel quite satisfied. And secondly, I alone have the responsibility of deciding where would be the best for my daughter."

Her father started for the door, Lydia's hand still in his strong hold. She followed him, her wet stockings stepping silently just a short pace behind his boots. At the doorway, her father turned to face Grandmother Brimmer, who stood now with a hand upon her chest and mouth agape.

"I thank you, Martha, for all you've done for my daughter and myself," said Papa in that same calm voice. "But I think it is time that we each move on. Lydia and I will pack our things tonight and sleep aboard the Heaven's Mist. Tomorrow I shall take her to Ponokanet."

Twenty-Eight

Lydia
On Ponokanet Island, still 1754

"Why won't he speak to me?" asked Lydia of Grandmother Constance. The two, Lydia and her grandmother, stood in the middle of a pokeweed patch, each filling their own basket with the plump purple berries. Her Papa had left her here two days prior, but Lydia was feeling comfortable with this second grandmother. She had been welcomed, just as she had hoped.

"I don't think he is able to speak," said her Grandmother.

At the far side of that patch of pokeweed, the boy Ethan bent down with the task of picking berries, his body square and far too large, resembling more an ox than a child only a year or two older than Lydia. And if she looked at his face too directly, it was frightening. The wide, high forehead could have been two of her own, and a slit began beneath the boy's nose and spread wide to where a top lip should be, exposing pink gums and large overlapping teeth.

Lydia forced her eyes away.

"Why is his face like that?" she whispered.

Constance sat her basket down among the broad green leaves and took up Lydia's hand. She patted the back of it. "Ethan was born that way," she said. "Both big and disfigured. But beneath that, inside where a person lives, he is a gentle boy. No one is put here on earth by accident, Lydia. Each of us has a purpose. And like the rest of us, Ethan will find his."

"I would like to speak to him, to say hello, but he won't come near enough."

"Give him time, dear. He's more than shy. Afraid, I think, of your ridicule."

"But I wouldn't tease. That would be cruel."

Constance picked up her basket and started again to collect the purple berries, plopping a few into the basket as she spoke. "Until a few months ago when Ethan's poor father died, the boy knew only people's cruel words, and worse."

Looking to the giant boy, Lydia could well-imagine the teasing Ethan would have been subjected to if he'd grown up along the docks of Boston. Many people were cruel, just as Grandmother Constance said, and Lydia grew more curious. "How'd he die ... Ethan's Papa?"

"He lost a hand while letting out the line of a harpoon. Then the poison set in. It was a difficult time, I'd guess." Her grandmother's voice softened in a way that spoke of the affection she held for that odd figure of a boy.

"Do you think Ethan saw him die?" Lydia had seen a man die once, one summer while at sea with her Papa. The man had been walking on deck and suddenly he'd grabbed at his chest and fallen down. She had watched with the others, useless as the man gasped for breath. Her Papa had said the man's heart gave out. What Lydia had hated, what she could still see sometimes in the dark of night, was the way the man's eyes stared open at her even after his heart stopped beating. She wondered if Ethan's Papa had stared wide-eyed at him. If it had been her own Papa, oh, she didn't know what she would have done.

"I don't know what Ethan saw," said her grandmother. "What I do know starts from the morning I spied Ethan stealing a loaf of bread from my window sill. He ran off, and when I couldn't coax him out of the woods, I went into the village to speak to his father. That's when I found the man lying on an old straw-filled mattress. The best I can determine is that Ethan likely left his father after he realized the man was dead. He probably hid in a packet ship, your Uncle Ralph's perhaps, and ended up here on the island alone and hungry."

"Then he's yours to keep? Ethan, I mean."

"No one has come to suggest otherwise."

Her Grandmother Constance moved along through the pokeweed. Lydia, too, began plucking the berries, but her mind filled with the ugly grin of the boy they called Ethan. She would need to get accustomed to the looks of him. Ethan did live there with them, after all. He slept in the smaller room just down the hall from her own. And other than Constance, he was the only company she would have while here on the tiny island, so removed from the village or any neighbors. Uncle Ralph lived there, too, of course, but Ralph spent his time sailing his small packet to Boston, carrying a few passengers and returning days later with rum enough to sop the villagers for a month. It seemed Ralph could not be counted on as company, either for the boy or for a newcomer such as Lydia.

Lydia worked her way in the direction of that great bulk of a boy. "Hello, Ethan," she said, quite loudly so that he could hear across the distance she'd left between them. His eyes grew so large she thought he would run, but Lydia went about her picking of berries. "It's all right," she said as she inched even a bit closer. "I don't mind that you don't speak. I can speak enough for the two of us."

She continued on to tell of the previous Monday's sailing across the bay from Boston and the former task of bringing the Heaven's Mist into Boston's harbor in the soaking rain the day before that, how she'd had to reef the sails and beat the forces of the wind as she held to the rigging, and that she was very glad to be rid of Grandmother Brimmer. She will miss her Papa though. And Caleb, too. And most of all she will miss being on the sea. "Have you ever sailed on the open sea?" she asked, standing up in the midst of the pokeberries to look directly at the boy for the first time since starting to talk at him.

Ethan stared back, but Lydia waited.

His eyes glanced to the woods at the edge of the clearing, but his feet remained planted in the pokeweed. Slowly, his head turned, first to one side, then to the other.

"Never? You've never sailed on a great ship out into the Atlantic?"

Again the misshapen face turned side to side.

"Well, we shall have to fix that. I shall take you out one day, and you will see for yourself just how grand a place a ship on the open sea can be." With that said, Lydia bent with her basket and plucked several berries from their stalk. "Grandmother Constance says each of us has a purpose. Mine is to be on the sea. I shall do something important there. I know I shall. And you, too, Ethan," she added as she moved along, the berries absently placed in the basket. "Grandmother said you also have a purpose, but you will have to learn what it is."

The conversation, though one sided, had taken an interesting turn, at least according to Lydia, but before she could pursue the boy's purpose any further, her grandmother called. "Come along, Lydia. Ethan. We have enough berries. Now begins the task of turning them to dye."

"Grandmother ..." Lydia slipped her hand around the rough, calloused hand of her Grandmother Constance. "Do you think Ralph would allow me to sail the packet?"

"Alone?"

"With Ethan."

"Oh, I don't think so, dear. The packet's so big. It's a ship."

"It's not a real ship, not like Papa's." Lydia paused but could see no sign of changed opinion on her grandmother's face. "Well, then," she countered, "does Ralph have anything smaller? The size wouldn't matter so long as it had a sail. I want to bring Ethan out onto the water so he might feel the wind on his face."

Constance looked to the boy, then back to Lydia. "There is the whaleboat. It's a bit heavy, and you'd have to row. It doesn't have a sail."

"A whaleboat?" A whaler was bulky and slow, and with only two to work the oars they'd never feel any wind. Still, she had to consider her options. "The whaler would do. At least we'd be out on the water," she said before she ran ahead to step in place beside Ethan.

The low red sun slid behind a cloud, and the beach fell under the shadow. But Lydia took little notice. "Come on, Ethan. Help me push this thing afloat." She strutted ankle deep out to the stern where it lay heavy in the bottom. With two hands she reached beneath the surface, dredged away a ridge of sand. That task done and with wet gritty hands resting high on her hips, she walked around front where she thrust her weight against the bow. The broad-bottomed whaler only dug in deeper.

"Come on, Ethan," she repeated. "If we don't catch this tide, we shall have to wait another entire day." She leaned again, her back readied against the solid wooden hull. Footsteps from behind ground upon the sand, and the great muscled hand of Ethan pushed against the bow. The whaleboat lurched forward, then bobbed afloat in the calm shallows.

"A right good job," she asserted while trudging knee-deep into the water. With a hard tug on the gunnel and a leap upward, Lydia was in the boat. She had worn her canvas breeches for the first time since coming to live on the island, and the freedom carried over into her gait, into her mind, and the day glowed. "It's your turn," she said, reaching out, offering one hand to the boy. But Ethan simply placed one leg, then the other over the gunnel, and he was standing in the boat.

When Lydia sat in the broad mid-section and insisted Ethan sit beside her, he motioned for her to move away, to sit across from him in the aft, but she would not. "I prefer rowing to watching," she said, and she reached for one long heavy oar, letting the weight of it fall into position, splashing water high as the oar cut through the surface. Ethan sat then at her side. He picked up the second oar and set it into the water, just as Lydia had done but with less splashing.

Right away the rhythm was wrong. Unbalanced. Lydia required long deep pulls on the oar, while the boy only dabbed the blade shallow beneath the surface. Even still, the boat veered off and away from her. Heat rose to her face from the effort. But soon it was worth the while. A rhythm established, and Lydia forgot the effort, for she was once again on the sea.

The boat slid along a golden path, a line afire or so it seemed because a blazing sun had emerged low beneath the line of cloud to cast its bold reflection over the indigo water. "Isn't it grand, Ethan? You'll never see the sun sink below the earth as clearly from land as you can while on the sea."

And so the two, the raven-haired girl and the giant boy rowed out toward the setting sun. Lydia rowed in silence because her thoughts flashed too quickly for words. She thought how beautiful the sky, how magical a sun that could turn from gold to red in a matter of minutes. She wondered if her Papa was watching the same sun at the same moment in time. She imagined her Papa at home in Boston, loading the new ship. It was a grand brigantine, with roods and roods of white sail. Not that she'd seen the ship. Only today would it arrive at Boston. Her Papa had needed to return there to see to the loading of cargo, then to set sail and be gone. But she wasn't going to think about that, not now. Instead, she would try to imagine her Papa at the helm of a new and different ship. The effort met with failure though, and only an image of the Heaven's Mist appeared, her Papa at the large worn wheel and Caleb at his side.

Off the bow of the bulky whaler, suddenly, the water roiled. The sea tossed and frothed as far as the eye could see. Great black fins and sleek black backs broke the surface. Tens. Hundreds. The air smelled of their oily flesh as all around her the giant blackfish rose up for air, rounded by their blubber, many of them as great as twenty links in length, and the stocky boat rocked in their wakes. At her side, the gunnel heeled low so that Lydia thought seawater would rush over the top. With her feet pressed to the slats, she pulled hard on the oar, using the blade as keel in the boiling sea.

"Heave deep to your side," she shouted to the boy.

Then the thud hit beneath her.

Her foot slipped, taking her balance out, and the boat lifted from the water, remained aloft – riding the back of a great blackfish, rocking, until the boat turned and flipped on its side. Lydia toppled over the gunnel, reaching for a hold to an edge that wasn't there.

She was sinking beneath the cold. Weighted by boots and canvas breeches, she wriggled, kicked with her feet, turned so she might look upward to find the light. Salt burned her eyes. Above, a smothering blanket of round white underbellies moved on the water, undulating, crisscrossing, blocking her way. Her chest craved a breath as she forced her way upward, sliding between the massive bodies, until at last her face broke the surface.

She gulped air.

Ethan ...

Her eyes darted over the water. Their boat bobbed bottom-up.

"Ethan," she shouted, pressing with her arms to stay afloat.

Her only answer was the roil of the sea.

"Ethan," she called again. But a fluke hit in front of her. The sea sprayed, filling her mouth, her lungs, and Lydia coughed it up until she could feel the air return. With both hands working under the water, she pulled off the boots. She let them sink, her feet freed, and she thrust her body deep beneath the surface.

In that cold wet world, Lydia swam, her eyes open in search of Ethan. But when she saw the one blackfish coming straight on, its large globular head pushing through the water with incredible speed, she stopped, hanging near to motionless beneath the surface. Forward the blackfish came, until suddenly, as if changing its mind, the mammoth creature slowed, its sleek body altering course ever so little, skimming so close to Lydia she could have touched the thick black skin. The bold white eye stared, and for an instant, there seemed a common curiosity, then the great blackfish moved on.

As her eyes followed the blackfish, she spied Ethan. He floated face down on the surface. To fight the urge to breathe, Lydia forced the last of the air out from her lungs, and with desperate strong strokes she kicked her way upward, taking her closer until at last her hand touched his shirt. Her face found air, which she gulped, while she tugged and pulled at the shoulder, until Ethan's great hulk turned over, his face now to the sky.

With one arm, Lydia pulled herself through water. The other she wrapped under the chin of Ethan, his great size blessedly buoyant in the salty sea. Ever so slowly they moved over the water toward the capsized boat.

She pulled and reached until at last at the whaleboat. She held to the bottom boards, taking a moment to breathe before she placed her own body under Ethan, pushing, nudging his head and chest onto the upturned bottom of the boat. And Lydia rested her own head on the wet boards.

The sea had stilled. The pod of blackfish had moved on. In the distance she could see the village's fleet of whalers. With oars in sync, several whalers headed toward Lydia and the capsized boat.

"Wake up, Ethan," she pleaded, and she pounded on his back with what little strength remained.

First he vomited seawater. His eyes fluttered. And Lydia grinned wide to the opened eyes of her friend.

Twenty-Nine

Sydney
The sailing lesson, still Monday, September 3

A soft wind presses the Sunfish out from shore. Ty turns them north, following the beach. When he lets loose the sail, the canvas flutters, and he hands over the tiller to Sydney. She draws it toward her until wind catches in the sail, and the Sunfish scoots over the water. Sailing, she discovers, works much like flying, the use of rudder and the sail together for control. She plays with tacking, a zig-zag route to the south, following the island shore toward its narrow sandy tip. When she heads the Sunfish out, away from the island, the boat rushes through the water, the wake splashes over, the cold sharp against her legs. She feels the smile on her face and allows it to stay.

"You take to this too easily," says Ty. He sits on the boat edge with the sun at his back, his eyes hidden behind dark glasses. Dried salt shows white on his tanned skin. "It's not fair to us who needed years to get close to being good."

"I have to admit, it's fun."

Tacking back takes longer. Ty seems content to listen to the trickle of their wake as Sydney works the Sunfish over the surface. The white cliffs of Ponokanet lie wedged between the equally brilliant blue of sky and sea. When the buoy off the tip of the island bleats, Sydney counts the twelve seconds until the next bleat. Day and night its signal warns sailors of the shoal that lies hidden beneath the water. Day and night, the same twelve seconds between bleats.

"Have you ever realized suddenly that what you once swore to be true was just a wrong idea?" says Sydney when turning to look at Ty, to the dark glasses, to the lean muscle of arms and shoulders.

"Like what, for instance?"

"Well, I was just thinking ... I grew up believing Ponokanet was my cage. It held me here against my will."

She supposes the confession is easy because of his sunglasses. With his eyes behind the dark shield, Ty is given a sort of anonymity. It gives Sydney the freedom to speak, to tell. She adjusts the sail and looks forward into the wind. "If not for Everett," she says, "I don't think I could've stayed here until I was eighteen. I probably would have run away and become ... I don't know, something other than what I did. But now, looking back, I realize that this place is what set me free."

Ty says nothing, and for a time he seems to watch a pair of gulls in the sky. Sydney aims again toward the beach, then feels the shift of Ty's weight, his own small adjustment.

"For many years after being left at the monastery, I believed my mother would one day come back for me." His words come slowly, thoughtfully. "I believed this without the slightest doubt. Then a day came when I was ten. I was pulling a weed from the damp soil one morning when I saw, as clearly as I saw the weed, that I had been wrong. I was going to have no savior. I was alone and any life I made from that day on had to be made by myself only. I know now that was not a bad thing. There's a freedom in being one's own refuge. A sort of peace. I work toward that place of peace every day."

"But you were so young. I can't imagine how you survived."

His hand drags beside the boat creating a small second wake. As water ripples away from his hand, he asks Sydney, "What about your belief that you'll never fly again? Is that a truth?"

"It may be the only truth." A gull flies low, dives into the water not far from the boat, but the gull emerges without a meal. "If I were to fly," says Sydney, "if I were to go up there again, I would relive the most horrifying day of my life."

"Aren't you reliving it all the time anyway?"

"Every day."

"So what's the sense? Why deprive yourself of flying if staying on the ground is just as bad?"

She pulls through her hair and listens for the buoy. "Because," she says, "it's my punishment."

"For what?"

"For being to blame. My mistake killed someone. Someone I loved." She bites her lip, hates it that tears fill her eyes. "No one believes me when I say it was my fault, not even Everett."

"You believe it. And for as long as you do believe it, for you, it is a truth."

Her gaze holds on his. "I do believe it."

Wind flutters in the sail, but when Sydney tightens the canvas the Sunfish lunges forward. To counter, she leans and their shoulders touch. The current is immediate, and she straightens, paralyzed by the notion that Ty felt it, too. It's impossible for one person to feel that electricity, that draw and the other not. She looks away into the cool of the breeze. And she holds her traitor body stiff.

"I'm driving Everett to Boston tomorrow morning," says Ty. "He's scheduled for another round of chemo and a CAT scan. Would you like to come along?"

Of course she wants to go. She wants to be with Everett as much as possible. But there would be the three of them. That changes everything.

"I think Everett would like it if you came with us," says Ty. "It would lighten the day up for him."

She keeps her eyes to the shore that grows closer. She wants to go. And the invitation is there. "Thanks," she says. "I'd like to go."

"We'll have to leave by eight."

Thirty

"The results of this morning's CAT scan are not encouraging." From where Dr. Sasaki sits behind her desk, she removes her eyeglasses and looks to Everett. Because Ty sits at Sydney's side, she cannot see him, not directly, but she detects motion, as if he too bristles at Dr. Sasaki's announcement.

Everett does not shift, not a hand or foot.

Dr. Sasaki slides her glasses on and refers to the report she holds in her hand. "I'm sorry, Mr. Dean, but the lymphoma is not responding to chemotherapy. There's no shrinking of the affected nodes, and lymphoma cells have spread into your bone marrow."

"With all the chemo, how could it spread?" asks Everett, his hands still holding to the arms of his chair.

"Sometimes, especially in recurring lymphomas like this one, the cancerous cells grow resistant to the therapy drugs."

Recurring. Resistant. Sydney's hands are damp with sweat. Yet, the room is cold, brought to bone chill by sterile white walls and controlled air that moves across the back of her neck. She wishes to be anywhere else. But Everett has asked her and Ty to be with him when the doctor discusses his scan results. The more ears, the better, he said. So Sydney struggles to sit still, to make sense of what is being said.

She glances to Everett, to the steadiness of his hands. He is tough. She has known this all along but never so completely as now.

Everett leans in, closer to Dr. Sasaki. "So what do we do now?"

"The most successful treatment in cases like this one has been stem cell transplants, if a donor match can be found."

"I'm not even sure what a stem cell is," says Sydney.

The doctor nods, recognizing Sydney's concern. "Stem cells are immature blood cells. They're found primarily in bone marrow, and they're extremely versatile. Stem cells can make more stem cells, or they can mature into blood cells … either white or red, or platelets that help the blood to clot, whichever one the body needs. In Mr. Dean's case, the cancer has invaded the bone marrow. It's destroying both the mature blood cells and the immature stem cells."

"But I can be given new ones from a donor?" asks Everett.

"Yes. We can take stem cells from the healthy donor's marrow and transplant those cells into the cancer patient. It's done through a simple IV hook-up, not unlike a blood transfusion."

Everett runs a hand over his bald head. "Sounds good," he says. "But I still don't get it. Why wouldn't the cancer destroy the new stem cells just like it did the original ones?"

Sydney's amazed at how quickly Everett can question, and she places her hand on top of his.

Dr. Sasaki rubs at her forehead, a possible sign that she, too, is human and not always at ease when offering last desperate options. "Before the transplant, you would undergo extremely high doses of chemotherapy, much stronger than any you have had thus far. At that high dose level, cancer cells seldom survive. We won't proceed with the stem cell transplant until all the cancer cells are gone."

"If those super chemo doses can get me cancer free," says Everett, "why do we need to do the stem cell transplant afterwards?"

"Well, technically, yes. You would be cancer free at the end of that high-dose chemotherapy," says Dr. Sasaki. "But treatment at that level will also destroy your own bone barrow. In order to survive the procedure, you will need new marrow cells from a compatible donor. It is those new donor cells that will eventually multiply, become your own and possibly save your life."

"Not a pretty picture is it?" This as Everett rubs his chin.

"No, I'm afraid it's not." Dr. Sasaki pauses but does not take her gaze from Everett. "You also need to know that, in addition to the usual weakness and nausea that comes with chemotherapy, for several weeks you'll be highly susceptible to infections and bleeding. It will be necessary that you stay here in the hospital during those weeks."

"My god," says Sydney. "He's already been through so much."

"I know," says Dr. Sasaki. "But it's the best treatment I can offer at this time."

Sydney rubs along her collarbone, restless, so much so that she stands up and walks behind the chair where she was sitting, seeing for the first time the narrowed eyes and worry on Ty's face. "So, let's talk about getting a donor," she says, "because I volunteer."

The doctor asks her, "Are you a close relative?"

"No. No, I'm not. But it's possible, isn't it, that a non-relative could be a good enough match?"

"We can do a simple blood test to see if there is an antigen match, but I should tell you that the odds are against it."

Dr. Sasaki looks then to Everett. "Do you have any immediate relatives," she asks him, "any siblings, a child, a parent?"

"Negative to all counts."

The doctor sits back in her chair, thoughts moving behind her eyes. "What I suggest we do," she says, "is take a blood sample from you, Mr. Dean, before you leave today so that we can determine your HLA type. It sounds foreign, but HLA simply put is a set of antigens that are found on the surface of cells. They appear in patterns or types. It will be important to find a donor that matches your HLA pattern as closely as possible. The body is very particular and will reject the new stem cells if the HLA is not at least a close match."

While biting on her lip, Sydney sorts the medical terms, absorbs their meaning, cell patterns and matches, until she realizes suddenly the doctor is speaking to her.

"As I said, Sydney, the chances are low that your HLA will match closely enough to that of Mr. Dean. But if you are willing, we will take a blood sample from you as well and see what happens."

"I am willing."

"Good. And if it's not a match, perhaps you'll consider listing your antigen type in our donor bank. You could possibly save someone else's life."

"I'd also like the antigen test," says Ty. "I don't expect a match with Everett because of our very different genetic past. But you can put my antigen type into the computer bank."

Tears fill Everett's eyes, and Sydney returns to her chair, places her hand again on top of his.

"So, Mr. Dean ... Everett," says Dr. Sasaki, "let's proceed as if a blood antigen match will be found. But I'm going to give you some literature on two alternative treatments, clinical studies that you can read about. Look them over and maybe have some questions ready just in case we need to decide on a second route. We'll meet again after the blood work has been checked. I'd like to make that appointment as soon as Thursday. At that time, we'll discuss the pros and cons and make a decision about the course we'll take."

"And if I go with the transplant," says Everett, "what kind of timeframe are we talking about?"

"That depends on the donor list. We have a national stem cell bank. As soon as we find a compatible match, we'll move ahead."

"And if there isn't a match?"

"One option is to wait until one is found."

"How long can I wait?"

"That depends. We don't want cancer cells spreading to other organs. We would have to weigh the risk of waiting against going ahead with one of the alternative procedures."

Sydney is nauseous. She hasn't eaten anything since early that morning, but it isn't the lack of food that's making her light headed.

At her desk, Dr. Sasaki writes orders for three blood tests to determine HLA type, the blood to be taken in the lab before they leave. They set a Thursday early afternoon appointment.

Ty drives, and Sydney is glad for the back seat in Everett's car. She's glad to be staring at the backs of heads, knowing Everett can't see her, because no matter how hard she blinks, silent tears keep coming. She meets Ty's glance in the rearview mirror, and she raises her hand, a signal for Ty to leave it alone.

With a shirtsleeve, she dries her cheek. She clears her throat and reaches into her leather bag for a tissue. "The office sign is almost finished," she says because the airport is what she wants to focus on. She admits to Everett how the paint colors at first ran together, but that she's finally getting the painting process down to a science. "What project should I start next? Maybe replace some cedar siding?"

"Let's hold off, Syd, until things settle down."

She doesn't want to hold off. She needs to do something more. But Everett sounds so weak and tired. For now, she lets the subject of Dean Aviation go dormant. As they cross the canal bridge onto the Cape, the low sun lays a golden trail across the water, and Sydney realizes how late it is. The day's been long for all of them. With head rested back, she lets the remaining miles tick away until she falls into a fitful sleep.

In sleep, she sees Everett ...

Everett soars high above her in the red and white Cessna. For a moment, there is a sense of pleasure in the watching, the Cessna graceful and its hum hardly audible so high in the air.

But the engine stalls.

The Cessna falls, nose-down into a spin.

Spinning downward.
Down.
Down.

Sydney tries to scream but wakes with the effort.

Thirty-One

"How you doing?" asks Ty when he drives them away from Everett.

Sydney shrugs, keeping her eyes straight ahead. They're in Ty's truck now, but they've left Everett at home in his small ranch house. She offered to stay the evening with him, the entire night if he wanted, but Everett said no, that he'd rather be alone for a bit, to read those pamphlets maybe and to get some sleep. "I should have stayed," says Sydney, "no matter what Everett said. If I was there, I could see that he's okay, that he's breathing."

"He's not going to die, Sydney. Not today anyway."

"You promise?"

The truck hums, rattles some over the back wheels, and Ty watches only the narrow road. A stubble of whiskers has come to his face since morning, making him look tired, and he asks Sydney, "This isn't just about Everett, is it?"

Sydney rests back against the seat and closes her eyes. "Maybe not."

"You want to talk about it?"

"No." She can no longer think, only feel – feel the fear of another death, the fear of being left again in a dark empty place. "How exactly did you survive when you realized your mother wasn't coming back for you? You don't get over something like that just because the monks think you should."

"No. And I'm not sure I'll ever get over it. Sometimes I'm still that little boy, sad, and angry at why it had to happen that way. But mostly I look at all of what I have today. I let the past in once in a while, to look at the pain, to understand it. But I can't let it define who I am."

"My God, you are stronger than I could ever be."

The bridge clatters as Ty drives them across, and the truck fills with the scent of salt and sea. The truck climbs, and they pass under the limbs of pine, the familiar shadows stretching long across the road. In front of the barn, Ty shuts off the engine, puts his arm across the back of the seat, his hand so close to her shoulder. The evening remains warm, yet Sydney hugs her arms to her chest. In the distance she hears the sea.

"I went looking for her once," he says. "But she'd already been killed. I spent a lot of years sorting that out."

"Is that why you went back to the monastery?"

"Yes. It was quiet there. A sanctuary. And it worked for a while, until I realized I was just hiding from life. That's when I knew I had to leave."

"Where'd you go?"

"Lots of places. Canada mostly. I taught there in a private school for a few years"

"You did that?"

"For a while. Then I came here to look up Everett."

Sydney pulls fingers through her hair, thinking that Everett has touched the life of Ty as deeply as he's touched her own. Everett, just by being who he is, has saved two young people. "Are you happy?" she asks, turning to look at Ty, to the black lashes of his eyes.

He hesitates only for a moment. "Yes. I am."

"I'm glad," she says while recognizing the low burn of envy. "Thank you, for taking me along today."

Sydney steps down from the truck and walks across the yard to the front porch. She looks back, intending to wave. But Ty already has left the truck and disappeared somewhere inside the barn.

For some time Sydney sits on the back deck watching the sun bleed into the bay. She thinks about the blood tests and the miniscule odds that she might be a match for Everett. She can only hope that the odds for finding another donor are not so small.

From inside the house, Alison's heeled shoes clack on the kitchen floor, stop at the doorway to the back deck. "Sydney, you have a visitor. It's Nora … the woman who works at the airport."

"Nora?" Fear pushes Sydney from her chair. "Did something happen to Everett?"

"I don't know," says Alison. "She didn't say."

Sydney steps past her mother, each stride wider than the one before. In the front hall, Nora stands waiting, one hand holding to the screen door. "Is it Everett?" asks Sydney. "What's happened?"

"Everett's doin' okay. He's asleep in his chair. I didn't come here because of Everett. At least, not like you were thinkin'."

"Oh, thank goodness," says Alison, surprising Sydney by being there so close at her back.

Nora looks to Alison, then to Sydney. "Sydney, could we talk, take a walk or somethin'?"

Sydney tries to find the reason in Nora's face, why Nora has this sudden need for a walk. She slips into the sandals she kicked off earlier, and she leads Nora out onto the porch, down along the gravel drive and onto the road. Dusk has come to blanket the island in grey.

Nora shoves both hands into chino pockets. "I wanted to talk to you alone," she says, "because what I have to say is between just you and me. For now, anyway."

"All right," says Sydney, walking, feeling her way.

"I came to talk about you and Everett."

"What about us?"

"Well, first of all, Everett told me what the doctor said about a stem cell transplant and the problem with finding a donor. And I know Everett might die if he doesn't get that donor."

"There are other options," says Sydney, defensive because she's spent the last half-hour convincing herself of that.

Nora stops in the middle of the road. "Look, what I'm about to say … it's never been any of my business. But because of what's happening to Everett, I'm gonna make it my business."

"Nora, I think you just need to get to the point."

Something determined sits hard in the line of Nora's jaw, and the hesitation is not like Nora, who usually has no filter on a word she says. At last she simply shakes her head. "I would bet my last dollar that you are Everett's daughter."

"What?" The question escapes on a gush of breath. "That's ridiculous. My father lived in New York."

"What's his name?"

"Antonio Ponti."

"Have you ever met him?"

"No."

"Why?"

Sydney shifts weight to her other foot. She rubs an arm where the cool of evening has settled, and in her mind she questions Nora's purpose – Nora's intended gain from this preposterous idea. It's totally ridiculous. Antonio Ponti is her father. Or was. Right after college, long before the flight team, before Rick, Sydney decided it was finally time to meet the man. She Googled his name and found a date of birth. But she also found a date of death in an obituary, in the archive of a little backwoods newspaper from upstate New York. She actually packed a suitcase and flew east to New York, unbeknown to anyone. She drove to the cemetery and stood at his gravestone. His name had been carved into granite. Antonio Ponti. She stood there in front of the stone, cried and then cursed, angry that she'd waited so long to find him.

"You can't be serious," says Sydney. "You can't possibly think Everett could be my father and I wouldn't know it."

"All I know is when I was in high school, the same class as your mother, I had my eyes set on Everett. All the girls did. He was a few years older and he'd come home from college and hell, he was good lookin' and smart. A pilot. Christ, no other guys came close. But I was a nobody, so I couldn't really expect Everett to give me the time of day. Alison Foster though, she was a whole different story. For one summer, that one summer after we graduated, Everett had eyes for one girl only and that was your mother."

"No. It couldn't have been. My mother went to New York that summer."

"Late August."

"That's not what she told me."

"Honey, if Everett wasn't so sick, I'd leave this whole thing alone. What's done is done. The man's already been robbed of raising a daughter. And I can't say for a fact that those two had been foolin' around. What I do know is that they were a real item. They spent all their time together, not seein' anybody else, from the day Everett came home from college in May until Alison left at the end of August."

"Then why would she tell me she left Wells Creek in June, right after graduation?"

"I can't tell you that because I don't know the whole story. But I can tell you, a few years after being away, your mother came home for a visit with you in tow, and there you were with his curly hair and Everett's same snappy eyes. I was convinced back then. I still am."

"You're wrong," says Sydney, her words shot with anger. The claim isn't fair to Everett. It isn't true. "It's impossible. I know who my father is."

"Sydney, I know this is got to be hard to hear. But I'm pretty damn sure, if you'd have one of those donor tests done, you'd be a match."

"I did have the test. Today."

"Well, now. Everett didn't tell me that."

"Probably because the odds are against me being a match."

Nora looks straight at her, holding the stare. "I'm willing to bet just the opposite."

Sydney walks away, heels heavy on the gravel, leaving Nora alone behind her. This whole thing is absurd. Why would she listen to any more of it? But she turns and walks back to Nora. "You're telling me my mother made up a whole life of lies. Why? Why would she do that?"

"Maybe that's a question you should ask her."

Sydney pulls through her hair, curls thick and dark, like Everett's, when he had some. She thinks of the picture in the album, Everett with his arm around her mother.

The possibility hits like a bolt, Sydney pressing a hand to her chest. If it is real, it means all her life she'd been denied Everett. Been denied an incredibly wonderful living man as her father. It means all these years Alison deceived everybody.

But all Nora has is a bunch of maybes.

Even so, if there's the slightest chance ...

Sydney wants to hear more, but she has to hear it from Alison.

Thirty-Two

Lydia
At age twenty-two, January, 1764

In the room that served as Ralph's office, Lydia sparked. "It's what I shall do with the money, no matter your argument." For ten years she had lived with Constance and Uncle Ralph, and in those years she'd come to love her uncle dearly. But he behaved sometimes too much like a man, not seeing her point of view at all.

"Your grandmother will not accept this," said Ralph.

"That I do regret, but I shan't change my mind."

"Lydia, be reasonable."

She was being reasonable. It was the rest of the world that was not. She plunked herself down on the one upholstered chair, wishing someone would understand her need. "This is what I must do, Uncle Ralph. The British deserve no less with all their bloody taxes."

"But you would be breaking the law."

"The law is wrong. By going direct to the Indies, I can half the King's price on sugar and coffee. And the greatest portion shall be saved on molasses. Why shouldn't we put the profit into our pockets rather than the Crown's?"

Ralph leaned forward in the chair behind his desk and set his elbows on the wide surface. "Lydia, need I remind you that you are a woman? In the name of God, you cannot go to sea as Captain of a ship. And certainly not a ship that smuggles against the British."

"I'm more than capable. So many times I've sailed to Boston's

Long Wharf and back that I could sail the distance with my eyes closed. And all these past years you've approved of me being in command of the packet."

"I shan't say that I approved of it. You talked your way in, that's all. Just as you're trying now. In the past, I chose to look away from the wrong of it."

"Then look away now." As if motion could release her frustration, Lydia stood again and went to the window that opened to the front yard. "What if I was a man? What if I was a nephew, twenty-two years of age and one of the best sailors you had ever come across?"

"The fact is, you are not a man. You wouldn't be safe."

Leather soles sounded on the wood floor. Her Grandmother Constance carried in a tray of tea, causing Lydia to heave a sigh.

"What is it now, my dear, you wish to do that is unsafe?" asked Constance while setting a tray of tea upon the desk.

"She wishes to purchase her own ship with sterling left to her by Martha Brimmer," said Ralph before Lydia's lips could part. "She wishes to become a smuggler of molasses. To sail her ship as far as the Indies."

The tea Constance poured splashed over the cup's rim onto the tray. "Your imagination has traveled too far, Lydia. Come to your senses."

"Why does everyone keep saying that? I don't know why Martha Brimmer chose to remember me in her bloody last will and testament, but I plan to use her money for the purchase of a ship … to go to sea and do some good."

Constance looked to Ralph. "You could say something here that would help me." But Ralph merely shrugged, and Constance turned again to Lydia. "What about the storms in the Caribbean? What about pirates?"

"Pirates scarcely exist anymore. Even Blackbeard is dead. And it's the Spanish ships that the renegades are after. Large, slow brigs loaded down with doubloons and eight. Not a swift little sloop carrying meager barrels of molasses."

Constance shook her head. "I can't allow it, Lydia."

"I'm sorry, grandmother, for the way this must be said, but it's no longer a matter of asking your approval. It's a matter of leaving with your blessing."

"I see," said Constance, her lips setting into a straight hard line.

"And I should think Ethan might wish to come along as well. We've learned to sail well together these years on Ralph's packet." Her words feigned nonchalance, a credit Lydia gave to determination. But within her heart lay a regret. It was selfish to take Ethan away. Constance cared deeply for him, as they all did, and now Grandmother Constance would be left without him. But with Ethan along, Lydia would be safe. Protected. The people of Wells Creek had come to know his gentle side, but during their trips to Boston's wharf, Lydia appreciated the wide path given to the brutish looking man that remained always at her side.

Constance lifted the hem of her apron and dabbed with it at the spilt tea, all the while clucking her tongue. "Ah, Lydia, your will outweighs your reason."

But Ralph leaned back in his chair. "If you are insistent on going, I agree you will need Ethan."

"I am going," she said.

Her grandmother gazed for some time out the window. "Come with me," she said when turning again to Lydia. "I have something to show you."

As Constance walked from the room, Lydia could only wonder at what argument might be coming next. No argument would change what she planned, but with determined spine she followed Constance into the hall and up the stairs.

She waited just inside the door of her grandmother's bedroom while Constance went to a high bureau and took from the bottom drawer a small and square wooden box. Constance sat with it on the bed, patting the patchwork quilt to suggest Lydia sit there with her.

The box had a cover of matching wood, and Constance ran her fingers over the cover as if deciding whether to remove it or not. "I have a story to tell," she said, her hands holding the box steady on her stout lap. "I promise that the telling will lead us back to your need to go to sea. You see, my mother was an English girl," said Constance as Lydia sat beside her, now intrigued. "Her hair was so fair it was almost white, and although she was prone to spells of quiet, she was generally full of life ... a snappy tongue much like your own. My father was a native from the Ponokanet tribe."

Lydia felt her own jaw slacken, her mouth open. "But how could that be? Your father was Zebadiah. Papa spoke of him often."

"No. My mother married Zebadiah, but she was already with child, the child that would be me."

A vein pulsed deep inside Lydia's ear as she tried to make meaning as the long ago words came back. Martha Brimmer's words. *Half-breed.*

"Then you are not English?" asked Lydia.

"I am half English."

"And you're not angry?"

"Angry? Why should I be angry?"

"Because your mother ... she allowed that to happen."

"Allowed herself to fall in love?"

"No, not that, but ..."

"Lydia, my mother loved a man named Mittark. I saw that love in her eyes and in the words that came from her heart when she told me all those years later. But Mittark would not have her, not as his wife, because she was not one of his people. The hurt he caused my mother must have been very deep. But I forgive him when I consider all of who he was, his people's way of survival and all that that entailed.

And I forgive my mother because she gave me life, a life conceived with a man whom she loved a great deal. I gained far more than a dark complexion from my mixed blood."

The implication was sudden and sharp. "But I am English," said Lydia. "I come from a long line of sea captains and ship builders."

"Of course, a larger part of you is English. But your great-grandfather was a Ponokanet by the name of Mittark."

With eyes wet, Lydia shook her head. "So, I am no longer who I thought I was."

"And who did you think you were?"

Lydia could only glare at her grandmother because the answer wasn't there.

"Were you not born with dark eyes and that raven hair from the start?"

"Yes, but …"

"Were you not always strong minded and willful?"

A smile happened despite Lydia's confusion. "Yes, I suppose."

"And ever since that first day your mother held you in her arms, you have been very special, such a strong, vital blend of all the best that came before."

Lydia bit on her lip, the words needing that moment before the meaning was felt, and she wrapped her arms around her grandmother, clinging to the warm softness.

"Now for the box," said Constance.

Constance lifted the cover and took from the box a necklace of sorts, a string of beads made from bone. Fifteen pieces of bone carved round, now porous and dry. They were placed in a pattern. Following every third white bone was a smooth thin slice of purple shell, looking to be cut from the hinged edge of a large sea clam. The chord that held them was old, made of some kind of hide, making the necklace even more unusual, raw and extraordinary.

Lydia looked to her grandmother for explanation.

"It was a gift," said Constance.

"From your father?"

"No. From his grandmother. The beads were worn for nearly a lifetime by Mittark's grandmother, a woman they called Weetamo. A short time before she died, Weetamo gave the necklace to my mother, a gift of friendship, one woman to another."

Lydia reached to touch on the beads but did not quite dare for fear of breaking one or doing some harm.

"My mother told me," said Constance, "that the necklace holds the spirit of the whale within the bones. She believed that the whale's spirit truly guided her, that without this necklace she would have been lost throughout her life. She would often take the necklace out from its box and simply hold the bone beads, asking them for the power to get through the darker days."

"That's so sad."

"For a while, for my mother, I imagine it was sad. But the mother I knew was not. She laughed. She was giving of herself and gentle and very brave. I would say the necklace guided her well. That's why I want to give the necklace to you. To hand the bone beads forward so that you may find your own way, to find what is in your heart, your destiny, perhaps."

Lydia looked to the string of beads, the coarse white and the thin slips of purple. "No, I couldn't," she said. "They are too much a part of you. They belong with you."

"And so they are a part of you," said Constance, and she slid the string of beads over Lydia's hair that had been coiled and pinned high off her neck. When the strand fell into place, coming to rest at her collar, as if on a second thought, Constance unpinned Lydia's raven hair, and with two hands shook it free. "I saw Mittark only a few times, when I was very young. But his look I remember. You resemble him and, I would guess, resemble Weetamo as well. You are lovely and wild and adventurous. And I shall miss you very much. Yet, I know you will go. When you do, when you leave for your adventure on the sea, I want you to take the necklace with you. Wear it and remember that you are on your own journey. Seek it out. And when necessary, draw on the courage that runs in your blood, the blood of Weetamo and of my mother, Ruth. And most importantly, return to me, dear. Return to me safely."

Thirty-Three

Lydia

On the Caribbean Sea, May of that year, 1764

The nimble sloop, the Prudence, struggled, riding the giant swell until the crest broke, fell away, and the Prudence plunged downward. The scream of pulleys rose above the howl of the wind and the shouts of men while rain and sea alike washed over the deck, and the hull creaked.

"Can you hold her, Seth? Can you keep her steady?" shouted Lydia, fighting to be heard though she stood close at the shoulder of the helmsman – he lashed to the wooden wheel in an effort to hold the rudder steady, and Lydia, too, clamped with lifeline at her waist.

"Aye, Miss, I can hold her," and the helmsman shook rain from his face.

The sky lit. The air crackled. Another swell ahead, a wall of sea, higher yet by twofold than any other, and Lydia gripped the safety line at her waist. The ship's bow turned upward. Through the rain, she looked to the blurred faces of her men. She feared for each of them, and for the first time, she feared for her own life. For a moment, the ship leveled, rested on the crest of the mountainous wave. A bolt of lightning, an earsplitting crack. The crest gave way. The bow dipped, fell, and Lydia's legs crumbled out from under. A terrifying feel – a disconnection, a lift in the pit of her stomach, and she tumbled down. She hit belly first. Slid fast over the angled deck, clawing at the slick planks, until the lifeline caught with a jolt and took all breath out.

The Prudence sprang upright, still buoyant on the raging sea. But Lydia remained flat, belly to the deck. Effort to draw in air failed. She waited, eyes shut against the scene until hungry gasps began and air returned. Daring to move nothing but her eyes, she took stock. Her fingertips were raw. Beneath a nail, a long jagged splinter had pierced the flesh, and her right arm had become ensnared in the lifeline, the arm wrapped and twisted at her back. The arm did not feel broken, but the shoulder it emanated from throbbed. And there was blood. With her freed hand, she touched on her forehead and found the source of warm thick liquid that mingled red with rain on the deck. She felt over the wound and determined it to be but a narrow gash.

Ethan appeared, bent over her as if arrived from the heavens. With those mammoth hands he tugged gently, cautiously on the lifeline, releasing its hold on her arm.

"Are you hurt," she asked, glad that her own shakiness did not show in her voice.

In answer, Ethan turned his head side to side.

With the oil lamp burning inside her cabin room, Lydia sat at the charts. The end of the storm had come suddenly. The rain had ceased, the moon having slid out into a black night sky. On the sea, the waves rolled round, their fury spent. A knock came at the door, and from inside the room Ethan opened the door. The first mate, Morley, stepped in.

"What is it, Morley?" asked Lydia, although her eyes did not lift from the sextant she used at the table.

"The sail, Miss. It be jury rigged and ready."

Lydia kneaded the ache in her shoulder before turning to Morley. The mast had been split, broken off to half its height, but they would make do. "Half sail is better than none," she said. "Send all but Seth and a watchman to their hammocks until dawn. That includes you, Morley. I shall need you fresh come morning. With the rigged sail, we scarcely move at three knots, but if winds stay steady, we shall put in at Sainte Eustatius before next day's end."

"Aye, Miss. And might I say you ought catch some sleep for yerself?"

"Perhaps. Thank you, Morley. And good night," she added as she stood to dismiss the first mate.

The door closed, and with Morley gone Lydia turned to face the quiet ever-present Ethan standing across the lamp-lit cabin room. Despite having changed earlier into dry clothes, the humid dampness remained and invaded muscle and bone.

"Go, Ethan. Get some rest," she said.

In his silence, Ethan jabbed a finger, first toward Lydia, then to the narrow bed that was her own.

"Yes, I shall try to sleep," she said, not wanting to argue the fact that there would be no time for sleep until the Prudence was safe in harbor. "Now go. Daylight will come too soon."

His mouth set as near to a frown as that freakish grin would allow.

"Go. I'll be fine," she said, nudging Ethan toward the door.

"Good night," she called, hoping he heard the affection before the door shut behind him. Then came the customary rap. "Yes, I'm locking it now," she said as she bolted the door from the inside.

She had not intended to sleep. She'd lain on the narrow bed fully dressed in breeches and man's doublet worn as a jacket, wanting only a brief rest. Now, in what seemed only moments later, it was as if she were rising from a deep faraway place. A rap at the door, once, twice, but she was not able to rise up, the heaviness of sleep bearing down. Another rap, loud.

"Yes. Yes, I'm coming," she called when rising near enough to the surface to open her eyes.

The room had filled with the odor of things too long wet. Thin daylight streamed through the row of windows at the stern. Lydia crossed the cabin room and opened the door. Standing there with Ethan was the young watchman, a spyglass held at his side.

"It be pirates, Miss Lydia," announced the watchman, words run together in his haste. "Their ship, it approaches off port side."

Lydia led the way, across deck to the port rail.

"Lend me your spyglass," she said, and she lifted the thin spyglass to her eye. A distant ship dipped with the motion of the sea. But with the help of the spyglass Lydia could see for herself the black flag, the white skull and bones that waved from the stern. She counted its cannon – four to a side.

Double the cannon carried by the Prudence.

Morley appeared at the rail. "I best get every man on deck," he said, "armed with all they have."

"Yes. Do." And to the young watchman she said, "In my cabin, there's a wooden chest. Inside that chest is a small store of sword and musket. Find them and hand them out."

Only Ethan remained at her side. Morning had come hot so that Lydia, with the back of her hand, wiped at the line of sweat that ran from her temple. With the same hand, she felt for the string of bone beads that rested always beneath her shirt. The Prudence was agile, built upon a sleek hull. But rigged as she was with half her sail, the sloop was no match for the ship that pursued. Although it was against the law for crew to carry arms, Lydia suspected more than a few of her men hid a dirk or pistol. A well-honed dagger lay concealed in her own boot. Those, along with the few sword and musket to be handed out, would have to be enough, though it be meager arms for facing pirates.

Lydia lifted the eyeglass. The ship, its skull and cross bones, moved steadily near.

A touch on her arm. Ethan.

"We won't resist using cannon," she said. "We are no match

for theirs. So we'll draw the rogues near, inside their cannon range. If then they try to board the Prudence, we shall fight. Not before."

Lines burrowed into the wide, misshapen forehead. A giant hand formed a tight, powerful fist that slowly rubbed over his heart.

"And I care about you, Ethan. Very much. But we have no choice. We make our lives no safer in surrender to scathing thieves than we do in the fight."

Ethan tapped on his boot, motioned for her to take out the dagger she had hidden in her own boot.

"Yes," she said, and Lydia pulled the pearl-handled dirk from her high boot. "I just pray that I shan't need it." She slid the blade upward beneath her sleeve, feeling the weight of it against her flesh. A bead of sweat trickled down along her nose.

The last of the crew scrambled up through the hatch, a total of twenty men, each showing the glint of blade or the butt of musket. "Conceal any weapons," she commanded. "Let them see no threat of attack."

A cannon shot blasted, landed to starboard, just short of the Prudence. The rogue ship moved closer. Closer, until the sails lowered and the great wooden hull fell abreast with the Prudence.

All went still – air and men.

Clear now to the naked eye was the vessel's name – Hawk – painted on the prow. Also clear were the men standing on its deck, two score or more, each dressed in brightly colored sash and bandolier.

"Show your Captain," demanded a bandit from across the distance, and Lydia looked to the one who spoke, the one with long twists of hair the color of wild carrot, a face clean shaven and leathered by the sun. He stood at the Hawk's rail, arms akimbo, his hands at rest upon the scarlet sash that wrapped his waist.

Morley stepped forward to stand beside Lydia at the rail. "The Captain stands to wait until yer intentions are made known."

Laughter gurgled from the throat of the pirate.

Blood pooled on her lip where Lydia bit through.

With his fist, the bandit struck at the air, bringing sudden end to his laughter, his hair like flame beneath the glare of sun. "Lower a line," he shouted. "And tell your Captain I be coming aboard, be it with ease or by force."

Lydia, matching shoulder to shoulder with Morley, spoke softly so only Morley could hear. "Tell the pompous infidel we offer no resistance. Tell him that the Captain asks only for mercy, that because of the storm we are a broken ship with a crew of broken men."

"But Miss…"

"Go on. Tell him. If I speak, he shall know I am not a man."

Morley gazed at her a moment, his thoughts hidden behind the spark of Irish eyes. Then he cupped hands to his mouth and relayed word for word his Captain's message.

A brace of wooly-haired bandits scurried to the Hawk's rail and to the winches. There was a clang of pulleys and a longboat was lowered from the Hawk. One by one, twelve pirates of the sea lifted themselves over the rail of the Hawk and skimmed down the lines into the longboat. Their leader followed.

In cadence, twelve oars cut through the long low swells, closing the distance. Lydia focused on the one who did not row. He sat at the back, a silent coxswain, rigid, without expression. He carried a sword, whereas the others did not. Likely it was that the others also carried a hidden weapon. Too many tales had been told of weapons stashed within the folds of a pirate's bandolier, and Lydia did not trust for a moment the show of unarmed men that pulled oar toward her.

She looked to the faces of her crew. A disparate group, outcasts and remnants of seagoing men, the few who had been willing to sign on with a woman as Captain. But each had proven worthy. They would count on each other now.

Lydia tossed a roped rat line over the gunnel rail. "We shoot the first to cross the gunnel," she said to her crew.

The pirate's longboat pulled in close, low in the water at the side of the Prudence.

Lydia's arm twitched with the wait.

A thud sounded against the hull.

A scuffle low on the rope line as the first climbed, until in front of her were the blue eyes of the first, his dark hair twisted into countless coils, and he swung a leg over the rail. "Now," she shouted.

From behind, a shot fired. The first bandit fell, only to be stepped over by the next and the next. They clamored up, cursing and hooting onto the Prudence. The air filled with the clash of steel gunshot. A sharp, blood-curdling scream came at her back, and Lydia turned to it, a bandit leaping through the air, the brilliant blue of his sash, the glint of silver pointed to her. Lydia stepped in, leading with the dirk, sinking its blade deep into the belly before the bandit could fall against her.

No blood spilled until she pulled back the blade from the flesh. The red oozed like molten iron through the blue of his sash.

Her gut knotted. Nausea rose up. But she turned to the scuffle of boots, only to see the leader, the frenzied hair, his scarlet sash and gleaming sword, rushing at her, he darting between warring shoulders. Lydia stepped back, the bloodied dirk ready again as the bandit stopped only a few good paces from where she stood.

"Call your men off," he ordered.

"Never."

The tyrant grinned. "Ah, so a woman speaks? How lovely. And you would spend your life to save a few ragged tars?" He raised an arm as the point of his sword swayed side to side. "How civil of you," he said. "How stupid."

Lydia trained her eyes on the sword, took another step back but felt the gunnel rail press against her spine. Only her bloodied dirk lay between her throat and the silver blade of the pirate's sword.

The heavy thud of feet – Ethan grunting, raging forward, his own dagger aimed to the fiery-haired leader that stood between him and Lydia. The leader turned the slightest to glance behind, and Lydia drove the dirk deep into the man's chest. The surprised eyes glared at her before the man fell forward, as Lydia stepped aside and the lifeless chin hit hard upon the deck.

Ethan scooped the limp body up in his arms, lifted the dead scoundrel high above his head and faced the fighting mob. As if a signal had shot out, the battle ended. Survivors, both merchant seamen and pirates, each tattered and bloodied, turned toward the giant. Three of the twelve bandits remained standing. Those three came forward and stopped in front of their slain leader. With no words exchanged, they took him up and carried him to the rail, his fiery twists of hair falling away, exposing the futile stare of the eyes. He was hoisted by the three over the side of the Prudence and down the line.

While the longboat inched its way back toward the Hawk, Lydia wrapped herself in her own arms in effort to stop the shaking. All around her, bodies lay bloodied. A mere seven were standing, including herself. On deck, a fallen Morley rolled onto his side and sat up, his shirtsleeve dark with blood.

"Fetch bandages," he commanded of the young watchman who stood near. "Can't ya see, ya tired tar, we need tend to the living."

Removing her doublet, Lydia let it drag as she turned back to rail. The scent on the air had changed. She lifted her face to the smell of earth – dry land, and for the first time in all her memory, she longed for the sight of it.

Thirty-Four

Lydia
The following day, May of 1764

In the hand mirror her lip showed split and swollen. A narrow cut angled above her left eye, and the flesh there was colored as a ripe plum. To touch it made her wince, but the wound was well closed. It would heal. With that thought, Lydia set the mirror onto the rumpled bed and carefully slid a stiff arm, then the other into the sleeves of the old leather doublet.

The Prudence lay tied at the winches, safe in the Dutch port of Sainte Eustatius. Both ship and body would require time to mend, but it was not the pain or stiffness that most disturbed Lydia. It was the killing. Decent men had been lost, men under her charge. And vivid was the image of her own bloodied dirk. She'd killed two. Both had been a scourge to mankind, but both had been men none the less.

She shook her arms, as if to shake off the mood. Death could just as easily have come to her as to the bandits. One day it would, soon or late, but not today. Today she was alive and there was business to be done. She pulled the old leather doublet across her bound breasts and did the buttons. She set the felt-rim hat atop her head, tucked the last stray strands beneath it, and walked out from the confines of her cabin.

All crew who were able had already left the ship for the feel of land under their feet. Except for the light clink of halyards, the ship lay quiet in the water. Lydia took the moment to breathe and to look out at the colonnade of buildings that lined the wharf, and to the village that had squeezed itself in between the sea and the steep green hillside of Sainte Eustatius. She crossed then to the starboard because Ethan waited there, patient as always in his own silence. His head cocked to the side as he touched with one hand on her bruised eye.

"Yes, but it shall heal," she said, and she started along the length of boarding plank toward the wharf, Ethan following close.

The air, softened by a breeze off the turquoise water, worked to lift her spirit. She walked past the counting houses and the smith's shop with growing curiosity for this foreign place, and after a stop at the shipwright to order a new mast, she decided to spend one brief hour exploring.

Beyond the wharf, a street led out both left and right. Either way bustled with people. Some were fair-haired with the square-cut jaw of the Dutch. But most who made their way along the front of shops had skin colored the rich brown of Old Mol's colt, their heads and bodies wrapped in brightly colored cotton. There were scores of them, and Lydia mingled slowly, listening to their thick voices conversing in a language she did not understand. She wondered if the darkies were perhaps slaves. In the colonies, even as far north as Boston, darkies could be bought and sold, owned by other human beings. It was one of life's unfortunate truths. On Cape Cod, however, it seemed to be looked at differently. Lydia knew of only one slave taken there for the use of labor. From her grandmother she had heard the story of Pomp. Pomp had been bought at auction in the West Indies by a Boston merchant trader and sold later for forty-five pounds to Hector Collins. Pomp had lived for a short time with Hector, a distance of some ten miles north of Wells Creek, but old Pomp had been found one evening hanging by the neck from the limb of a tree. He had taken his own sad life. Tired he was, her grandmother said, tired of loneliness. He missed his own kind and the wild jungles of his home, and the good Lord's heaven seemed the easier place.

As Lydia walked, the scent of seared meat cut in. "Oh, Ethan, did you ever smell anything so delicious," she said, and she followed the drifting scent but a short distance to the local tavern. Looking to its opened door, she stopped suddenly on the road. Her heart quickened. "No, it can't be. But it is."

There, on a wide stoop outside the door to the tavern, dressed in a fresh white shirt and trim breeches, stood Caleb Willoughby.

Ethan took gentle hold of her arm, tilting his head in question.

"It's an old friend," she said. "A friend from Boston who sailed with my father."

She must speak to him. But Caleb already was speaking to a man in uniform. Minutes passed as Lydia waited. People needed to step around her until at last Caleb and the man in uniform nodded their farewell. The uniformed man stepped alone inside the tavern door. Caleb placed a brimmed hat on his head and stepped down from the stoop into the bright morning sunlight.

"Caleb," called Lydia as she made way through the crowd. "Caleb," she said once more when at last she stood in front of him.

His expression was one of being puzzled. His eyes searched her face, scanned over her doublet and breeches. "Lydia?"

"Yes. It's me," she said.

"But ... How ..."

Without thought, Lydia placed her arms around his neck and his arms surrounded her, lifted her, swinging her in a circle. Twice they circled before Caleb set her down, and with their hands still held together he took a step back. "Let me look at you. It appears you've grown."

"It's been ten years. Of course, I've grown."

"Ten years? Has it?" He looked again at her from head to toe. "And what are you doing here? Are you all right? Your face, it's ..."

"I'm fine. It's my ship that's in need. She has a broken mast."

"Your ship?

"Yes. The Prudence. She's in the harbor."

"And just how did you manage that? No, not now. That's a story that likely takes a time to tell. We'll save it. But I'm not surprised. If any woman were to arrive here in this wild place on a ship of her own, it would be you, wouldn't it?"

"Yes, I suppose. But I couldn't have done it without Ethan," she said with a smile to the silent giant at her side. "Caleb, this is my dear friend, Ethan. We have been friends since my beginning on Ponokanet, and now we sail together."

Both men reached to shake the hand of the other. If Caleb made note of the freakish face of her friend, he showed no sign.

"Caleb," she said, "is Papa with you?"

Even with his eyes shaded by the hat, she could see that Caleb glanced away, avoiding for that moment the hope in her eyes. "No, Lydia. He's not. I don't sail with your father any longer."

"But why? And where is he?"

"Your father is well. He is on his way to Calcutta."

"I see." Her shoulders drooped as she looked to the dusty street. Her boots were covered with the white gritty powder – specks of silted coral uprooted from the reef and washed ashore.

"I'm sorry, Lydia."

"Don't be," she said. "I thought I might see him, that's all."

Caleb seemed to search her face, then a shift of weight, one foot to the other. "Lydia, I do wish to talk with you, to hear tales of your life of which I'm certain there are many. But it will have to be at another time. I have an appointment and I ..."

"That's all right," she said despite the slap of disappointment. "I don't mean to keep you."

"No, it's just that ... well, there's a ship here in the harbor, owned by the British ... the East India Company. It seems the former Captain died at sea, and just now I am on my way to discuss taking that position."

"You would work for the bully British?"

"I would be Captain of a ship. That has something to its credit, does it not?"

"Of course. And you have skill." Although she did not like it that such skill might go to the British, she added for the sake of Caleb, "You will be a good Captain."

"I suppose." Caleb glanced to Ethan, then away down the road. "Lydia, could I see you again? Perhaps take you to dinner this evening. I'll find the Prudence. I'll come for you at seven."

"I'd like that."

He extended his hand, and she took it as way to say goodbye. "At seven then," she said.

"Seven it is." This as Caleb turned and walked away through the multicolored cottons.

Lydia touched the split lip, feeling the tenderness. Oh, how she has missed Caleb, and she hadn't even known it.

The gentle giant hand touched on her arm.

"Yes, I know … we need to go," she said, the scent of seared meat forgotten. "The Prudence waits for its repairs."

Thirty-Five

Sydney waits in the rocker on the front porch, watching the moon that hangs yellow and round above the barn roof. She waits for the right moment to confront Alison. Edward has already made his way upstairs, and when the light in the living room clicks off, Alison's footsteps pad on the hall floor.

"Goodnight," says Alison through the screen door.

Sydney stops rocking. "Can I ask you something?"

The question hangs in the air much like the moon, but dark from the weight of it. The screen door opens, and Alison steps out – one step only. "What is it?"

She hears caution in Alison's voice. Things have been going better between the two of them, helped along, Sydney thinks, by having Edward there. His presence is a buffer, keeping conversation light and at a safe level. But real communication is still held together by a thread.

To have a clearer view of her mother's face, Sydney turns in the rocker, pulls one leg up under her. She bites on her lip because the courage to do this is thin. The only way is to jump in.

"Is there a chance that Everett is my father?"

Alison's eyes dart above and around Sydney but do not look at her. "No. Why would you ask such a thing?"

"Because I know you and Everett dated. Everett's told me that much, although apparently it never occurred to you to tell me."

A quick tucking of hair behind one ear, Alison's mouth holds open, as if captured on camera with nothing to say, the white of her teeth highlighted by the moon.

"Oh, my God," says Sydney on exhaled breath, as the last bit of disbelief disintegrates. "Go on. At least admit that you and Everett spent a summer together ... that you didn't leave Wells Creek until the end of the summer, not in June like you have always said."

"Did Everett tell you all this?"

Sydney straightens in the chair, the leg out from under her now and two feet on the floor. The meaning of it – Everett her father, and all these years ... "All these years, you lied. Why?"

"I'm going to bed, Sydney," and Alison starts away.

But Sydney is quick to step in front of her mother. She speaks low and definite. "This isn't a time to pretend. Everett could die. I need to know the truth before that happens. Is he my father?"

Alison tries to step past, but Sydney grips her mother's arm. "I'm not letting you walk away until you've told me the truth."

"I have."

Sydney shakes her head. "I don't believe you anymore. But go on denying it if you want. If the blood tests come back a match, I'll know the truth anyway." And she releases her mother's arm.

Alison remains in place, standing in the moonlight, and the usually arrow-straight shoulders slump. "Antonio Ponti was not your father," says Alison as if whispering to the night. "He gave me my first job on stage. But he was not your father."

"Then why, for all these years, did you let me think he was?"

"It seemed easier that way."

"Easier? That's your excuse? What about Everett? What did you tell him?"

"Nothing." Alison sits on the rocker, rubs on her forehead. "Everett didn't even know you existed for the first five years."

"But after that he did? Does he know?"

"No. No, he doesn't. I almost told him once. I came back here with you when you were five. I came back because my father had died. Dad had been living in Barnstable in a little rat-hole room of a motel, and because he owed several back months of rent, the owner wouldn't let me stay there. Because I had no money to stay anywhere else for the four days, I ate crow and asked Eva if you and I could stay with her. Of course, she wanted to bring you around ... into the village and to her friends. Somewhere in the course of those few days, Everett saw you. He came to me one night and asked me if he was your father. He said your hair and dark eyes were his, and I almost ..." Alison's eyes fill. "I couldn't tell him. Instead I told him he was crazy, that Antonio Ponti was Italian, what did he expect you to have for hair and eyes."

To contain rage, Sydney turns away, holds to the porch rail as if that might keep her from hating this woman who had lied all these years. A bat darts from an eave of the barn, visible in the white light of the moon, and just as quickly it disappears. "How could you do that?" she says to the motionless Alison at her back. "How could you lie so blatantly to everyone?"

Alison clears her throat. Sydney waits.

"In the beginning," says Alison, I was too proud. Ashamed. Scared. All of those things. It was a different time. Girls weren't supposed to get pregnant, not the good ones. By the time I knew that I was, I was in New York. I believed if Everett really wanted me, if he loved me, he would have followed me there."

Sydney turned at last to face her mother. "And done what? Give up his life here for your dream?"

"He could have asked me to come back."

"Would you have?"

Looking to her hands, Alison twists the diamond ring on her finger. "No. I would not have returned here. Not even for Everett." Alison rests her head against the high slatted chair, closes her eyes, and Sydney believes her mother's explanation is done. But Alison opens her eyes and sighs. "You might as well hear it all. Everett did ask me to marry him. That summer at the end of August, before I had even a clue that I was pregnant, he asked me to stay here in Wells Creek. He said he loved me, that he wanted to marry me if I would stay."

"So, all these years you and Everett could have raised me together. We could have been a family."

"It wouldn't have worked, Sydney. I was too young."

"You don't know that. Damn it. He's so … so wonderful, and he doesn't even know he has a daughter … that it's me." She pulls hard through her hair, every ounce of her held back from shaking her mother. "I need you to tell me something that I can hang on to … something that will keep me from walking away from you forever."

"Sydney, I was barely eighteen. I had dreams. I wanted to be an actress. I knew I could be a good one. And I didn't want to disappear into oblivion, a housewife with sand between her toes."

"I … I … I … Is that all there is to you?"

"That's all I had then. Myself and my dream."

"And a baby … me growing inside you." Sydney sees the hurt in her mother's face and looks away to the yard, to the moon and the chirp of crickets. "I went looking for him," she says. "I found Antonio Ponti buried in the ground."

"Oh, Sydney … I didn't know." Alison leaves the rocking chair and walks to the porch rail, stands with hands resting on the rail close to Sydney's.

Her mother's hands are small. Sydney remembers those hands pulling a brush through her hair while that young Sydney watched in the bathroom mirror, watched the hands pull through the tangle. And her mother's words, 'if your hair weren't so curly' …

"Sydney, I know nothing I say can change any of what I did or didn't do. I can't change what's already done. But you need to know how sorry I am."

"Bull."

"Let me finish, Sydney, please. I know in many ways I've been selfish. And I haven't been the best mother. But I have loved you from the first moment I held you in my arms. And I kept you. I didn't give you away. I didn't put you up for adoption like some of my actress friends thought I should. I didn't want someone else raising my baby. I wanted you."

"You did a good job at keeping that fact from me." It is the moon that Sydney looks to, not her mother. Never would be too soon to look at that lying deceitful face.

"Back then, I didn't know how to say these things. I didn't know how to show love to a child. But I do now. And I do love you. That's why I stayed this week. When I arrived and found you here, at first I wanted to leave. I was afraid we'd argue and only make things worse. But I stayed. I wanted to try, after all the years apart, to make a connection with my daughter."

"Why now?"

"Because I'm older. Hopefully wiser. And because I think Eva left this house to the two of us so that it could happen."

Sydney stared only to the darkness, stabbed by the mention of her grandmother.

"Please, Sydney, tell me you can understand, at least a little. Tell me that the last few days have made a difference for you, too."

"I can't."

"I'm sorry. I truly hoped things might be different."

Sydney hears her mother's footsteps cross the porch, hears the screen door open, then the latch click as it shuts. She hears the sea breaking on the beach. There is no forgiving Alison for the lie. Not tonight. Not ever.

Her heart beats, so tight with anger, and while the porch board creaks under the rocker, the moon fades from yellow to white. She watches the sky, keeps an eye to the moon that slowly shrinks from its large half-dollar size to a nickel. An effect of atmosphere. Even so, it amazes her how the eye is fooled. Just as she's been fooled all these years.

All her life she thought …

All her life she's lived without a father while Alison knew.

"Hi." The voice startles her. Looking up, she sees Ty standing just beyond the porch.

"I've been for a walk on the beach," he says. "When I heard the chair rocking up there on the porch, I thought it might be you. How're you doing?"

"Not a good time to ask."

"Want to talk?"

Sydney shakes her head. "I don't think so."

"How about a cup of coffee then? Or a glass of wine?"

It's late, and the day has been three weeks long. But sleep isn't going to happen tonight anyway. "Okay," she says. "A glass of wine would be nice."

Thirty-Six

While Ty opens wine, Sydney walks into the glass room, awed by the masses of color, some bold and large, most delicate and pale. The room holds a great deal of humidity. In addition to the plants' own breath, moisture comes from the several small statue figures with water trickling over stones at their feet. To one side, two wicker chairs sit by a slender tree, its broad green leaves poking out from a few high thin limbs. The limbs have blossoms, enormous yellow trumpets that droop under their own weight, and the fragrance they give is incredibly sweet.

A half-hour earlier she'd oozed with anger. But now, as she looks around this plant-filled room, she fills with a sudden realization – Everett Dean is her father. That truth rises to the top like a gust of wind, bringing with it a new feel, something very much like elation.

"You look better." Ty hands Sydney one of two glasses of dark red wine.

"It's this room," she says. "It's beautiful."

"I like it, too." Ty grins, and laughs a little. He is a man comfortable with himself. Sydney admires that. Over the past years she'd built up a kind of confidence of her own, but it's different than the ease she sees in Ty. His runs deeper, from a safer place.

She sips the wine. It is wonderfully dry, with a faint taste of licorice. She asks about the tree with yellow flowers, and learns that its common name is the angel's trumpet. As they talk about the knobby sedum that grows low among the stones by the fountains, and about the Buddha tucked in beneath a wispy fern, Sydney feels the growing need to keep distance. She avoids brushing her arm against his as she stretches to feel the slick dense leaf of what Ty calls the umbrella plant. Being in that room with him feels too easy, too warm. She tells him about her failure with the marigolds and says, "I was born with a brown thumb."

When Ty laughs, so does she.

"It's nice to hear you laugh," he says.

Sydney again sips her wine. "If I tell you something … and I have to tell somebody or I'm going to burst … you have to promise not to pass out or … or call me a liar."

"Should I sit down?"

"You better." She nods in the direction of the wicker chair.

"That's okay. I can take it," he says with yet another grin, and he stands there close with her and waits.

Sydney takes a breath before meeting the gaze of gentle dark eyes. "Everett is my father."

"What?"

"That's what I said when I first heard it."

Ty's grin is gone. "You know this for sure?"

Sydney only nods.

"And Everett doesn't know this?"

"I don't think so. My mother never told him. She finally told me tonight. I still can't quite believe it but … but I do."

By the taller of the fountains, Sydney lets the cool water run over her fingers, and she explains all that Alison said, how Everett questioned Alison after seeing Sydney for the first time, how Alison had denied that Sydney was his. "Everett believed her. We all did."

The wine has made her mind fuzzy, and she sets her glass down at the side of the fountain. When Ty steps in and stands at her back, she watches their reflection on the glass wall, and Ty places his hand on her shoulder. She watches his eyes when he tells her, "Having you as a daughter is going to make Everett happy. When will you tell him?"

"Tomorrow. I want him to know."

"This means you could be the donor he needs, doesn't it?"

"I think so," and she turns to face Ty, misjudges the distance and moves against him, the touch kinetic. The current lifts her, and she kisses his mouth, warm and lingering. But when his arms hold her close, Sydney pulls away. "I'm sorry," she says. "I shouldn't have done that."

With only a few steps she is out the door and running across the yard. She climbs the stairs of her grandmother's house, to the back bedroom that is her own, and she shuts the door.

What did she do? A kiss complicates everything. And it's unfair to Ty – and to Rick.

Thirty-Seven

Sydney
The next day, Wednesday, September 5

Alison has insisted on being the one to tell Everett, and by nine in the morning, the three sit in Everett's living room. Sydney looks to her mother's hands. Fingers of both hands, with nails painted magenta, are clasped to form a single fist. One thumb rubs the other. Everett also watches Alison's hands, as if rubbing of the thumb is the main event in the room.

"I was just as shocked," says Sydney.

Everett looks up with sunken eyes. "I'm not shocked, Syd. I'm not even all that surprised. I'm damn livid, that's all."

Alison stands. "I'm sorry," she says. "I should have done this year's ago. But now I've told you both, and I should go."

Everett lifts himself from his chair and walks with Alison to the door. "You're going to have to give me some time with this one," he says when he opens the door for her. Alison glances to Sydney but does not say goodbye before walking out the door.

Sydney is suddenly recalling the past Monday, when she asked Alison, 'did you love my father first or were you friends?' Alison's words – 'I loved him first.' Alison had loved Everett. If this was not her mother, Sydney might feel pity for the woman who spent all those years alone, not living with the love of a man or the love of what could have been her family. But Sydney was that child kept from knowing a father, and that child, even today, can hold no pity.

Everett rubs the smooth skin that stretches over his scalp, and Sydney crosses the room to stand with him.

"When I first heard," says Sydney, "I was so angry."

"I'm angry as hell," says Everett, "but not so much at your mother."

"At me?"

"No. Never at you," and he squeezes her hand. "But I should have known. Damn it. I told her you were my daughter."

"But she kept on with the lie. She lied to both of us."

"I should've had a test done or something. I knew, damn it. I should've followed my gut. And all these years..." Everett walks into the kitchen with steps stronger than Sydney has seen. He opens the refrigerator. Slams it shut. "Damn. No ginger ale."

"Hey," calls Sydney. "I think it's the best news I've ever gotten in my life."

Everett returns, a small grin at last on his face. "You know," he says while easing down onto his usual chair, "I'd look at you sometimes and see my expressions in your eyes. Or scarier still, my mother's look. But then I'd brush it off because I thought I was imagining it, like something you want so much that you start thinking it's true. Damn it, Syd, I'm sorry. You deserved more than that."

"You couldn't have known. Not for sure. And you know what? You were there anyway. You were always there."

"You're one hell of a kid, you know that?"

Sydney reaches to put her hand on top of his, again so amazed to think this man is her father. "What was she like at eighteen?"

"Your mother?"

"Yes." Sydney goes to the chair by the book case, sits to better listen because suddenly she wants to know everything.

"Ah, she was a knock-out, I tell you. Thing is, Alison didn't even know how beautiful she was."

"I find that hard to believe."

"Come on now, give her some credit. She was young. I should've known better. Cripes, I was twenty-two. I'd been away to college for four years. I'd been around some. But your mother … she was just blooming. Damn, she was lovely. And I fell for her. Hard. I loved her. You should know that, Syd. I mean, it wasn't just a casual thing for me."

"She told me you asked her to marry you."

Everett leans back in his chair, his hands coming to rest on its fabric arms. "I did," he says. "What a damn fool thinking an eighteen year old girl was ready to settle down out here in the dunes."

"I'd say she made the biggest mistake of her life."

"Careful now. That's a bit simple. Your mother had fire. Determination. She had to get out of here. She had to become a woman on her own. And it wasn't long before I was off flying helicopters for the U.S. of A."

Their eyes meet across the distance, and Everett gives a small shrug. "I'm sorry, kid. I wish it had been different. But I'm damn pleased to finally know the truth." A sparkle shows in his eyes – a light shining through.

"And tomorrow we get results from the blood tests," says Sydney. "I could be a match."

Everett winks. "Odds are looking better."

By afternoon the attic window is open. Any stuffiness has been cleared by a briny offshore breeze. The gold lettering is complete, and Sydney works on painting the contours of the plane, blending red on the pallet until it matches perfectly the red she remembers. She takes her time, enjoying the process, hands busy and her mind free to explore. She feels better about Everett. If the blood tests shows a match, and that's looking more likely, then she can give Everett the marrow he needs. He can get well.

But Alison?

Sydney hasn't spoken to her since the two were at Everett's earlier in the day. She's remembering Everett defending her mother despite everything. So Sydney, too, is trying to do better at this. She's trying to look at Alison's lie with a different lens – to 'look at it and let in the pain some times' – wasn't that the phrase Ty used?

When the sign is done, Sydney takes her time cleaning the brushes. She is beginning to like this space high in the eaves. It's good for thinking. But the grumble of an empty stomach takes her down the narrow stairs from the attic, intending to grab a late lunch. She walks the length of upstairs hall, but she stops at the sound of muffled sobs coming from behind her mother's bedroom door.

Sydney cannot take the next set of stairs. Something holds here, and she stands motionless outside her mother's door. There's been so much hurt, so many harsh words. Yet, of all the dumb things, after everything, she cares. She cares about this deceitful woman who sobs alone on her bed. The idea surprises. This caring survived somehow, like an orchid that lives and breathes with no soil to nurture it along.

Sydney knocks on the bedroom door.

From inside, the bed hits against the wall, as though Alison has sprung from it. "Who is it?" asks Alison, her voice strained and coarse.

"It's Sydney. May I come in?"

"The door's not locked."

Alison is sitting on the edge of the bed. Her hair lies flattened on one side and hunched up on the other. Mascara runs in dark smudge lines down and over her cheekbones like clown paint. On the bed, stretched out beside Alison, is Cat, the gray face looking up sheepishly at Sydney.

"I bet I look a mess," says Alison.

"Let's call it the earthy look."

Sydney sits on the bed. She isn't sure what to say, so she says only what first comes to mind. "Looking back, I'm glad you sent me here. I'm glad I had the chance to know Eva. And Everett."

Alison somehow laughs. But when the throaty laugh turns to tears, Alison wraps her arms around Sydney, holding a rigid Sydney close.

Thirty-Eight

Lydia
Still St. Eustatius, May of 1764

Lydia dropped the bundled purchases onto the bed. Her cabin room held still the smell of wet, and she left the door open to let in the Indies air. Through that open door, a fan of sunlight fell on Ethan where he stood just inside. Because he stared, Lydia asked, "What are you peering at?"

With a finger, Ethan drew a down-turned frown across the slit that was his mouth.

"I'm not sad," she said. "It's just that … I've been thinking." Lydia pushed aside the bundles and sunk onto the bed to sit. Seeing Caleb so suddenly out of nowhere had been wonderful. But seeing him also made her think of her father, a momentary hope that her father was here on Sainte Eustatius. She had glanced to the street in search of his full grand figure but was left with only the longing and the reminder that her Papa had chosen a life that suited only himself, those around him be damned. Not unlike herself. That fact had struck like a bolt of lightning. And she wondered if her Papa had ever killed a man.

She looked to her giant friend. "Ethan, what am I doing here?"

With his hand, Ethan brushed a wide arc through the air, as if presenting for the first time the array of dust motes floating in the light around him.

"I know. I sail my own ship," she said. "It's what I have longed for, is it not? But look at me. I dress in breeches, always hiding behind them. But hiding from whom? And what if I end up like my Papa, roaming the world alone?"

Ethan tapped on his chest, affection in his eyes.

"Yes, you are with me, Ethan. And each day I am grateful for that. But today I feel … I can't say what it is exactly. Ah, it's just a funk, and I shall get through it," she said, slapping coral dust from her breeches. "And I shall get through it best with a good washing."

Preparing for an evening with Caleb lifted the unease, and while alone in her cabin, after washing, Lydia held up the blue linen skirt she'd taken from the bundle. The skirt slipped easily down over her arms, and she tugged at the hem until the fabric fell into place at her ankles. She smoothed out the folds and admired once again the color. In town that morning, while purchasing dry goods at a shop, she had spied a small rack of lady's apparel, three skirts, each with matching bodice, all sewn from fine linen and set out for sale by the shopkeeper's wife, and Lydia had suddenly wanted to wear something other than breeches to dinner with Caleb. There had been but one skirt sewn to her size, but that one was the skirt she would have chosen. The color matched exactly that of a spring robin's egg. The color was a favorite, although Lydia never ceased to wonder how nature created such a blue from a bird the color of pumpkin and brown.

Lydia slid her arms into the sleeves of the matching bodice and laced it snuggly across the front. The bodice neck was cut low and square, exposing the straight line of white ruffle that was part of the shift she'd chosen as undergarment. She was pleased – with the fit and the look. Pleased, too, with her hair pinned high and off her face, which was the current style.

There was still the cut above her eye. Even so, in a day's time the bruised color had faded some, and in the hand mirror the darkest of brown eyes looked back at her. In them, Lydia could see Constance. The resemblance was uncanny and that brought the start of a smile, but also reflected in the mirror were the bone beads. They looked large and indeed out of place resting there above the delicate ruffle. The necklace had not been removed since leaving Ponokanet, and it took several moments to decide. Slowly, Lydia lifted the beads over her head. At the bottom of her wooden trunk, beneath a blanket and the second pair of breeches, she found the wooden box with its lid. She put the corded beads safely inside and returned the box to its place in the trunk.

A rap sounded on the door.

Her glance fell upon the chronometer. The timepiece hung on its gimbals, maintaining its horizontal position for accuracy, and her mind quickly converted meridian time to that of Sainte Eustatius. The time was two minutes to seven.

She waited for Ethan's customary second rap.

When the second rap didn't come, she called from her side of the door, "Ethan?"

"No. It's Caleb. Shall I wait on deck?"

"No need. Come in," she said, crossing to the door quickly and sliding the bolt free.

The door opened, leaving Lydia to face her guest.

"Where's Ethan?" she asked out of surprise only, for never had anyone appeared at her cabin door without him.

But Caleb only stared.

"Caleb, I've asked you a question."

"Yes. Yes, I know," he stammered. "But I seem to be at a loss of words. You're lovely."

"You're stunned to see me in anything other than breeches, that's all," she said, intending to sound put off.

"That is true," and a smile relaxed his face.

"But really, where is Ethan? How did you get by Ethan without him knowing?"

"I didn't. He greeted me with a handshake. I said hello, and he curtly pointed the way to your door."

"Did he now?" But Lydia understood completely. By remaining on deck, Ethan had spoken. He approved of Caleb, and he thought her safe.

"He's a serious chap, isn't he?" said Caleb.

"Not always. At times he can be fun. Truly he can be," she added when Caleb lifted an eyebrow. "It's his silence that makes you think him serious. He never speaks. Not even to me ... not once since the first we met in the pokeberry patch."

"You met him in a pokeberry patch. Ah, Lydia, you have a great many tales to tell, tales I am eager to hear."

She slipped her arm around his, then backed away, for she remembered the straw hat with the ribbon around its crown. She plucked it from the bed, set it at just the slightest angle upon her head before taking hold again of Caleb's arm.

Lantern oil lit the tavern, causing shadows to play on the wall behind Caleb. Much of the Dutch sausage and cabbage remained on Lydia's plate, for she had talked endlessly about Ponokanet, about the death of Martha Brimmer, and the decision to purchase the Prudence so that she might bring rum and molasses to Cape Cod. Sitting back now, she felt somehow released of energy, a calming that allowed her to look about the tavern room, to smell the rich scent of tobacco that filled the air, to listen to the murmur of the dozen voices in the room. Any of her cares could wait because at this moment, more than anything, she wished to hear of the years she'd missed in the life of this dear friend.

"It's your turn now," she said. "I've talked far too much. I should like to ask the questions."

"Such as?" said Caleb while stretching an arm over the back of the empty chair next to him, showing a breadth of fine tweed waistcoat beneath his jacket.

"Such as, how did the meeting go? Are you Captain of a ship?"

"No. Mr. Hartley and I could not reach an agreement."

"Really? Well, then, I'm sorry."

"Don't be."

"But I thought being a Captain was what you wanted."

If not for the light of the oil lamp on their table, she might not have noticed the small twitch of muscle just there on his cheekbone – just as Caleb leaned forward in his chair, setting his folded hands onto the table, slender hands, long fingered.

"I thought so, too," he said. "But when I sat in that room, it was dark. You know how the English are with their dark wood on all the walls and a heavy curtain over each window. So you see, it was dark and ornate and the room smelled of old air. Worst of all, Hartley was an oaf."

"An oaf." She couldn't help it, she laughed at the word.

"Yes. Now don't go laughing at me, for it's true. The man was an oaf. And in my mind I kept hearing your words."

"Mine? For Heaven's sake, which ones?

"The ones that berated the British. You were right. The British East India is run by fools. They are arrogant and ignorant … to the tip of their white wigs."

"Well, I don't believe I said quite that, but I wish I had."

"The British haven't a slightest hint of what to do with our colonies. Hartley would have me carry goods to Boston's port, have me charge British taxes against my own neighbors. They'll force us to do more than smuggle a few worthless hulls of rum and tea if they don't loosen their hold. Fight. That's what they'll force us to do. By God, I should have started it right there with Hartley."

"Start it? A fight? With the oaf?" Lydia did not try to contain her laugh, for it was just as before, those many years ago when Caleb would spillover with unbridled ideas and share them with her, never flattened by her lighthearted take on his fervor.

"It is true, I swear. If I had not walked out when I did, my time with that puffed up old man would have come to blows."

"I can't imagine that you would let it come to that," she said while at the same time reaching across and covering Caleb's rounded fist with her own hand. Both remained stilled until Caleb opened his hand and wrapped it around Lydia's, enclosing her hand in his. In the lamplight, she explored the familiar square jaw, the cleft of his chin.

Caleb was first to slide his hand from hers, and the gray darkened in his eyes.

"What is it?" asked Lydia. "What's wrong?"

He ordered a second ale as the tavern girl passed close to the table, but Lydia would not free him from the question.

"You can't get around it with me," she said. "Remember who it is you are sitting with."

"You always could read a person's mind."

"Only yours. It seems I haven't lost the knack."

The tavern girl brought the new tankard of dark ale. Caleb took a swallow of the frothy liquid. "Seeing you again, so grown, so lovely … you remind me of someone."

"Who?"

Caleb set the pewter tankard down onto the table. "My wife."

"You're married?" She could not hold back her surprise, her hand coming to her throat.

"Was. It was nearly three years ago. Your father and I spent a winter here on Sainte Eustatius. Your father met a woman and then … so did I. The difference was I fell in love. She was Dutch and had grown up here on a coffee plantation. Her parents were not pleased with me for I was, in their words, a 'bastard son of a barmaid.' Not that they'd heard it from me, but they'd done their research. Anna and I married anyway. We married secretly one night before I left for China."

Caleb stared at the ale, just briefly before pushing the tankard on across the table. "It was selfish of me," he said. "I shall regret it until the day I die. Yet, it was the best that ever happened to me. Can you understand that?"

"I'm trying."

"I wrote letters, but you know the time that passes with letters posted at sea. A year passed, and the first letter that I received told of a baby boy, our son she'd named Kees, named after her grandfather, she said. I didn't even know she was with child. None of the earlier letters had ever reached me." There was a break in his voice, and Caleb's eyes looked past Lydia. Lamp light flickered gold on his face.

"What happened Caleb? Tell me."

He did look to her then, deeply, and sadly. "That one letter I received had been scribbled by Anna the morning after Kees was born. The letter said nothing about how difficult the birth was or how weak it had left Anna, only that we had a beautiful boy. It wasn't until I returned here to Sainte Eustatius that I learned she had died. Her body simply gave out less than twenty-four hours after giving birth."

In spite of the close tavern air, Lydia felt the chill tremble through her. "I'm so sorry," she said. "What about the baby, Kees?"

A smile came to Caleb's face before it faded.

"It's ironic, really, but I didn't see it then. I left Kees here with his grandparents, just as your father had done to you. They resisted my seeing him from the start, but I did. He was healthy and strong looking, with hair the color of honey, like his mother's. His eyes though … those were mine, not quite blue. But what did I know of raising a son? All I knew was the sea. So, I ran to what I knew."

"But you came back. When?"

"I was gone a year before I came around to my senses. I had loved Anna no matter how short our time together was, and she had given me a son. I couldn't shake that thought. Then one day I handed your father a letter. I knew it was from you, for I recognized your script, and I wondered if your father truly understood how much you had missed him when you were young and he'd spent all those months away. That's when I decided. I wanted Kees to know his father. And I want to know him. So I came back six months ago."

"So where is he, Kees? How old is he? Can I meet him?"

"He's nearly three. He's with his grandmother at the moment."

"But I thought ..."

On the table, the lantern light went out, and Lydia struggled with the waiting as the tavern girl replaced their lantern with another. With a match, the girl lit the fresh wick. The new light fluttered to life, but Lydia saw that Caleb rubbed at the muscle in his neck.

"The boy's grandparents did not take lightly to my request for Kees. They suggested I live on the plantation in a small cottage near the main house. They have agreed to allow Kees to stay with me in the cottage because there at least they can continue to be a part of the boy's life. It seemed like a perfectly sound arrangement. In hindsight, it was foolish to think it could work."

"But you are with your son. Why is that foolish?"

"The VanWaals have made it clear that I am still not welcome. I am a stranger there but for Kees. So I played with the idea of going to sea again. I thought Kees could have come along. And I would have been no stranger on a ship."

"But you turned the British oaf down."

At last a real smile brought a sparkle to Caleb's eyes. "Yes, Hartley was truly an oaf. But aside from that, I decided I couldn't bring Kees to sea. He is still too young. I could not put him in all that danger. You would like him, Lydia." He leaned back then in his chair, more like the relaxed Caleb who had walked in with her. "Kees is gentle, and he adores me, I think."

"So what will you do now?"

"I don't know. I have a little money set aside. Perhaps I'll buy a piece of land and farm. It's what I should have done from the start."

"Do you ever think of returning to Boston? To live there?"

"No, I don't." He reached to the tankard of ale and lifted it to his lips, taking a long swallow. "I buried my mother in Boston, up on the hill. I have no reason to return."

"But you grew up there. It was your home."

"Your father's ship was my home."

"Yes, I suppose it was. All the same …"

"You're not one to speak of home," he said while resting an arm again over the back of the chair beside him. "You're sitting here in the Caribbean a stroll away from your own merchant ship. I don't see you clinging to a hearth. It seems that for you the Prudence is now home."

"Yes, I have my ship, but I'm confused, Caleb."

"Confused? You?"

She smiled because she understood. But the smile wasn't real and did not last. "I killed two men," she said, "I don't ever want to have to do that again."

"You were under attack. You did what you had to do in order to save your own life. Hardly an argument for giving up everything you ever wanted."

Lydia reached from habit to touch the necklace that wasn't there, and she let the hand rest at her collarbone. "It's more than that, Caleb. I don't want to end up alone, drifting like jetsam on a current, like my father. I used to miss him, but now I think I'm just angry. I haven't seen him in four years. He hasn't even come back to see his own mother, and she's getting old. And here I am taking Ethan and leaving her behind. I'm no better than my cursed father."

Caleb sat straighter, a stream of air blowing out over his lips. "You're going back to Ponokanet to stay, aren't you?"

"I didn't know it until this moment, but yes. I'm going home."

Thirty-Nine

The night lay thick with the scent of orchids that drifted down from the forested hillside of Sainte Eustatius. The daytime crowd had disappeared. As Lydia walked with Caleb back toward the ship, she heard only the scuff of their own footsteps on the cobblestone. Something had changed. Somewhere between her stories and Caleb's, a new warmth built thread upon thread, and she saw clearly now – what had come to sit inside her heart was love. Yet, here she was about to go home. Her time with Caleb was done.

They came so soon to the wharf, and Lydia stopped at the foot of the boarding plank that would return her to the Prudence. Above them, on deck, she saw the dark and motionless form, Ethan in silhouette beneath the dim light of a quarter moon.

She turned to Caleb, studied his face, the straight Anglican nose, the full soft lip. "I've missed you," she said. "I've missed our talks together very much."

"I still can't believe you are here"

"But we're saying good-bye, aren't we?"

"Perhaps I could take Kees for a sail sometime, to show him Massachusetts Bay and visit a friend."

"I'd like that."

His lips brushed lightly on her cheek, lingered so slightly before he stepped away. "Good-bye, Lydia. I wish you only happiness."

She nodded, then made her way alone up the boarding plank. She longed to look back, to draw her eyes over Caleb one last time, but she would not. His life was here now, on Sainte Eustatius with his son. Caleb was lost to her again. A sting of tears threatened behind her eyes, until no matter how hard she blinked, tears started, a silent line down her cheek as she traveled forward along the plank.

"Good night, Ethan," she said without meeting the question in his eyes.

She closed the cabin door, slid the bolt shut.

A rap sounded at her door.

"Go to bed, Ethan."

His usual second rap.

Lydia lay down upon the bed, and she pulled her knees to her chest. Why had their paths crossed if it meant only to lose Caleb again? A cry curled from her throat, and she did not hear the thud of Ethan's boots, the leather heels as he crossed the deck, as he walked down the boarding plank away from the ship.

Ethan turned north at the end of the wharf, followed the moonlit road toward the village. When ahead of him he recognized the form of Caleb Willoughby, he quickened his stride. In front of the tavern, before Caleb could climb the step and go inside, Ethan reached from behind and set his great hand on Caleb's shoulder.

Caleb spun around, drew a pistol from beneath his waistcoat, the barrel staring back at Ethan.

Hands held high, Ethan stood firm and waited for recognition to show on Caleb's face.

The barrel lowered.

"Damnation, Ethan. I could have blown a hole straight through you."

One giant hand remained high in the air, while with the other Ethan gestured for Caleb to come with him, to follow him.

"What is it? Is it Lydia? Is she all right?"

Ethan turned on the road, certain his opinion of Caleb would prove correct, that Caleb would follow him back to the ship. To Lydia. But a gun fired from within the tavern.

A small lean man staggered out through the tavern door, came to a listing stop at the edge of the stoop. He was without a coat and the bared white shirt stood out ghostlike in the meager moonlight, all but for the dark circle of blood on the shirt's center. The man looked to Ethan and to Caleb, stumbled, listing more to the right and fell from the platform to the ground.

Caleb lowered onto one knee, bent to examine the sprawled body. But a second man, older, in a broad hat, swaggered from the tavern onto the stoop.

"Ya swindlin' bastard," the words slurred from the man who stood now with the wide stance of a sailor on a rough sea. He waved a smooth-bore pistol in the air until his gaze fell upon Caleb. "Clear out. This ain't yer fight," he said with as much muster as the consumed liquor allowed.

Ethan eyed the pistol still held in Caleb's hand, saw Caleb's thumb go to the hammer. A click and Caleb raised the pistol – barrel to barrel with that of the man who stood just above him. "Now take it easy, old man," said Caleb.

"I told yer ta clear out," words rolling off the drunkard's tongue, the barking iron aimed square for Caleb.

A click from the drunkard's gun, the hammer set. And Ethan made one quick step in front, a solid shield.

A shot exploded.

The pain was instant, a torch piercing his chest. He was falling. Caleb's arms took hold, and the night went black.

Forty

Lydia pulled the last of the hairpins, and with a toss of her head the loosened strands fell long and black to below her shoulders. Already she had rid herself of the blue linen skirt, replacing that with her breeches and shirt. Too many tears had been spent. Tears changed nothing. She leaned to the wash bowl, splashed the cool water onto her swollen eyes.

What she needed was to be gone, on with her journey home, the feel of the fresh breeze and the Prudence cutting through the open seas, all on the morrow. She'd scarcely completed the thought when a thud of boots – several pair – clamored on deck, then came to a halt. Only one set of footsteps approached her cabin.

A rap sounded on her door.

"Ethan?"

"No, Lydia. It's Caleb."

Hand held to her chest, Lydia looked about the cabin as if there in that room she'd find the reason why Caleb was here.

"I have Ethan," he called from his side of the door. "I've brought him back to the ship."

"What do you mean back to the ship?" She crossed the cabin to the door, pulled the bolt aside and opened the door, only to see Caleb's blood-stained jacket and bloodied hands. "Good God."

"It's not me," said Caleb. "It's Ethan. He's been shot."

"Where is he?" But Lydia did not wait for the answer before stepping past Caleb. She hurried toward the starboard, toward the shadow-like figures of six village men who had carried Ethan from the street and huddled now in a small circle. Morley appeared, and he stepped in among Lydia and the men.

Lydia knelt to where Ethan lay sprawled and still. Morley held a lantern high to cast light across the stilled body, and Lydia set her hand on Ethan's chest where it had pooled with warm thick blood.

"Ethan," she whispered, but there was no response. Holding his giant hand in her own small one, she felt with her other for a sign of life pulsing at the side of his great muscled neck. A pulse came slow, too faint, and Lydia called out his name, "Ethan."

The lantern came nearer, its yellow light dim on Ethan's face.

"Ethan," she called, begging for an answer.

His eyes rolled beneath the lids.

"Ethan, stay with me. Stay with me, do you hear? I'll have Morley get some bandages."

A weak pressure gripped her hand. His eyes opened, and his gaze held on her face. In the eyes of this mute friend, he so practiced in speaking without words, showed a look that spoke of love. Never before had anyone looked to Lydia with such feeling. Tears that did not seem her own fell upon his shirt.

"I love you, too." As she spoke, Ethan slowly lifted his hand, reaching out past Lydia. "He's looking for you, Caleb."

"I'm here," said Caleb, and he, too, knelt close.

Ethan clutched Caleb's hand, and the hand belonging to that giant of a man shook in its weakness as it placed Caleb's hand onto Lydia's.

"I'll take care of her, Ethan. You have my word."

"No," cried Lydia, and she held hard to his shoulders. "You are not going anywhere, Ethan. Do you hear me?"

His mouth formed, as if for the first time he might speak, but only a bubble appeared. The bubble broke and a dribble of red pooled at his lip.

"Ethan. No. Stay with me." But not even her pleading could alter the wide cold stare that had fallen over his eyes.

She held to the shoulders and pulled herself against him. Her body trembled. She heard the scuffle of feet but did not look up. Rather, she looked within and saw the two of them, Ethan and herself rowing Ralph's whaleboat out into the bay. The sun was shining hot and both their bodies glistened with sweat and youth.

There came a touch upon her arm. "Lydia, let me help you."

"No. No, I'm fine," she said, and she clung tighter to Ethan.

"No, you're not." Caleb took hold of her arms and gently lifted. "It's all right, Lydia, let him go." And Ethan slid from her as she rose up. Caleb pulled her to him, his arms holding securely around her.

"He saved my life," said Caleb while still holding Lydia within his arms. "Your friend, Ethan had come to fetch me. He wanted me to follow him, but there was a scene. A gun aimed at me ..." Though Caleb paused, he did not lessen his hold and his breath was warm at the side of her face. "I'm sorry, Lydia. Your friend died to save me."

Her eyes had become accustomed to the night, and as she stepped away from Caleb's embrace and looked about the ship, she could see that the village men were gone. Morley stood at the starboard rail, at the far side of Ethan's body.

"I must take care of him," said Lydia, crouching down to dear Ethan. With a touch that lingered, she smoothed her fingers over his opened eyes so that the lids closed. "Good night, Ethan. I shan't say goodbye."

She stood, drawing away this time from the hand Caleb offered. "This wasn't your fault," she said. "What he did was just Ethan being Ethan." And she walked around the giant's body to Morley.

"This be a sad night," said Morley.

"Yes. And it appears I shall need your assistance awhile longer,

Morely. We'll need to prepare Ethan's body. He'll need to be bathed and put into fresh clothes. We'll need a casket box made ready for a burial. I'll make arrangements first thing come morning light. We will sail on the afternoon high tide as planned, after the new mast is stepped sturdy into place. Can you help with those tasks?"

"For certain, Miss. It'll take me but a minute to toss a man or two from his hammock to help us with the job. A shame is what it is," he said as he shuffled away, the lantern swinging in his hand. "A damn shame."

When Morley disappeared below deck, Lydia went to Caleb. "I thank you for bringing Ethan back to me," she said. "But, I'm going to be all right. You ought to go home to your little boy."

"I'm not leaving you. My promise to Ethan was real. I will sail with the Prudence, to return you safely to Ponokanet."

"I don't need your assistance. My crew may be few, but they are skilled. And trustworthy. I shall be fine."

"I don't believe you heard me."

"Go home, Caleb. You have Kees. You have a life here." She started for her cabin, but all blood seemed to be leaving her head. Her knees wobbled. Caleb stepped in, swept her up into his arms just as her knees gave out.

"What you need is a bed and rest," he said.

"No. I …"

"It'll do no good to argue."

Caleb tucked the two of them through the cabin door.

He pulled down the coarse blanket that served as top-quilt, and he set Lydia on the bed. "You need sleep, but I don't imagine it will come," he said while one at a time he tugged at her boots, placing them on the floor at the foot of the bed.

"I only need a few minutes alone."

"Then take them," he said, pulling the blanket over her until it reached her chin. "I'm going to leave the ship for a short time. On my way, I'll tell Morley that I myself shall make the arrangements to bury Ethan. I will return here at dawn to escort you and Ethan's body to a small graveyard just beyond the village. You will like it there, I think, as a resting place for Ethan. It has the breeze from the sea and the smell of orchids from the hillside. Will you let me do that?"

Lydia bit back tears. "Yes," she said. "And I thank you."

"I don't like it that I'm leaving you alone. Should I have Morley come sit with you?"

"No. I'm fine. Or I will be. I prefer to be alone."

"Then I'll concede on that. But like it or not," he said while reaching for the cabin door, "I am sailing with you on the morrow."

"What about Kees?"

"I think the day has come for him to visit Massachusetts Bay." Sharply as that, Caleb stepped out and the door closed between them.

Forty-One

Lydia
On Ponokanet, June, 1764

At last, after so many days at sea, Lydia opened her eyes to the bedroom at the back of her grandmother's house. She was home, a comfortable fit, like an old shoe, and as she looked around the room, to the tall windows and the gentle light of dawn, new calm settled over her. But she was eager to start the day, to feel the familiar sand solid beneath her feet. She would fetch some eggs from the henhouse. Make a breakfast. Fresh.

She stood in the yard in the early sunlight when deciding to let the noise of making breakfast wait. She would walk and let the others sleep. Behind the barn she found the path that would take her to the mammoth stone. Needles of pine had covered the path during the weeks she'd been away, but the path was familiar. She could have found her way with eyes covered. The path ended at the back of the great stone.

Lydia walked to the very edge, and she looked to the waves that broke on the shore below. This day would be a difficult one for her grandmother. Constance had stood strong when told yesterday the news of Ethan. Her eyes had filled. "I'm so sorry. We both will miss him dearly," said Constance, and she'd held Lydia within her arms. But today, for her grandmother, the real knowing will set in.

And Caleb? What would happen now, with him, was not clear. During the days of the return sail, she had depended on him, depended

on his listening and his willingness to share her sadness. Each day she
and Caleb had worked side-by-side on deck. They'd stood together at
the rail in quiet conversation beneath a starlit night. And she adored
Kees. How long the two would stay here on Ponokanet she did not
know. This morning Caleb and his son were asleep in the room that
had been Ethan's. As for tomorrow, she held no answers.

In quiet rhythm, the sea gently rolled. The whir of breeze spoke
its own cadence through the pines, and suddenly Lydia felt not alone.
Ethan was near. She turned to search but there was no one. Yet ...

Footsteps, muffled by the needles, came then along the path,
and Caleb stepped out into the clearing.

"Your grandmother told me I might find you here," he said. "I
hurried to ..."

Lydia put up a hand. "Hush."

"What is it?"

"He's here. It's Ethan," she whispered, as she closed her eyes
to the movement of air that came with the warming sun.

"Lydia ..."

"No, really," she said. "He is here. I know it as strongly as I
know my own name. Not in body, of course. But he's here." Her voice
trailed away as her hand came to rest at her neck. She wanted to believe
it – the part that had lived inside that giant body had come home, a
soul released to return here to Ponokanet. Ethan loved this island. He
loved to roam its forest, one side to the other. Would it not be to these
high cliffs that Ethan would return?

Caleb walked to her side. "I hope you're right, Lydia. I hope
Ethan is here. And I'm happy for you, that you have this place. It
seems you will find peace here."

"I will," she murmured, her mind still away.

She looked to the deeper blue of northern water and knew that
she would always love the sea – the sight of it, the smell, the lap of its
wake against the ship. But when her hand lifted to where the necklace

had been, she knew, too, that the bones had surely shown her the right path. This sandy chunk of earth would forever be home.

She turned to Caleb, looking to the gray eyes and to fair hair that had not yet been pulled back to its customary tail at the nape. "What about you, Caleb? Where shall it be that you at last find peace?"

A darker gray came to the eyes. "That's what I came to speak with you about."

"Are you leaving?" Her heart suddenly loud. "So soon?"

"No. At least I hope not."

"That's good because I'm going to miss you and Kees terribly."

"Yes, Kees. He certainly has grown fond of you." Caleb pulled through his hair, glancing out over the water. "I left him sleeping. I'm afraid he'll sleep 'til noon after last night's excitement. But I met Constance in the kitchen on my way out. She said she would listen for him."

Lydia felt the smile pull at her lips. "They're friends already, aren't they?"

But Caleb did not share her smile.

"And so, you were going to tell me something," said Lydia. "Something about you leaving?"

"Yes. Well, no, it's not about leaving," he said. "You see … I'm not sure how to begin."

"Caleb, it's me, Lydia. Since when has there been concern about where to begin?"

"Since seeing you on the street of Sainte Eustatius. Since sitting across from you with the lamplight coloring the soft texture of your skin." He tried at a smile, but the smile came a bit crooked, and Caleb pulled again through his hair. "I had to think about this, you see. I had to understand the sudden change in the way I looked at you. When you were a small girl, we had been friends … you such a feisty little sprout. Then there you were … a woman, a beautiful courageous woman. But you were on your way home. And there was Kees to consider. There was no time." Caleb slipped a hand around hers, their faces now so close. "Suddenly, we were given time," he said. "And each day while on the Prudence, the truth became clearer. I had fallen in love with you." The back of his hand was soft on her cheek. Lightly his lips pressed on hers. "It's you, Lydia, not a place that will give me peace."

At last her own smile won out. "You don't know how happy that makes me." And she returned the tender hunger of his kiss.

Forty-Two

Sydney
The next morning, Thursday, September 6

Thursday early, Sydney follows the scent of freshly brewed coffee into the kitchen, and she finds Edward alone at the table reading *Newsweek*. "Your mother's already out, doing some errands," says Edward while closing the magazine.

Sydney thought Alison was still in bed because she's learned that Alison is not an early riser. But she dodges the subject and pours herself a cup of coffee. She thinks about taking the cup out onto the deck, but it is awkward, this Edward thing, this having him around twenty-four-seven. Fortunately, he is easy to be around. "It looks like it's going to be a nice day," she says when deciding to keep it pleasant and to sit across from Edward with her coffee.

"Yes, I think so," he says, but Sydney feels him watching as she sips her coffee. "Your mother told me about Everett," he adds, a touch of pink coming innocently to his cheeks. "It must have been difficult to hear."

"It was."

"It must have been difficult to tell, too, don't you think?"

A staunch supporter. Of course, he would be. Yet, Edward is also right. "I suppose it was," says Sydney, and she leaves it at that. Understanding Alison is too new, too undeveloped, more like an embryo than anything that could walk and talk and breathe on its own. So when the knock on the door comes from the front of the house,

Sydney is grateful for the interruption, and she escapes to answer the door.

Ty stands in the doorway.

She sticks her hands into her pockets and takes one step back because she's been avoiding Ty since being with him in his room of plants.

"I know it's early," says Ty, "but I wondered if you'd rather I didn't go to Boston with you and Everett today."

Her hands come out of the pockets, so that one pulls through her hair. "Are you saying you'd rather not go?"

"I thought you might want the day alone with Everett. Time without me sitting in, that's all."

"Oh," says Sydney, having to think too quickly. "No, really, I'd like you to go with us. I don't know what we'll hear. If it's not good news, it would help if you were there."

"Then I'll be back here at eleven."

"Thank you."

His eyes hold hers for one long moment before he turns and walks back across the drive.

It's just an hour later when Nora holds the ladder, and from a high rung Sydney pushes the sign onto two bolts. She's using the early morning to hang the sign over the office door. Also, she wants to talk to Nora about an idea for Dean Aviation. "You were right about Everett," says Sydney. "He is my father. I want to thank you for telling me."

"Yeah, Everett's pretty pleased about the whole thing." Nora's face tilts upward, her long blond braid falling at her back.

With a two-handed grip on the wrench, Sydney works a nut over each bolt. At the same time, she listens to Nora tell about breakfast that morning with Everett, that Everett seems upbeat, one of his better days. The final nut at last is tightened, and Sydney slips the wrench into the back pocket of her jeans before climbing down the ladder.

"You know," says Sydney. "You and I could save this airport. We could open a diner in the room behind the office. Offer a good breakfast to the pilots who fly in. Maybe some burgers later in the day. And we'd have to ramp up the flight school. To do that we need the flight instructor. Do you have that license?"

"Me? Hell, no. Couldn't afford one even if I wanted it."

"Would you go for the rating if I paid?"

"Why don't you go for the rating yourself?" says Nora while resting one hand on the ladder.

"Because I already have it."

"Well then?"

Sydney bites on her lip. They'd have to get into this sooner or later. It might as well be sooner. "I don't fly anymore."

Nora shakes her head. "What a cop-out." Nora picks up the ladder and carries it toward the hangar.

But Sydney isn't done with her own argument, and she matches Nora's stride. "Call it what you want, but I need your help. Everett needs your help."

"Look," says Nora, stopping just outside the hangar. "You and I both know how important this place is to Everett ... how much it'd mean to him right now to know he didn't have to worry ... to know that this place is on solid ground. Knowing that would give him good reason to kick the shit out of this cancer. And would I go for my instructor's rating if I thought it would help bring in business? You bet your ass I would. What I want to know is what excuse you use to make it okay for you not to do it."

The air between them might as well have exploded. Sydney's mouth opens, then closes.

"So you lost someone you loved," says Nora, relentless with her whipping. "You think you're the only one? You should take a walk through town, knock on a few doors and ask if anyone ever lost someone they loved. Then come back and tell me how sorry you feel for yourself."

Tears well in Sydney's eyes, and she turns on a heel, walks past the hangar to the car. But the car won't start. She's flooded the engine, and she curses, resting her head against the steering wheel.

But when Sydney looks up, Nora stands at the car's open window. "My guess is," says Nora, "whatever excuse you use is big or you would've told me off. So, if part of the plan is to get me that instructor's rating, then I'm in."

Forty-Three

Sydney
Boston, Thursday afternoon

A team of five specialists, each starch-stiff, sit around the table in the conference room. While Dr. Sasaki taps the table with the tip of a pen, Sydney balances at the edge of her chair, waits for Everett and Ty to pull their chairs in and settle. This will be the group to decide what best to do to keep Everett alive, and with that thought Sydney exhales, trying to calm nerves in her stomach.

Dr. Sasaki clears her throat. "There's good news," she says. "We have an antigen match." Seeming to need a check of the data, Dr. Sasaki glances at the folder in front of her. "Sydney, the HLA antigens from your blood sample match five out of six. A near impossible coincidence, but it means, if you are still willing and Everett decides to go ahead with the stem cell transplant, you make an ideal donor."

"That's wonderful," says Sydney as she looks to Everett.

Everett rubs his sharp knees and looks to Sydney, a small grin on his face. "The match is not a coincidence," he says. "For the record, I'd like to make it known here that Sydney is my daughter, a fact that she and I just learned ourselves. Now, that said ..." And Everett sits back in his chair, the weight of thought moving behind his eyes. "I'd like to talk about one of the trial procedures. I was reading about the man-made antibody. The one with the radioactive molecule. That procedure wouldn't require a donor. And it might be just as effective."

"It might. But it's still in clinical trial. The true effectiveness is not thoroughly known or proven." She gives statistical data, how many have lived, how many not. "And," she adds at the very end, "it is still my opinion that a stem cell transplant has the best chance for success in your case. As ironic as it sounds, you're general health is still pretty good. There are no signs of infection such as a cold or respiratory problems. You have had no other forms of cancer prior to the lymphoma. Also, we now have an ideal donor willing to go ahead. I believe I am correct in saying it is the recommendation of this team to go with the stem cell transplant."

Four medical heads nod in agreement. Each speaks in turn, saying what amounts to a yes, stem cells are the way to go.

Everett looks to Sydney, his face gray and tired.

"I want to do this," says Sydney.

A long moment passes before Everett nods. "Okay. When do we start?"

"We'd like to have you admitted here on Saturday."

"That soon?" he asks.

"We need to start while your health is still good." Dr. Sasaki removes her glasses and sets them on the thick stack of papers that constitute Everett's medical file. "We'll start the chemotherapy doses Monday. The entire series takes about three weeks. So, Sydney, in two weeks I'll start you on five days of a medication that will increase the number of stem cells your body is releasing into your bloodstream."

"Then what?" asks Sydney. "How do you actually get the stem cells from me to Everett?"

"It's quite simple, really. On the day of the transplant, we'll take blood from a large vein, most likely the vein in your neck or in the chest area. As the blood is taken from you, it passes through a machine that removes the stem cells. From there the blood, minus its stem cells, is returned to you. The donated stem cells are then given to Everett in much the same way, inserted through a tube. The procedure takes four or five hours to complete.

"What about side effects for the donor?" asks Ty.

Sydney turns to Ty, sees the almost imperceptible narrowing of his eyes.

"The procedure is relatively painless," says Dr. Sasaki. "While we are taking her blood, Sydney may feel some lightheadedness. Some chills. Occasionally, people get numbness around their mouth. But the procedure requires no anesthesia. But Sydney," and the doctor looks to her, "you can expect a greater side effect from the medication you'll take beforehand. It can cause bone and muscle aches, headaches, sometimes difficulty sleeping. But these effects generally stop within two or three days of stopping the medication."

"So for a week I rest," says Sydney. "It sounds too easy."

"For you, relatively, it is."

The car crosses the canal onto the Cape, hums along the highway, the oaks and pines shorter, scrubbier than on the mainland. There's been little talk in the car. Everett has been asleep, and it seems Ty wants to honor the quiet as much Sydney. But Everett's head jerks involuntarily. Then he rubs his bald scalp. He is awake.

"There. I'm feeling better," he says.

"Could you handle a short visit to the sheriff's ranch?" asks Ty. "There's something there I'd like Sydney to see."

"Sure," says Everett, though he rests his head back against the seat. "I'm actually feeling pretty good."

Ty pulls off the highway onto a twisty road. They drive through a midsection of the Cape that Sydney doesn't recognize, and she asks Ty, "What am I going to see?"

"You'll have to wait." His grin shows in the rearview mirror just as the car turns into a long driveway. They pass a clapboard house, and when they stop in front of a red barn, three teenage boys walk across the yard. They stare at Everett's unfamiliar car, until Ty steps out of it.

"Hey, Ty," a boy shouts while running toward the car, and the others follow.

"I thought you wouldn't be back until tomorrow," says the smaller of the boys.

"That was the plan," says Ty, "but I wanted someone to meet our new Annie."

Sydney leans forward from her place in the back seat, asking Everett, "What is this place?"

"It's a program for young kids. Boys in trouble with the law. Every kid here's been a pain in the butt to the system long enough to earn a long-term stay on the ranch. Ty gives them three afternoons a week. He teaches them how to ride and how to care for the horses."

Ty walks back to the car. "Come on," he says while opening the back door. "I'd like you to meet Annie."

When Sydney looks to Everett, Everett waves her on.

Ty introduces her to the three boys, and the three follow along into the red barn. Inside, another teen is busy grooming a horse and a fifth is pushing a wheelbarrow in through the back door. Ty says hello to both.

"They're each assigned to a horse," says Ty. "So if they're not in the classroom, they're out here in the barn."

Ty leads her to the far end, to the very last stall. He slides the latch bolt and opens the gate. "Sydney, meet Annie."

A spotted mare stands protectively in front of a spindle-legged foal. "Our newest member," says Ty. "Go ahead in. Just kneel down."

Down on one knee, Sydney watches the foal wobble out from behind its mother. "Hello, Annie," says Sydney at not much more than a whisper. The foal moves close, and Sydney holds the tiny muzzle in the cup of her hand. "I've never seen anything so adorable in my life."

"She was born last night. I drove up early this morning to have a look at her," says Ty, who stands close by the gate with five teenage boys at his side. "Annie will be Eric's responsibility while he's here. It's a good match," adds Ty while resting one hand on Eric's shoulder. "Eric has a gentle way with the horses."

A smile spreads on the boy's face, and he clearly stands taller.

"You ready to go?" asks Ty.

Sydney looks again at the new foal. "Only if I have to."

When she backs away, the foal returns to its mother, shoving the tiny muzzle up onto a nipple, and Sydney laughs aloud.

The ranch is all they talk about the rest of the way home. At Everett's they eat soup and crusty bread that Ty has picked up at the market while driving through Orleans. Even Everett spoons the soup, until eventually he says, "I have to go to bed."

At the door he wraps Sydney in frail arms. "No matter what happens, Syd, you've been a gift, and I appreciate what you're doing. I want you to know that."

"It doesn't come close to what you've done for me."

Everett shoos them out. The thick drops of rain are a surprise. A gust of wind pushes them toward the green truck.

Forty-Four

By the time Ty pulls up in front of the porch, wind is whipping rain against the windshield. Sydney looks through the wet blur of the yard. "Thanks for driving," she says. "And thanks for Annie."

His smile shows white even in the absence of stars or moon. "I thought you'd like her."

"Where did you learn about horses?"

"At that private school in Canada. I taught French and math, but the program involved a lot of outdoor work, including taking care of horses."

Sydney turns, just enough to lean against the door. "Has anyone ever told you you're an interesting man? You're like an onion with layers that just keep peeling away."

"We all are, don't you think?"

"I suppose." She is aware of the drum of rain on the metal roof, soothing, reminding her of sleeping in a tent, camping with Rick in the Sierra Nevada.

Ty has settled back against the seat, one knee leaning against the stick shift. "Most of the things I've done," he says, "I did because I was still searching."

"For your mother?"

"No. The search for my mother took only a few weeks."

"Then what were you searching for?"

"Peace. Who I was. A place."

And did you find all those things?" asks Sydney, comfortable and somehow safe in this small space of the truck.

"I found out who I was ... what I stand for in the middle of everything else. After that, the rest just fell in line."

"That's what I'm doing now, isn't it?"

"Seems to be."

Sydney leans to the window. "A year ago I thought I had all that ... the peace and a place. I thought I knew exactly what I wanted. Then it all changed."

"Holding on to who you are can be tough," said Ty, "like tending a sailboat in rough water. Perceptions bounce around." His eyes hold on her face. A gust of wind blows rain.

Sydney looks out at the blackness. "What would you say if I told you that sometimes I feel my grandmother near me? That once, a few days ago, I even heard her talk to me?"

"I'd say, who knows what's possible."

Sydney crosses her arms and rubs, suddenly chilled by the dampness. "I know it was only the wind, and yet ..."

"So, you don't believe she really spoke to you?"

"I don't know. It sounds a little weird to say it out loud."

"So, what if I told you I think souls coexist all around us?"

"You do?"

Ty merely nods.

"I'd like to believe that," says Sydney, almost inaudible under the pummel of rain. "But honestly, I think it's just wishful thinking, a fairy tale like the Easter bunny and Santa Claus."

"Maybe."

"Dust to dust. That's what I think," says Sydney when resting her head against the window. A sheet of rain blows across the same window, and she flinches. "I'd forgotten that Cape Cod rain can blow sideways."

"It's a good old Northeaster."

"And it's been another long day. I should go inside." Sydney opens the truck door, climbs out into the rain. Ducking her head in one last time, she says, "Good night," then beelines onto the porch.

All night, wind thrashes the house, while Sydney lies in bed staring through the dark. What Ty said about souls – Sydney tries to imagine souls swirling around, perhaps even in this room. Swirling everywhere. And this makes her smile because the image is silly. If all the people that ever lived, billions and billions, if they were swirling around, imagine the stir. Every night would be like tonight, with wind thrashing from all the swirling of souls.

Forty-Five

Maddie
New York City, August of 1832

When Estelle Davenport eyed the clock, her eyebrows knit to a point, and she plucked her straw bonnet from the hat tree. To close shop at ten in the morning was no way to run a business, but she could see no alternative. Something was wrong. Her young employee, Margaret, was a good worker. Dependable. In the near to two years she'd been employed in the dress shop, Margaret had never once been late. Yet, Monday the woman had not come in at all. And here it was mid-morning on Tuesday and still not so much as a word sent.

Estelle worried that the little girl, Margaret's daughter, might be ill. Madeline, or Maddie as the mother called her, had been born just weeks before Margaret started work in the shop. At first the small thing had simply been brought along to the dress shop in a basket where she slept most of the day. But when the child started to crawl and demand much of her mother's time, Estelle had helped to find a sitter, a widow that lived just three doors down from the dress shop, and Maddie had begun spending her day hours away with the sitter. Estelle had missed the baby's presence as much as Margaret did, missed the opportunity to hold the soft sweet bundle on the few occasions when she would cry. And oh, the unspoken envy she had felt while listening to the teary-eyed mother go on about the difficulties of working while raising a child. Estelle had grown attached to that little child.

Estelle turned the sign, showing CLOSED through the glass of the shop door, stepped out and locked the door. Dropping the key into her satin reticule, she pulled the drawstring shut and started down Orange Street towards the tenements of New York City. The sidewalk was already dusty and scorching. All of August had been this way. Day after day, the sun baked down without mercy upon the streets and shops, wood and brick alike.

With a nod of her head, she greeted Mr. Hoffman who washed the window outside his bakery, and she hurried on. At Five Corners, where Orange met with Park, she crossed, making way between the hack drivers and their bony horses. She kept her eyes forward as she passed the door fronts of keno houses and grog shops, one after another until she came to the tenements of Pearl Street.

Were she not so concerned, she'd go no farther. Here on Pearl Street the squalor of swine rooting in garbage was made worse by the overcrowding of tenement living. Since the Irish, many of the once lovely homes and business fronts had been sectioned off into tiny spaces, rented out to the immigrants and the poor. Some families, so Estelle had heard, huddled in with as many as eight or ten living in one room. Her husband, Henry, had talked of moving farther out from the crowded district. Easier it was for him to consider, he being a reporter for the *Tribune*. But for Estelle, moving elsewhere was impossible. Ten years of her life had been devoted to the dress shop. The business of sewing apparel for New York's wealthier women had become quite sound. Henry knew it as well as she – the shop was a success because of her own business sense and her knack for dressing the city's well-to-do. Every few months the argument would reappear, but each time, in the end, Henry had agreed to stay in their quarters there above the shop on Orange Street.

The ground floor at 424 Pearl Street was yet another grog shop, and Estelle skirted around the shabby doorway, looking up to the third story windows. She pondered which window it was that Margaret's late husband, the Mr. O'Brien, had leapt out before falling face down onto the street. Poor Margaret had shared the details of that story sometime after she'd begun work at the shop. It seems Mr. O'Brien was an artist, traveling from town to town in search of portraits to paint. That was how Margaret had met him. He'd been to Massachusetts, far out on the peninsula of Cape Cod, in a small village where Margaret lived.

The name of the village Estelle could not recall as she looked to the high windows, but the name didn't matter. What mattered was that while having her portrait painted, Margaret had fallen in love. With an Irish Catholic. "You can well imagine the ruckus," said Margaret in telling the story, and in fact Estelle could very well imagine. It didn't take the emotion-packed heart of a parent to know that a Catholic of any sort and a New England Congregationalist could not mix – not for long. But as it was, religion had not been the wedge between Margaret and her husband. It was his moods. The man suffered from vast swings across high to low, but the young Margaret had not witnessed the extreme lows until she'd already run off to New York and married the man, cutting herself off from her family's affection, for Margaret's own father apparently refused to communicate at all. Yet, Margaret did assert that times were not all bad. When her husband's mood had been at his best, he painted with a flourish and business would be quite good. However, the down times grew more frequent, and it was during one of those long dark periods that the man had thrown himself out the window.

Coward is what he was. Imagine leaving a wife and soon-to-be-born child that way.

In the narrow alley between the grog shop and the tenement next door, Estelle found two boys busy at the game of mumblety-peg, one tossing the knife so its blade stuck straight into the parched soil.

"Do you know a Mrs. Margaret O'Brien?" asked Estelle.

"Aye. She lives there. Up two flights, top floor," said one as he pointed to the outdoor stairway at the back of the grog shop.

Estelle climbed carefully, for the stairs were rickety and she did not wish for a splinter from the rail. When she knocked on the door, no voice answered from inside. She knocked again. Still no one – neither the patter of feet nor sounds of chatter that one might expect with a two-year-old running about. Only the dissonant tune, a drunkard's song, wafted up from two floors below. When Estelle tried the latch, surprisingly, the door swung open.

The stench struck her first. Not the smell of soured, old filth. In fact, the room she entered was particularly clean and organized despite the congested accumulation of table and shelves and a wide wooden chest. The stench was that of rotting flesh. As Estelle raised a hand to her nose in effort to block the suffocating odor, she spied the source. On the far side of the room, half hidden behind the chest was a mattress set on the floor. At first only the woman's legs were visible, but Estelle crept closer, forcing herself forward until she could view the entire length of the body.

The bitter taste of bile rose in her throat. Yet, the scene was so gruesome, she could not turn her eyes away. Margaret O'Brien lay clad only in a white cotton nightgown. The taut skin of face and arms and feet had turned black, the entire body bloated as if filled by a fire's bellows. Clearly a death by cholera.

And lying with Margaret, her tiny body curled around the dead woman's head, was the little girl but two years old. All that moved were the fingers of one dainty little hand, tiny dimples creasing each knuckle, fingers that twisted back and forth on a lock of her mother's dark hair. The child's hair, however, was not so dark but red, short and tight with curls, eyes wide-set and green, eyes nearly swollen shut from crying or lack of sleep or both. Estelle could only guess how long the child had lain there by a mother cold and dead. Because cholera was an expedient death, a person could fall sick and die in as few as twelve hours or as many as twenty-four. Margaret's death might have been during the night or as long ago as two days prior. And all that length of time the child had been on her own. The thought of it tore at Estelle's heart.

"It's all right, Maddie. You're going to be just fine." Estelle spoke softly while reaching for the child. But the child clutched tightly to the mother's hair. Each time Estelle tried freeing those tiny fingers, the child screamed the one word, "Mama," and clenched her fist all the tighter around the hair. "Come now, Sweetie. Come see Estelle. We'll take care of Mama, but first come see Estelle." On and on she spoke, pleading gently even as the child cried out, sobbing now as Estelle unraveled hair from her fingers. At last the tiny hand was freed, and Estelle lifted the girl into her arms.

Quickly, she went to the door and stepped out to the top of the stairs. The air, as hot as it was, helped clear her head of the horrendous odor. The child's crying had lessened but the little chest rose and fell in short, broken breaths while the arms wrapped around Estelle's neck. Maddie smelled of soiled diaper. She needed to be washed. Days could have passed since she'd had either food or drink. Estelle needed to do something, and it was only a matter of seconds before she knew exactly what.

"Young man." She called down to the boy who played in the alley. "As fast as you can, go and fetch a constable. I saw one at the corner of Park. Tell him it's another case of cholera. Mrs. O'Brien is dead."

With the child clinging, the sweaty face hot against Estelle's neck, she went back inside. Hastily, she found a child's faded dress, looking much like a hand-me-down, wrinkled but clean inside the chest. She folded it and placed it within the bodice of her blouse only a moment before the constable's boots thumped on the stairway.

"Mrs. O'Brien is behind the chest, Constable. I've covered her with a blanket which I found on the shelf." What she didn't say was that she had covered Margaret so that the child would not have to look any longer at a mother who had left this world.

The constable cursed when looking to the far side of the chest. The child called out, "Mama," and the constable turned to Estelle.

"If you don't mind," said Estelle, "I'd like to answer any questions you have as quickly as possible so that I can get myself and my daughter out and away from this smell."

Maddie whimpered all the way to Orange Street, but Estelle patted the child's back, talked of milk and biscuits until, with her one free hand, she unlocked the door to the shop. She left the CLOSED sign as it was and ignored the work that waited in the back sewing room as she climbed the stairs to the kitchen of her apartment on the second floor.

"We're going to heat some water for your bath. And get you a cup of milk. Would you like that, Maddie?"

The tears stopped sometime during the preparation. But the child's face was smeared with sticky mucous, and there was the fear of a startled animal in those beautiful green eyes. "I know you want your Mama." Estelle spoke as she moved about the kitchen. With the child resting on Estelle's one hip, Estelle filled the teapot with water, struck a match and lit the stove. "Your mommy is gone, Maddie. She was sick, very sick, and she had to go away. You're too little to understand all this now, but I'm going to take care of you. You'll be all right." She filled a cup with milk and found a biscuit from last night's dinner. It was while she held the child in her lap, held the cup to the child's lips and watched her sip, that Estelle took a deep breath and admitted the enormity of what she had done.

"Are you mad? You can't just walk away with someone else's child."

"Henry, that someone is dead."

"Yes, from cholera. What if the child gets it? And you?"

Estelle and her husband stood at the side of the makeshift bed created from a bureau drawer. In the drawer was the sleeping child, so Estelle lowered her voice. "Henry, the city is full of cholera. We might fall prey to it with or without Maddie. I figure that's in the Lord's hand. But He's clearly put the child in mine. I couldn't just leave her there."

"Of course you could have. You should have, Estelle."

"What you mean is, you'd rather I had left that little waif alone and on her own to become just another Pearl Street guttersnipe, begging and thieving in order to survive."

"She wouldn't have been put out on the street. She's too young. The authorities would have found her a home."

"With whom? If there's no relative to take them in, the orphans have no one. You know that. The streets are full of them. Henry, think about it. I don't even recall the name of the village Margaret was from, so I couldn't give the authorities a place to look for any relatives, even if they do exist. Margaret's own mother has been dead for years. Margaret told me so herself. And her father has had nothing to do with her since her marriage to that Irishman. As I see it, the child has no one, except for me. And we have had no children. I believe this is God's way, Henry. We've been given a little girl. Her name is Maddie."

Forty-Six

Maddie
Four months later, December, 1832

In December, while Maddie played on the carpet stacking wooden checkers, Estelle shuffled through the letters just delivered. Two were addressed to Henry. The third, written in an open feminine script, was a letter addressed to Estelle. She sat on the Sheraton chair with its tapered legs and lyre-shaped back, and she studied the unfamiliar handwriting. The return address in the upper left was written as *Wells Creek, Massachusetts*. It was a town name Estelle had not remembered, but now seeing it there in script, the name startled her so greatly that she set the letter down. She rose from the chair to pour a cup of tea, took a cracker from the tin and gave the cracker to Maddie, pushing a coil of curls back from that round little face before returning to the letter. Only then did she break the seal and unfold the page.

Dear Mrs. Davenport,

It is my greatest hope that this letter reaches you and that you can be of assistance. My name is Beatrice Chase. I am sister-in-law to an employee of yours, Margaret O'Brien. Margaret was never very good at correspondence. However, she did write to me on occasion, and your name was once mentioned in her telling how she did enjoy her position in your dress shop. I have not heard from Margaret in nearly a year; whereas, I myself have posted two letters since summer. As you can well imagine, my concern is growing. I do not mean to meddle if it is Margaret's decision to remain apart from her father and her brothers, but I do wish to know if she and little Madeline are well. Would you be so kind as to inform me of their welfare.

Most sincerely,
Mrs. Beatrice Chase
Wells Creek, Massachusetts

The letter dropped to Margaret's lap.

A deafening pulse pounded in her ear. She went to the child – her child now, and she scooped Maddie up into her arms. Maddie's face was spattered with cracker crumbs, her cheeks red as cherries from the brisk December outings with Alice, the young woman that now helped out in the dress shop.

So much love invested. And the lies to friends and neighbors, to anyone who asked, saying Maddie had been taken in, all legal through the channels. But now, with this letter ... a relative ...

She called to Alice. She bundled the child against the soft snow that fell outside and placed her into her carriage. As the two, Alice and Maddie, left for a stroll along Orange Street, Estelle waved through the glass, and she felt the relief of her decision. Circumstances need not, in deed would not change. But she must act quickly.

From the office desk, Estelle withdrew ink and pen, and she placed them methodically on its flat surface. Then the stationery. She adjusted the chair, pulled it closer to the desk before dipping the pen to ink.

Dear Mrs. Chase,
It is my deepest regret to inform you of the death of Margaret O'Brien.

Setting the pen down, Estelle considered what more to say. When the words had been well planned, she dipped the pen again and continued.

This past August, Margaret and the child, Madeline, were stricken by cholera, a dreadful disease that took both their lives. It was I who found them lying together on the bed in Margaret's home. Except to say there had been a rift due to her marriage, Margaret never spoke of home or family in Massachusetts, and as the husband, Mr. O'Brien, was previously deceased, there was no known family we could notify. I was greatly saddened by Margaret's death. She had become friend as well as employee. Please accept my deepest condolences.

Yours truly,

Mrs. Estelle Davenport

With the blotter, Estelle patted the wet ink. She then folded the letter and addressed it to Mrs. Beatrice Chase at Wells Creek, Massachusetts. From the rack by the door, she gathered her wool coat and slipped it on. Her letter of response she put into the wide pocket. The letter received by her from Welles Creek was picked up and carried to the coal stove where Estelle tossed the letter in. The page burst into yellow flame, crinkled only a moment before disintegrating as ash.

Estelle went to the door and turned the sign to CLOSED before heading out to post her letter of condolence.

Forty-Seven

Maddie
Sixteen years later, July of 1848

Maddie, at age eighteen, was among the youngest of attendees at the lyceum that day, but she was not put off. Wearing her simple white linen work dress, she inched her way between shoulders, struggling to catch a glimpse of the speaker, Agatha Lamb.

"And injustice will continue unless we, the other half of creation, unite together, and unite we will."

The lyceum was bursting at the seams, with women standing like packed pins behind those more fortunate seated on the benches.

"Our history is one of repeated injuries, mankind seizing both power and privilege without thought to his degradation of women."

Even those with the luxury of a bench seat were now on their feet, cheering in agreement with the speaker, and from the tips of her laced boots, Maddie stretched tall so that she might see between the forest of pearl-studded turbans and brimmed bonnets. Stretching, however, was futile, and she gave out a great sigh of frustration. She hadn't walked all that way, given the single hour she had been granted away from the sewing, simply to listen. Determined, Maddie hitched up her skirt and climbed the nearest bench.

Agatha Lamb was slender, and in fact, rather severe in appearance. Near fifty, if Maddie were to guess. Yet, Miss Lamb seemed not to understand the contention that women ought to age quietly. Her voice rang out. Every eye was upon her, chins nodding in agreement.

"And so I tell you, just as we must not concede to those who sanction the owning of one man by another based on the color of one's skin, we must not sit idle while man continues to relegate women to lower status."

Maddie looked over the nodding heads, feeling a lift of hope at seeing a near dozen men sprinkled among the crowd. But on close inspection, a goodly number of those angular masculine chins showed no expression of agreement, the faces marked instead with reddened cheeks as Agatha Lamb poked at the air with a sharp finger.

"In one week's time, on Wednesday thus, I shall speak to the convention at Seneca Falls. The intention is that we create there a Declaration of Sentiment, and in that declaration we will set in writing the changes that must take place. Our efforts must not cease until women are guaranteed all the rights now enjoyed by mankind … social, civil, and political."

Promptly, Agatha Lamb left the podium. Applause rose until Maddie thought the rafters would shake. A great amount of that applause came from the exuberant Maddie, and in her exuberance, one boot slipped from the bench. Her back arched and she was falling – arms flailing until she felt another's arms catch under her own.

Her head struck against a firm chest, and she wobbled before getting both feet steadied on the floor. "Thank you," she said as she straightened the Colburg bonnet that had gone crooked at the side of her head. Only then did she manage to look to the one who had broken her fall.

The man stood a head taller than she, and appeared to be in his mid-twenties or thereabouts, with brown eyes and a grin that seemed to be at her expense. "I'm glad to know we men are still useful for something," he said.

Heat spread on Maddie's cheeks. "I suppose it's safe to say then that you don't agree with the sentiments of Miss Lamb." Her chin lifted perhaps too high, and as she spoke, Maddie opened her clenched palm. On the palm lay an unfamiliar dark button. The button matched perfectly the others on the front of this man's finely tailored paletot jacket, except that one was missing from the jacket and a small rip showed where the missing button ought to be. "Oh, my," she said, "I'm afraid I've torn your jacket."

"Don't worry about it," he said as he brushed at the torn fabric.

"But you will need it repaired."

"No doubt. But it will wait until I get home."

"Then you'll stitch it yourself?"

"Me? Sakes alive, no." And his grin grew wider still.

"Then perhaps your wife …"

"Sakes alive, no to that, too."

Maddie couldn't help it – she laughed, only to be bumped by a shoulder from behind, causing her to stumble forward, once again bumping up against the man.

"Let's get out of here before we both end up injured," he said, guiding Maddie by the arm, weaving them through the clusters of chatter that clogged the doorway.

When at last they stood together beneath the bright sunlight, Maddie considered the button still in her hand. What she wanted to do was bold. Never in her eighteen years had she dared to do such a thing. Never had she wanted to.

"My name is Maddie O'Brien," she announced. "I work as a seamstress in a shop not far from here. I would like to repay you by mending your jacket … that is, unless you are in a terrible hurry."

"Well, Miss Maddie O'Brien, today I am a man without need to hurry. And as this is the only jacket I have with me, I will accept your offer."

"Your only jacket?" asked Maddie when starting off toward Orange Street, the man with the torn jacket at her side.

"It's all I packed. I'm visiting here," he said. "From Cape Cod, that turned-up arm that connects to Massachusetts. When packing, I hadn't thought to be wrestling with New York's most staunch advocate in the fight for women's rights."

"So then," she said while hurrying along the sidewalk, "you don't agree with Agatha Lamb."

"I don't think I ever said I disagree with your Miss Lamb."

"She's not my Miss Lamb. She represents all women."

"Yes, I would guess that she does."

"You laugh with your eyes, you know. You can't hide it."

"Do I? Well, it's not meant to offend. In fact, I am quite sympathetic to the cause of women's rights. With two sisters to tout the cause, I've given it some thought. And I agree. It's time the gentler gender gets its due."

At the corner of Orange, she crossed briskly. Time had passed beyond the hour she'd promised to be back at work. And there was this matter of bringing home a man. Estelle may disapprove. Even so, Maddie walked on, forward along the bluestone sidewalk of Orange Street. "Are you in New York on business?" she asked.

"Not exactly. I came to see the launching of a clipper. The Sea Witch. She's a beauty, with a mainmast of one hundred forty feet. I'd read about her and wanted to see her before she sailed for China."

"You traveled from Cape Cod to New York to see a ship?"

"A man has to love something."

"Yes, I suppose. But it's such a long distance. I should think Cape Cod could give you your fill of ships."

He laughed, much to Maddie's pleasure. And too quickly, or so it seemed, they had come to the Davenport shop. "This is it," said Maddie. "This is where I work."

Entering with a man in tow, Maddie chose to ignore the raised eyebrow offered by Estelle. She would be safe from any line of questioning as long as Estelle remained with the favored customer, a Mrs. Hoffman, browsing the many bolts of fabric meant for dresses.

"Agatha Lamb was extraordinary," announced Maddie. "But there was a near accident, and I'm afraid I tore Mr. ..." She realized she did not know the man's name. "It seems I've torn this man's jacket. I've offered to mend it."

"Good afternoon, Ma'am," he said, his hat held in his hand. "My name is Wyatt. Wyatt Hamilton. As I am a visitor here in the city, your Miss O'Brien has kindly offered to repair my one jacket."

There was that eyebrow lifted again. "Did she now? Well, that was very kind of her, I'm sure. Go ahead, Maddie. Fetch the thread."

Maddie slipped into the back room, having to trust that Estelle would not say anything to frighten Mr. Hamilton away. She and Estelle had never discussed men. Not in any way that was ... was of a personal nature. Maddie almost mentioned recently her concerns about Henry and his drinking, and the way he looked at Maddie sometimes. But in the end, she couldn't bring herself to speak against the man Estelle cared for. So men remained a non-topic. Although heaven knows she and Estelle had talked hours on any other subject. She loved Estelle. Maddie had told her so many times. And she believed to her very center that Estelle loved her equally in return. That belief was a spring of strength during times Maddie might otherwise slip into that under-water feeling of not knowing truly who she was.

In the back room Maddie set her turban on the table, ignoring the coils that sprang out to frame her face. Near the new lock-stitch machine, she found the box of threads and a hand needle, and she returned to store front with them.

Mr. Hamilton stood with his face to the wall, his attention now taken by a painting that hung there. Maddie waited, not exactly in one room or the other, chastising her heart because it beat too loudly. In a breath, she gathered her demeanor and stepped into the room. "What is your opinion of the painting?" she asked.

"It's good. And the artist ... M. O'Brien. That's you, isn't it?"

"Painting is what I do whenever I can steal the time." With a button still in the opened palm, she held out her hand. "Your jacket, Mr. Hamilton. If you slip it off, I shall mend it."

"Ah, yes, the jacket."

The jacket slid off easily, showing the crisp white shirt and tweed vest, the vest tailored perfectly sung against the breadth of the man, and Maddie turned away, feeling the heat again rising on her face. Not that his appearance and manner were anything but proper. Nevertheless, extremely grateful for the distraction of mending, Maddie carried the jacket to the oval-backed chair generally used by waiting customers.

"It's quite beautiful," his attention again on the framed work on the wall, "Amazing, actually, how you've created sky behind streams of sunlight, the rays of sun you rarely see but when you do, you fill with awe. You're very talented."

His glance caught her staring.

"Do you paint, Mr. Hamilton?"

"Sakes no. The only thing I know about painting is how to spread white lye in the hen house to keep the feathered ladies clean."

Maddie laughed, causing her to prick her finger. She put her finger to her mouth to sip away the drop of blood.

"Have you ever been there?" he asked. "The scene looks to be painted from high in the Catskills, west of the river. I ask because to paint with such authority, I would think the artist would need to have been there."

"I was once." With the rip was now mended, Maddie tied off the thread and started to resew the button where it belonged.

"My brother lives right about there," said Mr. Hamilton, his finger pointing to where the Hudson valley flattens before the river. "I visited him for a few days before coming here. He seems happy there, but the valley's so … so quiet. Rather like Irving's Tarrytown, if you ask me."

"Mmmm. A sleepy hollow," she said, looking up from the button. "How does it go? 'A little valley, or rather lap of land among the hills, which is one of the quietest places in the whole world.' "

"That's Newell's valley exactly."

And they laughed together.

"Then you've read Washington Irving?" he asked.

"Over and over." With button tight in place, Maddie stood and carried the jacket to Mr. Hamilton.

"I thank you," he said as he slipped the jacket on, leaving it open at the front while examining her work. "Nicely done."

"Then you're very welcome, Mr. Hamilton."

"I wish you'd call me Wyatt. Mr. Hamilton sounds so old." He began buttoning his jacket, but stopped on the third. "Maddie, while I was walking today, I believe it was along Chatham Street, I passed a theater. The Merry Monarch is playing there. Did you know that Irving was one of two writers of that script? I saw his name on the marquee."

"Yes," she said. "An article in the *Tribune* said it's quite good."

"You haven't seen it then?"

"No. I haven't." Heaven knows she'd begged Estelle enough. But Estelle seemed still peaked after her winter bout with fever and catarrh. By evening she always gave the excuse of tiredness. Henry had offered twice to accompany Maddie, but she's kept a wide distance from Henry for some time now, since his lingering eyes began making her uncomfortable.

"Then would you consider keeping me company tonight," he said, "and come with me to the theater?"

"Me? I …"

"Don't tell me you have another engagement, please. This is my last night in the city, and I would very much like to spend the evening with you."

She would have to ask permission. However, Estelle and her customer had retreated to the back room for sizing. Estelle might be talked into allowing her to go, just as she'd done today when Maddie asked to go to the lyceum. But Henry ...

Henry need not know, not until she was out and gone. After that, anything Henry said could not prevent her going.

"I would like to go with you to the theater, Wyatt. Very much."

Forty-Eight

Sydney
The next morning, Friday, September 7

By dawn, though the wind remains strong, the rain has faded to mist, and Sydney falls gratefully into sleep. It seems only minutes pass before a knock sounds on her bedroom door. She nestles into the pillow hoping the knock is part of some forgotten dream. But the knock comes again.

"Sydney, are you awake?" Alison calls through the door. "You have a phone call. It's Ty."

"Ty?" She lifts her head to the clock. Six fifteen. Immediately she thinks of Everett. Still in the fog of denied sleep, she starts for her cell phone until remembering Ty doesn't have that number. He'd have to call her on the house phone. "I'll take it in the kitchen," she says as she hurries past Alison.

"What's happened?" asks Sydney without saying hello.

"Don't worry. It's not Everett. But I could use your help."

"Me? Doing what?"

"You'll need a bathing suit, under some warm clothes. I'll be there in a minute to explain."

"Explain what? Ty…"

The phone clicks off.

She is on the stairs still zipping her jeans when footsteps scrape on the porch. She meets Ty at the door, he wearing a dark blue slicker.

"What's this about, Ty?"

"Some pilot whales have stranded on the beach not far from here. I'm on my way to meet up with other volunteers to see what we can do."

"And you want me to go? What would I do? "

"You'll work with me. I'll show you. And I promise it'll be worth it. We're missing one of our rescue team. Michelle. This time she's too pregnant. She's been delegated to coffee duty, but she's bringing her suit for you."

"Suit?"

"They call it a dry suit. To keep your body temperature up while you're in the water."

Her eyes open wide. "You don't really think I know what you're talking about?"

"Okay. There's a dozen or so whales lying on the beach a few miles from here. The surf was rough last night, and they stranded just after high tide. That was six hours ago. There's not much chance of saving the ones on the beach, but there's two trapped in a river. The river's been cut off from the bay now that the tide's out. But the two whales have a chance of surviving if we can keep them calm until the tide comes back in."

"I'm going to save a whale?"

"Or give your best trying."

Through mist, Ty turns into the parking lot, and Sydney reads the sign for First Encounter Beach. Two trucks are already parked. In one is a man Ty introduces as David. "Sydney's using Michelle's suit," says Ty. "So she can work in the river with me."

She's introduced to a Ken Walters. Walters is head of the Cape organization whose job it is to save stranded whales. "Welcome to the group," he says, just as another car pulls into the parking lot. A women swollen by the late stages of pregnancy waddles from the car. Michelle at last. And Michelle brings to Sydney the polypropylene suit.

Stripped down to just the bathing suit, Sydney pulls the polypropylene up and over her body. Michelle is not quite as tall but the suit is forgiving. Once on, it covers neck to knees, and full length down the arms to her wrists. Feeling every bit alien, Sydney begins to walk with Ty along the beach, their destination a river estuary.

On the beach, the wind still blows strong, pressing at their backs. It takes Sydney's equalizing lean just to keep from being blown along while Ty explains. "Last night's moon wasn't visible because of the storm, but it was a full moon. Its gravitational pull created the extreme high tide, somewhere around midnight, and this morning an extreme low tide. So we've got a long wait, four or five hours before the whales can get out of the river."

The water line is far out from the dunes, perhaps as much as a quarter mile or more, though distance on the flats is difficult to judge with any certainty. Beyond the muddy flats, the sea rumbles in its turbulence. Ahead of her, at first, Sydney sees only the black mound that stands out against the sand. But as Ty and she walk, the rounded shape of a stranded whale grows closer. Lying on its side, the white of its belly shows.

When only an arm's length from the beautiful creature, Sydney stops on the sand. One visible eye stares up at Sydney. The look is deep, and Sydney cannot look away. It is as if she is falling in and the creature's fear becomes her fear, the pain of suffocation burning in its lungs while the black center of the eye pleads for breath to be put back in, pleads for Sydney to do it.

The whale thrashes, lifting its great head as the tail beats down hard on the sand. With the effort, air bursts from the blowhole at the top of its head. Body fluid pours from the orifice by its tail. It is life at a most desperate moment. A most humiliating. Instinctively, Sydney rests her hand on the whale. The body calms, but the visible eye again seeks Sydney, the fear so real in the animal's eye.

"What can we do?" asks Sydney, her hand still on the whale.

"Someone else will keep her wet with buckets of water," says Ty, nearly shouting to be heard above the wind. "But it's five hours before the next high tide. She probably won't live that long. They may have to put her down."

"You mean kill her?"

"If they decide she's only going to suffer more anyway."

"Oh, God. Why did you think I could do this?"

Ty takes hold of her one free hand. "Come on. There's another whale waiting in the river. One that we can probably save."

"No. I can't just leave her like this."

"Look." Ty points up the beach. "There's the group with the buckets. They'll keep her wet and do what they can. You and I have to move on. Our work is in the river."

Ty pulls her forward, and Sydney moans as her hand drops away, and the massive body begins again to thrash.

Sydney stands with Ty at the edge of a riverbank. With the low tide, only a narrow channel of water is left to snake its way through the marsh. A wall of muck and peat line the river bank. The black back and dorsal fin of two pilot whales can be seen suspended, buoyant in the channel, the creatures held captive because the channel now is cut off from the sea by the long stretch of exposed flats of sand.

"What we have to do," says Ty, "is walk with the whale, slow in the channel. Keep one hand on its back, and sort of guide it. The touch seems to keep them from panicking. Without us, they get desperate and try to escape. They end up driving themselves from the channel up onto the beach, just like the others."

Sydney looks out at the two whales in the river. "Do you really think we can save them?"

"It's worked before."

On a deep breath, Sydney starts down the banking. One foot, then both sink deep into the bottom mud. She pulls each foot through the muck and through the cold of water that inches up, until she is walking breast deep in the center of the channel. As she pushes through toward the whale, miraculously her body warms inside the suit.

"You stay on this side of her," calls Ty through the wind. "I'll go to the other side. All we have to do is keep her moving in the deepest part of the channel."

Sydney moves with the whale. David, along with Michelle's husband, holds the second whale. In tandem they guide the animals, following the gentle bend of the riverbank. Sydney keeps one hand rested just behind the head of the whale and speaks to it as they move through the water. "You have to wait," she says. "Freedom is just a few hours away." She pushes through the water feeling as if she is not really there, but rather above the river, separated from her own body for one purpose – to see herself in the sea with one of its most magnificent creatures.

She is startled back to the moment when, from the other side of the whale, Ty's hand takes hold of hers. "How you doing?" he asks.

"Okay. Just don't ask me to leave. Not until this one is back in the bay, alive."

When nearing the shallow mouth of the channel, they turn the whale, guiding it, nudging its great head to turn, and they start again following the river up into the marsh. They repeat this pace again and again, and Sydney learns from Ty that the pilot whale is not actually a whale at all, but a type of large dolphin. It's often called the blackfish. Centuries ago these blackfish were found in large pods all around the Cape. Men hunted them for their meat. Today their numbers are less, but they still come into the bay. And occasionally, like last night, they run headlong onto the beach in what is called a suicidal stranding. No one knows why. There are only theories. One is that there used to be a deep river passage here near First Encounter Beach, and that river cut through from the bay, across the Cape and into the open Atlantic. Currents and time have filled in much of that former river, but genetic memory pulls the whale forward, thinking it is on its way to open ocean. A second theory suggests that during storms the water becomes stirred up with sand, reducing visibility and the use of sonar. The whales cannot navigate, get confused and misjudge the water's depth until it is too late, and they are caught, heavy on the beach.

Sydney looks to the sky. The day is drying out, and the sun shows behind the clouds. But high tide is still two hours away. When she and Ty are sent replacements, Sydney gives the whale over because she is promised she can return, that she and Ty will be out of the water only to eat and to rest.

In the parking lot, Sydney stands with a circle of volunteers, eating a sandwich but feeling restless, eager to be back in the river. The man Walters walks from the sand flats onto the parking lot and joins the group.

"The news isn't good about the whales that stranded on the beach," announces Walters. "But we did save two young males." He goes on to tell that the two males were taken in a front-end loader to what he calls the Salt Pond, and they will be transported later to Boston, to the aquarium to be examined and treated for any health problems. If all goes well, both whales will be released later back into the sea with another pod. "But five had already suffocated on the beach. Three others had to be euthanized."

Sydney turns from the group, tosses the sandwich she's been eating into a bag of trash. Her heart is racing. She needs distance, and she doesn't slow until her feet feel the soft sand of beach. In her mind is the pleading eye of the whale. No one can tell her why the whale beached itself, why a whale will drive itself out of the sea. There is only theory and speculation. Conditions beyond the whale's control … something gone wrong …

Something gone wrong …

The notion hits hard.

Rick was a great pilot. Even so, something went wrong. It may have been weather or mechanical. But something else could have gone wrong. Something out of Sydney's control.

She doesn't know there are tears until she wipes at the wet on her cheek. Then Ty is at her side.

"Are you okay?" he says.

Behind Ty, she sees the small group of volunteers. "I want to go back to the river."

Forty-Nine

Ty watches her as they walk the channel, the whale between them. But if he wonders about her silence, he doesn't ask. Sydney moves through the water, trying to understand, trying to maneuver through what could be true – Rick's death wasn't her fault. The possibility has to sink and settle, like a rock tossed into a rushing river, rolling and rolling until at last it is comfortable on the bottom.

The water rises to just under her arms. The whale, sensing the new water, begins to fight against Sydney's hold.

"Hang on," says Ty. "It's too soon to let her go. Where the river leads out, it's still too shallow. But soon."

Sydney grips firmer, two hands now, one guiding the head, one on the sleek black dorsal fin. For hours she has been part of this great animal, held to it by the common goal of its survival. This one life can be saved.

"It's time," says Ty. "We can lead her out."

Together they turn the whale to the direction of the river's mouth, staying as close to center in the deepening channel as possible, guiding the whale this time across what had been a barrier of silt and now is covered again by the sea. In sudden realization of its own freedom, the great blackfish shudders, and with one undulating motion lunges forward and is gone. Only its black fin is visible above the water and soon that too is out of sight.

Behind it follows the second whale. Sydney cheers along with the others, four pairs of hands raised and held together in the air.

The entire group of volunteers gathers in the parking lot, each one looking tired and wet. Most complain now of the sudden cold. Michelle's husband puts his arms around his bulging wife and invites everyone back later to his house for pizza. "At four o'clock," he says. "Come dry and hungry."

When all eyes turn to Michelle for consent, her arms rest on the shelf that is her stomach. She tells them, "Just bring your own beer."

Sydney rides in the truck wrapped in a blanket that Ty has brought along. Every muscle aches with exhaustion, and she rests her head back, thinking only of how today she saved a life.

Some died. But some lived.

When she closes her eyes, what she sees is the image of Rick, in the plane he flew. She can see him as clearly as if flying wing tip to wing tip, looking out from her cockpit to his. On his face is a smile. He nods. Then he is gone.

Rick is letting her go. That sense is heavy. She, like the whale, has been sent back to the sea, with places still to discover, a life to live.

"You up for pizza?"

Sydney opens her eyes. The truck has stopped in front of the barn without her knowing. "I don't know," she says. "I'm really beat."

"We'll only stay for the pizza. Not long."

She thinks about going. Thinks about the people who are now her neighbors, future friends. They are good people.

"So," says Ty. "Do we go?"

Sydney considers the choice – new friends or in her room alone, and she turns her face toward the caretaker they call Ty. It seems he guides far more than whales. "We go."

Fifty

"Ty never comes to anything that resembles a party." Michelle is barely old enough to be called a woman. Yet, Michelle, near popping at the seams with enormous belly, seems happy with the way things are, the simple cottage, the husband surrounded by his friends. "Ty gives us the same excuse every time," she says. "He tells us he's not a social animal. So thanks for getting him here tonight."

"Don't thank me," says Sydney, not quite finished with the task of stuffing used paper plates into a trash bag. "Ty makes his own decisions."

"Maybe. But I think he's finally been snared," says Michelle who ties off the bag and sets it by the back door.

From the kitchen, Sydney can see Ty. He talks with David in the living room with his back to Sydney. As if he feels her watching, he glances over a shoulder, raises the bottle in his hand in salute.

"You see," says Michelle. "He's got 'I'm snared' written all over his face. He grins just looking at you."

Sydney shakes her head. "No, he's just ..."

But by then Ty comes to stand in the kitchen doorway. "You ready to go?" he asks. "It's getting late."

Ty parks in front of the barn. They stayed longer at the party than planned. Even so, Sydney enjoyed it. She'd laughed more than she has in a long time. And now, while sitting here in Ty's truck, she looks to a clear sky. All clouds have been blown out, and above the barn hangs an orange moon. "Who would believe the day could end as lovely as this?" she says, before climbing out from the truck onto the gravel. The tired ache has been replaced by a deep quiet in her bones, and she hears herself asking Ty if he wants to walk on the beach.

"Sounds good," he says.

He follows as Sydney takes the path down onto the beach, where they leave their sandals at the path's end. Sand shows white under the moonlight, and as they walk, waves left behind by the storm roll in and break with a frothy crash.

"In northern California," says Sydney, "in the mountains near Tahoe, the night sky can sparkle with literally millions of stars. But here by the sea, even with the moonlight, there seems to be more. The horizon is low here. It's like having a bowl over my head with cut-outs lit up all the way down to the rim."

"Last time I flew to Europe," says Ty, "it was at night, and it was like looking into an endless circle ... the black and the stars."

"Exactly," and Sydney lifts her face to the sky. "And from up there, just before the sun appears in the morning, you can look into a kind of hollow horizon and see the first color ... a brilliant molten pink like you'll never see anywhere else."

"That I haven't seen," says Ty. "But I'd like to."

They walk where the waves break in snakelike strings of white winding along the shore beneath the moon. The cold laps at Sydney's ankles. She feels Ty at her side, his nearness just a half-pace behind her own.

"I made another discovery today," she says. "A huge one."

"And what was that?" asks Ty, never breaking the rhythm of their steps.

"I realized Rick's death may not have been my fault. That Everett was right. Rick was too good a pilot. Something went wrong ...

something between Rick and his plane, but it was not because of my mistake in timing. Rick was too focused. Intense. And so, I can't blame myself anymore."

When Ty stops on the sand, Sydney turns to him. He touches her cheek, pushes aside a coil of hair that has fallen over her eye. "I'm glad for you, Sydney."

The moon is bright on his face. His eyes seem to watch hers, and Sydney is remembering being connected to the whale, each looking into the other, just as she and Ty are doing now. Then his lips touch on hers, tender and soft. Sydney takes in the slight scent of beer and the sweetness, as her own hunger rises. Among the shadows of moonlight, she starts with the buttons on his shirt.

They lie together on the sand. Their hands, at first, are slow, allowing time, until his body moves over her, his breath hot. The moon lights his skin and hers, and their bodies move together, intense now, on fire.

But when at last they lie quiet and spent, Sydney lies back against the cool damp sand. "I think I'm learning to like the beach."

Ty laughs as he rolls away. "Let's swim," he says. And they run into the ink-black sea, the cold engulfing.

Fifty-One

Sunlight bursts into Ty's room through a window to strike her face, and Sydney rolls to her side. Ty lies beside her, still asleep. Last night they walked here from the beach, made love again and slept, their bodies folded together. Being with him – it felt good and right.

But a sudden image cuts into that thought – the image of one painting. The portrait. The woman with the beads. It surprises Sydney, and she shakes her head. It makes no sense, but she needs to see that painting again. The notion is so strong that it pulls her from the bed.

Ty turns onto his side. "Good morning," he says in a groggy sleep voice.

Sydney smiles but puts on the shirt left last night on the floor. When Ty reaches for her, she backs away. "I have to go."

"Why?"

"You're going to think I'm crazy."

Ty lies back on a pillow, hands tucked beneath his head. "Not crazy. Just beautiful and ... well, maybe a little crazy."

Sydney tosses the other pillow at Ty. "I'm serious." She kisses his cheek. "I'm sorry, but I have to leave. I'll explain later. I promise." She is half out the door when Ty calls, "Remember, we have to pick up Everett at eleven to go to Boston."

The house smells of coffee when Alison meets Sydney at the door.

"Have you had breakfast?" asks Alison while eyeing Sydney's crumpled shirt.

"Yes, I ate earlier," she says, a lie for the sake of escaping to the attic.

"I need to talk to you," says Alison. "I have an idea."

"I'm leaving soon. Everett's being admitted today."

"I only need a minute. I have a way to help Everett keep his airport. So, please, just have a cup of coffee."

Sydney looks to the top of the stairs. "Okay but ... I'll be right back."

She climbs both sets of stairs, wondering if maybe she is a little crazy. She can't believe she's left Ty for this. But the painting feels important, and here she is, climbing stairs, headed for an old portrait of an unknown woman. Why did Eva leave it there on the rack?

Sydney walks past the easel to the sloping wall, to the rack of unframed paintings. She sorts through to the last one, the portrait of the woman wearing a bead necklace. Picking up the painted canvas, Sydney looks closely. The face is no one she recognizes. But Alison might.

Sydney carries the canvas down to the kitchen, holds it up for Alison to see. "Do you know who this woman is?"

"No," says Alison, glancing while at the same time pouring two cups of coffee. "But I have seen that bizarre looking necklace before."

"Really? When?"

"Oh, a long time ago. Eva had it." Alison sits at the table, sips from her coffee. "She wanted to give it to me, but it was all too creepy, the bones, I mean. Not that they were human bones. I think she said they were whale bone."

"Whale? Well, I suppose that makes sense. There used to be a lot of whales around here." She sets the picture on the floor, leaning it against the wall, and she looks at the painted face again. "There's a reason Eva kept this painting, don't you think?"

Alison places both hands around her mug of coffee, watching her own hands as she does this. "I wouldn't know. But Sydney, I do know of a way to save the airport."

"Yes. So you said." Sydney goes to the cupboard. Pours herself a bowl of cereal, remembering too late that she said she'd already eaten. She takes the bowl back with her to the table. "I have a few ideas myself. Nora's going to help"

Alison's eyes open wide. "Nora?"

"Yep. She's going for her instructor rating, so we can bring in some student pilots. And I'm hoping my friend, Jean, will come east to be our engine mechanic."

"Well, hoping isn't going to save the airport. What I have in mind will bring in real cash."

Sydney says nothing because odds are against Alison knowing how to save an airport.

"Honestly, Sydney, what I have in mind will bring in a lot of people. Something you could do just on weekends."

Sydney sets her spoon down. "Okay. I'm listening."

"Well, first of all, you would have to fly."

"Then forget it," says Sydney, and she pushes her chair away from the table.

"But if you would fly," says Alison, "you could act out a drama, a live play like in the theater, except your stage is the sky."

"I'm not flying. I could panic up there. I could make some dumb mistake." Sydney bites on her lip where the cut has healed. "I don't know … maybe I'm just plain afraid."

"But you're such a good pilot. You need to fly, Sydney. You just need to do it. Just once, that's all. You'll see. And you know it would help the airport. I mean, if an air show brings in more money, isn't it a good thing?"

"I guess, but …"

"We could make up a skit," says Alison, pushing as if she has a foot in. "A comedy, maybe. You could act it out in a plane. Fly low over the airport. You could build in a few of your aerobatic stunts. People who are interested in planes and flying ... they would buy tickets, just like they would in any other theater."

"Acting in the sky? I don't think so."

Yet, Sydney has seen it done at other small airports, at fly-ins and air shows. It isn't exactly a new idea. That kind of thing does bring in an audience, even families, people of all ages – potential student pilots.

"I know you're the flight expert," says Alison. "But I could help with the comedy part."

"The comedy?"

"Sure. You could have characters. Maybe two or three planes. Like a Larry and Moe and Curly."

"The Three Stooges? You can't be serious."

"I am. Well, not about the Stooges. We'd have to create our own characters. But think about it. It could work."

"Not with me as pilot."

"Sydney, you came back here for a reason. And in spite of Everett being ill, in spite of me, on occasion I have seen you smile. I've seen you emerging again. It's time, don't you think, to get back into a plane."

Sydney stands, backs away, and stumbles over the portrait. "I'm not going to fly. I can't," she says before picking up the picture and walking out from the kitchen.

She is under a hot shower, the air filled with steam, when her shoulders give in. Alison's idea ... it's not so ridiculous. In fact, it could help. Nora, maybe even Jean if she'd come, they could do the flying. And from the ground, Sydney can make it all happen. An airshow really could help save Dean Aviation.

Fifty-Two

Maddie
After leaving the theater, July of 1848

"May I ask you something?"

"You may ask me anything, Wyatt. It's the answer that may or may not be given." Maddie grinned and slid in across the seat of the carriage Wyatt Hamilton had hired as they left the theater, a carriage to return them to Orange Street.

"Fair enough," said Wyatt as he stepped in and settled into the carriage beside her. He called to the driver to start away, and the carriage lurched before falling into the rhythm of clopping hooves. "You see, all evening I have wondered," said Wyatt. "With eyes as green as a summer meadow and a name like Maddie O'Brien, why do you speak without the brogue of the Irish."

"Ah, that," and Maddie turned her face to the drizzle of rain beyond the carriage. She was not so much a Miss Innocence that she couldn't recognize a man's compliment. His words felt good, like the first sip of tea warming her belly on a cool morning. "My real father killed himself before I was born," she said, wanting to speak truthfully. And with as few words as possible she told how her mother had worked for Estelle, how her biological mother had died of cholera. "When Estelle found me, she simply picked me up and took me home. I was two."

"I see."

Beyond the carriage, along the curb, street lamps burned. Each lamp's reach was short, leaving all things beyond that small circle of light in the darkest shadow. Inside the carriage was no exception. Maddie could scarcely make out the line of Wyatt's shoulder, or the place where his face should be. But she didn't need to see his face to know his thought. "You needn't feel pity for me," she said. "It was a long time ago."

"But it was your mother. I don't believe time ever completely heals that loss."

"Why do you say that? Have you lost your mother?"

"No. But I can't imagine my life as a boy if I had."

"I was so young. Estelle is the only mother I've known."

"You don't recall your real mother at all?"

"No. At least I don't think so." Maddie looked again to the light rain. "There are times, at night, I dream of sinking through total darkness, and I wake myself up crying. When I was younger, Estelle would come to me and say that it was my remembering. But there's no picture. No mother's face. That's the part I wish I could remember. But it doesn't matter, really. Estelle and Henry have given me a home, everything I've needed. Even my bloody proper English."

She heard Wyatt laugh a little, just as the carriage wheel thumped up and over some unseen obstacle in the street, tossing Maddie sideward. She may as well have been hit by lightning. The firm feel of a man, her arm pressed against his, it sent a bolt that traveled through her, head to toe. It was wonderful and frightening, both at the same time. She straightened herself, brushed a wrinkle from her skirt and folded her gloved hands on her lap before she could think of where the conversation had been.

"And what about you?" she asked while shuffling her senses back into some sort of order. "What makes Wyatt Hamilton such a lover of ships that he travels for days just to look at one?"

"I build them. Not clippers. Rugged working ships for the men who fish the banks. As for the rest, mine is a far more ordinary story."

"But that's not fair. I go on and on about me. Then you tell me your story is much too ordinary to share."

The carriage came to a sudden stop at the curb. The door to the dress shop waited in the darkness beyond the lamppost. In an upstairs window, a light still burned. Although she dared hope it be Estelle sitting up, wakened by some late night sound on the street, Maddie suspected otherwise, and she bristled at the probability of facing Henry.

"The evening was far too short."

"Yes, it was," she said, grateful for being brought back to the moment and to the man who sat beside her. "The play was wonderful. Thank you, Wyatt."

"I enjoyed it, too. I enjoyed the entire evening. In truth, I would rather be sharing my own ordinary story than leaving you so soon." He turned on the seat, his arm stretched easily across the seat back, so close. "Maddie, I sail early in the morning, which makes it impossible to see you again before I leave. But may I write you?"

"I'd like that."

"I will then."

For a moment, the quiet of night filled the carriage, then Wyatt opened the door at his side and stepped out. Accepting his hand, Maddie stepped down and walked with him to the door of the shop.

"Good night," she said, before going inside and closing the door at her back.

She leaned to the door. Such a glorious evening. Her heart should be merry. Instead, in her heart, she felt the loss of something – a possibility – the loss of someone wonderful.

Reluctant and keeping her footsteps light, Maddie started in. The smoke of a cheap long-nine cigar reached to the stairway, causing her to cough, and Maddie put a hand to her mouth to stifle the need. When the floorboard creaked as she entered the kitchen, she cringed. But Henry made no sound. She glanced through to the sitting room, to the hand that rested on the arm of Estelle's favorite Louis XV chair. The hand wrapped a cup, and in it, no doubt, was Henry's favored gin-sling, his gin with a required squeeze of lemon.

Since winter, since Estelle had grown so sickly, Henry passed the nights by downing the liquor. At first, Maddie felt sympathetic, offering to keep him company with a game of cards or at times reading aloud. But the gin brought out the worst in Henry. It made him curse and talk vulgar, his glare upon her feeling dirty, and she would take to her room, lie awake until his snoring started.

Tonight, as she placed her beaded turban on the hat rack by the door, she wondered how many lemon rinds and how many stale ends of cigar she would need to toss out come morning.

"So, it's come to this. You sneaking around in the night with a man."

She stopped there in the kitchen, wondering how to answer. "I wasn't sneaking, Henry. Estelle knew where I was." She heard him sip on the gin-sling and curse the empty cup. "Is Estelle in bed?" she asked.

"Where else would she be?" He looked at the empty cup as though it had betrayed him, and Maddie thought he might throw it. Instead, he rubbed it with his thumb. "She's sick again. Gone to her room hours ago with a dose of quinine."

"I'll look in on her then." With intentional poise, Maddie moved toward the room where Estelle would be sleeping, keeping her eyes from the ones that bore upon her as she walked in front of his chair.

"What's his name?"

"Whose name?" she asked, putting distance between them.

"Don't play stupid, girl. The man you were with, who is he?"

"His name is Mr. Wyatt Hamilton," she said with her hand on the doorknob to Estelle's room. "He's a ship builder," and she slid into the bedroom, closed the door at her back. She heard the floor in the sitting room creak, but the footsteps gratefully scuffed toward the kitchen, to replace the gin, no doubt.

"Estelle, it's me, Maddie. Are you in need of anything?" she whispered. But Estelle's breathing remained deep, heavy from the quinine, so Maddie took advantage and hurried through the empty sitting room, down the short hallway to the room at the end that was hers.

She lit the peg lamp and set it close to her bed. Slipped from her clothes into the nightgown kept beneath her pillow. And quickly she climbed in beneath the quilt.

But heavy footsteps fell along the hall. Then pounding on her door.

Maddie sat upright, fear like a drum in her chest.

A fist struck again on her door, and the latch fell away. Henry took just one step into the room before taking a large swallow from the cup in his hand. Without need to reach far, he set the cup beside the burning lamp, and he wiped the gin from his lips. "I've come to get my due."

Maddie pulled the quilt to her chin. "You're drunk, Henry. Go to bed."

But Henry leaned in, both hands resting on the edge of her bed, his face inches from her own. His eyes narrowed. "It's not right," he said. "Another man's not getting a taste of you before the man who took you in … the man who gave you everything."

With knuckles white, Maddie gripped the quilt. "Get out. Get out of my room," she shouted.

Henry stumbled, but caught his balance as he yanked the quilt from her hands. And he was there, pushing her down, his weight upon her. His cold hand pawed at her flesh, took hold of her breast so that it hurt. With her one hand that was not pinned under his weight, Maddie pushed at his chest, pounded on his arm. "Get off me." But cold fingers slid down over her stomach, along her thigh.

With the one free hand, Maddie found his face and clawed with her nails using every bit of strength she had. A loud curse sprayed spittle. The arm that had held her down lifted and came back with a slap on her cheek, but it was the single moment she needed.

Maddie tumbled from the bed. As she ran from the room, she heard a crash that sounded much like a drunken Henry falling to the floor. She grabbed the shawl from the back of Estelle's chair before sprinting down the stairs and out onto the street.

She dared not stop until she stood in front of Hoffman's Bakery. Her body trembled beneath the light drizzle, and she pulled the shawl around her. She did not want to wake the Hoffmans, not in the middle of the night, for there would certainly be questions. But she had nowhere else to turn except to Yvonne.

Yvonne was Maddie's closest friend. She lived above the bakery with both parents and two sisters. Early on, Henry had forbidden the friendship because the Hoffmans were Jews, he said, as if it were a disease. Regardless, the friendship had grown. Tonight, while holding to the ache that had come to her cheek, Maddie looked to the alleyway that ran in beside the bakery, and she schemed a way to wake Yvonne.

Along the curb beneath the lamppost, she found pebbles. She gathered several and made her way down the alley, to just beneath the window of the room Yvonne shared with her sisters. Maddie tossed a pebble to the window. It struck and fell back at her feet. She tossed another and another, creating a tap, tap, tap against the glass. After six tosses, a face appeared in the window. The older sister peered at Maddie through the glass, then disappeared.

Maddie shivered beneath the shawl and waited. When the window slid open, it was Yvonne who looked out at her.

"What is it? What's wrong?" whispered Yvonne.

"May I ..." With the words, tears broke through, and Maddie covered her face with her hands.

"I'll be right there," said Yvonne, and the window closed.

In what seemed an eternity, Yvonne stepped into the alleyway with a cloak over her own sleeping gown. "Come inside," she said. "And we'll talk."

"I don't want to talk. I just need a place to stay the night. Is that all right?"

"Of course, it's all right." Yvonne put one arm around Maddie, holding her close, and the two walked together through the back door and up the back stairs. Like two mice scampering noiselessly across the floor, they tiptoed, each barefoot, through the kitchen, along the hallway to the bedroom shared by the sisters.

"What happened to your face?" asked the younger.

"Be quiet and go to sleep," whispered Yvonne as she sat Maddie down at the edge of her bed, taking the damp shawl from Maddie's shoulders. "You're shaking," said Yvonne, and she took the extra blanket from the foot of her sister's bed and wrapped it around Maddie. "What's happened to you?"

"It's nothing. Please. Can we just go to sleep?"

"If that's what you want." Yvonne went to the lamp and snuffed out the light. She took the blanket that was around Maddie and spread it as an extra layer over her bed. "Slide in," she said.

Maddie moved to the far side. In the dark, her friend slipped in beside her. "I'll need to borrow a dress," said Maddie. "Just for the morning. Then I'll return it."

"We'll get you one of Dena's. Mine are too narrow."

"Thank you, Yvonne." Maddie turned to the wall. The room went quiet. She closed her eyes, but the image of Henry – the heavy feel of him – forced her eyes to open. And while her body would not stop trembling, she forced herself to consider tomorrow. She needed a plan. A place to go and a story to tell Estelle. She couldn't tell the truth of what happened. What if Estelle blamed her? What if Estelle thought her dirty, soiled somehow? No. The truth would remain known only by Henry and herself.

Fifty-Three

Maddie
The next morning

Since dawn Maddie had crisscrossed the city. Her feet begged for release from the cramped leather shoes she'd borrowed, gathered from the Hoffman sisters like every other article that covered her body. She'd had a night of little sleep. But this morning, the time spent walking had been good for thinking. When at last she was certain Henry had left for his work at the *Tribune*, Maddie headed toward home, to talk to Estelle and to pack her things.

She turned the corner onto Orange Street feeling a heavy jumble of anger and humiliation and sadness – all three warred inside while on the curb she slipped off one shoe. She rubbed her toes, forced her foot back in and began the last length of walking.

Her fabricated story was ready. She would tell Estelle that last night she'd had another of her black sinking dreams and in the confusion she'd fallen out of bed. That would explain the bruise that lay darkened purple across her cheekbone.

The door to the shop was locked, the CLOSED sign looking out at her through the glass. It was a turn of events Maddie had not considered. She had no key. She rattled the brass knob. When the door would not open, she looked up to the front window.

Precisely then, the door swung open.

"Oh, thank goodness," said Estelle, who stood in the open doorway, and she hugged Maddie close.

"I'm sorry to make you come down the stairs," said Maddie as she stepped quickly inside. "I forgot my key."

"I've been waiting right here," said Estelle, but the coughing began. Estelle coughed into her handkerchief and held it to her lips until breath came more easily. "I was worried. And Maddie, what's happened to your cheek?"

"Nothing really. I'll explain, but let me make us some tea first." Holding to Estelle's arm, Maddie supported the thin frame as they climbed the stairs and turned into the kitchen.

Maddie made tea while an unusual silence settled around them. In her head, Maddie practiced her story. But when at the table Maddie poured tea into Estelle's cup, Estelle broke the quiet "I've been to the Hoffman's this morning,"

"You? You've been out?"

"I thought, if you were to go anywhere, it would be to see Yvonne. Yvonne admitted to your spending the night there. But either she couldn't or would not say why you had gone there in the middle of the night. Nor could she say where you'd gone to this morning."

"She couldn't because I didn't tell her," said Maddie while setting a slice of corn bread on a plate in front of Estelle. She poured her own cup of tea and sat then across from Estelle.

"Henry hit you, didn't he?"

Maddie needed to swallow the sip of tea. "No …"

"You can tell me the truth, Maddie. Henry hit you. Was it because I allowed you to go out for the evening with Mr. Hamilton?"

Maddie's mouth opened. She wanted to contradict …

"That explains his ornery mood," said Estelle while shaking her head. "He cursed the whole time I searched the house for you. Then he went off to work, slamming the door before I'd even thought of going to the Hoffman's."

Maddie nodded, slowly as she considered. Estelle's idea was near half the truth and as likely a story as the one Maddie had made up.

And Estelle's version better supported Maddie's decision to take a room in a nearby boarding house. "It's done, Estelle. And I'm fine."

But Estelle traced the rim of the cup. "As I said, Henry was upset," she offered without taking her eyes from the cup. "So upset he wouldn't explain the deep scratch that runs the length of his face."

Maddie boldly set her jaw. She would tell no more of the truth. "I don't know about any scratch, Estelle. When Henry hit me, I ran. That's all."

Estelle stood and crossed to the stove. She brought back the pot of tea and refilled her cup, though she had taken only a few sips. While returning to the stove, the cough started again, and Maddie went to her, took the teapot and set it back on the stove.

"Sit down, please," said Maddie. "I've made a large decision, and I want to tell you about it."

"Oh, Maddie, I'm so sorry," groaned Estelle as she sank onto a chair, her face covered by her hands.

"You have no reason to be sorry for anything," said Maddie. She sat beside Estelle, took hold of the hands that had worked so hard at giving a life to an orphaned girl. The hands were thin, the knuckles large, and the fingers wrapped around Maddie's. "I want you to know," said Maddie, "that I love you as any daughter loves her mother. To me, you have been the best of mothers."

Set deep in a face gone gaunt with sickness, Estelle's eyes filled. But a smile, as meager as it was, turned her lips. "It was so easy to love you, Maddie. You were the daughter I could never have."

"Yes, I know. But I need you to understand that it is time I go out on my own."

The smile was gone. "What do you mean, 'out on your own'?"

"I mean, I plan to take a room in a boarding house. I shall have to add to the wages I earn here. I know that. I'll get a second position, perhaps sewing for another shop. Or anything at all. It doesn't matter what. But it is necessary that I move out from here."

"Because of Henry."

"Because I'm eighteen. I wish to be more independent."

Estelle smoothed the napkin on the table. "If that's what you say." She sipped at the tea, holding it in her throat as if the warmth of it would fortify her. "I will help you in any way I can, Maddie. But first, I must tell you a story."

"It isn't necessary. Talking will start the cough."

"Maddie, this is very necessary. And very difficult to say. But I'm feeling tired and old. I knew one day I'd have to tell you. I thought I would dread it. I do, some. But it's the right thing to do. I should have told you a long time ago."

"Tell me what, Estelle? What is it?" asked Maddie, trying to read the something dark in Estelle's eyes.

"Oh, how to begin. At the beginning, I suppose," and Estelle set the cup of tea down on the table. "It was August when I found you. Your mother had spoken of her own father only once. They'd had an argument before she left home with William O'Brien to come here to New York. But your mother never mentioned where that home was, or if she did I chose to forget it."

"Yes, I know. But you took me in. You gave me a home and family. I can't imagine what might have happened to me if you hadn't. You did a wonderful thing."

"That's what I told myself the day I found you. But Maddie, there's more." Estelle coughed, using the napkin to cover her mouth, her shoulders wracking.

"Don't, Estelle. You need to rest," said Maddie.

"No. I need to tell you everything." Estelle took in breath that lifted the frail shoulders. "Just four months from the day I found you, a letter came. It was from your aunt."

When Maddie's mouth opened to question, Estelle held up one hand. "No, let me continue. This woman, your aunt, was married to your mother's brother. She did not give the brother's name, but hers is

Beatrice … Beatrice Chase. She was inquiring about your mother because several letters had gone unanswered. Maddie, you have family. You could go to them and see for yourself who they are and from where you came."

Maddie could only blink, trying to make sense. "No," she said. "You are my family. They, whoever they are, are not real. They did not come here looking for me. They didn't take me in and love me. You did that."

"Oh, Maddie, I did something terrible. Perhaps unforgivable. I wrote a letter back to Mrs. Chase. In the letter I told of your mother's death by cholera. I also said that you, the little daughter, had died alongside your mother."

Maddie turned the round saucer that nested her own cup, turned it one way, then the other.

"I suppose you're angry," said Estelle. "And with good reason."

"I don't know what I feel, but I'm not angry. I was only thinking … all my life I've assumed I have no family … no blood relative. And that was all right. It was. I'd accepted it. Now, I have to wonder, do I care."

"Of course you do," said Estelle. "Or you will when you've had time to think about it."

Maddie looked to the tired and grayed face of Estelle. She felt sorry and felt the ache that Estelle must feel.

"You should go there, Maddie. Meet your family. There must be someone, some relative still there even if this Beatrice Chase is not."

"Where is she? Where does this aunt live?"

"In Massachusetts. In a town called Wells Creek."

"Wells Creek?" asked Maddie, her spine sitting straight.

"Yes."

"But that's so strange. Wyatt Hamilton lives in Wells Creek."

"Really?"

Maddie never believed in coincidence. Things happened for a

reason. Someone or something pulled strings like a puppeteer – or at least that's what she liked to believe. Her mother's death, for example. If it had been just a coincidence, a mother dead and a child left without one, it would mean that life was simply cruel. Far easier to accept that the spirits, or God, or someone had good reason. That there was a heavenly benefit more important than the heartache felt by the mere mortals here on Earth.

"What is it you want to do, Maddie? Tell me, and I will help."

Maddie dug through feelings. Dug through all she'd learned. What was clear was that she could not leave Estelle, not while Estelle was so very ill. "I want to pack my things," she said. "I want to get a room somewhere near here so that I can be near you, to help you, and I'd like to continue to work in the shop, if I may."

"What about Beatrice Chase?"

"I don't know what to do about her." Maddie picked at a loose thread on her skirt. She needed time. "First things first," she said. "Today, what I need to do is find a room."

"That won't be easy. People don't look favorably on young single women living out on their own."

"I've thought of that. I'm going to tell them I'm married. I was married in Paris where my husband continues with his work."

"Paris?"

"Or someplace like that. It has to be far away. Too far for any occasional visits. I will tell them I grew homesick and have returned a few months ahead of my husband to be near my mother."

"That might work," said Estelle, a thin eyebrow lifting.

Fifty-Four

Maddie
One month later, August of 1848

As hot as days can get in August, this one broke the back of all others. So heavy was the air that the leaves on the tall maple drooped, stilled without even a flutter. Maddie stood beneath its limbs. Far off, a jagged line of lightning split the sky, and she counted the seconds until the gentle rumble rolled across the top of the wrought iron fence and over the circle of mourners dressed in black, those who had come to say their final goodbye to Estelle.

A large wet drop fell from above, avoiding somehow along its way the dense green cover of leaves as it coursed downward and hit on Maddie's cheeks. She did not brush it away. Instead, she held to the few pink roses she'd collected from behind the boarding house, and she let the soft cool feel of the raindrop linger as she studied the familiar faces, women mostly, who had gathered around the black hole into which the boxed body would soon be lowered. As she looked at each face, Maddie tried to recognize why each had come.

Words were being read by Reverend Jones, words that had been written thousands of years ago, penned by one who had never known Estelle Davenport. That point caused Maddie to want to scream out, to demand that the man throw down the Good Book and speak from his heart. But Maddie held her anger as tightly as her tears. While here among the tombs and stones, she would not have her knees give out, only to slide down into a heap upon the grass.

When Maddie raised her gaze, that gaze settled on Henry. She had expected Henry to be there, of course. But Maddie had not, until that moment, even so much as set eyes upon Henry. Even last night, she'd refused to go to visiting hours above the shop where friends gathered to view the stilled body of Estelle. She refused to stand next to that man and pretend. Yet, she had to wonder. Henry and Estelle were married for thirty years. Could a man as horrid as Henry be faithful to a wife? Could he have loved Estelle? That was beyond her imagination. But she did know with all certainty that Estelle would want Henry here today. Estelle had loved Henry. Love seemed a strange thing. Did it make women blind to all else

At Maddie's side, Yvonne nudged with an elbow. All eyes were now staring at Maddie, and Yvonne whispered in her ear. "The Reverend has asked if you wish to say a few words."

Maddie looked once more to the faces. She swallowed, trying to loosen the tightness in her throat. "Estelle often spoke to me of her friends, of how much she appreciated each of you. And I'd like to thank you for coming ..." Maddie's voice broke, just as the sky seemed to empty itself, and Maddie stepped forward to the grave. On top of the casket, she placed the pink roses she had held since noon. "Goodbye, Estelle. And thank you, for everything."

With only a nod of her head to Yvonne, Maddie turned and began the long walk alone back to the boardinghouse.

Wearing only a dry chemise, Maddie sat on the corner chair, looking down at the threadbare carpet at her feet. Today she must decide what best to do with the rest of her life. Henry was selling the shop. He found a buyer just three days before Estelle died. And Estelle had insisted that Maddie get one half of the proceeds. At first Maddie had protested, but tomorrow morning at ten she would meet with Henry's attorney to receive her share of the shop's worth.

Maddie walked to the small desk by the window and took from

it Wyatt's letter. The letter had arrived at the shop two days previous, while Maddie visited for the last time with Estelle. By now, she had memorized the page – a friendly note and newsy about his ship building.

From the desk Maddie took a fresh sheet of paper, pen and ink. Today, she would write back to Wyatt Hamilton. And she would ask him that one enormous question. Did a Mrs. Beatrice Chase exist there in Wells Creek?

Fifty-Five

Early in October of that same year, 1848

Shortly after sunrise, in a town with the English name of Yarmouth, Maddie climbed into a stagecoach that had been painted in shades of gaudy yellow and a red. Pulled by a team of four horses, the coach lurched forward and she was on her way, the final day of her journey to Wells Creek. She had sailed by ship to Boston, had been terribly seasick through a storm and had vowed to travel the remainder of her journey on dry land. Thus, since Boston, the stagecoach had been her means of travel.

The morning shone with bright sunshine, but the coach was cramped, Maddie tucked in among six other passengers, the diverse group sharing only two bench seats. Hours passed with vistas across lush lowland, the tall grasses turned to autumn's gold and sided up against twisting rivers snaking their way to the sea. And sitting back from the road were large stately homes with spreading lawns, so unlike the city. But as the sun lowered well into the afternoon, even the vistas grew old. The day seemed endless, even though it had been broken up mid-morning, again at noon, and again at nearly three, as they made rest stops at taverns along the Old King's Highway and passengers could refresh themselves.

After that third chance for refreshment, the interior of the coach smelled horribly of breath tainted by whiskey. Maddie could only hope this last leg of her journey might be smoother, for truly, she could not withstand one more wheel stuck in sand or one more tussle against the somber Widow Doane who sat beside her.

On that very thought, the coach careened over a rock, sending Maddie into the air, only to land on the widow's lap. The look received by Maddie left her with barely enough courage to apologize, and she settled back onto the bench seat, to again watch the road and the textured bark of the passing oaks.

With back aching and her beaded turban stiff with dust, Maddie felt the coach at last roll to a stop. The driver announced that they'd arrived in Wells Creek, at Commercial Street.

The sun sat low, making colors sharp, and the air was scented by the salt of the sea. But the air, too, was crisp, and Maddie raised the collar of her light coat, while at the same time getting her bearings. To her right, just as Wyatt's letter said it would be, was Foster Mercantile. Directly across the road from the mercantile ran a row of wooden structures fronted by business signs, and Maddie, her satchel heavy, began to walk the row.

She could hardly believe she was here. Somewhere in this town she had family – an uncle named Thomas Chase, and his father who was in fact Maddie's grandfather, John Chase. Wyatt had written that Maddie's uncle lived in the village with his wife, Beatrice, but that the elder, John Chase, lived alone on a small island not far out beyond the harbor. Also in the letter Wyatt offered to take her to the island and introduce her, if John Chase agreed to the meeting. But Maddie had not waited to receive further news of her grandfather's response. She'd been too eager. She started for Cape Cod as soon as she'd heard a grandfather existed, having taken time to merely send off a telegram to Wyatt to say she was coming. If John Chase or any of them refused to see her, then so be it. She would live with that. At least she had come. At least she would see the town that had once been home to her mother.

Her telegram to Wyatt had said to expect her in a week, but

only six days had passed since. As her feet carried her toward him, she feared she was too early. Perhaps she asked too much of Wyatt. But here she was – in a strange town, nearing dusk. Little choice remained but to proceed. When at last Maddie neared the end of Commercial Street, she looked up at a sign that read Hamilton Shipyard. A deep breath lifted her shoulders, and Maddie opened the door.

A young lad, who could be no more than fourteen, greeted her in a front office room. His trousers and shirtfront were blotched with black tar. Fair hair fell disheveled every which way. But he smiled as he approached Maddie. "Might I help you, Ma'am?"

"Yes, please," she said, resting the satchel down onto the floor. "I'm looking for Mr. Wyatt Hamilton. Would he be here?"

"He's in the back. Would you like me to get him?"

"If you would. Tell him Miss O'Brien is here to see him."

The boy's eyes grew twice as large. "You're Miss O'Brien?"

"Yes. That would be me," she said, trying to sound light while the boy stared.

"That makes us cousins," said the boy, as if it were the most wonderful thing in the world. "At least that's what my father has told me. My father is Thomas Chase. My name is Sam. I work here when I'm not in school." His hand came forward, and Maddie took hold of it, shaking hands though her head was spinning.

"It's very nice to meet you," she said. "I didn't know I had a cousin."

"You have two. Me. And Clara. She's seven and a nuisance, but I guess she's pretty cute."

"Your sister, then?"

"Yep." The boy shoved both hands into his pockets. "Well, I guess I better find Wyatt." The young Sam disappeared then through a door at the back of the office.

Maddie rubbed the small of her back where stiffness had set in from a long day of sitting, and she moved around the office looking for clues – more to learn about Wyatt. One large table crowded the far end of the room, the table strewn with detailed drawings, lines and angles among graceful curves, all ships' hulls, if she guessed right. On the back wall, done in oils, hung a painting of a sleek ship on the sea, the sails full, and Maddie leaned to look more closely.

"Maddie, it's good to see you."

She turned to the voice, to the face she had tried to remember each time she'd read his letter. The look of him warmed her. "It's good to see you, too."

"How was your trip? Are you exhausted?"

"The trip we won't even discuss. Exhausted? Yes." And with the nod of her head came her laugh, small but real.

"Then I'll let you decide what you want to do," said Wyatt. "I must tell you though, your grandfather made me swear I'd bring you to him as soon as you arrived. Day or night, he said. He doesn't care which."

"Then he's not upset? He's not going to disown me before we even meet?"

"No. On the contrary. When first I told him I had met you and that I'd learned the story of you being found by Mrs. Davenport, the poor man's face went a bit pale. But he recovered quickly, and you're all he's been talking about throughout town."

Her hand went to her chest, the reality of her situation truly setting in. "Can we go there ... now? Are you free to take me?"

"If that's what you want. If you think you might want to rest first, I can get you a room for the night at the inn on Main Street."

"I don't think I could sleep."

Young Sam appeared at the door, shifting feet, seeming caught between curiosity and the work that waited. Wyatt slipped an arm across the boy's shoulder. "Let's close up shop, Sam. Call it a day. When you get home, tell your father that his niece has arrived and that I'm taking her out to the island. If he wishes to meet her, as I know he does, tomorrow morning might be a good time for him to ride out to Ponokanet. Miss O'Brien will be staying the night there."

Sam came to Maddie and shook her hand. "Goodbye, Miss O'Brien. I'm happy to have met you."

"I think, because we're cousins, you should call me Maddie."

The boy glanced to Wyatt who winked an eye, and the boy's grin grew wider still. "I'll tell my father and mother that we've met." With that, the boy ran out the door.

Wyatt leaned back against the table. "It truly is good to have you here," he said.

"And I'm so grateful that you are here. It's strange, isn't it? You living in the very town where my mother was born."

"Life is meant to be full of surprises."

"I suppose. Mine certainly has been." For a moment their eyes lingered on one another, the room quiet, and Maddie smiled.

"So," said Wyatt as he gave up his lean on the table and stood. "Are you ready to meet your grandfather?"

"Yes. Very."

Wyatt locked the front door and picked up Maddie's satchel. "Good Lord, that's heavy."

"It's all I own," she said, and she walked with Wyatt out of the office into a deep grotto-like room behind.

Enormous wooden ribs rested on frames. "The start of a new hull," said Wyatt. The space smelled of cut wood, a fresh clean scent Maddie had not expected, and she drew it in like one would the scent of a rose. The great room seemed much like Wyatt, full of energy and creativity, but Wyatt walked quickly, guiding her by the arm as he led her out through a back door.

There, behind the building, narrow wharves stuck out like fingers into the river. Vessels of single and double mast were strung cheek to cheek along the length of each wharf. Wyatt led her onto one of the shorter wharves, he carrying her satchel in one hand, and he held

Maddie's hand in his other. They boarded one of the smaller boats. On deck, the air held a chill, and Maddie huddled beneath her coat.

"You might want to go below, out of the wind," said Wyatt.

"No. I don't want to miss a thing."

He pulled a wool jacket from a compartment on the portside, and when he offered it to Maddie, she wrapped the jacket across her shoulders. She watched from the rail as Wyatt raised the sail, and the sail caught in the light wind. The boat cut through the water, taking them beyond the wharf, out of the river and into Cape Cod Bay.

The setting sun reflected red, a molten path across the indigo of water, and the sea rippled low against the bow.

"Is that it?" she asked when seeing the distant cliff. "Is that the island?"

"Yep. That's Ponokanet."

The island grew closer, the cliff higher. Its top showed dense with green forest. "It seems so ... so isolated. Are there other houses out there?"

"No. Just the Chase house. But it's not so isolated anymore. Not since your grandfather built the bridge." Wyatt pointed to the far right of the island. "At that end, the mainland is fairly close. About ten years back, John Chase had the bridge constructed. Anyone can get there now by horseback or carriage, and many of his friends do. He loves big parties."

Maddie sat back, hands clasped on her lap, one thumb rubbing the other nervously as she tried to imagine the house and a grandfather that loved parties.

"You'll fit right in, Maddie. They're good people. The family's been here just about forever."

"And what about you? Have you always lived here?"

"Always. My folks still live in the village. I keep my own place, a few rooms in the same building where I do my work. It's not luxury but it's home."

"It's very fitting," she said, "that your home is with your ships." Maddie fell into silence then as the boat pulled up to a short wharf, and she thought she'd never felt so nervous.

Fifty- Six

Maddie
April of the next year, 1849

Having lived several months on this tiny island, looking out from the high cliff, Maddie turned up the collar of her coat. A light rain had started, but she wanted another minute here by the stone. Winter had passed so quickly, it was difficult to keep up with the days. But in this spot, looking out over the constancy of the sea, time slowed, and she could almost forget the sadness of missing Estelle. While huddled under her coat, hardly with a breath, Maddie concentrated on the rhythmic wash of waves on the beach below, and like magic, the ticking of her heart fell into rhythm with the sea.

And today, Maddie tried to imagine her biological mother standing here by the stone struggling with the decision of love – love for her family or love for a man who would take her away. It seemed an ironic twist of fate that Maddie's love for Wyatt Hamilton had done just the reverse, that her growing love for Wyatt held her here while she learned to love the same places and people her mother had left behind. She felt sorry about that. Sorry for her mother, that her mother, in the end, had lost both.

Maddie knew now, at least, what the face of her mother had looked like. A portrait of Margaret Chase hung on the wall in the living room. Where Margaret's brother, Thomas, was fair-haired, Margaret's hair had been black as night and her eyes nearly as dark as the hair. According to Thomas, Margaret was a quiet girl, a reader of books and with encouragement, a great one to tell stories.

With her face lifted to the rain, Maddie felt the cool spatter on her cheeks. This place was becoming home, and she was ready now to walk back to the house and check in on her grandfather.

She found her grandfather settled in on the sofa, his feet stretched close to the blazing hearth. He was a square-built man, large framed and fit for his seventy-two years, and he smiled to Maddie as she entered the room. He patted the far side of the sofa and asked her, "Any chance you could sit here with me for a while?"

"Would you like me to get you something hot first, some coffee or hot tea?"

"No, thanks. You're making me stout, Maddie," and he patted his belly though in truth he was no more stout than when Maddie first arrived.

She sat with him on the overstuffed sofa, but the comfort Maddie felt came not so much from the sofa as the newly rooted place within her. "A note came today," she said, "from Wyatt's parents. They accepted your invitation to join our dinner party Saturday night. That brings us to a count of twenty-five."

"Good. I want all our friends and family here," he said. "It isn't every day my granddaughter turns nineteen."

There'd been half a dozen parties since Maddie arrived here last October. The house had filled with aunts and uncles and cousins and the multitude of her grandfather's friends. Saturday's party would be just as large and rowdy.

"And Wyatt? He'll be here Saturday night, won't he?"

"You know he will," said Maddie, feeling the warmth on her cheeks give away her feelings for Wyatt as loudly as any words.

"Just making sure." Her grandfather grinned, but when looking away to the fire in the hearth, the grin melted. "I think that fellow's going to take you away from me before too long."

"Never. Not away from Wells Creek."

John Chase combed fingers through his white head of hair. "Maddie, you can't know what it means to me to have you here. This old man's been given a second chance."

"Because of my mother, you mean."

"That's right. Before she left, when she told me about the artist … the man that would be your father, I hung onto so much anger. And over what? Over how one believes in God? It was short-sighted and cruel. There's nothing more important than my children. So many times, so many nights I've stayed awake asking why I didn't know that then." His eyes welled with tears. "Come with me, Maddie. There's something I want to give you."

Maddie walked behind, while her grandfather climbed the stairs to the second floor. But, too, he climbed the narrow steep staircase that took them both higher to the attic under the eaves. Sharp brittle rain sounded on the roof, and the air chilled as John led her to the window at the front gable end. Tucked in beneath the window sill was an old low wooden chest.

"This should have been your mother's," said John. "Now I want you to have it."

Maddie knelt on the floor, drawing her hand over the worn pine wood of the chest, the rich dark patina.

"Open it," said John. "And we'll take a look at what's inside."

Maddie lifted the lid, took out first a piece of tattered canvas, which she let unfold. It appeared to be a pair of breeches but were too small to be worn by any man.

"These belonged to a young woman named Lydia, an ancestor of yours." John went on to tell that Lydia had captained her own ship, had smuggled against the British just before the Revolution. "But Lydia returned to Ponokanet and married. She raised two kids here, so the story goes. Now, take out that small box."

Maddie took from the chest a square thin box, and she removed the cover, only to discover a circle of beads held together on a rawhide string. Beads made of bone and each set of three divided by a purple slice of shell. Maddie held them up to better see.

"It's beautiful," she said. "Did this also belong to Lydia?"

"Yes, eventually. But the necklace traces back much earlier than Lydia, all the way back to the 1600's, to a young woman who had come with her family to settle here. My own mother claims the necklace was given to the girl as a gift from a native Ponokanet woman who lived near where the harbor is now, in a village of domed huts. The larger beads are made from the bone of a whale. Legend says the whale's spirit lives on in those old bones, to guide whoever wears them along life's journey."

Maddie traced a finger over the porous beads. "It's a lovely story," she said. "Do you believe it?"

"Don't know. But I want to. And who's to say. So, the necklace is yours now, Maddie. Keep it with you. Let it guide you on your journey."

Fifty-Seven

Sydney
Still Saturday, September 8

She hurries, thinking she is late, that she's spent too much time with Alison and with the old portrait. But it's not quite eleven when Sydney hauls herself up into Ty's truck. "Good morning," she says. "I'm sorry I ran off this morning."

"Me, too," says Ty, and he reaches for hand.

"Ty, you need to know my leaving this morning had nothing to do with you."

"I didn't think it did."

"Really? That's good. Because … there's something I should tell you. Something I want to tell you."

Ty slips his hand away and lets it rest on the steering wheel. "Sounds serious."

"It is." The sun breaks over the roof of the barn to strike on Sydney's face, and she turns from it to meet his dark quiet eyes. "I loved Rick," she says as way of jumping in. "I never loved anyone else. Growing up, there wasn't time and probably not the trust for a relationship. And I was so hell-bent on flying. But when Rick came along, it was like no one else existed. We flew together. We loved together. When he was killed, I didn't think …"

Sydney waits until the tightness in her throat releases. "Until last night, I thought falling in love again, with someone else, would be wrong. Disloyal because of the way Rick died. Because I was there. I know now it wasn't my fault, but I never thought I could move past that. Now I keep coming to these places, these walls I've put up, and I discover that they're all artificial, that I've been mistaken. What's happening between you and me is not wrong. The way I feel when I'm with you is very right. And I'm not running from it. Not anymore."

Ty touches her hair and softly kisses her before he grins. "Let's go get Everett."

And the truck drives down off Ponokanet and over the bridge.

"I'm not wearing any damn pajamas in the middle of the day," says Everett, sitting dressed in street clothes and propped by pillows on the hospital bed. The admitting process has taken hours. It is four-thirty, and Everett's pallor has gone to gray.

"Just so long as you rest," says Sydney, careful not to look across the bed to Ty, or she would grin and give them both away.

"You two don't have to pretend in front of me," says Everett. "You've been tip-toeing around me all day."

As easily as that, Ty's smile admits everything.

"Okay, so you were right," says Sydney. "Ty's a nice guy."

Everett gives a nod in approval, just as a nurse walks in with a dinner tray. She is young, wholesome looking and full-breasted, and as she leaves the room Everett winks at Ty. "Not a bad place," he says. But he rests his head back against the pillow and closes his eyes. "You know, you two don't have to come all the way in here every day. It doesn't make sense. It's too far. And it isn't necessary."

"Well, it is necessary for me," says Sydney. "But we'll go for now and leave you to rest if first you'll eat some of the soup."

Fifty-Eight

Sydney
Sunday, September 9

The next morning, Sydney carries the portrait up the narrow stairs to the attic. It's where Eva had left it. For now, it's where it belongs. Yet, Sydney sets the painting against the rack rather than on it, so that the unknown face looks out to the attic space. With Cat at her heels, Sydney crosses to the gable end, and she sits there in the chair. But Cat, as if eager to explore, climbs onto the middle shelf of the bookcase, tries to make herself comfortable against the stack of old art magazines that are piled on that shelf. The magazines start to slide, Cat fidgets, and one after the other the magazines slip down and into a heap on the floor, while Sydney groans at the mess. "Look what you did," she says to Cat who ignores Sydney, choosing to leap to the floor, far from the mess of magazines, and slicks down any ruffled fur on her back.

Sydney, too, gets down on the floor and starts to restack the mish-mash of pages, but there, uncovered now on the middle shelf of the bookcase, is a white cardboard box, more like the size of a shirt box. On the cardboard cover, written with marker in Eva's script are two words – *For Sydney*. The box is heavier than it looks, and Sydney sets it on the heap of magazines. The cardboard cover fits loosely and lifts off with little effort.

Inside lies a smaller, thin wooden box. Beneath the wooden box is a notebook, the spiral kind with a purple cover like Sydney would have used in high school. She lifts the wooden box as she sits cross-legged with it on the floor, and she removes the perfectly fitted lid. The bone necklace from the portrait lies coiled inside. Fifteen round bone beads, with thin shards of purple shell that separate the bones into groups of three. All are strung together on an old rawhide cord. Sydney touches the dry white bone. It is eerie – haunting and beautiful, and she cannot resist. She slips the necklace over her head.

And Sydney opens the notebook. Each page is filled with Eva's handwriting. Sydney turns to the first page.

My dear Sydney,

If you are reading this, it is because you have come up here into my painting space and found the box. I knew one day you would, when at last you were ready to understand the bone beads. My own grandmother recounted to me years ago the journey these beads have made and why. On the following pages, I have written that story down so that you may know it, and so that you in time may hand it on to a next daring woman because we must each be daring, my dear, if we are to be all that we can be.

Lovingly yours for eternity,
Eva

With the hem of her shirt, Sydney blots the wet of a tear that has dotted the page.

"Sydney, are you up there?"

She startles at the sound of her mother's voice. "Yes," she says. "I'm here."

"Come down, will you. It's important."

There is earnest insistence in Alison's voice, so Sydney puts the notebook back into the cardboard box, to be cherished later. And while still wearing the bone beads, she takes the narrow staircase down.

"Look what I found," she says when seeing Alison there at the bottom of the stairs.

"That's it. That's the strange necklace." Alison reaches to the necklace but pulls back her hand. "Whale bone or not, I can't even touch that thing."

"But there's more. There's a whole story ..."

Alison puts up a hand, cutting in. "I'm sorry to interrupt, but you know I'm going home to Connecticut this afternoon. And you're going to Boston to see Everett. But there's something I need you to do before that. Something you need to do this morning. Actually, you need to do it right now."

"Now?" Sydney is shaking her head, that small amount of distrust creeping in.

"I need you to go to the airport," says Alison. "To Everett's. There's going to be a delivery. It's for you, and you have to be there when it arrives."

"What kind of delivery?"

"I don't want to tell you. It's a surprise. And I wouldn't push except you need to be there."

"But it's almost ten. I don't have a lot of time."

"Please, Sydney."

"I ..." But Sydney is empty of more argument. She does have time, if she goes right now. "Just where do I pick up this delivery?"

"Just park by the office. I'll follow you in my own car, so you can stay longer if you want."

"I'm not staying. I'm going to Boston."

"Yes. Yes. Whatever. But first, we have to go to the airport."

In the parking lot by the hanger, the car's clock reads 10:14.

"Should we go inside?" asks Sydney, stepping from the Subaru to stand with her mother.

"No. Let's wait here."

Sydney's eyes lift to a high-pitched hum off at a distance. With one hand, she shades her eyes to search.

"There," says Alison, pointing out the plane.

But Sydney has already spied the glint of white, the two pair of wings. The Pitts approaches low over the runway, stripes of red that spread fanlike across white wings and tail. With a wave of its wing, the plane rises high again, rolls into a gentle loop before banking into final approach. Both women, mother and daughter, watch as the Pitts lands on the runway.

"It's yours," says Alison.

"What is?" asks Sydney, because she hasn't yet made the connection.

"I wanted you to have one. Your own plane. For the theater in the sky."

"You? You bought a Pitts?"

"Right from the factory."

Sydney's heart is pounding. She pulls through her hair. "How could you do that?"

"I told you. I wanted you to have it."

The Pitts taxies toward them, stops in front of the hangar and the engine is shut off. The pilot slides back the canopy exposing the cockpit to the salt air of Cape Cod.

"This is insane," says Sydney.

"You have to admit you like it."

"You've known all along I won't fly."

"You haven't yet, that's all," says Alison.

"You still don't get it. I can't fly." Sydney's voice breaks, and ridiculous tears start spilling down her cheek. "What am I supposed to do with a plane if I can't fly?"

Alison slips a hand around Sydney's. "You could sit and look at it. It's pretty enough."

The Pitts is more than pretty. It's perfect. Designed with symmetry and balance, made for one purpose – aerobatics. But Sydney pulls her hand away from Alison.

She kicks at a stone on the parking lot. The Pitts is useless. No one else knows how to fly the thing. Not even Jean can fly a stunt plane like the Pitts.

"You're out of your mind," says Sydney. "How could you do this without asking me, without considering how I might feel?"

"I did consider you. I considered what it might take to get you into the air again."

Sydney looks to the squat little plane. She bites on her lip, and her hand goes to her throat, touching on the forgotten bone beads. "But you bought a Pitts, Mom. You bought a damn Pitts."

"Yes, I did. And with no strings attached. So you decide. Do we send it back with the pilot there? Or do we keep it?"

"I can't fly that plane. Can't you see? I'm afraid," says Sydney. "What if I panic up there?"

"What if you don't?"

The pilot waits by the wing. But Sydney shakes her head.

"If you believe you can't," says Alison, "then you're right. But Eva told me once to follow my own path. Now I'm saying it to you. Flying is your passion, Sydney. It's been your path … your life, and it's a good one. A hard-earned one."

Sydney roughs fingers through her hair and looks again to the Pitts. The Pitts, it could be hers. Flying could be hers again … if she dares.

Each of us must be daring …

Digging so deeply that she feels the pull in the pit of her stomach, Sydney starts out across the parking lot, toward the wing of fanned stripes.

"Are you sure you can fly this thing?" asks the delivery pilot.

She tells him yes, that she's flown the exact plane hundreds of times, and she scribbles her signature on papers that release the plane and makes it hers. She circles the Pitts, giving a slow full preflight test to ailerons and rudder. And holding back breath, her heart loud in her chest, she steps up onto the wing and into the cockpit. Her hands are sweaty. Yet, she closes the canopy above her and locks it with a quick turn of the latch. In front of her is the instrument panel. At her knees rests the control stick. All so familiar.

With a press of a button, the claw propeller churns. Sydney clamps on the headphones, and Nora's voice crackles over the radio. "You go, girl."

Sydney focuses – suddenly calm. She reads the identification number, 142Y, that is etched on the metal plate to the left of the controls. She speaks into the small dot microphone at her chin. "This is 142 Yankee requesting take off."

"Request granted, 142 Yankee."

Sydney taxies to the start of the runway. Lines up the nose to the oncoming wind and tests the engine, revs it before letting the Pitts have its way. The old pavement slips beneath her. Wind buoys the wing, and the wheels lift. A light pull on the stick and the nose angles up. Fifty feet. Five hundred. A thousand.

At two thousand feet, she levels off. She is flying.

She tries an easy turn. The Pitts responds, its wings bank, the engine hum incredibly beautiful.

Sydney looks out to a distant herringbone cloud. Eva – is she there, lanky arms raised in the air, waving? Sydney wants to believe she is. Perhaps with Rick, he with his crooked grin.

With a quick press to stick and rudder, the Pitts makes a four point roll, stopping at each ninety degrees to make it pretty, and she levels out for a count of seconds. A pull back on the stick brings the nose up to vertical. A straight climb. Then over onto the plane's back, and into a dive. The earth rises up close until again Sydney levels the plane. And it is fun.

When the Pitts rolls to the hangar, Alison runs toward her. Sydney cuts the engine, opens the canopy and climbs to the ground.

"I'm so happy for you," says Alison, taking Sydney in a tentative embrace.

"You had more faith in me than I did."

"I'm discovering that's what mother's do."

"They don't buy planes, Mom."

"Well, this one does."

Sydney is still shaking her head when she wraps her arms around her mother, feeling the pull of a smile, a pull stronger than Sydney has felt in a long time.

Fifty-Nine

Sydney
In late October

"I can't stay in bed. I'm too wired," says Sydney as daylight fans across their bed. She reaches to Ty, kisses the back of his neck.

Ty moans, a garbled 'good morning' that tells Sydney he, too, is now awake. But Sydney is up. Finally, it is the last Saturday in October. Today there is the airshow, and the Pitts will begin to earn its keep. Better than even that – Everett is coming home. He's doing well and in just a few hours he'll see that Dean Aviation, like himself, has survived hard times.

Hot water from the shower streams across her shoulders. She has noticed recently that her body is filling out. Arms and shoulders are not quite so thin. She needed to eat healthy and often to be ready for the stem cell procedure. For Sydney, the actual giving of her stem cells was the easy part. The few days following the transplant slowed her plans. But she gave in to the deep muscle aches and a lack of energy, and she rested. Good food and rest – a combination that has brought a glow to her face. Today, however, her excitement is for what lies ahead.

When Sydney steps from Ty's rooms within the barn out into the sunshine, she sees Jean already waiting on the front steps of the house. Jean's use of the small upstairs bedroom is a temporary arrangement. Eventually, Sydney will help her find a place of her own, but there hasn't been time for house hunting. There's been too much work, too much planning involved in getting ready for this one day. Not only has Jean signed on to be the mechanic for Dean Aviation, Jean will also play a key role in today's theater in the sky. She plays the role of Ludwig, terror of the sea. And Jean was easy to convince to come. 'I guess it's BFF,' that's all Jean said when Sydney offered the idea, and two weeks later Jean was here on Ponokanet.

"Your mother's making coffee," says Jean when Sydney sits beside her on the porch step.

"Alison is awake?" asks Sydney because Alison is still surprising her by being someone Sydney barely recognizes.

"Said she couldn't sleep ... she's too excited."

"Guess that makes three of us."

Bleachers have been brought in and made permanent at the side of the runway, and today they are filled with ticket holders, an audience that has paid money to watch this new theater in the sky. But it's nearly two o'clock, and Sydney stands by the hangar, peering down the entrance road in search of Ty's green truck. Earlier, in the morning, he left for Boston, but he ought to return any minute now with Everett beside him in the truck.

Sydney checks her watch.

Only twenty minutes remain before show time. She wants Everett to see every minute of what's to come. She scans the faces that still wait in line for a ticket. If all goes well, and it will, the day is a success.

"Come on. We should be getting the engines warmed up," says Jean, who comes from inside the hangar. Sydney laughs at the sight – Jean decked out in a wild red wig ready to portray the fiery-haired pirate.

"Where's Nora?" asks Sydney.

"She's in the Cessna, a little too full of stage fright but she's ready to go."

Sydney looks to the announcer's booth that has been built high at the rear of the bleachers. From the booth, Alison waves a purple scarf. Alison is in place, prepared to read the script they wrote together. That one task was actually fun, made easier after reading the notebook Eva left behind.

"Testing. One. Two." Alison tests the audio, talking through the speakers, then waves again to Sydney with the scarf.

Sydney is reluctant to start without Everett here, but she walks with Jean to the field where the planes wait – the Pitts, built so perfectly for the rigors Sydney will soon put it through, and next to it the restored single-wing Aeronca C3 with its pugged face and thick body, an antique attraction that will be piloted by Jean. There, too, waits the old Cessna. In it is Nora, who shouts, not surprisingly, "Get your asses movin'."

The Pitts is first to leave the ground. To please the crowd Sydney waves her wings, then climbs to three thousand feet in little more than a minute. She banks the wing and turns away from the field, needing to circle the airport while waiting for Jean and Nora to be in the air. While waiting, far below Sydney spies the green pick-up driving in along the road. As it pulls up close to the airfield in the parking space left purposely open, Sydney smiles and takes position.

Through the audio speakers on the ground and through headsets clamped to pilots' ears, Alison narrates and the story begins –

"The mid-1700's were a hard time for colonists here in the new world. The British wanted money in the form of taxes. Those who refused to pay paid in blood."

Sydney rolls to the right, buzzes low over the field before climbing vertical. She rolls into a loop, as Alison narrates –

"Fortunately for Cape Codders, there was Lydia."

The Pitts appears again over the runway, does a four-point roll, levels out and climbs. The crowd cheers.

"Lydia was a woman with strong will and spine. To bring profits to Cape Cod, Lydia defied the King. In her own ship, she smuggled into Wells Creek hundreds of barrels of rum and molasses from the Caribbean."

Belly to the sky, the Pitts passes low over the runway, Sydney hanging in the harness. The crowd is on their feet, as she rolls upright and flies off to the south. In sync, Nora, as one of the King's men, flies the red and white Cessna in from the west.

"But everywhere, danger lurked. The King's men patrolled the seas. They boarded ships in search of lawbreakers who would smuggle goods into small hidden harbors rather than pay the King his share."

From two thousand feet above the runway, Nora dives into a simple slow loop before flying off – just as Jean, the red-haired Ludwig, flies in low, a skull and crossbones flag waving from the plane's tail, and the pirate Ludwig waves her wings to the crowd.

"And there was Ludwig, terror of the Caribbean Sea."

Like an aerial dance, three planes crisscross the sky in mock battle. With daredevil stunts, Lydia combats the perils of both King's man and the terrifying pirate, while Alison goes on to tell the story of the girl from Wells Creek who outsmarted the British – Lydia Fenton who was Captain of her own ship and battled pirates with her own hand. And through headphones, Sydney hears the crowd laugh and cheer.

"So, Ladies and Gentlemen, that ends our show today. I ask that you welcome our Lydia and her defeated foes back to earth. For a small fee, a plane ride is offered.

We guarantee an unmatched view of Cape Cod and a possible sighting of the whales that are here feeding in our waters."

Sydney is first to land. She is first to step out onto the tarmac. She sees him then – Everett waiting by the hangar, standing on his own. Ty stands beside him wearing his quiet grin, whereas Everett uses the back of a hand to wipe at tears.

> *ACKNOWLEDGMENTS* <

A huge thank you goes to Anne Lamott for the invaluable lesson offered in her book, Bird by Bird, for surely that is how this novel was written. Many thanks also go out to the friends who listened as the story grew and who listened again and again through revisions.

I offer thanks to Carol Lindemann for the time and attention she gave to editing and whose suggestions made the story tighter and a better read. A thank you also goes to Clement Walsh for improving the quality of the cover photo.

Gratitude is given, too, for the happenstance of that one particular erratic boulder that has stood in place on the Outer Cape since the melting of glaciers, the maiden's face profiled and waiting. Inspiration comes often where least expected.

Finally, I thank Jim for his constancy, his encouragement and his insight.

Judith Manchester lives on the outer spine of Cape Cod and has long wanted to bring to life the beauty and romanticism of that sandy peninsula. She has been a teacher, a free-lance journalist, and a writer of award-winning short stories. *Sisters of the Stone* is her first novel.

www.judithmanchester.com